"A comic extravaganza, deftly plotted... funny. Jonathan Barnes combines a lo... ...bsurdity worthy of Edward Gorey with the surrealistic invention of a London-obsessed García Márquez. This parody penny dreadful is one of the classiest entertainments I've read in a long, long time."

—Christopher Bram, author of *Exiles in America*

"Jonathan Barnes puts a perfectly good Oxford education to mischievous misuse.... A cheeky tale ... salvaged from the sensationalist novels of the past three centuries.... It doesn't take an English-lit wonk to appreciate the antic mind that would name two of the grotesquely deformed prostitutes in Mrs. Puggsley's brothel after virginal victims of Count Dracula—and find a role in these shenanigans for Coleridge."   —*New York Times*

"Magical, dark, beautifully odd—and utterly compelling—this is an astonishing debut."   —Michael Marshall, author of *The Intruders*

"The Victorian era lends itself to fantastical literature, and in recent years there has been a surge of novels set in the nineteenth century. *The Somnambulist* is one of the best.... The plot is complex and helter-skelter, and Barnes plays with the reader's expectations: Is this a detective novel, an occult thriller, a horror yarn, or all three? It's certainly a grotesque and compelling debut."   —*The Guardian* (London)

"Four score and nine years ago, old Doc Caligari opened up his famous cabinet and unleashed his slinky somnambulist. Now Jonathan Barnes has given us a different sort of sleepwalker, a milk-swilling golem around whom swirls a literary maelstrom in which we glimpse not only German expressionism but Conan Doyle, Edgar Allan Poe, Wilkie Collins, Mary Shelley, Dr. Who, Mr. Hyde, Hammer horror films, and a Lovecraftian eldritch unnamable or two, all of it served up with macabre wit and stylistic panache. Parliament should immediately pass a law requiring Barnes to write a sequel."   —James Morrow, author of *The Last Witchfinder* and *The Philosopher's Apprentice*

"This promising debut subverts its nineteenth-century predecessors amusingly. Inventive and often witty. A cabinet crammed with curiosities."   —*The Observer* (London)

"Sneaky, cheeky, and dark in the best possible way, Jonathan Barnes's massively entertaining *The Somnambulist* manages to make the familiar daringly unfamiliar. I enjoyed the heck out of this novel." —Jeff VanderMeer

"A compelling and highly entertaining read.... Highly recommended."   —*Library Journal*

Amelia Wallace

About the Author

JONATHAN BARNES graduated from Oxford University with a first in English literature. He reviews for the *Times Literary Supplement* and lives in London. *The Somnambulist* is his first novel.

THE
SOMNAMBULIST

JONATHAN BARNES

HARPER

NEW YORK ■ LONDON ■ TORONTO ■ SYDNEY

HARPER

This book was originally published in the United Kingdom in 2007 by Gollancz, an imprint of the Orion Publishing Group.

A hardcover edition of this book was published in 2008 by William Morrow, an imprint of HarperCollins Publishers.

FIRST HARPER PAPERBACK PUBLISHED 2009.

Designed by Jessica Shatan Heslin/Studio Shatan, Inc.

Library of Congress Cataloging-in-Publication Data has been applied for.

ISBN 978-0-06-137539-2

09 10 11 12 13 WBC/RRD 10 9 8 7 6 5 4 3 2 1

For my parents

ACKNOWLEDGEMENTS

In the U.S.—Diana Gill for expert advice on making the book better.

In the U.K.—Simon Spanton for championing the book; Lisa Rogers and Adam Roberts for notes and corrections; Bede Rogerson and Ben Marsden for invaluably honest read-throughs; Tony Fullwood for pantisocracy.

At home—Amelia Wallace for changing everything; my parents for their patience and support.

1

Be warned. This book has no literary merit whatsoever. It is a lurid piece of nonsense, convoluted, implausible, peopled by unconvincing characters, written in drearily pedestrian prose, frequently ridiculous and wilfully bizarre. Needless to say, I doubt you'll believe a word of it.

Yet I cannot be held wholly accountable for its failings. I have good reason for presenting you with so sensational and unlikely an account.

It is all true. Every word of what follows actually happened, and I am merely the journalist, the humble Boswell, who has set it down. You'll have realised by now that I am new to this business of storytelling, that I lack the skill of an expert, that I am without any ability to enthral the reader, to beguile with narrative tricks or charm with sleight of hand.

But I can promise you three things: to relate events in their neatest and most appropriate order; to omit nothing I consider significant; and to be as frank and free with you as I am able.

I must ask you in return to show some little understanding for a man come late in life to tale-telling, an artless dilettante who, on dipping his toes into the shallows of story, hopes only that he will not needlessly embarrass himself.

One final thing, one final warning: in the spirit of fair play, I ought to admit that I shall have reason to tell you more than one direct lie.

What, then, should you believe? How will you distinguish truth from fiction?

Naturally, I leave that to your discretion.

2

We begin with Cyril Honeyman.

Honeyman was a gross, corpulent little man, permanently sweaty, whose jowls flapped and quivered as he walked. His death is a matter of pages away.

Please don't get attached to him. I've no intention of detailing his character at any length—he's insignificant, a walk-on, a corpse-in-waiting.

But you should, perhaps, know this: Cyril Honeyman was an actor, and a bad one. And by "bad" I mean more than simply incompetent. He was wholly and irredeemably awful, an affront to his profession, a ham who had bought his way into theatre and squandered on plum parts the vast allowance he was granted by his overly indulgent parents. At the time of his death he was preparing to play Paris in a production of *Romeo and Juliet* at some luckless fleapit desperate for cash, and on the night itself he was out carousing with the rest of the cast, the majority of whom were almost as wretchedly talentless as he. He left them around midnight, saying that he was returning home to work on his lines, though he had, in truth, a different destination and quite another pastime in mind. He walked for the best part of an hour, leaving the theatre district behind him and moving with clammy-palmed purpose towards one of the seamiest parts of the city. Just being there excited him. He enjoyed the sense of transgression it gave him, its whiff of illegality.

He moved through the streets for what felt like an age, breathing in the noisome air of the place, revelling in the dirt and degradation of its inhabitants. The train station had been closed for hours, any respectable residents had long since retired to bed, and the streets found themselves given over to venality and vice. Honeyman shook with illicit pleasure as he ventured further into this latter-day Gomorrah, through the darkened alleyways and thoroughfares lit only by the sickly, guttering light of the gas lamps. A mist had descended, lending the streets an eerie, phantasmagoric sheen, and the people Honeyman passed seemed vague and insubstantial, only partially real, like characters in a story book. They called out to him, begging for food or alms, promising clandestine pleasures or offering themselves for money, but Honeyman strutted past them all. He had been here too often, had become jaded and bored and accustomed to the sight of mankind sunk to its lowest and most degraded state. Tonight he sought new and baser pleasures. He wanted to fall further into corruption.

Silhouetted beneath a gas lamp stood the figure of a woman. She was well dressed for her surroundings, a new bonnet perched decorously upon her head, and her figure, lissom and lithe, was lent emphasis by a dress which showed a good deal more flesh than polite company would ever have allowed. Her skin looked as though it had once been a porcelain white, but now was pitted and scarred and crusting over with a layer of grime. The city was cruel to women like her.

Honeyman drew closer and doffed his hat in greeting. Even beneath the greasy ochre of the lamp her youth and beauty shone through. A fallen woman, certainly—but only recently. A woman of the unfortunate type but one still new and fresh to the game.

"Looking for something?" she asked.

Honeyman stared back, his eyes licking her shamelessly. Surely she couldn't be more than eighteen. Almost a child.

He gave a furtive grin. "Might be."

"Want to know how much?"

He mumbled: "Go on."

"Enough to get me a bed tonight. That's all I ask."

"My dear. You're far too precious a thing to be dawdling out here. You're a pearl amongst swine."

If she noticed his crude compliment she gave no sign. "Want to come with me?"

"You have somewhere in mind?"

"Somewhere safe. Private, like. So we can get more intimately acquainted." Doing her best to play the coquette, the woman gave a crooked smile. She was tired, probably drunk, and the pretence was obvious, but Honeyman, his ardour now inflamed, saw only a lascivious girl, a wanton, a sylph waiting to be conquered. She moved away and he followed without thinking. Before long his thighs grew sticky with perspiration, rubbing uncomfortably together as he walked. He grimaced, half in pleasure, half in pain.

"How much further?"

"Not far."

They walked in silence for a time before the woman paused and pointed upwards. "There."

Honeyman stopped short as a vast structure reared out of the darkness above him—a thing horribly out of place in the modern age, perverse in its anachronism. Wreathed by the night, illuminated only by the anaemic light of the moon, it resembled some primeval monument, a slab of Stonehenge wrenched from Salisbury Plain and thrust unaltered into the depths of the city.

"What is it?" he whispered.

She spat upon the pavement and Honeyman tried hard not to show his distaste at her vulgarity.

"Don't worry about that. You coming up?"

"Up there? Why?"

"Best place to do it." Her client looked unconvinced. "You'll like it," she wheedled. "It's more of a thrill this way. More exciting. More dangerous."

Honeyman gave in. "Let's go up, then," he said, and noticed as they drew closer to the tower that it appeared to be constructed entirely from a smooth, sheer metal which glinted ominously in the moonlight. The woman produced a key and let them inside, and Honeyman warily followed, taking especial care to bolt the door behind him.

By the trickle of light from the street he could make out a spiral staircase winding upwards into pitchy blackness. The woman had already started to climb and he could hear her moving above him. Nervous, but spurred on by the promise of pleasure, Honeyman began his ascent, the handrail cold to the touch as he groped his way uncertainly up the staircase in the gloom. His companion refused to slow down and the actor found himself wheezing and short of breath as the climb went on for what felt like hours. To calm himself as he was drawn further and further into darkness he began to recite some of his lines.

"Immoderately she weeps for Tybalt's death,
And therefore have I little talked of love,

For Venus smiles not in a house of tears.
Now, sir, her father counts it dangerous
That she do give her sorrow so much sway,
And in his wisdom hastes our marriage
To stop the inundation of her tears."

As the words echoed round the tower, Honeyman, suddenly uneasy, fell silent. He sensed movement at the periphery of his vision, felt an irrational certainty that there were presences here other than the woman and himself. Suppressing a shudder, he moved on.

He reached the top of the stairs and walked into an enormous room full to bursting with the very last thing he had expected: profound, improbable luxury. A four-poster bed stretched out across the floor, a table beside it buckled beneath an immense feast, a bottle of champagne lay unopened and the air smelt sweet as though tempered by incense or perfume. The room's sole window was made up of delicate, clear panes of glass held together by strips of lead, geometrically arranged—a window better suited to a church or chapel, to some forgotten cathedral, than to this ominous tower, this giant finger of fate raised in imprecation against the city. Honeyman walked across to admire the view. The streets lay spread out before him, the railway station crouched amongst them, the jutting spire of a nearby church glimmering in the moonlight.

The woman stood behind him. "Not what you expected?"

"How many men have you brought here?"

She sighed—a low, guttural sound. "You're the first," she said and slowly began to unbutton her dress, revealing a tantalising layer of petticoat. Honeyman bit his lower lip hard in excitement.

"Take off your clothes," she demanded.

He wiped his forehead. "You're impatient."

"Aren't you?" She dealt with the last of the dress and set to work on her undergarments.

Honeyman prevaricated. "Shall we have a drink? Seems a shame to waste such good champagne."

"Later." She smiled. "I've a feeling you won't last long."

Honeyman shrugged, then eagerly complied. He unlaced his shoes, kicked them aside, took off his tie, unbuttoned his shirt and trousers. Folds of fat and unexpected bits of skin kept getting in the way and it took him far longer than it ought, but eventually he stood before her naked, febrile and tumescent. To his disappointment she was still in her petticoat.

"I want everything off," he snapped. Then, with another involuntary nibble of his lower lip: "May I help?"

The woman shook her head as from the street below there came a deep, sonorous, metallic sound as though something vast had struck the side of the tower.

Honeyman felt a jolt of fear. "What was that?"

She tried to soothe him. "Nothing. Nothing. All is as it should be."

He heard the sound again, louder this time, and Honeyman was afraid: "Someone knows we're here."

As if on cue, a figure unfurled itself from the shadows in one corner of the room. "Cyril?"

He spun round to confront the intruder—a grim, heavyset woman lost somewhere in the outer regions of middle age. He gasped at the sight of her. Tears pricked the corners of his eyes. "Mother?" He stared in horror. "Mother? Is that you?"

A part of him refused to take in the sheer wrongness of her presence and he flailed desperately about for some reasonable explanation. The happy thought occurred to him that this might be the result of some especially fevered poppy dream—certainly it had about it all the garbled, wonderland logic of the opium den. Maybe he had overindulged in some Eastern dive or other and this was all a horribly vivid dream. An uncomfortable thing to endure, to be sure, and most likely a stern lesson in the perils of narcotic excess, but there was nothing dangerous here, nothing life-threatening. All this unpleasantness would pass away soon enough. Why, no doubt he'd come to at any moment to find himself slumped upon a divan, some concerned Oriental type shaking him awake to offer him another pipe or two. He closed his eyes, willing away this terrible mirage.

When he opened them again his mother was still there, her thick arms folded like hunks of meat, wearing her angriest and most exasperated expression.

"Mother?" he managed feebly. "Mother, what are you doing here?"

"You always were a disappointment." She sounded almost conversational, as though there were nothing at all extraordinary or remarkable in the scene. "Your father and I have become accustomed to your failures. But this . . ." She gestured vaguely around her. "This is too much."

"Mother . . ." Reality kicked hard against him, and faced with so unexpected and unprovoked an assault, Honeyman could do little more than whimper. He made an unsuccessful attempt to cover his nakedness with his hands. "I don't know what to say."

"Better you stay silent." She turned to the fallen woman. "Thank you, dear. You may get dressed now." The woman curtseyed and busied herself rearranging her skirts.

Honeyman looked on, wide-eyed and terrified. From outside there came another tumultuous crash. "You knew?"

His mother smiled.

He heard the sound again, turned and peered from the window. To his utter disbelief and horror, a figure was climbing the tower, clattering noisily up the side of the structure, scuttling towards the top, crawling ever nearer as effortlessly as a lizard moves along a wall.

Cyril wept. "Mother?"

The figure came closer and a moment later a face appeared at the window, its nose squashed tight against the glass, its breath frosting the panes. It had the form, the size, the shape of a man, but there seemed no trace of humanity about it, as though it belonged to some species all its own. Its sallow skin was covered in a multitude of vile grey scales which hung in grotesque flaps from its cheeks, lips, chin and eyelids, like molten cheese spread lumpily over toast. It was a face of melted candle wax.

Honeyman was paralysed by fear. The creature grinned evilly at him and began, quite deliberately, to pick away at the fragile strips of lead which clasped the panes together.

Honeyman screamed, "Mother! It's trying to get in."

She smiled benignly. The fallen woman, now fully dressed, appeared at her side and together they blocked Honeyman's only possible route of escape. The figure picked away some more at the window. It may just have been Honeyman's imagination, but he could have sworn that the creature was whistling cheerily as it worked.

"Mother! Mother! Help me!"

The thing at the window continued to work away, only minutes from getting inside as the lead came off with a horrible, piercing, scraping sound.

"At least tell me why."

Through the cracks in the window, Honeyman could feel the cool night air scratching at his neck, tickling the back of his spine.

His mother sighed. "You allowed yourself to be defiled. The city has corrupted you."

"I'd take it back, Mother. If I could. Oh please. I'd undo it in a heartbeat."

"We're doing this for the poet, Cyril. This is his vision. And I doubt he'd consider you worthy of the merest shred of clemency."

Behind him, a bony finger poked its way into the room and tore away a section of the window. The thing dropped it outside and they heard it crash and splinter on the street below.

"You really are a disappointment, you know. We had such high hopes for you."

"Mother, please. Whatever I've done—however I've disappointed you—I'm sorry. I'm sorry. *I'm sorry.*"

With impossible strength and apparently impervious to pain, the thing pushed aside the last of the glass and thrust its way into the room. It squatted athletically beside the actor and leered malevolently up at him, like some maleficent vision from Bosch stepped, still wet with paint, glossy and glistening, from the canvas.

Mrs. Honeyman smiled again. "May the Lord have mercy on you." She nodded at the creature, which leapt obediently to its feet and moved towards its victim, forcing him back against the shattered window. Honeyman screamed in anguish and mortal terror. He tried to mouth some final plea but before he was able to speak the monster was upon him, pushing him further and further back until, with a final, deceptively gentle shove, Honeyman disappeared through the window altogether and sailed out into the cold, merciless air.

He screamed all the way down. Seconds later, the creature followed suit, leaping out of the room, scuttling down the tower, darting away into the night.

Upstairs, Mrs. Honeyman and the fallen woman linked hands.

"God be with you," said one.

"God be with you," echoed the other.

Hand in hand, they left the tower and vanished into the city.

Cyril Honeyman was still alive when they found him, his dying moments witnessed by a cluster of curious residents and a single police constable. It passed into local legend that his last words were also those of his final character:

> *"O, I am slain! If thou be merciful,*
> *Open the tomb, lay me with Juliet."*

A ham, then, to the last.

3

I do not like handsome men.

Mostly this is jealousy, I know—this instinctive hatred of mine, this old, irrational animosity. When I compare my swollen flesh and pockmarked features with the supple frames of the young and the beautiful, I find myself achingly wanting. Even today, I am quite unable to look upon a comely youth without wishing to beat his exquisitely proportioned face into a bruised and bloody pulp.

So you can scarcely imagine my joy when I realised that Mr. Edward Moon was losing his looks.

All that silken hair, those perfect cheekbones, that preternaturally well-defined jaw—Moon had once been elegance personified, style and dash incarnate. But now, past forty and barrelling towards his sixth decade with what felt to him like indecent haste, his appeal seemed at long last to have faded. His hair had started to thin and the keen observer could discern the first few flecks of grey. His face, already sagging and crinkled, had begun to display an inclination towards corpulence, had lost its handsome lineaments as the testimony of his sins and vices wrote itself across his features in lines and furrows and wrinkles.

The night Cyril Honeyman tumbled to his messy death, Edward Moon was dining with acquaintances (not friends, you'll notice, never that) at a party in an especially fashionable part of Kensington, surrounded by some of the most prominent of the city's chattering classes. Time was when he would have sat amongst them as their most honoured guest, the evening's star attraction, but nowadays his hosts seemed content merely to tolerate him, inviting him (he strongly suspected) chiefly out of habit. A few more years and he would be dropped from these gatherings altogether, his name erased from the guest lists, become a non-person, an also-ran.

Moon swiftly found himself tiring of their company, and at the end of the meal when the women retired to giggle and gossip and the men lit cigars and reached for the port, he excused himself from the table and strolled out into the garden, leaving his companion to fend for himself indoors.

Moon had once enjoyed a reputation for dressing exquisitely, his wardrobe always just that vital inch ahead of fashion. But now, as his dapperness ebbed away, he had begun to look lost in the new style, had come increasingly to resemble a leftover from the last century, a relic from an earlier, mustier age. His Savile Row jacket had seen far better days and his shoes, handmade and paid for with several months' earnings, were grown scuffed and weary. He wore a black armband, still in mourning for the Queen though she had passed away some months before. He was a creature of the old century as surely as she.

The year stood just on that cusp of the seasons when winter begins to clench its fist about the days, and the trees, robbed of their leaves and colour, stand stark sentinel like empty hat-stands. The air was clammy and chill; fog had stretched itself out from the lower parts of the city, and illuminated by light streaming from the house, the garden shimmered and shone with a strange lustre. Moon strolled away from the building, the long, damp grass soaking his shoes, the bottoms of his trousers, the tops of his socks. He lit a cigarette and inhaled with relief as the smoke percolated soothingly through his lungs.

"Mr. Moon?"

There was a man standing behind him, one of the dinner guests, an American whose name Moon had already allowed himself to forget. The tip of the stranger's cigar glowed angrily in the half-darkness. "Enjoying the evening?"

Moon ignored the question and took another drag on his cigarette. "What can I do for you?" he asked at length. "Mr. . . . . ?"

The American gave a lopsided smile. "Stoddart."

Moon smiled smoothly, meaninglessly back. "Of course."

"I have a proposition for you. I publish *Lippincott's Monthly Magazine*. Perhaps you've heard of us."

Moon shook his head.

"We're a periodical—not entirely an unfashionable one, if I may say so. In the past I've commissioned some of your most prominent authors. Arthur Doyle contributed—"

"A hack, Mr. Stoddart. A journeyman."

The American tried again. "Oscar Wilde—"

Moon gave an expansive yawn, refusing to be impressed. "Why are you telling me this?"

"I'd like you to join them."

"I'm not a writer. I have no stories to tell."

The publisher tossed aside his cigar and ground out what was left of it with the toe of his boot. "But you do, sir, you do. I'm not asking for a work of fiction. I'm in pursuit of something infinitely more engaging."

"Oh?"

"I want your autobiography. A life of such vigour and colour as your own should make for compelling reading—would even, I fancy, have some considerable historical value."

"Historical?" Moon grimaced. *"Historical?"* He turned back towards the house. "My career is not done with yet. I've no interest in writing my own eulogy."

Stoddart chose his next words very carefully. "Let's not be coy. We both know your best work is behind you. Since Clapham your stock has fallen considerably."

Moon was defiant. "There is still one last great case."

The man persisted. "You owe your public the truth. Our readers want to know how you solved the Limmeridge Park Murders. How you tracked down the Fiend. The Adventure of Smugglers' Bay. The so-called Miracle of Mile End. Your rumoured involvement in the Crookback Incursion of Eighty-eight."

Moon eyed his inquisitor suspiciously. "I wasn't aware that incident was public knowledge."

"Name your price," the publisher replied and suggested a sum which even today would amount to a small fortune.

Moon reached the house and turned back to face the American. "My past is not for sale, Mr. Stoddart. There. You have my answer." He slipped inside and pulled the door shut behind him.

He strode through to the billiard room. His companion sat alone and silent, a glass in one hand, a smouldering cigar in the other, a wide smile spread blissfully across his face.

Moon spoke curtly to their host. "Get me a cab. The Somnambulist and I are leaving."

To describe the Somnambulist simply as an unusually tall man would hardly do justice to his memory. He was abnormally, freakishly large—indeed, if the rumours which circulated after his death are to be believed, he stood well in excess of eight feet tall. He had a thatch of dark-brown hair, cultivated a substantial pair of side-whiskers and had about him a likeably innocent air which belied a prodigious strength. More curious still, he carried with him at all times a miniature slate blackboard and a stub of chalk.

The journey home was entirely silent. Exhausted by the effort of maintaining his composure in the face of the evening's relentlessly cheerful rounds of socialising, Moon said nothing, but as the cab neared the end of its journey the Somnambulist reached into his satchel and drew out his blackboard and chalk. In straggly, childish characters he wrote:

WHAT DID HE ASK

Moon told him.

With a massively oversize thumb, the Somnambulist rubbed out his message and wrote again:

WHAT DID YOU SAY

On hearing the reply, the giant put away his chalk and board and did not write again till morning.

Edward Moon was a conjuror by profession. He owned a small theatre in Albion Square, just at the border of the East End, where every night except Sunday he performed his magic show with the silent, indefatigable assistance of the Somnambulist. Naturally, they were both far more than mere stage magicians, but I shall come to that in time.

Their show was a quiet phenomenon, opening to modest houses in the early 1880s until, at the very acme of his popularity, Moon could count it a disappointing night if the stalls weren't filled to capacity and half his potential audience turned away for lack of space. At the time, the city had never seen anything quite like the Theatre of Marvels. In a single production, it synthesised magic, melodrama, exoticism and real, heart-stopping spectacle. But the audiences came to see one thing above all others, the mystery at the heart of the performance: the great and silent enigma of the Somnambulist.

The theatre itself was a little over fifty years old, a modest building with the look of a minor college chapel about it. A gaudy hand-painted sign took up half the front wall and proclaimed in foot-high letters:

THE THEATRE OF MARVELS
starring
MR. EDWARD MOON
and
THE SOMNAMBULIST

BE ASTONISHED!
BE THRILLED! BE ENLIGHTENED!

By the time of our narrative, the theatre had ceased to be truly fashionable and audiences had begun to dwindle in numbers and enthusiasm.

The night after Moon's encounter with Stoddart was typical—a small crowd, a half-hearted line outside the entrance, nothing like the glory days when by five o'clock, a full three hours before the performance was due to commence, a queue would start at the box office and snake its way out of the theatre and into the street, stretching as far as the doors of a nearby public house, the Strangled Boy.

Inside, the theatre had a grimy, run-down quality, exacerbated by its omnipresent scents of sawdust, liquor and stale gas. Unbeknown to our protagonists, I was there myself that night, seated in the front row, the fourth or fifth such occasion on which I had attended.

As the audience idled to their seats, a ragtag orchestra played in the pit at the front of the stage, heroically struggling through a medley of popular standards almost physically upsetting in their coarseness and banality. There was a time when audiences had been drawn from all strata of society—from local working-class families to professional men, paupers to priests, doctors to drapers, even on one memorable occasion a minor scion of the royal family—until quite abruptly and without apparent cause the higher orders had ceased to come, leaving only local people, the idle, the curious, those who merely wished to get out of the rain, as well as a peculiar crowd of what can only be described as "regulars." These were a gang of mild obsessives and social misfits who visited the theatre repeatedly, had seen the show a dozen times or more and could (no doubt) recite the act by heart. Always outwardly courteous, privately Moon harboured nothing but contempt for his disciples, despite the fact—or more likely because of it—that his livelihood appeared increasingly to depend upon them.

Mercifully, the orchestra limped to the end of its minuscule repertoire, the lights dimmed, and backed by a persistent drum roll, Edward Moon took the stage. He bowed, to immediate applause. Noticing a phalanx of his fans occupying the entirety of the fifth and sixth rows, he acknowledged their presence with a cursory nod. Then, professional smile in place, he began the well-worn routine, confident that his audience, though small, was sympathetic.

He was careful to eschew what was expected, the staple tricks of the magician. At the Theatre of Marvels there were no rabbits, no hats, no shuffling of cards, no coloured handkerchiefs, no rings, cups or balls—Moon's act was altogether more recherché than that.

To roars of approval from the regulars, he produced from thin air what appeared to be a large Galápagos tortoise and watched it totter its wrinkled way amongst the crowd before it inexplicably disappeared in full view. He brought forth an entire set of encyclopaediae from his apparently bottomless pockets, even after a

member of the audience had certified them empty. At his com-
mand a live ape materialised in a puff of magenta-coloured smoke
and capered and gibbered delightfully for a time.

In preparation for the first major trick of the evening, the monkey picked a gentleman from the audience who, on Moon's instructions and accompanied by encouraging whoops and cheers
from the stalls, got reluctantly to his feet and made his way onstage. Upon the man's arrival, Moon snapped his fingers and the
ape scampered obediently away.

"Can you tell us your name, sir?" Moon asked, with a wink to
the audience who laughed knowingly along, fully cognisant of
the fact that one of their number was about to be discomfited,
patronised, mocked or—better still—humiliated and openly rid-
iculed.

"Gaskin," the man replied in an insouciant, disagreeable tone.
"Charlie Gaskin." He was stocky, barrel-chested and had cultivated (unwisely, in my opinion) a flaccid, patchy approximation
of a walrus moustache.

Moon held Gaskin in his gaze. "You are a valet," he said. "You
are married with two children. Your father was a tailor who died
of consumption last year. For supper tonight you ate a stale kip-
per, and you spend many of your leisure hours building and maintaining a collection of antique clocks."

Gaskin was visibly astonished. "All true," he said.

The audience burst into applause. The man's wife, sitting three
rows from the front, stumbled to her feet, clapping wildly.

Gaskin laughed, red-faced. "How the devil did you know
that?"

Moon arched an eyebrow. "Magic," he said.

J can imagine you now, all dewy-eyed and eager for an explanation of how it was that Moon had come to know all this, for a

detailed post-mortem of his deductive processes. Sad to say, I have to disappoint you. What follows can be no more than a tentative reconstruction of his methods.

As I see it, there are three chief possibilities.

The first is that this uncanny display of insight was a deception, that Gaskin was a plant, that he and Moon had arranged their patter in advance. In short—that it was all a trick. What took place immediately after, however, surely rules this out as a serious supposition.

The second is that our hero was an unusually brilliant observer of minutiae, a man of rare deductive skill, a master of intuitive ratiocination cut from the same cloth already stitched and darned by Sir Arthur and Mr. Poe. If the second conjecture is correct, then this—an extrapolation from the few known facts—is my attempt to re-create his methodology.

That the man was a valet was obvious from his air of sullen servility; that he was married from his wedding ring; that he had children from the two toffee-apples bulging stickily from his pockets, purchased (one presumes) as gifts for the little ones. That his father was a tailor was clear from the quality of his jacket (unnaturally fine when set against the threadbare quality of the rest of his clothes); and that the unfortunate parent had died from consumption was elucidated by the faint graveyard scent of mildew and disease which still lingered insidiously about it. A distinct whiff of fish on Gaskin's breath, and behind it an undercurrent of decay, made the man's supper simple to deduce, and the distribution on his fingertips of a rare oil used only in the restoration of antique clocks rendered his chief pastime as plain as if he had tattooed the same upon his forehead.

But doubtless you will say that such things happen only in cheap novels and upon the stage. Perhaps I have allowed myself to become unduly influenced by the yellow-backed vulgarities of sensational fiction.

The third possibility seems on the face of it still less persuasive. Namely, that Edward Moon possessed powers beyond the understanding of conventional science, that he saw into Gaskin's soul and somehow understood him, that—bizarre and outré though I know it must seem written down—he really was a mind-reader.

*T*he applause died away.

"Mr. Gaskin? I must ask you something."

"Anything."

"When did you intend to tell your wife?"

A shadow passed across the man's face. "I don't understand."

Moon addressed his next remark to the unenviable Mrs. Gaskin who still stood in the third row of the stalls, puce-faced and flushed with pride. "My sympathies, ma'am," he said. "It gives me no pleasure to inform you that your husband is a liar, a cheat and an adulterer."

A few delighted sniggers from the audience.

"For the last eleven months he has been engaged in intimate relations with a scullery maid. And for the past fortnight they have begun to worry that she has fallen pregnant."

A hush descended on the theatre and the smile fled from Mrs. Gaskin's lips. She looked imploringly at her husband and stuttered something unintelligible.

Gaskin snarled. "Damn your eyes!" he cried and made as if to spring at Moon. But before he could strike, a figure glided onstage and moved wordlessly between the two antagonists, like some animate portcullis lowered in the magician's defence.

Gaskin looked up to realise that he was standing opposite the Somnambulist, his face approximately level with the giant's sternum. The big man shielded Moon, as silent and impassive as an uprooted Easter Island statue. In the face of so irresistible a force, so immovable an object, the man sloped swiftly and shamefacedly away, gabbling his apologies and leaving stage and theatre at a craven trot. His wife followed soon after.

Moon allowed himself a private, faintly malicious smile at their departure before flinging wide his arms. "Applause," he cried, "for the city's most remarkable man! Asleep! Awake! The celebrated sleepwalker of Albion Square! Ladies and gentlemen, I give you . . . the Somnambulist!"

The audience bellowed their approval and the giant managed a stiff, embarrassed bow.

At the back of the stalls, somebody called out, "The swords!" His fellows took up the cry. "The swords! The swords!" Soon most of the audience were chanting the same.

Moon clapped the Somnambulist affectionately on the back.

"Come along," he said. "We mustn't disappoint our public." *Sotto voce* he added: "Thank you."

Moon disappeared, returning with half a dozen wicked-looking swords (borrowed on long loan from Her Majesty's Coldstream Guards). The orchestra struck up a familiar melody, and at this signal the Somnambulist removed his jacket to reveal his spotless, starched white shirt.

The theatre was silent as everyone waited for what they knew was coming. A member of the audience was brought up to test the genuine nature of the weapons and to certify that the Somnambulist himself was not wearing any padding, device or piece of mechanical trickery. This accomplished, Moon drew out one of the swords. Under the pitiless gaze of the lights and in full view of the crowd, he plunged the blade deep into the Somnambulist's chest. The tip entered the giant's body with a slippery, sucking sound before emerging seconds later, with stomach-churning inevitability, from the centre of his back. The Somnambulist did not so much as blink in response. Some of the audience cheered, some gasped, others stared on in goggle-eyed amazement. Several ladies (and more than one gentleman) were seen to swoon at the sight of it.

Another drum roll and Moon renewed his attack, this time pushing the blade deep into the thick of the Somnambulist's neck and out through the back of his head. Without respite, he did the same again, now skewering the man's thigh, now his chest, and lastly, and most painfully of all, his groin.

Like a bored commuter waiting for his train, the Somnambulist yawned in response. He remained still for the whole of his ordeal, immune to what must surely have been the most exquisite agony. Any other man would have fallen long ago but the giant stood resolute throughout.

Perhaps the most startling scene of the performance arrived at its conclusion. As Moon removed the swords from his assistant's body and held them up for inspection, I saw that not only was there not a trace of blood discernible on any of the blades but also the Somnambulist's shirt, though pierced and torn, remained an unsullied white.

Both men bowed, to genuine applause. The most celebrated part of their act, it had not disappointed.

No doubt the audience assumed that what they had seen was an optical illusion. Some may have speculated idly about trick swords, elaborate sleight of hand, gimmicked shirts, smoke and mirrors, but whatever their theories they never doubted that what they had seen had been anything other than an unusually impressive piece of prestidigitation. It was a parlour game, surely. A conjuring trick.

The truth, as you shall see, was infinitely stranger.

The remainder of the performance took place without incident and the audience seemed to go home satisfied.

But still Edward Moon was unhappy. He had tired years ago of giving the same routine every night and went on with it now only in an attempt to stave off ennui. He was chronically, terminally, dangerously bored.

After the show, it had long been his habit to leave by the stage door and stand in the street, to smoke and watch his audience disperse. Well-wishers sometimes lingered on and he was happy enough to spend a moment or two with each of them, making small talk and acknowledging their compliments. A small knot of admirers waited that night and he dealt with them all with his customary courtesy. One woman stayed longer than the rest. Moon stretched and yawned. He wasn't tired, but in those days and months when boredom took him in its grip he would often sleep his days away, slumbering twelve or thirteen hours at a time. "Yes?" he asked.

The woman seemed incongruous in Albion Square. Patrician, elegantly middle-aged, she had an aloofness about her, a haughty *froideur*. In her salad days, he thought, she must have been a considerable beauty.

"I am Lady Glendinning," she began. "But you may call me Elizabeth."

Moon, doing his best not to look impressed, affected a nonchalant expression. "Pleased to make your acquaintance."

"I enjoyed the performance."

He shrugged. "Thank you for coming."

"Mr. Moon?" She paused. "I've heard rumours about you."

The conjuror raised an eyebrow. "What have you heard?"

"That you're more than a magician. That you investigate."

"Investigate?"

"I have a problem. I need your help."

"Go on."

Lady Glendinning made a strange snuffling sound. "My husband is dead."

Moon managed a reasonable simulacrum of sympathy. "My condolences."

"He was murdered."

That last, heady word had a tremendous effect on the conjuror. Moon felt giddy at the sound of it and it was only with an enormous effort of will that he was able to stifle a grin.

"I'm determined to see justice done," she continued, "but the police are quite hopeless. I'm sure they'll bungle the whole business. So I thought of you. I confess that, as a girl, I was quite an admirer of your adventures."

Moon's vanity got the better of him. "As a *girl*?" he asked incredulously. "How long ago was that?"

"Some few years. But one finds one rather grows out of detective stories, doesn't one?"

"One does?" said Moon, who had never felt any such thing.

Lady Glendinning gave him a chilly smile. "Will you help me?"

Moon took the woman's hand and kissed it. "Madam," he said, "it would be an honour."

*E*dward Moon and the Somnambulist lived, rather improbably, in a cellar beneath the theatre. They had converted the basement into a comfortable living space with the result that two bedrooms, a well-equipped kitchen, a drawing room, a considerable if hopelessly cluttered library and all conceivable conveniences lay below the Theatre of Marvels. Needless to say, their audience remained entirely ignorant of this subterranean domesticity, this sunken home-from-home.

Moon said goodbye to Lady Glendinning with a promise to visit her the following day. The prospect of relief from boredom cheered him no end and as he strode towards the strategically placed rhododendrons which masked the wooden steps leading down to his lodgings, something like a smile hovered discreetly about his lips.

As usual, Mr. Speight sat, or rather slouched, upon the steps.

Speight was a derelict, a pauper whose presence Moon had long tolerated, allowing him over time to become something of a fixture. Unkempt and raggedly bearded, the man was hunched inside a filthy suit, a stack of empty bottles nestling miserably by his feet. Propped up beside him was the wooden placard which he spent his days carrying through the streets of the city. Its message had begun to fade but it still read in thick, gothic letters:

SURELY I AM COMING SOON
REVELATION 22:20

Moon had never asked Speight why he found it necessary to carry this notice wherever he went nor why he had chosen that particular piece of scripture as his motto. Frankly, he rather doubted he would have understood the answer. Speight slurred a bleary "Good evening." The conjuror responded as politely as he was able, stepped over the vagrant and let himself indoors.

Inside, beside a pot of tea simmering aromatically on the stove, Mrs. Grossmith was waiting for him. A diminutive, maternal woman, she took Moon's coat and poured him a cup of Earl Grey.

Moon sank gratefully into his chair. "Thank you."

She shuffled deferentially. "A successful performance?"

He sipped his tea. "I think they liked it."

"I see our Mr. Speight's outside again tonight."

"As he surely will be till the End. You don't mind?"

Mrs. Grossmith sniffed disparagingly. "I suppose he's harmless enough."

"You're not convinced."

She wrinkled her nose. "Frankly, Mr. Moon . . . he smells."

"Should I invite him in? Offer him a bath? Is that what you'd like?"

Grossmith rolled her eyes in exasperation.

"Where's the Somnambulist?"

"I believe he's already retired to bed."

Moon got to his feet and placed his tea, not half-finished, upon the table. "Then I think perhaps I should join him. Goodnight, Mrs. Grossmith."

"Your usual breakfast in the morning?"

"Make it early. I'm going out."

"Something interesting?"

"A case, Mrs. Grossmith. A case!"

Moon walked through to the bedroom he shared with the Somnambulist. They slept in bunk beds, Moon on top, the giant below.

The Somnambulist had changed into a set of striped pyjamas (due to his excessive size, these had to be produced for him bespoke) and was sitting up in bed, chalk and blackboard by his side, engrossed in a slim volume of verse.

He was also entirely bald.

Every morning, using an especially tenacious brand of spirit gum, the Somnambulist applied a wig to his scalp and false whiskers to either side of his face. Each night before bed he removed them. On this point, I wish to make myself absolutely, unequivocally clear: the Somnambulist was more than simply bald—he was utterly hairless, unnaturally smooth, billiard ball–like in his depilation. It was a secret he and Moon had guarded fiercely for years. Even Mrs. Grossmith had only found out by accident. The giant was not without his own, unnatural vanity.

As Moon entered the room, the Somnambulist put aside his book and looked up with drowsy eyes. His bald pate shone comfortingly in the gloom.

The conjuror was barely able to contain his excitement. "We have a case!" he cried.

The Somnambulist smiled lethargically, but before his friend could explain any further he rolled over, closed his eyes and went to sleep.

His dreams, their precise contents and nature, sadly lie beyond my jurisdiction.

The next morning, the body of Cyril Honeyman, almost unrecognisably contorted after its unwinnable struggle with the laws of gravity, was laid to rest at a small private service attended by close family and a smattering of theatrical acquaintances. Moon, meanwhile, was racing off on a wild-goose chase—an unfortunate missed opportunity and a sad misjudgement which, as things turned out, were to cost more than one innocent life.

It might be of some trivial interest to learn that chief amongst the Somnambulist's many idiosyncrasies and peccadilloes was a passion for milk—not a fondness, you understand, or a liking for, nor

even a mere partiality, but a *passion*. He guzzled whole pints o
stuff at a time, pouring it down his throat long after his thirst had
been assuaged and, in all the years he had spent with Moon, had
never once shown the slightest interest in any other beverage. He
drank compulsively, it seemed, bibulously, as though he could not
live without it.

It was far from unusual, then, that when the detective got out
of bed and slouched through to the kitchen he found the Somnambulist at the breakfast table with three large glasses of milk
lined up before him. On his entrance, the giant took a big, slurpy
sip from one of the glasses, splashing his drink in a broad white
swathe across his upper lip. Moon motioned discreetly towards
the spillage and watched, indulgent, as the Somnambulist wiped
it away.

"I'm going out presently," he said, tussling with teapot and
kettle. "Thought I might drop in at the Stacks. See what I can dig
up on this Glendinning business."

The Somnambulist inclined his head in a manner which made
his lack of interest abundantly clear.

"Would you like to visit the scene of the crime?"

A half-hearted nod.

"We've an appointment with Lady Glendinning at noon. Meet
me by the library gates at eleven." Moon gave his friend a stern
look. "And by that I mean eleven sharp. This is important. We
can't afford to be late."

The Somnambulist rolled his eyes. Moon poured himself some
tea and disappeared back to their bedroom.

As usual, Mrs. Grossmith had laid a freshly ironed copy of the
Times upon the breakfast table that morning, its headline shrieking something about the savage execution of a fat actor in the
seamiest district of the city. Unfortunately, those words were almost wholly obscured by a large bottle of the Somnambulist's
milk, with the result that Edward Moon, his mind hopelessly

aflutter with the Glendinning business, had glanced at the paper
once and then given it no further thought.

Some time later, he left the house alone and hailed a cab to the
West End where he made his way directly to the Reading Room
of the British Museum. Despite the earliness of the hour the place
was filled almost to capacity as people reserved their seats for the
day, their crumbling volumes heaped before them, hoarded as
fiercely as dragons would their gold. Moon recognised a few of
his fellow regulars and they exchanged polite, noncommittal
nods. For many of them the Reading Room was a second home,
the eternal hush of the place, its tangible atmosphere of scholar-
ship, a sanctuary from the relentless clamour of the city.

He presented himself to one of the librarians, a sandy-haired,
neatly scrubbed young man freshly down from one of the universities.

"I'm here to see the Archivist."

The librarian looked at him uncertainly, then glanced warily
about. "You have an appointment?"

"Naturally."

"Quickly, then. Follow me."

He led Moon towards the rear of the room where a small black
door was situated, cobwebbed, unprepossessing, paint peeling
from neglect. Checking that no one was watching, the librarian
fished an oddly shaped key from his jacket pocket. Moon noticed
that his hand shook slightly with nerves and that he experienced a
moment's difficulty slipping the key into place.

"Good luck."

Without reply, Moon stepped inside.

Not bothering to hide his relief, the librarian shut the door
smartly behind him and Moon heard the key creak and complain
as it turned in the lock.

The room beyond was so poorly lit that it was impossib
first to see how far the space extended. In the gloom it seer
cavernous, resembling less a man-made structure than something
hewn out by the Earth itself, formed by the processes of time. The
place was filled with paper—shelves of it, vast stacks and racks,
acres of documentation, books, journals, manuscripts, pamphlets,
periodicals and ledgers—stacks stretching almost to the ceiling
and lending the room a dizzying, vertiginous air.

"Mr. Moon. It's been too long." The voice came from behind a
pile of leprous-looking newspapers, all of them faded, curling at
the edges and stacked so high that they would dwarf even the
Somnambulist. The speaker stepped into the light. She was a
woman in the furthest reaches of old age, enfeebled, bent all but
double with decrepitude. She looked up at Moon with a milk-
white blankness where her eyes should have been.

You've heard of the Archivist, I suppose? She knew every inch
of that place. She was its guardian and tutelary spirit, and through
her files and records, she felt, physician-like, the fevered heartbeat of criminal London.

"You may turn up the light," she said. "One of us, I know, has
need of it."

Obediently, he adjusted the lamp and the room was illumined
by a gentle glow.

"I take it you're working on a case?"

"Yes, ma'am. The Glendinning business."

"Ah. All most unpleasant, from what one's heard. I gather it
was poison. Such a cruel method. But will we ever see an account
of your investigation? I understand Mr. Stoddart has made you an
offer."

Moon wondered how she had come by this information. "I doubt
it, ma'am."

"Pity." The Archivist tugged a handkerchief from her sleeve
and blew her nose, noisily and at length. Moon could hear the

mucus rattling through her system like an old boiler filled with air. "You're bored," she said.

"I've not had a case to test my abilities for a year or more."

"Since Clapham," the old woman commented quietly.

Moon ignored the aside. "Pulling rabbits from hats is no way for a man of my talent to make a living."

"I've visited your theatre, Mr. Moon. I saw neither rabbits nor hats. But I mustn't keep you. You've a killer to catch. Let me see what I can dig up." She tottered precariously away amongst the stacks.

Moon took a seat by the door, but no sooner had he done so than the Archivist returned, half a dozen musty ledgers in her hands, as though she had known all along what he had come for and had set aside the relevant volumes accordingly.

She put a wrinkled hand on his shoulder. "You've got two hours. I've a visitor at eleven."

"I don't suppose it's worth my asking for a name?"

"You ought to know the rules by now," she answered, unsmiling.

Chastened, Moon flipped open the first of the books.

"Tell me if you require anything further."

"Of course," he murmured, already engrossed. The Archivist patted him gently, maternally, on the shoulder and vanished into the depths of the room.

The Stacks were a secret known to fewer than a hundred men in England. Edward Moon was proud to be one of them.

When he emerged by the iron gates of the museum at eleven o'clock sharp, he was gratified to see that the Somnambulist was already waiting, hirsute again.

Were YOU SUCSESFUL

"Very," said Moon, trying not to grimace at the spelling.

Shouldering aside a newsboy who was busy straining his larynx by hollering about the death of an actor in bizarre and scandalous circumstances, Moon hailed another cab, gave the driver Lady Glendinning's address and, clearing his mind of all external distraction (especially, unfortunately, the child still bellowing outside), began to prepare himself for the main event.

Lady Glendinning lived in Hampstead, in a grand town house, grossly outnumbered by servants, butlers, cooks, drivers, gardeners, scullery maids—all the human paraphernalia, in fact, of the seriously rich. When they arrived, the conjuror leapt excitedly from the cab, leaving the Somnambulist to pay the driver.

Moon had hoped for an opportunity to employ his usual modus operandi: to examine the murder room, interview the suspects one by one, size up the likeliest culprit and summon them all into the drawing room to unveil the killer. But as soon as they arrived he saw that the house was alive with activity—bustling blue-coated policemen, swarms of scribbling reporters, the idle public gawping at the sport of it all.

Lady Glendinning must have observed Moon's arrival. She walked up the drive towards him—press, police and hoi polloi parting before her as though she were some terrible queen whose slightest glance might mean death. She stopped mere inches before him.

"You're too late."

"If you'll permit me to say so, ma'am, I think we're absolutely punctual. Though I'm surprised at all this activity. I hope to goodness the police haven't trampled over too much of the scene."

"No, I mean you're too late. Hard cheese, Mr. Moon. It's over."

"Over?" Moon asked, but the woman had already turned away and was returning to the house.

The Somnambulist frowned.

In the distance, they heard probably the most inappropriate noise possible at a murder scene: a raucous, slightly dirty laugh. At a nudge from the giant, Moon looked up to see a familiar figure strolling towards them, waving delightedly. "Mr. Moon!" The man drew closer, beamed and stuck out his right hand in greeting. "Edward."

The conjuror could muster little enthusiasm. "Good morning, Inspector."

Bulky, ruddy-cheeked, fanatically jovial and sporting an extravagant pair of muttonchop whiskers, Detective Inspector Merryweather was in look and manner powerfully reminiscent of Mr. Dickens's Ghost of Christmas Past. He chuckled. "Seems you've missed the boat, old man. Early bird and all that—"

"I'm sorry?"

"Case closed, I'm afraid. Murder's been solved. We've got the killer in custody."

Moon gave him a sceptical look. "Are you sure? This wouldn't be the first time you've arrested the wrong man."

"True enough, and don't say I haven't admitted it. But not here. It's a simple business. Open and shut. We've got a confession."

Moon's disappointment was palpable. "Oh."

The Somnambulist gave him a discreet pat on the back and Moon brightened a little at the gesture. "May I ask . . . who did it?"

Merryweather laughed again, another tremendous *profundo* exhalation. "Let's just say"—he winked—"that it was one of the domestic staff."

A gaggle of uniformed policemen strode past, escorting a tall, soberly dressed gentleman in handcuffs. He had shifty eyes and was muttering bitterly under his breath. When he passed the inspector, he spat theatrically on the ground.

Merryweather gave the man a jocular wave and clapped Moon on the back. "I shouldn't worry about it. Believe me, it wasn't worthy of you. It was too ordinary. Predictable and . . . what's the word? Formulaic."

"I'm bored, Inspector. I need a diversion."

"The lads and me are going to the pub to celebrate. Care to join us?"

Moon sniffed. "Not today. We've a show to do."

"Well, then. I'm sure we'll meet again before long."

"Perhaps."

Merryweather looked nervously towards the Somnambulist. "Goodbye."

The giant waved and the inspector strode back towards his men, palpably relieved.

"We should leave," Moon said gloomily. "We're redundant here."

They started back towards the theatre, the detective silent and lost in contemplation.

"I think it's gone," he said at last. "I had a bit of talent once but I think it's vanished."

The giant did his best to cheer him up.

UNLUCKEE

"P'raps my time's past. That's all. I've gone to seed."

The Somnambulist gave him a glum smile.

"I need something more. Something . . . gothic and bizarre. Like the old days."

A sudden gust of wind sent a flurry of litter eddying around them, entangling a single sheet of yesterday's *Gazette* around Moon's shoes. Its headline screamed:

HORRIBLE MURDER!
HAM ACTOR THROWN FROM TOWER!
POLICE BAFFLED!

But so caught up was he in his introspection that the detective didn't even notice. He screwed the paper up into a ball, tossed it over his shoulder and trudged forlornly on.

5

Edward Moon was bored.

He had been smoking for hours, lying stretched out on the couch in a corner of his study, enveloped by the tobacco fog which blanketed the room, thick and suffocating as a nicotine peasouper. He yawned and extended a languorous arm for another cigarette.

Mrs. Grossmith bustled in, a half-glimpsed figure amongst the fug. "Mr. Moon?" she asked in a querulous voice which suggested that she stood in her usual posture of disapproval, hands on hips. The atmosphere was too hazy to be certain, but from his long experience of the woman, Moon thought this entirely likely.

"Bored again?"

"I'm afraid so." He lit the cigarette and settled back into the couch. "Sorry to disappoint you."

"You get bored," the housekeeper said sternly, "the way other men get the clap."

Moon gave a thin-lipped smile. "Very good."

"You'll have to stop smoking in here. Given that we live in a house without windows, I absolutely refuse to tolerate it a moment longer. You'll poison us all if you carry on like this. You're a positive menace."

The conjuror blew out a long grey stream of smoke. "You're not the first to have said so. But I must confess that coming from you it stings a little more."

"Be reasonable."

Ruefully, he stubbed out the remainder of the cigarette and got to his feet. "No doubt you're right. Besides, I think I'm starting to get bored with ennui."

Mrs. Grossmith snorted disapprovingly. "You're quite impossible when you're like this."

"And you're a saint to put up with me."

"Can't you get out? Go for a walk. Take some air."

Moon seemed unconvinced but Grossmith persisted. "It'd do you good. This atmosphere can't be healthy." She gave a phlegmy, melodramatic cough.

"Perhaps I shall go out for a little while."

Mrs. Grossmith sounded pleased. "You can't expect a mystery every week."

"Can't I?" Moon looked disappointed, like a child on Christmas morning who wakes to find his stocking filled only with a farthing and a bruised orange. "You know, I long for a world where violent crime is so commonplace that I'm kept in constant employment."

"A strange wish."

He sighed. "Not that villainy is what it was. The age of the truly great criminal is past. Since Barabbas . . . Mediocrity, Mrs. Grossmith. Mediocrity as far as the eye can see. A case in point: You remember the robber the Somnambulist and I foiled a couple of years ago? The man who'd planned to burrow his way into the Bank of England but ended up digging into the sewers instead?"

"I remember, sir."

"His name escapes me at present. Can you recall it?"

"I'm afraid not."

"You see? Forgettable. All of them—to a man—forgettable."

Mrs. Grossmith forced a smile. "This boredom will pass, sir. It usually does."

"Yes," Moon almost whispered to himself. "I know the remedy."

"You're going for a stroll, then?"

"That's right. For a stroll."

Moon walked away and Grossmith heard him move through the house, trotting spryly up the hidden steps, past the rhododendrons, out onto the street.

The Somnambulist ambled in from the kitchen, an enormous jug of milk in one hand. He gave Mrs. Grossmith a quizzical look and gesticulated a brief message.

"Where's he gone?" she asked. "Is that what you mean?"

The giant nodded solemnly.

She sighed. "I think we both know the answer to that."

The Somnambulist did not reply but, head sunk low onto chest, milk cradled to his bosom, made his way mournfully back towards the kitchen.

❖

After exchanging a few slurred words with Mr. Speight (who had wedged himself into what looked like a surprisingly comfortable position on the steps), Moon left the Theatre of

Marvels and headed towards a disreputable district of the city, well known to him and to those others who shared his regrettable predilections. It was a route he knew by heart and he covered the distance in less than an hour, having no desire to hail a cab. He needed this time alone to prepare himself. Indeed, so intent was he on his journey that he entirely failed to notice that for its final fifteen minutes he was most expertly followed.

His destination was a dilapidated flat at the end of an alley a few minutes' walk from Goodge Street, in that unprepossessing area of the city still a decade or so away from being known as "Fitzrovia." The shutters of the place were tightly drawn but an enticing glow escaped at their edges. Looking quickly about him to make certain he was alone, Moon knocked six times in a precisely ordered pattern. As he waited, he was certain that hidden eyes were watching him from the other side of the door, and felt a profoundly uncomfortable conviction that somewhere within the house he was the subject of scrutiny and debate.

The door opened at last. An enormously fat woman stood before him, bathed in greasy yellow light, reeking of cheap perfume. Titanically vast, she relied upon a walking stick to support her stupendous bulk. "Mr. Gray!" She beamed. "It's been too long."

Moon shuffled his feet uncomfortably on the doorstep.

"Bored again?"

He nodded sheepishly and the woman gave a low, blubbery laugh. Hobbling forward, she ushered Moon over the threshold and closed the door behind him.

Inside, the air was thick with incense and the smell of desire. Moon walked into a large reception room, opulently and lavishly furnished, dripping with the trappings of immoral wealth. He moved swiftly across it to sit in one of half a dozen luxuriously upholstered chairs. This was a place and procedure he knew hor ribly well.

The woman gave a coarse smile. "We've got a new one in to-night."

*O*f all the brothels in London, Mrs. Puggsley's was by far the most distinguished, catering as it did to a select and discerning clientele. The men who patronised her establishment came there for services which could not be provided by any other of the city's houses. They had special, unique tastes—preferences which, to the innocent, unjaded eye of the reader, may seem distasteful and even repugnant. Don't say I didn't warn you.

*D*oes she have a name?"

"Mina," the woman purred. "You'll like her."

"And Lucy? Mary? Where are they tonight?"

"They're with other clients at present. Why don't you meet our Mina, Mr. Gray? I promise you shan't be disappointed."

Moon winced inwardly as Mrs. Puggsley used his pseudonym again. He was certain she had realised long ago that it was an as-sumed name, and in his darkest moments feared even that she had stumbled upon his true identity. He wondered occasionally if she used "Gray" to tease and taunt him, as a way of telling him she knew.

He nodded. "Show her in."

Puggsley gave an oleaginous bow. "Settle back, Mr. Gray. Relax. See your darkest dreams come to life before your eyes."

Six soft taps came at the front door, the same code Moon had used moments earlier.

"Excuse me." Puggsley waddled across the room, peered

through a small hole bored at eye height and let out a wet, gurgling giggle. "It's Pluck."

She unbolted the door and admitted her latest customer, a short, balding, well-fed man with painfully pockmarked skin. The madam spread wide her arms in a florid gesture of introduction. "Mr. Gray? Meet Mr. Pluck."

Warily, the two men shook hands. Pluck's handshake was moist and feeble and Moon was barely able to resist the impulse to wipe away the stranger's dampness from his palm.

"Charmed," he said acidly.

"Gentlemen, talk amongst yourselves. I'll be back shortly with a little slice of paradise." With a final bow and a chubby flourish, Mrs. Puggsley disappeared from the parlour and vanished into the bowels of the house. Pluck pulled up a chair.

"I love it here," he confided. "Come whenever I can. Whenever I can afford to, you understand. You know, before I discovered this place I thought nobody on earth felt the same way as me, I thought I must be ill. You understand, Mr. Gray? I thought I was a freak."

"Quite so," Moon said vaguely.

"Course. I knew you'd understand. We've prolly got a lot in common. This hobby of ours, for one. Tell me—when did you realise that you shared our . . . inclinations?"

Moon, having no desire to dignify the man's question with an answer, took a cigarette from his pocket and lit up. For courtesy's sake he offered his neighbour the same. Happily, Pluck accepted, and for a few moments there was just smoke and blissful silence.

"I hear there's a new girl," Pluck said between puffs. "Any idea what she'll be like?"

"None."

"Seems we're about to find out." Pluck managed a rough approximation of a light laugh—an awful, anxious, scraping sound.

Mercifully, Mrs. Puggsley returned at that moment, rolling back into the room with her usual mastodon grace. In her wake was a most unusual woman who nonetheless, at first sight, appeared wholly unremarkable. She was fetching enough (one would expect nothing less from the Puggsley stable) with a pleasingly symmetrical face and a smooth, attractively dimpled complexion. She was dressed in a filmy white gown tied at the waist by a slender piece of cord, clasped tight enough to accentuate her natural curves. But what marked her out from the legions of similarly pretty but unassuming women one passes every day on the street was that she also sported a monstrously bushy black beard.

"Is it real?" Pluck asked, his voice hushed and reverential.

Mrs. Puggsley acted scandalised. "Mr. Pluck! What do you take me for?"

"May I touch it?"

Puggsley turned to the girl. "Mina?"

She nodded and simpered with practised coyness. Pluck reached out to her facial hair and stroked, eyes half-shut, transported in bliss. "You're so beautiful," he murmured. Mina gave a smoothly professional smile which suggested she was well used to this kind of compliment.

Moon yawned. "Anything else?"

"You always want more, don't you, Mr. Gray?"

"I pay you for it."

Puggsley ushered Pluck back to his seat, then untied the cord around Mina's waist, gently slipping away her gown to leave the girl naked before them. Her body had a ripe, plump sensuality but was not in itself remarkable.

Dangling between her breasts, however, was something extraordinary—a curious deformity, a grisly pink piece of flesh which bore a ghastly, visceral resemblance to the severed arm of an infant. It flopped and twitched slightly as they stared, almost as if it were aware of their fascinated attention.

Moon licked his lips. "Magnificent."

"Gentlemen." Puggsley beamed with pride. "She's yours for the asking."

Moon and Pluck smiled wolfishly as one.

"What am I bid?"

Pluck named a sum most likely equal to his wages for a week. Without hesitation, Moon doubled it. Pluck suggested a modest advance, only for his opponent to instantly double the offer again. Crestfallen, the little man admitted defeat. "She's yours."

"Use her well," Mrs. Puggsley said sternly.

"I'll use her as I please." Moon took Mina by the hand and led her from the room, heading for a boudoir on one of the upper floors of the house. As he left he could hear Puggsley doing her best to cheer up the loser.

"Bad luck, sir. But I've plenty more as would love to meet you. The seal girl will be free in an hour. The pinhead's ready now. And if you're happy to wait a bit, we've got a new Siamese coming in later."

Edward Moon disappeared upstairs and heard no more. And for the next three luxurious hours he gave himself up to the caresses of a bearded lady.

Moon stepped out of Mrs. Puggsley's house, gingerly pulled shut the front door and looked cautiously about him. Mistakenly thinking himself unobserved, he walked to the end of the alley and turned left into Goodge Street, starting for home. The pavement was deserted, eerily silent, and his footsteps rang out loudly as he walked, but he had gone no more than a few yards before the still of the night was interrupted by a discreet, dry cough. Startled, Moon turned to see a man standing close behind him.

He was neat and small and fussy in appearance, with a pair of gold-rimmed pince-nez balanced precisely on the tip of his nose. His complexion was chalky and unusually pallid; his hair pure white.

A look of grim recognition crossed Moon's face and he nodded with icy politeness. "Mr. Skimpole."

The albino gave a courteous bow. Despite his faintly comical appearance there was something threatening about him, a tangible air of menace.

"I didn't see you," Moon explained.

"People rarely do."

"And how long have you been following me?"

Skimpole brushed the question aside. "Give my regards to Mrs. Puggsley."

"What do you want?"

The albino stared impassively at him, the lower halves of his eyes magnified weirdly by the pince-nez. "I need your help."

Moon snorted in reply and began to walk away.

Skimpole hurried after him. "Wait."

"I've refused before. My answer has not changed."

"There is a plot against the city. Some conspiracy has been set in motion. The Directorate needs you. Your country needs you."

"Find another stooge."

"Something's happening. Can't you sense it? Some great crisis is upon us."

Moon stopped dead in the street and turned to face his tormentor. "Must be your imagination, Mr. Skimpole. Too much cheese before bedtime."

"I could make you . . ." Skimpole spoke lightly. *"Mr. Gray."*

Moon said nothing.

Skimpole's pale face contorted itself into a semblance of a smile. "You'll help me."

Moon smiled back with excruciating civility. "Even I have

...e scruples. You'll have to put a gun to my head before I'll help you."

He strode away and Skimpole watched as he melted into the distance. "It may come to that," he said softly. Then, more firmly: "It may yet come to that."

*T*he following day did not start well. The ape Moon had used in his act for the past two years fell unexpectedly ill and was prescribed by his veterinarian a rest cure of indefinite duration. The zoo sent a replacement but he was an obstreperous, troublesome fellow with none of the natural talent of his predecessor. Asked to caper with enthusiasm, he gibbered listlessly; required to materialise with style and panache, he limped onstage with all the eagerness of a condemned man queueing for his final meal.

It was with relief, then, that Moon returned home at the end of the show, the Somnambulist choosing to linger upstairs a while longer in an attempt to cajole some semblance of a performance from the recalcitrant chimp.

When Moon let himself inside, Speight was dozing uneasily on the steps. On hearing his arrival, Mrs. Grossmith hurried out to greet him. "There's somebody waiting for you. I said it was late but he did insist."

"Who is it?" Moon lowered his voice to a whisper. "Is it the albino?"

Someone out of sight laughed uproariously.

Moon walked into the kitchen to find an ungainly figure sprawled in his favourite armchair.

"Albino?" The visitor laughed again. "Really, Moon, I swear your friends get odder each time we meet."

Moon allowed himself a small smile. "Inspector."

Detective Inspector Merryweather got to his feet and shook

Moon warmly by the hand. "Pleasure to see you again. I wish that one day we might meet under happier circumstanc

As Mrs. Grossmith retired discreetly to her room, Moon produced a bottle of whisky and a set of glasses, sat opposite his guest and poured them both a generous draught. "I take it this is a professional visit?"

" 'Fraid so. I apologise for the lateness of the hour but I'm at my wits' end."

"You mean you have a case for me?"

"You've seen the headlines?"

"The Honeyman business? I've followed your lamentable lack of progress with no little disappointment, Inspector. I'd hoped by now that you might have learnt something from my methods."

"We've done our best. But take my word for it, it's the strangest one yet. The most baffling case of my career."

Moon arched an eyebrow. "Aren't they all?"

"This one's special," the man insisted. "There's something queer about it, something grisly and gothic and bizarre. So you see why I thought of you."

"It sounds perfect."

Merryweather laughed again, another raucous, splenetic bellow. "Mrs. Grossmith told me you were bored. You know, by rights, I shouldn't be here. My colleagues don't approve. They think I've got rather an *idée fixe* about you. Still, since that business in Clapham—"

The conjuror flinched.

"Well, they're not so inclined to turn a blind eye any more."

HELLO INSPECTOR

Merryweather had always felt oddly discomfited in the presence of the Somnambulist, and on the giant's entrance the inspector's natural good cheer was immediately muted.

The Somnambulist sat down, tore off his tie and poured himself a tot of milk. He had just raised the glass to his lips when Moon got to his feet and turned to the inspector. "Well, then," he said impatiently, "I want to see where it happened."

❀

An hour later, the three of them stood at the top of the tower where the late Cyril Honeyman had taken his final, ignominious curtain call. The window through which he had fallen had not yet been repaired and the room was bitingly cold. The smell of decay congealed in the air, its source a table stacked with putrid, long-abandoned food—what was once a great feast made stinking and corrupt.

"My apologies for the smell," Merryweather said. He was wrapped up in a thick woollen coat, a black slab of scarf knotted about his neck. "There was a bottle of champagne here as well but the boys polished that off days ago."

Moon ran a finger along the table, stained gangrenous and grey by dust and mould.

"What was this place?"

"No one's quite sure. We think it might be some sort of water tower. Disused," he added rather desperately. "Can't find it on any maps. Doesn't seem to exist officially."

"I don't think it's a water tower, Inspector." Moon stood by the window, gazing absently down at the street. "I think it's a watchtower."

"Sorry about the mess. The Met boys seem to have trampled your evidence half to death."

Brandishing his chalkboard, the Somnambulist tapped Moon on the shoulder.

SUEISIDE

Moon dismissed the suggestion with a brusque wave of his hand.

"You know the reputation of this district," Merryweather said. "Given the food and the bed, we think he may have been lured here."

Moon hardly seemed to hear him. "I should have thought that was obvious." He knelt at the foot of the shattered window and picked up some broken pieces from the floor. "See the way the glass has fallen. If Honeyman broke the window when he fell, I would expect to find glass only outside. There's far too much in here for that to have been the case."

Merryweather furrowed his brow. "What are you implying?"

"That someone—or something—broke the window from the other side. From outside the tower. Something got in."

"Impossible. No one could possibly climb this high."

"Curious, isn't it?"

Merryweather sighed. "Will you take the case?"

Moon did not reply.

"I don't understand. You've been longing for something like this. Something knotty, you said, something complex, like the old days. Something with the stamp of real criminal ability about it. By rights, this ought to be a dream for you."

"Dream?" Moon repeated absently and began to shift the glass shards about the floor, rearranging them in a fresh pattern free of any discernible order.

"Will you take the case?"

Moon gave a distracted nod. "Against my better judgement."

"What does that mean?"

"It means that there is something wrong here, Inspector. It means that this is no ordinary crime, that it has some larger meaning. That we're on the edge of something terrible."

Merryweather laughed. "Good God, do you always have to be so gloomy?"

Moon gazed unblinkingly back, silent and solemn, shaming the inspector into silence.

The Somnambulist pulled a childish face and wrote another message.

FRIGHTENED

Moon did not smile. "You should be," he murmured. "We all should be."

6

The murder of Cyril Honeyman was the sixty-third criminal case to be investigated by Edward Moon. It was the nineteenth in which he had enjoyed the assistance of the Somnambulist and the thirty-fourth sanctioned by Merryweather and the Yard.

It was also to be the last of his career.

He began, as was his custom, by immersing himself in the minutiae of the killing, by haunting the murder site and trawling the streets for clues, interviewing witnesses, speaking to the most tangential of bystanders. But despite his diligence these efforts bore little fruit. It was as though the evidence had been somehow erased from existence, the ground of his enquiries swept clean, become a blank slate, a tabula rasa. He spent long days in the Stacks but could find no trace, not a shred of a clue on the Honeyman affair, nothing to shed light on the man's demise.

nd of the first week, more out of courtesy than any real
ould materially aid his investigation, he and the Som-
t visited the parents of the deceased. They lived in a
ntry house, miles beyond the furthest reaches of the city
and isolated by several acres of green and pleasant land.

An hour after their arrival, during which time they had been
left to wait in the hallway as though they were little more than
common tradesmen, a retainer shuffled out to inform them that his
master and mistress—already severely inconvenienced by their
presence—felt able to receive only one guest. The Somnambulist
was happy to forgo the pleasure and so, shortly after, Moon was
ushered into a draughty office.

The Honeymans sat at the far end of the room, enthroned
behind a great oak table. Neither of them got to their feet when
he entered but gestured silently for Moon to sit several feet
away. When he explained the purpose of his visit (having to
speak more loudly than was natural because of the distance between them) they reacted without any visible sympathy. Mr.
Honeyman, a grey-faced, harassed-looking man trussed up in
pinstripe, explained that they had already told the police everything they knew and that this kind of intrusion was certainly
unwarranted and probably illegal. Moon retorted that he did not
represent the police, going on to remark (somewhat immod-
estly) that he had a better chance than anyone of bringing the
case to a successful conclusion. The man blustered and harrumphed in reply until his wife intervened, fixing Moon with a
basilisk gaze.

"My son is dead. We have answered all these questions before.
My husband and I are satisfied that the police are doing everything in their power to settle the matter. And we most certainly
do not require the services of an amateur." She spat out that last
word with some vigour, as if trying to dislodge an awkward piece
of gristle trapped between her teeth.

"My wife is a devout woman," Mr. Honeyman added mildly, as if that explained everything.

They rose to their feet and filed silently from the room. Evidently, Moon's audience was at an end.

The Somnambulist was waiting outside, standing by the fish pond and engaged in a conversation with a gardener about the finer points of tree surgery. The giant turned away and wrote Moon a message.

CLOOS

Moon shook his head morosely. "Nothing," he said, and stalked away into the foliage.

Later, aboard the train, he sounded almost angry. "Could it just have been random? Motiveless malignancy?"

The Somnambulist shrugged in response.

"But it seems so premeditated. There's something planned about it. A sense of . . . theatre. Grand Guignol. This is not the work of a common hoodlum." He fell silent, brought out his cigarette case and, to the exasperation of his fellow travellers, proceeded to fill the carriage with thick, acrid smoke.

The following evening, Moon and the Somnambulist were invited to a party.

Their hostess was Lady Glyde, a valuable patron in the early days of the theatre and the woman largely responsible for introducing Moon to high society. Her house in Pall Mall was an ugly, ostentatious place, a shrine to wealth and vulgarity, a warren of interlinking rooms and chambers which, despite their considerable size, tonight brimmed almost full.

A manservant took their coats and hats and led them through

the teeming throng into the drawing room. A string quartet were plucking their way through some baroque sonata or other but were all but drowned out by the babble of conversation, the tinkle of polite laughter, the chink and clink of glasses, the sounds of insincerity. The servant stood at the doorway and announced, with the po-faced solemnity of a pastor reading the last rites: "Mr. Edward Moon and the Somnambulist."

The volume dropped momentarily as heads swivelled and turned to ogle these new arrivals. Moon—once the toast of the best soirées in London—offered his most dazzling smile, only to watch his fellow guests glance at him briefly with glazed indifference before returning to their conversations as though nothing of any significance had taken place. A decade ago, dozens would have dashed forward, jostling to the front to be the first to greet him, to shake his hand or fetch him a drink. Many would have asked for autographs. Today, there was only the barest flicker of interest before he was dismissed by the herd.

The servant thrust drinks into their hands and vanished, abandoning them to the uncertain mercy of the mob. The Somnambulist gave Moon a warning nudge as a dumpy, pugnacious-chinned woman pushed her way towards them.

"Mr. Moon!"

The conjuror raised his voice in order to be heard above the tumult. "Lady Glyde."

She reached them at last, clasping Moon's hand with all the feverish pertinacity of a drowning woman. "Edward," she gasped. "I'm quite sure I don't know who half these people are."

The conjuror laughed politely and even the Somnambulist's face cracked a dutiful grin.

"You have drinks?"

"Thank you, ma'am, yes."

She looked curiously at the Somnambulist. "You always choose milk?"

He nodded.

"Come with me," she said, "there's someone you simply have to meet." And she thrust her way back into the scrum, her new companions trailing reluctantly behind. "Are you engaged on a case at present?" she called back.

Moon told her.

"Really?" She seemed genuinely fascinated. "I gather the papers speak of little else. It must be quite a challenge, even for you. Are you very close to a solution?"

"I'm quite lost at present," Moon admitted. "I've yet to find a suspect."

"Well, if anyone can crack the case, I'm sure it's you."

"Thank you, ma'am."

"I must say, you've recovered wonderfully well from that dreadful business in Clapham. Most unpleasant. A lot of men in your position might have given up after that. Thrown in the towel."

Moon did not have time to respond before Lady Glyde stopped beside a small group of women gathered about a young man holding court. Moon caught a little of what he was saying—from the sound of it, something unnecessarily contentious about America.

Squat, freckled and sporting an ugly shock of ginger hair, the fellow cut an unprepossessing figure amongst Lady Glyde's social elite. Stoop-shouldered and stuffed into an ill-fitting tuxedo, he seemed an alien there, an interloper, a moth amongst the butterflies. His face was made up of an unusually revolting set of features and he appeared to be missing a finger on his left hand.

"Enjoying the party?" asked Lady Glyde.

The ugly man beamed. "It reminds me of a marvellous little soirée I went to once before in Bloomsbury . . ."—he paused before delivering his punch line—"in 1934."

Moon took an instinctive dislike to the man. Lady Glyde giggled in a manner quite unbecoming for her age.

"Mr. Moon," said Lady Glyde, with the air of an impresario introducing a music hall act. "Meet Thomas Cribb."

"We've already met," Cribb said quickly.

Moon glared. "I doubt it."

"He won't remember me, but I know Edward well. In fact, I think I'd go so far as to say we're friends."

Lady Glyde laughed and Moon eyed the man with a good measure of confusion. The Somnambulist's reaction, however, was unexpected. On seeing the stranger a kaleidoscope of emotions crossed his face—what almost seemed like recognition, then suspicion, then anger, then rage, then fear. He turned away and disappeared back into the party. Nobody saw him leave.

"Mr. Cribb," said Lady Glyde, "it sounded as if you were having the most fascinating conversation when I arrived."

"Oh yes. Go on, do," squealed one of the women, and the others chattered their empty-headed approval.

Cribb made an unconvincing dumb show of embarrassment before bowing, inevitably, to their demands. "I was speaking of America," he explained, "of what she will achieve a few short years from now."

"And what is that?" one of the women asked. "Civilisation at last?" She snorted at her own waggishness.

"She becomes a great power," Cribb said soberly. "A mighty nation that eclipses our own. Our empire withers and dies."

With the exception of Moon, everyone laughed at this. Lady Glyde all but whooped in delight. "Oh, Thomas," she gasped. "You are wicked."

The man gave what he mistakenly believed to be an enigmatic smile. "I've seen the future, madam. I've lived it."

*T*homas Cribb was an enigma.

As is often the case with men like that, there are innumerable rumours and theories about his origins. He may have been a genuine eccentric, a man with simply no conception of his oddness. He may have been a professional charlatan, a canny self-publicist who had started, disastrously, to believe his own press. More plausibly, he may just have been someone who made up stories to get invited to parties.

He claimed to have knowledge of the future, to have lived there and seen the city a century from now, but whether anyone actually believed this is irrelevant. What mattered was that his stories granted him a colour and theatricality which would otherwise have been quite beyond his grasp. Whenever he spun those yarns, women hung on his every word for what was almost certainly the first time in his life. Middle-aged widows like Lady Glyde adored him. He had cut a swath through polite society and become a fixture at these events, where he was regularly brought on as a kind of semi-comic turn. Above all, they made him interesting.

There is the outside possibility that he was something altogether more significant, but I'll come to that in time.

I met him only once or twice and, frankly, thought very little of the man. But I insist you make up your own mind.

*O*nce Lady Glyde, whispering huskily into his left ear, had told Moon exactly who and what Cribb claimed to be, the detective was so singularly unimpressed that he called the man's honesty into question.

"Mr. Moon!" his hostess exclaimed in mock indignation. "I believe every word he's told me."

"You disappoint me."

Moon stayed for another hour or two, mingling half-heartedly with the other guests, yearning all the while to continue his investigations. The Somnambulist, meanwhile, had found himself an empty chair and a jug of milk and had settled down for some serious drinking.

Moon quit the party as soon as politeness allowed, upon which Lady Glyde took barnacle-like hold of his arm to escort him to the door. They passed Cribb on the way.

"Goodbye, Mr. Moon. I shan't see you again."

"I suspect I'll stand the disappointment."

A sly grin. "But you misunderstand. This may be the last time I see you but it most certainly is *not* the last time you see me. A deal has to happen yet before you see the back of me."

The conjuror just stared. "You're gibbering."

"I'm a two-legged contradiction, Mr. Moon. You'll learn." Cribb gave an oddly wistful little smile, bowed his head once and disappeared back into the crowd.

"Quite something, isn't he?"

"I'm glad he amuses you," said Moon, as Lady Glyde squeezed his arm a little tighter than was really necessary. "But I'm afraid you'll have to forgive me. I must go."

"So soon?"

"I've work to do."

"See you again?" she asked hopefully.

Moon offered a final, tight half-smile. "Goodbye, ma'am."

His obligations for the evening satisfied at last, Moon stepped out into the night.

He had gone barely five paces before he was stopped by a voice, whining and almost familiar. "Edward!"

He turned around. Someone stood silhouetted at the doorway—the ugly man.

"What do you want?" asked Moon, not bothering to hide his irritation.

Cribb grabbed the conjuror's left hand and clasped it in his. It was almost certainly his imagination but Moon could have sworn that the ridiculous little man actually had tears bulging in his eyes.

"Mr. Moon." He trembled, his voice thick with feeling. "Edward."

Moon did his best to extricate his hand but Cribb held it tight. "Please. Let me speak. Let me say this. We've been through so much together."

"Nonsense. We've barely met."

"Oh, we've faced death together, you and I. We've looked the worst this city has to offer in the eye and lived to tell the tale. I'd like to say what an honour and a privilege it has been to know you. To . . ." Choked with emotion, Cribb stopped, gasped in desperate lungfuls of air. Recovering his composure, he finished forlornly: "To have been your friend."

Moon assumed the man was drunk and tugged his hand away.

"You don't understand me now. But you will. I promise. You'll regret this. You'll regret not saying goodbye."

Moon strode swiftly away. The ugly man chose not to follow but, sadder and more solemn than before, turned and walked slowly back inside.

❦

As if by instinct, Moon returned to the site of the murder.

Despite the lateness of the hour the streets were filled with the same human flotsam that had accosted Cyril Honeyman on his final journey. But at Moon's approach, they drew swiftly back, aware perhaps that he was not a man to trifle with. The conjuror barely noticed them as he moved, wraithlike, through the alleys and backstreets of the place, heading inevitably for the tower.

He could feel the weight of the past pressing down upon him as he walked, the waters of history closing about his head. He found himself recalling the notion of *genius loci*, that fanciful conviction that a place itself materially affects the individuals who pass through it. If this place had any tangible effect upon its inhabitants, then it was surely a malign one. The topography the district had a uniquely malevolent quality; it seemed to draw to its bosom all that was most loathsome in the city, most monstrous and sinful. The place had a hunger to it; it craved sacrifice.

Moon reached the silent hulk of the tower, made his way to the top and found it entirely deserted. It was clear that no transients had pressed the place into service as an impromptu boarding house—in an area beset by poverty of the most acute and pernicious kind, this fact ought to have surprised him, though, strangely, it did not.

The summit was bare now and cleared of rancid food and Moon mused again on the particulars of this troublesome case, the suspicious paucity of physical evidence, the tantalising sense he had of something greater lurking just beyond his grasp. He sank to the cold floor, fumbled in his pockets for cigarette and lighter and sat and smoked as the night slipped away, cross-legged, eyes tight shut, like some latter-day Buddha waiting patiently for he knew not what.

Mrs. Grossmith's many years of service had inured her to her employer's eccentricities, practicality immunised her against his quirks and idiosyncrasies. Consequently, her near-hysterical reaction on Moon's return home was no small cause for alarm.

"Mr. Moon!" she wailed. "Where have you been?"

"That's no business of yours."

"No need to be rude," she snapped.

There was a long pause. Moon sighed. "My apologies. What is it? What's the matter?"

"There was a man here for you. All night."

"Who?"

"Gave me the proper chills, he did. Right upset me. He was a little man. All small and white."

"An albino?"

Grossmith scrunched her face up in a frown. "I think that's the word."

"What did he say?"

"Just that he wanted to see you and that it was important." She reached into her apron pocket and passed him a small white rectangle of card. "He left you this."

Moon glanced down. "It's blank."

"I know. I asked whether it was a mistake but he said no, that you'd understand. I don't mind admitting I was worried. What kind of a man leaves a card like that?"

Moon tossed the thing onto the kitchen fire where it was satisfyingly consumed by the flames. As it burned, he came to a decision.

The Somnambulist shambled into the room, his monolithic frame swaddled in a florid purple dressing gown. Moon bade him good morning; the Somnambulist yawned in response.

"I'm cancelling the show tonight. It's time we went on the offensive."

The Somnambulist stretched and yawned again. He scrawled a message.

WHERE

When he heard Moon's reply, the Somnambulist lost his bleary-eyed torpor and found himself suddenly and uncomfortably wide awake.

They waited until dusk before leaving the theatre, creeping past a disapproving Mrs. Grossmith and an inebriated Speight already settling down for the night. Moon raised his hat in greeting, to which the man managed a sottish sort of reply.

A coach waited for them a few minutes' walk from Albion

Square. Moon and the Somnambulist climbed silently aboard, saying nothing to the driver who sat draped in black, his face obscured by muffler and scarf. He was an associate of the inspector, a fellow renowned for his tact and discretion.

"Tonight is a hunting expedition," Moon explained once they were inside. "We're after information. Just fishing. I don't want a repeat of your behaviour last time."

The Somnambulist nodded sagely.

"But if things become unpleasant—as I fully expect they might—I trust I can rely upon your . . . expertise?"

Another nod.

"Thank you. There's no one else I'd rather have by my side on these little excursions."

The giant smiled shyly in response and the coach rattled on through the night.

Less than half an hour passed before they arrived at their destination, a squalid alley deep in the bowels of Rotherhithe. This was an evil place, a collection of vile tenement buildings, doss kitchens and tumbledown slums. The streets were putrid with the stench of neglect and its people seemed more animal than human, their faces grimy, leprous and grizzled. It was a part of the city that cried out for civilisation, for mercy and—yes, I do not hesitate to use the word, however unfashionable you may happen to find it—for *love*.

Midway down the street, amongst a row of crumbling houses leaning drunkenly together, between a pub and a lodging house where the very poor paid tuppence a night for the privilege of sleeping slumped up against a rope, stood an establishment well known to Edward Moon. An aged, drunken Lascar stood guard, and as they approached, Moon nodded politely—just as one might to a doorman at the Ritz, to the gatekeeper of some exclusive club of which one is a lifetime member. The Lascar studied them with rheumy and suspicious eyes but, too inebriated perhaps to offer much resistance, let them pass without comment. They walked down a crooked, well-worn staircase into the main body of the building, its poisonous heart, a gigantic cellar reeking of sin—the notorious opium den of Fodina Yiangou.

The cellar was wreathed in a fog of livid yellow smoke and the floor was thick with human bodies: contorted, ugly and unnatural. A young man sat lost in some heaven or hell of his own creation, the very portrait of ruin, mouth agape, eyes wide open, pupils shrunk to pinpoints. Hunched beside him was a broken-down soldier, still dressed in the scarlet livery of his regiment, filthy and ragged from years of neglect. Their hands like claws, they clutched feebly onto their opium pipes—granters at once of ecstasy and torment. Made drowsy by the poppy, they lolled listlessly on their couches, their pale, pasty faces illuminated by the light of the oil lamps, helpless as puppets shorn of their strings. Moon and the Somnambulist picked their way amongst them, and almost as one the men shuddered as they passed.

"Lotus-eaters," the conjuror murmured. His companion gave him a quizzical look, but before he could write anything in reply a stooped Oriental materialised beside them, his face cracked and raw as though ravaged by some hideous disease.

"Mr. Moon?" His voice was thickly accented, insidious, sly.

The detective bowed politely.

The Chinaman jabbed angrily at the Somnambulist. "Why he here?"

Moon did his best to placate him. "The Somnambulist has come as my guest. You have my word he'll be on his best behaviour."

"He not welcome," Yiangou insisted.

"Don't say that." Moon grinned toothily. "You'll hurt his feelings."

Yiangou snarled. "What you want?"

"What do I want?" Moon asked nonchalantly. He moved towards the Oriental and pinched his pug nose hard between forefinger and thumb. "I want information, Mr. Y. I trust you'll be happy to oblige."

The Chinaman yelped in reluctant agreement.

"Capital," said Moon, releasing his nose. "Now let's see if we can manage a more civilised conversation. I'm investigating the murder of Cyril Honeyman."

Yiangou nodded sullenly.

"I'm sure a man of your intelligence could hazard a guess at my next question."

Yiangou laughed. "You must be desperate to come here," he said. "I think you fail. You fail!"

"I never fail," Moon replied stiffly.

"Clapham!" The Chinaman cackled triumphantly. "I think you fail there."

The shadow of the Somnambulist fell across Yiangou, and the Chinaman immediately fell silent.

"I want names," Moon demanded, "anything you might have heard. Any whisper, any clue let slip by one of your poppy-addled clientele. Every evil thing in London comes through here at some time or another. One of them must know something."

Yiangou gurgled a sigh. "I no help you, Mr. Moon."

"I could persuade you."

"I think you could not."

Moon glared. "Do you know something?"

The Chinaman gave an elaborate shrug, only to give himself away by giggling.

"You do!"

He shook his head.

"Given our long friendship, Mr. Yiangou, I rather think you owe it to me to say."

Yiangou simpered.

"Alternatively," suggested Moon matter-of-factly, "I could ask my friend here to break your fingers one by one."

"Ah." The Chinaman sighed. "I been told to expect you."

He clapped his hands and two burly men appeared by his side, stripped to the waist, awesomely muscled, prolifically tattooed, glistening with perspiration. Yiangou snapped his leathery fingers. At this signal both men drew out alarmingly vicious-looking swords and advanced towards Moon and the Somnambulist.

"You've been told?" the conjuror said thoughtfully. "By whom, I wonder?"

One of the men lunged eagerly towards him, his blade cutting the air inches from Moon's face.

"You're making me nervous, Mr. Yiangou. And you used to be such a generous host."

The man swung his sword again and Moon took an instinctive step backwards, silently berating himself for not bringing a gun with him. He gulped and wiped a trickle of sweat from his temple.

The other thug brandished his sword at the Somnambulist who, unlike the conjuror (never at his best in any physical confrontation), stood resolutely firm.

"Run away!" Yiangou squealed as Moon muttered something about the better part of valour. "You come to me," the Chinaman went on. "You threaten. You disturb my customers. You aggravate for many years."

"I can close you down any time I like," Moon protested, rather out of breath. "The only reason you're still here is because you're of use to me."

It was quite the wrong thing to say. Yiangou clapped his hands. "Bored now," he said, and the thugs moved in for the kill, their eyes aflame with the promise of murder. Moon leapt aside as one of them tried to skewer him, but was forced back against the wall. Exhausted, he knew he wouldn't last much longer.

But still the Somnambulist stood firm. The other man ran roaring towards him and, like some especially ferocious javelin-thrower unable or unwilling to let go of his spear, thrust the blade deep into the giant's belly.

The Somnambulist looked down at the wound, his face a picture of mild curiosity, looked up again and smiled. His would-be assassin gazed back in disbelief and then in real terror as, without betraying the slightest outward sign of pain, the Somnambulist strode forward, thrusting himself further onto the sword to reach his attacker. Expecting his quarry to fall at any moment, the man kept tight hold of the hilt but still the Somnambulist came relentlessly on, unstoppable as the sword slid smoothly into his belly and emerged unstained on the other side. The man held tight until the Somnambulist was almost upon him, when, shrieking inchoate curses, he let go of his weapon and ran in terror from the scene.

Disturbed by the noise of the rumpus, some of the opium slaves started to stir in their sleep, a few shambling to their feet, mumbling and howling confusedly. Yiangou squealed in frustrated rage and barked an order to his remaining servant. Foolishly, but with admirable loyalty, the man ran at the Somnambulist and buried his sword in his back. The giant swatted him easily aside and, still unflinching, plucked both blades from his body. Just as at the Theatre of Marvels, the swords were clean of blood. Moon walked to his side.

"Thank you," he gasped. They turned to face Yiangou. "Now. Who the devil told you to do that?"

Numbly, the Chinaman shook his head.

"Mr. Yiangou," Moon said reasonably, "you said someone had told you to expect me. All I want is a name."

Yiangou seemed terrified. "I can't. Mr. Moon, I can't."

"Very well. I'll just have to ask the Somnambulist to be gentle with you. But as you've seen, he's not a man who knows his own strength."

One of the pipe smokers, a whiskery fop who had hitherto lain silent, suddenly lumbered to his feet and yelled something unintelligible into the air. Startled, Moon and the Somnambulist turned towards him, but as they did so Yiangou saw his opportunity and took it. He ran, vanishing from sight almost immediately, disappearing deep into the warren of his establishment. The Somnambulist set off in pursuit but Moon called him back.

"No good. Yiangou knows this place far better than us. I fear we've lost him for tonight."

The Somnambulist seemed disappointed.

"Are you all right? That must have taken its toll even on you."

The giant frowned.

"You don't look well. I think we should get back."

They left the opium wrecks behind them and headed home, looking forward to the broth Mrs. Grossmith had promised to prepare for their return, but as the coach drove into Albion Square, they saw Detective Inspector Merryweather waiting on the steps outside their lodgings. He stood next to Speight, evidently uncomfortable in the vagrant's company, even if the latter seemed in the midst of lively conversation, talking loudly and gesticulating at his perennial sandwich board.

SURELY I AM COMING SOON
REVELATION 22:20

"Gentlemen!" Merryweather called out as the pair descended from the cab.

"Inspector."

"What have you been up to this time?" he asked, eyeing their torn and bloodied appearance.

"Solving your case," Moon replied, a little tartly.

"It's bad news."

The conjuror sighed. "Go on."

Merryweather drew himself up to his full height and paused dramatically.

"Well?" Moon was in no mood for theatrics.

The inspector swallowed hard. "There's been another one."

7

As the coach sped back into the city, Merryweather explained it all.

"What was his name?" asked Moon. He seemed alert again, re-energized, whilst the Somnambulist, exhausted by the battering the night had already given him, had begun to drift off into a pleasant doze.

"The victim's name is Philip Dunbar. Wealthy. Like Honeyman, an only son, an idler and a wastrel. Like Honeyman, he fell from the tower."

"The same site?" Furious, Moon clenched his hands into fists.

"Dunbar was lucky."

"Lucky? How?"

"He survived, Mr. Moon. He survived."

*P*hilip Dunbar lay close to death. He may once have been a handsome man but now it was almost impossible to tell—teeth smashed, face ruined, he writhed helplessly on the bed, its sheets already stiff with sweat, blood and urine, more like some shattered beast than a young man whose whole life had stretched uncomplicatedly before him only hours earlier.

"How long has he got?" Moon asked.

"Doctor says it could be any time now. Frankly, it's a miracle he's still with us at all."

Dunbar thrashed about, muttering indistinctly.

"Poor devil's delirious. From what we can make out he says he was attacked by some sort of creature. A kind of ape, he says, its face covered in scales."

"Scales?"

"The doctors have given him a hefty dose of morphine. We can hardly blame him for getting a little fanciful."

"Anything else?"

"Keeps talking about his mother. Said he'd seen her."

"His mother?" Moon gave the policeman a curious look.

"First person a chap calls for, I imagine, when he's in a spot like this."

Dunbar shouted again, the words more distinguishable this time. "God be with you."

"What?" Moon seemed almost alarmed. "What was that?"

Shuddering, the man struggled to sit up. "God be with you," he muttered. "God be with you." He let out a feeble moan and fell back into bed, silent but still breathing, the cord which tethered him to life frayed and worn.

Merryweather sighed. "He's too far gone. Sooner it's over for him now the better."

Moon turned and walked away. "I want to know when he dies."

Merryweather protested, "You mustn't take this personally."

"There's a pattern here. Why can't I see it?"

Outside, the Somnambulist was still dozing in the coach. The driver shivered on top.

"Take us home."

The man nodded.

"Inspector?"

"Mr. Moon."

"I want to see Honeyman's body."

"I'm afraid the family had it cremated last week."

"Cremated?"

"I'm sorry."

Moon frowned. "I'll be in contact again soon."

"You realise we've got to stop this," Merryweather insisted. "It has to end."

Moon told the coachman to drive. "Give me time," he called out. "Give me time!"

*P*hilip Dunbar passed away an hour or so after Merryweather had wished him a speedy death, screaming out his agony to the last. Regrettably, Moon's response was to throw himself back into the coils of degeneracy. Two days later, he returned to the house of Mrs. Puggsley.

Deliciously exhausted, he lay stretched out on a couch in the reception room, his modesty covered only by a woman's filmy dressing gown. Mina, the girl with the beard and the vestigial limb, placed a lit cigarillo between his lips and shimmied demurely from the room. The procuress beamed and rubbed her hands together in delight. "I trust Mina proved satisfactory?"

"Admirable. She's quite become my favourite."

Sitting around the room were three other girls, former favourites all, and at Moon's remark they affected distress, pulling mock-disgusted faces. One of them, a pinhead named Clara, across to him and began to softly stroke his neck. Moon tossed her a few farthings and she gambolled happily away.

"Must be a slow night for so few of your girls to be working."

"Oh it is, sir. It is. You've been our first john all evening. Point of fact, it's been rather a slow week."

"Really?" Moon made an unsuccessful attempt to blow smoke rings, much to the amusement of one of the women, a grey-faced creature with a painful-looking skin condition and flippers for hands. Mrs. Puggsley chided her softly. "Mr. Gray" was a regular customer and was not to be openly mocked.

"No doubt business will pick up soon."

Puggsley shook her massive frame in what was probably intended as a shrug. "Not till the travellers leave," she muttered, and the others murmured their assent.

Moon sat up, pulled the negligee tight about him and stubbed out his cigarette. "Travellers?" he said.

$\mathcal{I}$ once put it to Moon that his patronage of Mrs. Puggsley's bawdy house was a reprehensible lapse in an otherwise approximately moral character, that his perverse attraction to these poor discarded accidents of nature was a predilection utterly unworthy of him. In reply, he maintained that these liaisons were the mark of an inquisitive mind and an experimental spirit and (somewhat more persuasively) that Puggsley's was not in itself evil but merely a symptom of an unjust society. Mrs. Puggsley, he argued, provided a sanctuary for these girls from a world which would otherwise hate and fear them.

As it turned out, he was right about society. It *was* our society, of course, and not Mrs. Puggsley that was responsible for forcing these vulnerable women into their unfortunate positions. I believe I may have remarked something to the effect that I would give my life to change that society, to improve and re-engineer it for the better. But whatever philanthropic qualities Puggsley may have possessed, one thing is certain—that night she provided the key to the Honeyman-Dunbar killings.

$\mathcal{J}$ell me about the travellers."

One of the girls tittered.

"They're show people," Puggsley explained. "A carnival. Novelties and funfair rides mostly. But some of their freaks turn tricks on the side. I don't mind telling you, they're hurting my business."

"What are they like?"

Mrs. Puggsley groaned. "They've got all sorts down there— mermaids and midgets and a girl who can blow balloons up with her eyes. How can we possibly compete with that?"

Mina came back into the room. "We shouldn't have to," she said, absently running a comb through her beard. "It's a proper disgrace, the way they've muscled in on our business." She sat down beside Moon, gave him a perfunctory, passionless kiss on the cheek and returned to the disentanglement of her facial hair.

Moon barely noticed. "How long have they been here?"

"Rolled in about a month ago."

"Are there acrobats? Gymnasts? Tumblers? Anyone who'd be able to scale buildings?"

"I shouldn't care to say," Mrs. Puggsley said haughtily. "I've no wish to visit such a place."

Clara, the pinhead, spoke up. "I've been," she said. "I saw this man there do this act where he climbs a church steeple and dances on top. He can crawl up anything, they say. They call him 'the Human Fly' because of it—and on account of the fact he doesn't quite look right."

"Describe him."

"It's horrible to see, sir. He got these scales all over his face—"

"Scales? Are you sure?"

Clara nodded vigorously.

Moon got to his feet. Showing no obvious signs of shame, he flung the negligee aside and hurriedly dressed himself before the assembly of women. "Where is this fair?"

"Is it important?" Clara asked.

"More than you could know," he replied, struggling with his cuff links.

"South of the river. A mile or so beyond Waterloo."

Moon gave her his thanks and ran for the exit. Mrs. Puggsley lumbered to her feet.

"Always a pleasure, Mr. Gray. Can we expect you again soon?"

"You may rely upon it," Moon called back. He left the house, ran back through Goodge Street, hailed the first hansom cab he saw and raced towards Albion Square.

*W*ell," Mrs. Puggsley said as she moved with fleshy inelegance back to her easy chair, "there goes one satisfied customer, at least."

*M*oon dashed up to the doors of the Theatre of Marvels to find a street arab loitering conveniently outside. "Boy!" he shouted.

The child, a ragged, underfed scrap of a thing, looked up. "Sir?"

"I've a sovereign for you if you can deliver this message to Scotland Yard." He scrawled a note and handed it over. "Deliver it into the hands of a man named Merryweather. Have you got that?"

"A sovereign?" the waif asked, wide-eyed.

"Two if you hurry. Now go."

Needing no further encouragement, the child ran headlong into the darkness.

Moon pelted down the steps to his flat, Speight grumbling sleepily as he passed.

Mrs. Grossmith was making herself a nightcap when Moon burst into the kitchen.

"Been for another walk?" she asked, her voice dripping with disapproval.

Moon ignored her. "Where's the Somnambulist?"

"Asleep, sir, these past three hours."

"Then we must wake him," Moon cried, running towards the bedroom.

"Has something happened?" The housekeeper was unsurprised to receive no reply.

Moon shook his friend awake. "We have him!" he shouted. "We have our man!"

*H*alf an hour later, in grim, persistent rain, Moon, Mrs. Grossmith and the Somnambulist stood assembled by the steps outside the theatre. Speight tottered across to see what all the excitement was about. "What's going on?" he asked. Everyone ignored him.

"This is no night to be out in," Mrs. Grossmith complained.

"We've no choice," Moon retorted.

"Where is it you're going at this hour, anyway?"

Before he could reply, a four-wheeler clattered into Albion Square, pulled up by the theatre and disgorged a beleaguered-looking Merryweather and two beefy plain-clothes policemen.

"You'd better be right," he said. "You've dragged me out of bed for this."

The Somnambulist nodded in weary sympathy.

"We'd best be going before this weather gets any worse. If what you say is true this'll be the arrest of my career."

"Have I ever failed you before, Inspector?"

It may be for the best that Merryweather's reply was lost to the wind and the rain.

As the coach drove from the square, Grossmith and Speight walked back to the theatre ruefully shaking their heads in an unexpected moment of camaraderie. The vagrant settled stoically down upon the steps and Mrs. Grossmith felt a sudden pang of conscience.

"Mr. Speight? It's a cold night. Might I offer you some broth?"

The tramp nodded gratefully, clambered back to his feet and the two of them retreated indoors to the warm and merciful pleasures of the housekeeper's kitchen.

By the time they reached the carnival the rain had become torrential, and worse yet a thick fog had begun to descend, lending even the most innocuous of scenes an eerie, minatory air.

The travellers had settled a mile or so west of Waterloo, colonising a small heath beside a row of residential houses. A church sat some way off in the distance.

The fair itself comprised nothing more than a dozen or so caravans grouped together in a rough circle at the centre of the heath. A few of them carried signs and placards promising contests, games, spectacles and the like, but everything was long since boarded up and covered over for the night. Most of their owners had retired but for a couple of uncouth, unshaven men sitting listlessly about a guttering, sickly fire. The plaintive wail of what sounded like a penny flute drifted through the camp.

As the investigators walked towards them, one of the men looked up, belligerence glinting openly in his eyes. "What do you want?" he asked. Attached to his left ear was the kind of large metal ring more usually to be found dangling from the noses of cattle.

Merryweather (well used to dealing with persons of this class) chose not to reveal his profession but stated instead that he wished to see the proprietor with a view to exchanging a sum of money for information. The man with the earring shot the inspector a suspicious look but got to his feet nonetheless and slouched away into the mist. The bolder of the two plain-clothes policemen (Moreland by name) unwisely attempted to make conversation with the remaining Romany, an offer ungraciously declined by means of a single, brusque hand gesture.

At length the proprietor appeared, and the fog must have descended still more heavily than before, as there was little or no sign of his approach—he seemed to materialise fully formed mere inches from the Somnambulist's right elbow. He looked the giant up and down like a farmer eyeing up livestock at the county fair. "Shouldn't you be with us?" he asked.

He was a slippery, weasel-faced squirt of a man who introduced himself as Mr. King. "What can I do for you, gents? Must be something devilish important to get you out here at this time of night and in such weather, too."

"We're looking for a man," Merryweather explained.

"Lot of men here," King replied unhelpfully, and sniggered.

"He is known," Moon interjected, "as the Human Fly."

A leer spread itself across the proprietor's disagreeable face. "It's the Fly you're after, is it? What's he done this time?"

"What makes you think he's done anything?" Moon said carefully.

"Oh, he's been in trouble before. He's sprightly, that one." King's tongue darted out to dampen his lower lip. "Very sprightly."

"May we see him?"

The proprietor shrugged. "I shouldn't like to wake the boy.

He's got a big day ahead of him tomorrow. Being one of our star attractions, you understand."

Merryweather produced his wallet and pulled out a five-pound note. "I'll double this when you take us to him."

King gave a greasy bow. "Follow me, gentlemen. Stay close. This fog can be treacherous."

They had good reason to take notice of his warning, as the fog had degenerated into a London particular, rendering vision more than a foot in front of them practically impossible. The fog clutched at their bodies, muzzled clammily up against them and permeated their clothes, dank and cold and seeping through to the skin. As the Somnambulist shivered, Moon touched his arm.

"I know, old man," he said. "I'm sorry."

King led them towards a peeling, canary-coloured caravan set apart from its fellows, the runt of the litter. As they drew closer, Moon saw that painted on either side was the legend THE HUMAN FLY and beside it a strange, daubed symbol: a black, five-petalled flower.

King hammered on the door.

"Visitors!" he shouted. "Visitors for you!"

A muffled snarl issued from somewhere within.

"They have money," King wheedled.

Another snarl, fierce and animal.

"We only want to ask you some questions," Moon said reasonably. "We're prepared to offer a substantial reward."

The door swung reluctantly open and a bizarre figure thrust his head into the light. At first it was barely apparent that the thing was even human. He seemed a second Caliban—bestial, ferocious, his face covered with vomit-coloured lumps and scales. He looked down at them and growled.

Merryweather coughed nervously. "He always look like that?"

King simpered. "Like I said. He's sprightly."

Moon ignored them. "We're not here to hurt you."

The Fly looked uncertainly back. He growled again and this time it sounded horribly like a word, each syllable crawling broken and mangled from his lips. "Poet . . ."

"Poet?" said Moon, who was trying his best to sound encouragingly cheerful. "I'm no poet. Who do you mean?"

Another inchoate growl.

"My name is Edward Moon and this is my associate, the Somnambulist. We're investigating the deaths of Cyril Honeyman and—"

Before he could go any further, the Fly yelped in shock. "Moon," he pointed and screamed in a guttural, unearthly tone. "Moon!"

Moon smiled. "Well done!"

"Moon!"

"That's right. Have you heard my name before?"

Ignoring his questions, the Human Fly thrust past them and vanished into the thick banks of fog. He moved so swiftly that they were all—even the Somnambulist—too shocked and too slow to stop him.

"Looks like he didn't take to you." King smirked and put out his hand. "Now as to the matter of my fee—"

Moon shouldered the man aside. "Devil take your fee," he cried and ran into the fog, disappearing almost immediately.

Merryweather turned to his men. "Follow me."

Accompanied by the Somnambulist, they dashed after the conjuror, leaving King to shrug and saunter back to camp.

*M*oon could just make out the figure ahead of him, a horrible, indistinct shape loping in and out of view. He cursed the fog. Behind him, he could hear the shouts of his friends as they struggled to find their way.

The Fly fled before him, across the common, into the streets beyond. Moon could hardly believe the evidence of his senses as he saw the man leap onto the side of the first house and scamper up to the roof with all the grace and agility of a jungle cat loose in suburbia.

"Please!" Moon called out helplessly. "I only want to talk to you."

The Fly hissed something back. It may have been his imagination but Moon could have sworn the thing was still shouting his name.

"Stop!" Moon screamed. "Come down!"

The creature took no notice and began to race along the roof of the building. When it reached the end it jumped onto the adjoining house and moved relentlessly on, heading for the church in the road beyond, squirming, wriggling, leapfrogging its way down the street, a vile shadow scampering grotesquely across the skyline. Merryweather and the others appeared, panting and too late, by Moon's side.

"Where is he?"

Silently, he pointed upwards. The creature perched upon a rooftop several houses away. For a moment it tottered uncertainly, then righted itself and scurried on.

"Good God." Merryweather crossed himself. "Is it real?"

"I'm afraid so."

"Looks like we've got our man."

"He knew me, Inspector," Moon shouted. "Someone had told him to expect us. This man did not act alone."

"When we have him in custody," Merryweather said in his most pedantic voice, "remind me to ask him."

Above them, their quarry clattered across the rooftops. As they approached the church they lost him in the fog, but an instant later the mist cleared and there he was, atop the steeple, clinging to the weathercock and howling at the sky.

"Come down!" Moon shouted. "Please!"

The creature screeched obscenities into the night.

Moon turned to the Somnambulist. "Could you——?" he began, but the Somnambulist interrupted him with a gesture. He scribbled something on his chalkboard.

FRAID OF HITES

"Marvellous," Merryweather muttered, and the conjuror shot his friend a disappointed look. The inspector turned optimistically towards his men, but before he was able even to ask the question, they shook their heads as one.

"How in God's name are we going to get him down?" the inspector asked.

Moon called up again to the Human Fly. "Please!" he said. "We won't harm you. You have my word."

The Fly screamed again.

"What's he saying?" Merryweather asked.

"I think I can make it out," said Moreland (famed in the force for his preternaturally acute hearing). "Sounds like . . . God be with you."

"What?" Moon said.

The Fly wailed.

Moon shouted up to the steeple: "Please, whatever you're about to do——stop. We can help you."

But it was too late. The Fly shouted again and this time they all heard it quite distinctly, a prosaic and common enough phrase in everyday life, but here somehow unsettling, shocking in its incongruity.

"God be with you."

With this final cry, the Fly threw himself from the steeple. Mercifully, the fog masked his fall, but they all heard with sickening clarity the terrible, bone-snapping crunch as his body hit the ground.

Merryweather ran across to him and felt for a pulse. "Quite dead," he confirmed.

Moon stood over the unfortunate creature's corpse. An oddly frail thing it seemed in death. One could believe it almost vulnerable. "The death of a human fly," he murmured.

"Quite right." The inspector chuckled. "Looks like we swatted him."

Moon stared at the policeman, distaste etched upon his face. "This is not the end," he said softly and disappeared into the fog.

8

One week later, on London Bridge, the conjuror met the ugly man again.

"Mr. Moon!"

Hunched halfway along the bridge, a curious figure stood shouting Moon's name and waving his hat in greeting. He resembled a gargoyle crawled down from the roofs of the city and left to roam its streets with impunity. "You're a little later than I'd expected."

Moon eyed the squat-featured stranger suspiciously. "Have we met?"

The ugly man seemed palpably disappointed. "Surely you can't have forgotten me so soon?"

"Mr. Cribb?"

A sudden grin. "The same." This said more as proclamation than confirmation, as though he believed his name to be instantly recognisable. He held out his left, four-fingered hand.

Moon ignored the gesture. "I thought you promised we'd never meet again."

Cribb wore an infuriatingly amused look. "Did I? Well, doubtless that was true from my perspective. From yours . . . let's just say that time runs differently for the two of us."

The detective snorted in irritation and began to walk away.

Cribb shouted after him, "I can tell you the truth about the Fly."

Moon stopped short but, his face blank and unreadable, did not turn back. "What do you know?"

A smile insinuated itself across Cribb's unlovely face. "Walk with me."

"Why?"

"Because this is what we do. What we must do, will do, have done already. Viewed from a certain angle, of course, we did it months ago."

"I'm too busy," Moon protested, but already he could feel curiosity, his old, persistent mistress, tugging at his coat sleeves.

"Just walk with me."

A moment's hesitation and uncertainty. A heavy sigh. An ostentatious glance at his watch as if to imply some deliriously hectic schedule. Then a nod, a half-smile, a reluctant agreement. And as they strolled back across London Bridge, Cribb began to talk.

"The Vikings were here," he said, apropos of nothing in particular. "Nine hundred years ago they tore down this bridge." He began to gesticulate expansively like an overzealous don keen to impress at his first lecture, his intonation shifting from the conversational to the rhetorical. "The Norsemen tied their ships to the scaffolding of the bridge, chained them to its beams, its bolsters and supports—and they rowed. Dragged downriver, the ships dislodged the structure of the thing, brought the whole, glorious enterprise toppling into the Thames. London Bridge is falling down. You see? But it was built, rebuilt, many times. The city endures."

"Why are you telling me this?" Moon asked, bemused by the impromptu history lesson.

Cribb did not reply, as though he thought the answer entirely beneath him. Instead he turned to Moon and said: "You're not a man accustomed to failure."

"True."

"You're used to solving crimes after an hour or two in the Stacks, to unravelling riddles from your armchair, to coming up with vital insights in the arms of some misshapen girl at Puggsley's."

Moon sounded almost afraid. "How do you know all this?"

Cribb shrugged. "You told me. Or rather you will. But there is so much you have to learn. You never understood the Honeyman case. You don't know why the Fly recognised your name. You have so many questions and so terribly, achingly few answers."

"If you know something, I suggest you say so at once. If need be, I can bring down the full weight of the law to support me."

"Please." Cribb's tone was that of a disappointed but still indulgent headmaster. "There's no need to bandy threats. My hands are tied. There are rules."

"What do you want?"

"All crimes have a context, Mr. Moon. All murders take place as the result of an intricate sequence of events. Occasionally that sequence may be a matter of hours or days or weeks. More commonly, it is a question of months or years. But in a few—in a very few remarkable instances—a single death may represent the work of centuries. You lack perspective. I have in mind a modest tour. I'd like to show you the city."

"I've seen it."

"London is spread out before us like a great book. Follow me and I shall teach you how to read."

Leaving the bridge behind them, they walked swiftly along Upper Thames Street, into Queen Street and from there to Cannon Street, where they paused outside a forlorn, neglected-looking church.

"Saint Swithin's," Cribb explained, in the peremptory manner of the career tour guide. He strolled inside. Moon followed.

Between services, the church was all but deserted. The smells of must and incense hung heavy in the air and a handful of the faithful sat scattered amongst the pews, a few deep in prayer or meditation but most asleep or, in the case of one row of bulbous-nosed old lushes, stupefied by drink. Of any priest or rector there was no sign—theirs was a foundering flock, deprived of its shepherd.

Moon watched his companion crouch beside the altar, peering intently at something just out of sight.

"Edward!" he called in a hoarse whisper. "Over here!"

Moon bridled at the man's overfamiliar manner. "What are we doing?"

Cribb pointed. "There. Do you see it?"

Built into the dark fabric of the wall, set high above the altar beneath two mildewed cherubim, was what appeared to be a large chunk of masonry, dappled with spongy patches of damp, etiolated by age and gloom, utterly alien to the rest of the building. Lime, perhaps, Moon guessed, or sandstone.

"What am I supposed to be looking at?"

"The London Stone," Cribb breathed, his voice tinged with reverence.

The detective flung him an exasperated look.

"There are many stories about the origins of the city," the ugly man began, ignoring the glances of irritation directed towards him by those still-conscious faithful. "According to legend, its founders were the children of the Greeks. Brutus is said to have sailed here guided by a dream from the goddess Diana in which she foretold the whole of London's history. 'Beyond the setting of the sun,' she said." At this point in his narrative, Mr. Cribb adopted a slightly embarrassing approximation of a woman's voice. "'Beyond the realms of Gaul, there lies an island, once occupied by giants, now desolate and empty. I have prepared it as a sanctuary for your people. In years to come, it shall prove a second Troy. A race of kings will be born there from your stock, and the round circle of the earth shall be subject to their rule.'"

Moon yawned.

Cribb forged on, the old story flowing easily from his lips. "The goddess gave Brutus this stone. She promised that as long as it endured, so the city would flourish. But her warning was clear—if the stone is lost then the city shall perish." He looked about him at the church's shabby interior. "Frankly, I think we ought to take better care of it."

"A pretty fairy tale," said Moon, peering again at the stone.

"This has always been a sacred place. Where we stand now Boudicca razed to the ground. In a few years' time, archaeologists will find her revenge marked upon the earth beneath us in a seam of red soil, a scarlet thread running through London's history. Even now there is a certain . . . thinness here. Can't you feel it?"

Moon grimaced. "Listen," he said, as reasonably as he knew how, "why don't we forget all this and find ourselves a drink?"

"You need to understand the nature of the city," Cribb said, rising to his feet. "Come. There is more to see."

Riled by the man but still, despite himself, intrigued, Moon followed as they headed up Cannon Street and towards the centre of the financial district. This was not an area of the city he had ever felt the need to wander in—despite its easy affluence there was something indefinably depressing about it, something grey and oppressive. Flocks of black-clad businessmen strutted through its streets, self-important crows oblivious to the passing of the conjuror and the ugly man. A distinctive scent, largely unfamiliar to Moon, was omnipresent: the acrid perfume of commerce, everywhere the rich, dry, second-hand smell of money.

They turned into King William Street and cut through to Threadneedle Street by way of Change Alley.

"Much of this district will be bombed," Cribb said matter-of-factly.

"Bombed?"

"Destroyed, obliterated by explosives from the air."

"Impossible."

"Saint Swithin's, for one, will be reduced to rubble in forty years. They build a bank on top of it. There's nothing left to say the church ever existed."

"How can you possibly know that?"

Cribb's repulsive little face darkened for a moment. "I've seen it. More than once. The first bombs fall a decade or two from now, no more."

Moon laughed. "You're joking."

Cribb smiled infuriatingly in response, then walked away, compelling Moon to adopt an undignified trot in order to catch up. They emerged onto Threadneedle Street where the twin centrepieces of the city reared up before them—the great Guildhall and the Bank of England.

"I've always wondered about those," Moon said idly and pointed up at a pair of statues which stood weather-beaten, monolithic guard over the doors of the Guildhall, two stone giants wielding wooden clubs and dressed in animal skins.

"So you *are* willing to learn."

"I'm curious."

Cribb rattled off the information with the self-assured authority of some articulate encyclopaedia. "They are Gog and Magog. The last of England's giants, brought here by Brutus to guard the city gates. Legend says they were banished from London by King Lud after a bloody quarrel."

"How did you come to learn so much about the city?"

"I cannot leave. I am circumscribed by its limits. But this is not why I brought you here." Cribb nodded towards the Bank of England. "Look."

"I stopped a bank robbery there a few years ago," Moon said conversationally. "The Somnambulist and I still laugh about it from time to time. Fellow tried to burrow into the vaults, hoping to get at the gold reserves, but ended up waist-deep in sewage. Thoroughly entertaining at the time."

Cribb seemed irritated by the digression. "I want you to look at it. Really look at it. Try to see its true self, see the skull beneath the skin. Understand what it represents."

A moment's silence.

"The poison heart of London!" Cribb spluttered, suddenly splenetic with rage. "A monstrous canker at the centre of the city! We are oppressed, Mr. Moon, and all around us are the signs and symbols of our subjugation."

"If you say so."

"Make no mistake: the city is at the heart of this business, the prime mover in these crimes. Now I have one more thing to show you."

He walked away and Moon followed as they retraced their steps through King William Street and hurried onwards to the Monument (an enormous Doric column erected in the seventeenth century in memory of the Great Fire).

*F*orgive me if the above sounds condescending—I add this last detail only for the benefit of the ignorant and for tourists. I should hope my readers educated enough to recognise the significance of Wren's achievement without it being explained to them, but regrettably it remains the case that one must always make allowances for dullards. I cannot police the readers of this manuscript and it is a sad and tragic truth that I have never yet succeeded in underestimating the intelligence of the general public.

*C*lose by the Monument on King William Street some construction was under way.

"Trains," Cribb said briskly as they strode past. "They're renovating the Underground."

The two men paid for their tickets at the little booth outside, entered the Monument and climbed the corkscrew stone staircase to the top, emerging eventually into the chill autumn air, sweaty and panting. A flimsy metal rail seemed the only barrier between them and a queasily high drop.

The last visitors of the day were leaving (there had been several awkward moments on the stairs as various parties had attempted to squeeze and manoeuvre their way around one another) and for a few minutes Cribb and Moon had the view entirely to themselves.

They looked out across London. It had begun to rain, a thin colourless drizzle, and it was as though some drear and dusty veil had been draped across the panorama.

"Ugly, isn't she?" Cribb said. "You see her now as she really is, without her make-up, without her rouge. After the Fire, Wren wanted to build a new city—the London of his dreams, a new

Jerusalem, a shining metropolis constructed upon pure mathematical lines."

"What happened?"

"The city defeated him. It refused to be bent into shape; it stayed a wilful, sprawling, sinful place. It even told him as much. When he walked through the gutted wreck of old Saint Paul's, he tripped and fell over a piece of rubble—a tombstone. When he got to his feet and dusted himself down he saw that it read, in Latin, 'Resurgam'—'I Will Rise Again.'"

"Are you trying to tell me something?"

"I'm doing my best. But there is a limit to what I can say."

"Are you always so cryptic?"

Cribb grinned toothily. "The Monument is two hundred and two feet tall. Coincidentally the exact same height as the statue of Nelson in Trafalgar Square."

"Is that significant?"

"Secret geometry, Mr. Moon. The city is filled with it."

A guide appeared and pedantically informed them that opening hours were over and that they were to leave at once.

"Where now?" Moon asked once they were outside.

"Tea and scones, I think."

Despite his many disreputable and insalubrious qualities, there was something arresting, even magnetic, about Thomas Cribb. Or so Moon assured me—I was never able to see it myself. Still, over tea and scones in a Cheapside coffee house, Moon found himself warming to the man, quizzing him incessantly on his knowledge of London history and trying to prise from him whatever it was he knew, but refused to tell, about the Human Fly and the Honeyman-Dunbar murders. Halfway through his second cup of Earl Grey, Moon asked a question which he had no idea how to verbalise without sounding foolish. In the event, he favoured candour. "Why do you tell people you travel in time?"

Cribb toyed with his coffee spoon. "I say nothing of the kind. I admit merely that I have lived in the future."

"I don't believe you."

"What you believe is your own affair. But I can tell you this: Nine years from now, the King will be dead. Thirteen years from now we will be at war and then again less than three decades later. In nineteen fifty-two, hundreds of Londoners will be killed by poisonous fog. Ten years later and the city's skyline changes for ever—new buildings soar and scrape the sky. And a century hence great and terrible temples will be built where now our docks and shipping yards thrive and prosper."

Moon stared at him, in genuine admiration for the man's effrontery. "How can you possibly claim to know all this?"

"I've lived it," Cribb said simply.

Moon laughed, a little uncertainly. "Your patter's good. I'll give you that."

Before Cribb was able to reply, an unwelcome figure appeared beside their table and coughed politely.

The albino, Mr. Skimpole, stood before them. He nodded in greeting. "Gentlemen."

Moon ignored him.

"Skimpole," Cribb said quietly.

"Have we met?" the albino asked uneasily.

Cribb waved the question aside. "You won't remember me."

"No." Skimpole stared at him. "No, I don't. Here. My card." He passed him a blank square of cardboard which Cribb examined with obvious distaste.

Skimpole peered over his pince-nez, a glazed smile hovering about his lips, the very picture of insincerity. "So sorry to interrupt, but I must crave a brief audience."

Moon glared at him. "Have you been following me?"

"Thank you for the tour. Most instructive."

Cribb looked back at him with undisguised curiosity. "My pleasure."

"What do you want?" Moon snapped.

"What I've been asking of you for weeks: your help. Nothing more or less. I give you my word you'll be handsomely rewarded."

"You already have my answer," the detective replied, barely able to keep his anger in check.

"Please," Skimpole pleaded. "The city is in danger."

"So you say."

"I'd have thought after Clapham you'd be champing at the bit. Don't force me to use drastic measures."

"Never," Moon spat, his hackles rising at the pale man's threat.

The albino heaved a melodramatic sigh. "Then I'm afraid you leave me no choice." He bowed and sloped from the room. "We'll meet again."

"Unpleasant fellow," said Cribb once he had gone, chewing pensively on a muffin. "You're not friends, I take it?"

Moon shook his head. "Skimpole exploits human frailty," he explained flatly. "He feeds off petty jealousies and weakness. Believe it or not, he has the full force of King and country behind him. He works for a department in the government. It calls itself—absurdly—the Directorate."

"You have some history with him?"

"Before I met the Somnambulist," Moon said darkly.

"Before?" Cribb looked faintly surprised. "You seem as though you've been together for ever."

"Before . . . Years ago, I had a partner." Moon paused. "A young man. He possessed my critical faculties to a greater degree even than I. He might easily have outstripped me. In a kinder, better world he would have. Oh, but he was so beautiful, Mr. Cribb. Strikingly, heart-stoppingly beautiful."

Cribb sipped his coffee politely, taken aback by this unexpected outpouring of emotion.

"I shan't go into particulars, but Skimpole found his Achilles' heel. An unfortunate incident, a minor indiscretion, a moment's weakness, nothing more. But the Directorate hounded him for it, blackmailed him into working for them. The dear boy followed the albino's orders only to avert a scandal—as much for my sake as for his." Moon closed his eyes in grief. "In the end his sacrifice cost him everything. In the course of his work for the Directorate he was . . ." Another pause. An embarrassed cough. "He was lost to me. So you understand why I can never work for Skimpole, why I can barely restrain myself from shooting him on sight."

"I'm concerned as to what he meant . . . Something about drastic measures."

Moon shrugged. "I'm well able to take care of myself."

"Has the Somnambulist mentioned me to you?"

"No. Why? Should he have?"

"I might be wrong, but I thought he recognised me."

"Recognised you?"

"Impossible, of course. I'm sure I'd remember. But I'm curious—how did the two of you meet?"

"Surely you've learnt all about us in the future?" Moon said sardonically. "Am I not studied in the universities of the future? Are there not statues of me in the streets?"

"You're forgotten, I'm afraid. You're a footnote, Edward. One of history's also-rans." Cribb didn't seem to notice how hurt Moon looked at this. "But we've digressed. You were about to tell me of the Somnambulist."

"I was not," Moon retorted. "You were asking."

"Please."

"He came to me. I found him one night a few Christmases ago."

"Snow on the ground?" Cribb asked. "Carol singing in Albion Square? Ragamuffins building snowmen in the street?"

"Yes, as it happens," Moon said, surprised. "Why?"

"Just setting the scene. Go on."

"There's not a great deal to tell. I heard a knock at my door and found him outside, shivering in the cold."

"Like a stray cat."

"I prefer to think of him as a foundling. Though I've no idea why I've told you. I trust I may rely upon your discretion."

Cribb nodded.

Moon rose to his feet. "We must finish. I've a performance to get back for."

Out in the street Moon flagged down a hansom. "Thank you for the conversation," he said as the cab pulled up sharply before them. "I'm not sure how much I understood but it was certainly diverting."

"My pleasure."

Moon stepped into the cab and instructed the driver to hurry back to Albion Square.

"Can we meet again?" Cribb asked as Moon was settling himself for the journey.

Moon thought for a moment. "I'd like that."

As the cab began to pull away, Cribb seemed suddenly to remember something. "Mr. Moon! I forgot! I have to warn you! Don't see the—"

Whatever else the man may have said was lost to the clatter and rattle of the cab's departure, as it left the financial district behind and carried Moon gratefully towards home.

Detective Inspector Merryweather was in the audience that night, cheering and clapping with the rest of them despite the fact that he must have seen the show a dozen times before.

Afterwards, in the Strangled Boy, he congratulated Moon and the Somnambulist, roaring with laughter the whole while, clasping their hands and thanking them effusively for solving the Honeyman-Dunbar murders. "It's case closed, then?" he asked hopefully.

Moon had seemed listless and out of sorts all evening. "I think not."

"But we've found our man," the policeman protested. "We've got him rotting in the morgue." He turned to the Somnambulist. "Help me out here, lad. Back me up."

The Somnambulist sat by the bar, his stool tiny beneath him, a half-drained pint of milk in one hand. He shook his head morosely and went back to his drinking.

"There's no motive," Moon said suddenly. "He was an itinerant fairground attraction. Why? He wasn't killing for profit."

Merryweather brushed these objections aside. "He was escaped from some institution or other, I shouldn't wonder. People like that don't need motives. You and I both know he wouldn't be the first."

"There's a connection here. The Fly knew my name. He recognised me."

Merryweather looked unconvinced. "You were tired. We were all confused. You may have misinterpreted things . . . Seen and heard things that didn't happen." Pleased with himself, the inspector gulped down the last of his beer. "Excuse me," he said and disappeared into the recesses of the bar.

The Somnambulist tugged at Moon's sleeve but the conjuror seemed annoyed at the interruption.

"What is it?"

WARE WERE YOU

For a moment he did not reply. Then: "With a friend."

CRIBB

"Were you following me?"

The Somnambulist shook his head in vigorous denial.

"He thinks you recognised him, you know."

BAD

"Actually, he's rather interesting once you get to know him. You really must try not to be so judgemental."

The Somnambulist began to write a reply, but in a sudden display of irritation, Moon knocked the chalk from his hand.

"Later," he muttered.

The inspector returned, his glass brimming over with an oily, evil-looking liquid.

"I've come to a decision," said Moon. "Our investigation is not over."

"Please," Merryweather interjected. "I understand you must be bored but this is ridiculous. There'll be another case along soon."

The detective ignored him. "We need an expert opinion."

Merryweather's eyes narrowed. "What do you mean?"

"There is only one man in London who possesses my faculties to a greater degree than I."

Merryweather raised an eyebrow wearily. "Who?"

Moon grimaced as though he'd accidentally swallowed something bitter. "Barabbas."

The Somnambulist gave him a quizzical look, but the name had a very different effect upon the inspector. Aghast, he set down his drink untasted on the bar.

"You can't be serious."

Moon was already heading for the door. "I want to see him tonight."

Merryweather and the Somnambulist traded long-suffering glances.

"Not possible," the inspector protested.

"Make it happen," Moon barked. "Call in favours. Pay whatever it takes to grease the wheels. I'll see you both in an hour." With an imperious wave of his hand, he was gone.

The Somnambulist scribbled a message for the inspector.

WARE WE GOING

Merryweather groaned. He seemed haggard suddenly, drained of all his good humour and mirth. "Newgate," he said.

9

*N*ewgate squatted at the heart of the old city, Hell's chief out-post on Earth.

At that time in its history, in its last few years of life before it was torn down and replaced with something less obviously Hadean, the gaol held only those criminals sentenced to death and awaiting execution—sinners for whom all appeals were past, all hope lost, whose only chance for reprieve lay with a higher court. It was a place without charity or love, an urban cancer whose every fibre and essence pulsated and trembled with death.

They arrived a little after midnight. The sky was black with storm clouds and it had begun to rain again, dolefully, a grey drizzle.

"Why is it always raining?" the inspector complained as they stepped from the coach.

"Hadn't noticed," Moon snapped. He strode towards the ebony gates of the penitentiary, Merryweather and the Somnambulist reluctantly in tow. The giant looked up at the immense, brooding structure and shuddered. Two guards eyed them truculently as they approached. Merryweather took the lead.

"I'm Detective Inspector Merryweather. This is Mr. Moon and the Somnambulist. We are expected."

One of the men nodded grimly, his face the same colour as his grimy uniform. After much rattling of keys and pulling back of bolts and shutters, the trio were allowed to pass through a small inner door which nestled like a convict's cat-flap at the bottom of the main gate. An empty courtyard lay inside, lit only by the moon, shadows crouching in its every nook and corner. At its edge a man stood waiting. His appearance was incongruous. Dapper, well dressed but severely balding, he wore what little hair he had left in a plait so long that it hung halfway down his back, greasy and unsightly like a moth-eaten pelt inexplicably stapled to his scalp. He waved in greeting.

"Mr. Moon." He shook the conjuror's hand with a warmth and clammy vigour that made the conjuror flinch. "Such a pleasure to see you again." He turned to the others. "My name is Meyrick Owsley. Delighted to make your acquaintance. Barabbas is waiting for you." He walked briskly away and the others followed—Moon by his side conversing in low, urgent tones, Merryweather and the Somnambulist lagging tactfully behind.

Owsley led them from the courtyard and down, down into the warren of Newgate. Every door and barrier they passed had to be unlocked, each of them guarded by a gaoler, heavily armed and with the flint-faced look of one who is every day confronted by the worst excesses of his fellow man. Owsley took them through corridors and passageways whose dingy walls dripped with fungus, damp and grime; past cell after cell peopled by the solitary condemned, their cries and lamentations filling the air, as choking and mephitic as smoke. Some peered out at the intruders between the bars of their cages, a few wailed or hissed obscenities, but most sat slouched in their own filth, too dissolute and jaded to care, resigned to their imminent appointment with the noose. The air was dank and close, and as the four men moved through the innards of the place, little things with fur and teeth skittered and scuttled past their feet.

No doubt you think I'm exaggerating, colouring the truth for dramatic effect, that even back then conditions in our prisons can't have been quite that mediaeval. But it grieves me to admit that the above is an entirely honest and accurate account of the state of Newgate during the last years of its life. If anything, I have toned down my depiction in order to spare the delicate feelings of any ladies who may ill-advisedly be reading and for those of you who suffer from a nervous or hysterical disposition.

The Somnambulist gave Merryweather a meaningful poke in the ribs and nodded towards Owsley, still striding ahead of them, his long plait of hair flopping comically up and down as he walked.

"Meyrick Owsley," Merryweather said. "A former lawyer, and a good one. Chancery's finest before he met Barabbas. Now, so far as anyone's able to tell, he's become his servant."

Owsley must have overheard because he turned back and leered at the policeman. "More than that, Inspector," he said, his eyes wide with fervour and belief. "I'm his *disciple*."

Merryweather cleared his throat uncomfortably. "I stand corrected."

At the very end of the passageway they stopped before the final cell, tiny, bare, dimly lit by a stub of candle. They could just make out a figure within: an amorphous black shape slumped at the corner of the cell. Then they heard the voice, half-croak, half-whisper: "Meyrick?"

Owsley essayed a little bow. "Sir. I brought you a cigarette." He passed something through the bars. Filthy fingers groped for it in the gloom before the cell was illuminated first by the scratchy flash of a match, then by the dull glow of the cigarette.

Visiting time at the zoo, thought Merryweather—who only the previous week had stood with his wife and five children and watched the perambulations of a Bengal tiger as it stalked anxiously to and fro behind the bars of its cage.

The voice again, rasping and hoarse, but with the merest hint that it had once belonged to a sane and civilised man. "Is he with you?"

Meyrick Owsley whispered back, "Yes, sir."

There was something almost tender, the inspector thought, in the way Owsley spoke to the inmate—like a mother to her child, or a woman to her lover.

The prisoner spoke again but too faintly for anyone to make out what was said. Owsley seemed to understand.

"Barabbas will see only you, Mr. Moon. The other gentlemen are to wait at the gates."

Moon spoke briskly. "Very well."

Merryweather thought he ought to put up a token protest. "As a police officer I should be present."

"Please, Inspector. This is important," Moon insisted.

"Damned unorthodox is what it is."

"This is the only way he'll speak to me."

Merryweather was relieved to admit defeat. "I understand."

The Somnambulist touched Moon's arm, his face a picture of concern.

"I'll be fine. Wait for me outside."

Owsley took a bundle of keys from his pocket and unlocked the cell. "I can give you fifteen minutes. No more."

Moon stepped smartly inside and the door slammed shut behind him.

Owsley turned back towards the others. "Gentlemen. With me."

Merryweather was grateful to follow him back down the corridor and escape into the sanctuary of the courtyard. The Somnambulist trailed silently, unhappily behind.

*B*arabbas lay at the furthest corner of his cell; corpulent, naked to the waist, his fleshy face framed by rings of Neronian curls. His belly was covered by an elaborate tattoo, its intricate design distended and rendered unintelligible by enormous rolls of pale white fat. He had grown an unkempt beard since his incarceration and at the sight of it Moon was reminded, with an uncomfortable start, of Mina.

Barabbas sucked greedily on his cigarette. "Edward," he rasped. "You'll forgive me if I don't get up. I would offer you a seat but as you can see . . ." He gestured lazily about him. "I'm a little embarrassed at present." He pinched a meaty roll of belly fat between forefinger and thumb, then idly released it, watching with glassy fascination as it slopped back amongst the swathes of flesh swaddling his body.

"I see they let you keep your hair," Moon said mildly.

"Owsley arranged it for me. A small indulgence. One of many. He brings me these little chinks of beauty, lays them before me as tributes. Like offerings to some savage god."

"He seems to have the run of the place."

"He's a persuasive man. Also sickeningly wealthy. In a place like this, such things have influence." Barabbas coughed painfully on the remnants of his cigarette. "Incidentally, I heard about Clapham."

Moon flinched.

"Why are you here?" the fat man asked—pleased, it seemed, by Moon's reaction.

"I need your advice."

"A case?"

"Of course."

"You've never visited me before."

Moon looked away. "This . . . troubles me."

Barabbas stubbed out the last of his cigarette and tossed the butt carelessly to the floor. "Give me another," he said. "Then you may tell me everything."

Moon reached into the inside pocket of his waistcoat, took out his cigarette case and passed it to the condemned man. "There," he said. "Keep it."

Barabbas seized it greedily. "Another piece of beauty," he said. "A bauble for my collection." He stared at it, then sighed. "You'll take it back, of course, once I'm dead and gone?"

"Naturally."

Fumbling, Barabbas prised a cigarette from the box. "Light," he whispered. Moon struck a match and another flare briefly illuminated the cell, casting Barabbas's monstrous form into stark relief. The prisoner cackled and sucked in a lungful of smoke. "Now go on," he said, "my dear fellow."

"We begin with Cyril Honeyman," Moon said. "He was a gross, corpulent little man, permanently sweaty, whose jowls flapped and quivered as he walked . . ."

The conjuror told him everything about the murders and his investigation, beginning with Merryweather's summons and ending with the broken body of the Human Fly. When he had finished, Barabbas sighed. A smile crept halfway along his mouth but was swiftly banished, disappearing as quickly as it had arrived.

"Well?"

"You say he knew you?"

"By name," Moon said stiffly. "And he mentioned a poet."

"A poet? Is that so?"

"Why are you smiling? Does that suggest something to you?"

Barabbas gurgled. "It's really too perfect, Edward. I wouldn't want to spoil it for you."

"Damn it, man!"

Barabbas stifled a belch, only half-successfully. He leered at the conjuror through rows of yellow tombstone teeth, flanked by moustache and tangled beard. "You're in danger of letting this become an obsession. I've never seen you so excited. You should calm down. Do something to relax." A mucous cough. A grin. "How is Mrs. Puggsley, by the way?"

"You're the last person to lecture me on morality."

"Remember what I told you," Barabbas confided, his voice dripping with honey, rising and falling with the silken cadences of the practised liar. "I'm above morality now, beyond good and evil."

"The case," Moon insisted.

"You know, I don't think these squalid homicides are the real mystery."

"No?"

"I think they're a symptom. There is a corrosive influence abroad, Edward. There is a plot against the city and these murders are only the tip of the iceberg."

"What do you know?"

In response, Barabbas moved silently forward, his grotesque frame slithering across the floor like some Brobdingnagian slug.

"Let me out, Edward. Help me escape and together we can discover the truth."

Moon stepped hurriedly back, falling against the iron bars of the cage. Behind him, Owsley emerged from the shadows.

"Time's up," he said, producing a ring of keys from his pocket with an officious flourish.

Barabbas wailed and thrust out his hands in supplication. "Edward! Edward!"

The door was unlocked and Moon stepped sharply back out into the corridor.

Owsley said, "Your friends are waiting."

Barabbas brought his face up to the bars and peered out into the darkness.

"Edward?"

Moon turned around.

"Will you come back?"

"Perhaps."

"I hope I've been of some small assistance."

Moon spoke carefully. "Maybe you have."

"All the colour has seeped from my life. Next time, bring me scarlet. Bring me violet and vermilion and gold."

"I'll come back," Moon conceded.

Barabbas grinned in triumph. "Then you still need me," he hissed. "Even now." Overexcited, he suffered a violent fit of coughing. "Edward," he said more gently, once the attack had passed. "Edward, if I were you I should go home."

"Oh?"

"I should hurry, Edward."

Something was needling at the back of his mind. "What do you mean?"

"Something terrible is happening," Barabbas said simply. "Go now." The prisoner's face vanished from the bars of the cell and he dissipated back into the gloom.

Moon felt a sudden surge of panic. He turned to Owsley. "Let's go," he said, and they set off along the corridor almost at a run.

*T*hey were several streets away from Albion Square when they saw that Barabbas was right.

The sky was lit up by flashes of crimson. Thick black smoke poured past, as though a storm cloud had been dragged to earth. Seeing that some disaster lay ahead, the coachman refused to take them any further, so Moon leapt from the vehicle and ran on alone to the square. Despite the lateness of the hour, the whole of the East End seemed to be abroad and Moon had to battle through droves of idle onlookers to reach his destination. When he eventually emerged from the gawping masses he saw the truth of it. The Theatre of Marvels was aflame.

It was horribly clear that nothing could be saved. The blaze must have started shortly after they had left for the prison and now the building was burning down to its skeleton, its flesh and features long since scorched away. Its windows were empty, blackened sockets, its door a melted heap of slag. Of the sign which had read:

THE THEATRE OF MARVELS

starring

MR. EDWARD MOON

and

THE SOMNAMBULIST

BE ASTONISHED!

BE THRILLED! BE ENLIGHTENED!

a mere fragment had survived and only the half-word "LIGHTE" was still visible.

A group of men had formed a line to pass buckets of water to and fro from the disaster site but their valiant efforts were in vain. The theatre was lost, and as the flames began to spread, licking greedily at the adjoining buildings, they were forced to transfer their attentions elsewhere.

A man was standing beside Moon in the crowd. "Pity, isn't it?" He grimaced, displaying more gaps in his mouth than teeth. "Saw the show there once. Bored to tears, I was."

"How did this happen?"

"Why you asking? You local?"

Moon pushed him aside and ran towards the theatre. Hammered by waves of heat, stung by smoke, eyes streaming, he staggered helplessly back.

"Grossmith!" he shouted. "Speight!"

Even against the roar and crackle of the flames he recognised a horribly familiar sound, one so hateful to him that he would have given anything not to hear it at that moment—a discreet, dry, ticklish cough.

"Mr. Moon?"

He spun round.

"Good evening to you," said Skimpole.

The conjuror snarled, "What have you done?"

"Drastic measures. I did warn you." Flames reflected in the lenses of his pince-nez, lending his eyes an infernal aspect. Moon lunged forward but the albino stepped nimbly aside. "Your temper does you no credit," he chided. "Your friends are quite safe. They were removed before the fire was set. The monkey, I'm afraid, refused to leave. No doubt he's fricasseed quite nicely by now."

"You admit to it?" Moon asked furiously. "This was your doing?"

"I told you we were desperate. By rights you should be flattered."

Moon was speechless, choked by rage. "You've gone too far," he managed at last.

Skimpole flashed a quick smile. "I did think that might be your reaction. So I brought this." The albino produced a bulky manila file from his briefcase. "Take a look."

Moon snatched the thing from Skimpole and riffled through it. As he realised its full significance, even he was momentarily at a loss for words. "How long have you had this?"

"We've kept a dossier on you for years," Skimpole said coolly. "Of course, I'd hoped never to have to use it—but then you can't say we didn't ask nicely."

"You wouldn't use this, surely?"

"I might. The Puggsley material is here, of course. But some of the other items . . . Even the release of my records on our mutual friend in Newgate would mean your public ruin and disgrace."

Moon cursed, loudly and at length. This is not the place to reproduce such colourful material verbatim.

"I'll ask you a final time," said Skimpole. "Will you help me?"

The fire was reaching its zenith, throwing out furnace waves in its final rush to consume the last flammable matter. Moon staggered under the blast, dizzy and faint, flailing about to regain his balance.

"Mr. Moon?" The albino was insistent. "Will you help us?"

Feebly, the conjuror nodded.

Skimpole smiled. "Very good," he said briskly. "We'll be in touch." And he strutted away into the crowd. Left alone, gasping for breath as the Theatre of Marvels died before him, Moon tried to run in pursuit of his tormentor only to stumble and fall. Strong arms helped him up, and as Moon staggered to his feet, he looked into the eyes of the Somnambulist.

"We've lost," he muttered.

The giant looked gravely back, surveying the ruins of his home. Remarkably, a few tears ran down his cheeks. Behind him,

Merryweather emerged from the crowd with Mrs. Grossmith and Speight.

Moon gripped the Somnambulist's arm. "Barabbas was right," he gasped. "It's over. We've lost. Checkmate."

Then, for the first and last time in his life, Edward Moon fainted—swooning into the arms of the Somnambulist.

Grossmith, Speight and the inspector ran towards them. "Mr. Moon!"

Speight still had his perennial sandwich board with him, its cryptic message now the theatre's sole survivor:

SURELY I AM COMING SOON
REVELATION 22:20

The events of the evening seemed to have roused him into a semblance of sobriety. "Christ," he said, gazing at the devastation. "What will we do now?"

10

*B*eneath the city, far below the streets and pavements of the everyday, the old man dreams.

Cocooned in the underworld, time is lost to him and he has no notion of the span of his slumbers: years may have passed in the world above or he might have dozed for mere hours.

There is little logic and no pattern discernible to the dreams of this subterranean Rip Van Winkle. At times he thinks he dreams of the past, at others of what seem to him to be shadows of the future. Occasionally he is shown things that appear unrelated to any experience of his own—fragments, shards of memory from other people's lives.

A thin, reedy snore escapes him; he sighs, rolls over and returns to the past.

He is back during his last days at Highgate. The vision is so vivid and so real he can catch the very scent of his old room, the close, murky stinks of sweat, snuff, dirty linen, stale farts. Gillman is there, fussing about him as usual, medicine bottle in one hand, slop-pot in the other. Another figure, too, dwarfish, silhouetted against the window, his face in shadow. The old man strains to remember, but before he is able to identify the stranger, the scene ebbs away to reveal another, much earlier time. He is young again, in Syracuse—his wife, heavy with child, long since abandoned to the uncertain mercies of family and friends back home. He chances upon an excavation, stands and watches for long, dusty hours, enraptured as men tease and extricate from the earth the headless statue of the Landolina Venus—a thing of beauty returned from dust to the waking world. He sees sand and mud brushed away from the delicate traceries of the madonna's marbled bust, sees the decapitated, variegated stump where her head once stood—with a face, it was said, of achingly exquisite beauty. Mute, he watches this perfect being, this stone Olympian, raised to the surface.

With an infuriating disregard for chronology, the dream shifts and he is old again, back in that malodorous room, Gillman buzzing about him with medicine and pot, the dwarf at the window still obscured by shadow. Despite the prosaicism of the scene, the dreamer feels sure that this is some flashpoint in his life, some pivotal moment whose true significance has yet to be revealed to him.

The stranger turns, steps into the light and begins to speak.

The old man groans softly and stirs in his sleep. Above him the city roars giddily onwards, oblivious to the threat which slumbers beneath it.

*N*ine and a half miles away, Prisoner W578 received a visitor.

"Master?"

Barabbas waddled to the bars of his cell. "Have you brought it?"

"It's here, sir." Meyrick Owsley's plump, stubby fingers darted between the bars of the cell to push a small purple box into the hands of its inmate. Barabbas grabbed the thing with all the gluttonous excitement of a spoilt child and disappeared into the corner of his dungeon. Owsley caught a momentary glimmer, a glint of something shiny, metallic and expensive. Barabbas snapped the box shut and added it to his meagre store of treasures, bundled up in an oily rag and hidden behind a loose slab of masonry.

"Another glimpse," he hissed, quivering with fleshy excitement, "another flicker of beauty." He wrapped the item up, pushed it back into the wall, then dumped himself onto the floor, exhausted from his brief exertions, his body wracked by long, suety shudders.

"I thought you should know, sir—Moon and the Somnambulist—"

"Yes?" Barabbas suddenly seemed alert, curious, his stash of beauty temporarily forgotten.

"They're working for Skimpole, sir. Blackmail, if the rumours are true. The Directorate has a reputation. I'm worried he's getting close."

The prisoner laughed—a strained, prickly sound.

"Sir? May I advise caution?"

Barabbas seemed oddly jocular. "You may not. I think we can expect another visit from Edward. Don't you?"

Owsley did not reply, his disapproval obvious.

The fat man grinned, baring his cankered teeth. "I'm going to enjoy this."

The hotel Skimpole had provided for Moon and the Somnambulist was widely considered to be the most exclusive, and was certainly amongst the most expensive, in the city. Their quarters comprised a small network of rooms, painfully tasteful in their furnishings and design: bedroom, reception room, drawing room, study—all sumptuous and ostentatious, quite beyond anything they had known before. A distinctive scent wafted through the building, a soothing cocktail of wax, polish and the fruity after-taste of a really good bottle of wine—the old smells of wealth and luxury. On arrival, guests were assigned a personal valet, a ser-vant dedicated to fulfilling their every need, the slightest opportu-nity to pamper or please sending them into paroxysms of fawning delight.

It was, in short, a horribly gilded cage.

In the three and a half weeks which had passed since the de-struction of the Theatre of Marvels, Moon had been allowed out of the hotel on just four occasions and then only when accompa-nied by his valet—a gentleman's gentleman who, it transpired, owed his allegiance to Mr. Skimpole. Defeated and humiliated, Moon found himself so trapped in this genteel gaolhouse that the Somnambulist had begun to fear for his friend's sanity. He was oddly relieved, then, when on their twenty-third day under house arrest, their tormentor came to call.

The albino lowered himself gingerly onto the divan, reached into his pocket and produced an exquisite silver case.

"Cigar?"

Both declined in surly silence.

"Ah, well." Reverentially, Skimpole helped himself and lit up, something like satisfaction flickering fitfully across his face. "I trust you're comfortable? For myself, I've always found this a charming little hideaway."

Moon grimaced. "I shan't forget this."

"Please." Skimpole exhaled thin ribbons of smoke from his nostrils. "I've come to ask for your help. So sorry I've not been able to visit sooner but things have been absolutely frantic. You understand, I'm sure."

Moon and the Somnambulist glared back.

"To business, then. My profuse apologies for your enforced stay. I know you've not been able to pursue your extracurricular activities, Edward, but we had to make certain you wouldn't renege on our agreement."

"What do you want?" Moon's voice was studiedly neutral, the barest intimation of menace discernible.

Skimpole sucked in a lungful of smoke. "My colleagues and I are in possession of information which strongly suggests that a plot is at work against the city." He spoke baldly, matter-of-factly, as if this were an ordinary conversation, as though disaster were an everyday occurrence, catastrophe the common currency of his life. "We believe that during your investigation into the Honeyman and Dunbar murders you may have stumbled upon some tangential element of this conspiracy, a loose thread in the skein of the thing. A thread which we may yet succeed in tugging loose."

As if struck by a sudden thought, the Somnambulist scribbled something down.

FLY

Skimpole favoured the man with a ghost of a smile. "I don't think any of us believes the Fly acted alone, my friend. As I understand it, the man was mentally subnormal."

Skimpole paused a moment and looked the Somnambulist up and down, as though troubled by the thought that he might inadvertently have caused offence. "No," he continued more firmly, "the feeling is that he was a pawn at best. A minor player. My congratulations on catching him nonetheless. Such a pity he died so abruptly. But his demise is so very typical of what we've come to expect from you two. Like something torn from the pages of a penny-dreadful. Needless to say, it would never have happened had you been working for us. We pride ourselves on our prosaicism, our practicality and common sense. There's no room at the Directorate, gentlemen, for melodrama."

Moon and the Somnambulist exchanged glances.

"What I'm about to tell you is known to only half a dozen men in the country, all of whom exist at the pinnacle of our organisation. This is a state secret, so I suggest you keep it to yourselves. It's a snorting great cliché, of course—and I rather wish I didn't have to say it—but men have died for less. For the past five months, my organisation has been receiving vital information from—how shall I put it? From an unorthodox source. A woman. Since one of my people dug her up last year, my colleagues in Whitehall have begun to lean on her somewhat. More, in fact, than may be considered entirely healthy. Her advice is now thought to be so absolutely crucial on certain matters of policy that it would be no exaggeration to say that without her, the last war in which this country took a part would have ended much less happily indeed." Skimpole looked down at his feet, embarrassed, like a weak-willed schoolboy caught stealing apples. "I fear we've let things get a little out of hand."

"Her name?" Moon asked.

Skimpole took a deep breath. "Madame Innocenti."

Moon did his best to mask a smile.

"She's a medium," Skimpole finished, his chalk-pale cheeks tinged incongruously with scarlet. "A clairvoyant. Lives in Tooting Bec. Claims to receive messages from the spirit world."

Moon steepled his fingers, savouring the moment. "In essence, Mr. Skimpole, what you appear to be telling us is that for the past five months, British Intelligence has allowed itself to be led on the say-so of a backstreet fortune-teller."

The albino winced at Moon's candour. "Are you shocked?"

"Not at all. There's something oddly comforting about discovering all one's worst suspicions to be true."

The giant smirked, and Moon pressed home his advantage. "How far does this woman's influence extend? How high does this go?"

Skimpole sighed. "To the top, Mr. Moon."

"Tell me . . ." Moon was enjoying Skimpole's discomfort. "What has she to do with us?"

"For some time, Madame Innocenti has been warning us of a conspiracy directed against the state."

"Details?"

"Nothing specific. Just as you'd expect—vague, oracular warnings, phrased in the most purple and prolix terms. We'd like you to see her for yourself and discover the truth."

"I'm afraid I still don't see why this should interest us."

Regretfully, Skimpole stubbed out the ashy tip of his cigar. "Madame Innocenti has mentioned three names in the course of her auguries . . . Cyril Honeyman. Philip Dunbar."

Moon nodded calmly, as if he'd been expecting this.

Skimpole swallowed hard. "And Edward Moon," he murmured.

For the home of a latter-day Cassandra, Madame Innocenti's house was disappointingly unprepossessing. No doubt it was respectable enough in its own way—a modest two-storey semi-detached building which might have been more than acceptable as the property of a schoolteacher, say, or that of a clerk or an accountant, but for a seer of Madame Innocenti's supposed power and influence, frankly it was almost suspicious. It had a tired, uncared-for look, a forlorn atmosphere of abandonment and decay.

Moon stepped up to the rotten-looking front door and, as gently as he was able, knocked by means of an ancient brass knocker that looked as though it might at any moment crumble into rust.

The Somnambulist looked about him at the dreary greyness of the place, the glum homogeneity of Tooting Bec, and wrinkled his nose in distaste. Albion Square, the Theatre of Marvels, Yiangou's opium den—all of these, however unpleasant they may individually have been, were nonetheless alive with colour; they had a glossy, lurid quality redolent of the spit and sawdust of the stage. There was none of that about Tooting, this so-called Delphi of London—it was too ordinary, too monochrome, too wearily everyday.

The door opened and a gangling, nervous man stared out, startled-looking and suspicious. Still young, his hair had begun to recede and he was afflicted with a pair of owlish, too-thick spectacles. "Yes?"

"I'm Edward Moon and this is my associate, the Somnambulist. I believe we're expected."

"Of course." The man nodded repeatedly and with such ungainly vigour that Moon wondered if he might not be suffering from the early symptoms of some hideous degenerative disease. "Come through. My wife will join us shortly."

He led them down a grimy corridor and through into a darkened reception room, barely illuminated by a dozen or so spasmodically flickering candles. A long, narrow table stood at its centre, nine chairs set empty around it.

"It happens here," the man said portentously. "Tea?"

Moon answered for them both; their host bowed and disappeared.

"Fed up?" Moon asked, but before the Somnambulist could scribble a reply their host bustled back.

"Tea and milk on its way. In the meantime, allow me to introduce my wife."

He stepped back and a woman walked—or seemed, rather, to glide—into the room. She was comfortably into her middle years but looked more striking, more elegant and infinitely more re-markable than any debutante half her age. Feline, sleek, her face framed by a halo of chestnut curls, she was laced into a snug-fitting auburn dress which deliciously accentuated the soft, undulating swell of her breasts. Moon was unsure what he had expected—some toothless Romany, perhaps, a chintzy, obvious fake, gaudy earrings and paste jewellery—but never so exquisite a vision as this.

She smiled, exposing a set of perfect, pearly teeth. "Mr. Moon. Somnambulist. An honour. You'll have to forgive me if I seem flustered. I must confess to feeling a little in awe."

"Of me?" Moon began, obviously flattered, only to be silenced by a discreet but brutal nudge in the ribs from his companion. He corrected himself. "Of us?"

"I must have seen your act five times at least. My husband and I were great admirers." She turned to her balding consort. "Weren't we, my dove?"

He mumbled something in the affirmative.

"Such a pity what happened," Madame Innocenti mused. "So tragic. You have my condolences."

"Thank you, ma'am." Moon bowed his head and, remarkably, a hint of a blush appeared to suggest itself.

"Señor Corcoran has spoken of you. I understand you're here on behalf of Mr. Skimpole."

"That's correct."

She gave a sniff of disdain. "Are you friends?"

"Not friends, ma'am," Moon replied carefully. "Associates, perhaps. Reluctant colleagues."

"So glad. My husband and I can't stand him. Frightful, whey-faced little man. You must excuse me, I have to prepare. You're rather early but the others should be along shortly. You don't mind waiting?"

"Of course not."

"We're expecting seven tonight—you gentlemen and five others. Have you attended a seance before?"

"Never, ma'am."

"Well, there must be a first time for us all," Innocenti said, turning to go. "Even for you, Mr. Moon."

She drifted out and they were left once again with her husband—as disappointed as though some empress had swept from the throne room, stranding her subjects with a mere footman.

"Wait here," he muttered sullenly. "I'll fetch your tea."

Tea was served in tandem with a plate of unappetisingly dry biscuits, and as Moon and the Somnambulist pecked politely but unenthusiastically at these refreshments, the other guests arrived. They were a curious group, all of them smelling strongly of desperation, all prepared to pay whatever it took to receive Madame Innocenti's brand of wisdom.

First to appear were a couple, Mr. and Mrs. Salisbury, both of them settled into the plump, comfortable final stretch of middle age. They were followed by an unusually ugly young woman who introduced herself as Dolly Creed—her face, sagging and acutely unremarkable, further marred by four evenly sized brown warts clustered around her left nostril. After her a Mrs. Erskine appeared—hunched, elderly, walking-sticked yet oddly nimble, she moved with brittle, scuttling grace. The biscuits had all been eaten and the teapot run dry by the time the final guest fetched up, a gingery, skittish young man who passed out his card to all present—Mr. Ellis Lister, B.A. (Oxon.). He was evasive about his profession, stating only that he worked in a wing of the Civil Service. Moon and the Somnambulist recognised him immediately, however, as a Directorate man.

Eventually, Innocenti's husband skulked back into the room.

"Take your seats. My wife is here."

They moved obediently to their chairs, Moon and the Somnambulist careful to place themselves at the head of the table on either side of the seat reserved for Madame Innocenti herself.

Heralded by the satiny music of her gown, the medium walked through the room, lovelier than ever, basking in the puppy-eyed adoration of her clients. Her husband withdrew to the edge of the room and discreetly pulled shut the door, once again sinking the place into candle-lit gloom.

"Welcome," said Madame Innocenti.

A discreet round of applause ensued as, after a graceful curtsey and a brief fumble of handshakes and kisses, the medium took her place at the head of the table.

"Death is not the end," she said soberly. "Life is not snuffed out with our frail physical forms. There are worlds beyond our own, realms inhabited by the dead, planes of existence ruled by forces beyond our comprehension. Believe me, I know. I know that the soul endures. I know because I have seen beyond the veil. I have spoken with the departed and they have chosen me—unworldly vessel that I am—to be their voice in the world of the living." Innocenti laughed. "But enough. I've no wish to bore you. I'm sure you've heard this kind of thing before."

"Link hands," her husband instructed, and they all obeyed, each grasping the hands of their neighbours, forming around the table a daisy chain of sweaty palms and twitching fingers. Moon and the Somnambulist exchanged glances, checking to make sure they had a firm grip on the medium.

"You are right to be cautious," she said. "We understand your unwillingness to believe. The spirits will forgive you."

"Glad to hear it," said Moon.

Madame Innocenti spoke grandly. "I shall leave you now. I will remove myself from the mortal plane and ascend towards the sunlit realms of the dead. When I speak to you again I shall not be alone. My body will become the vessel of another. My spirit guide. A Spaniard from the age of Elizabeth. He is known to us all as Señor Corcoran."

Murmurs of earnest assent around the table.

"Don't be afraid." With that, Innocenti sighed deeply and slumped back into her chair.

The old woman, Mrs. Erskine, cried out in alarm.

"Don't break the circle," hissed the medium's husband.

A moment's silence, then Madame Innocenti sat up. Her eyes remained closed, but whilst to all intents and purposes she seemed the same woman as before, something almost imperceptible had changed about her—some small shift in the alignment of her face, a subtle alteration in the cast of her features. When she spoke again, her voice was deep and rich and tinged with a European accent, maddeningly unclassifiable. "I sense you have many questions. Who amongst you would speak first to the ranks of the departed?"

Mr. Salisbury spoke up eagerly. "My son. Is he with you?"

A strained smile passed across Innocenti's lips. "I need a name," she said, still speaking in Corcoran's pseudo-Spanish tones.

"Albert," the old man murmured. "Albert Salisbury."

"Albert?" There was a long pause. Madame Innocenti screwed up her face, as though she were grappling with some intensely complex problem. "Albert?" She exhaled loudly. "Yes, there is one here called Albert." For a terrible moment, Innocenti's body juddered and convulsed, bucking and writhing on her seat as though electricity was being passed through her body. Throughout these contortions Moon and the Somnambulist were careful to keep tight hold of her hands. When she spoke again, it was in the singsong tones of a child. "Papa?" she breathed. "Papa, is that you?"

Mr. and Mrs. Salisbury sobbed as one. The latter was content to leak her tears discreetly but her husband, half-laughing, half-crying, all but screamed: "Yes, my boy. Yes, it's me!" There was something pitiable in the sight—bald, bullet-headed, with the look about him of a retired headmaster, the kind of man who'd gleefully have thrashed a classroom's worth of boys before

breakfast—weeping and gnashing his teeth, womanish in his
hysteria.

Madame Innocenti giggled childishly. "Papa," she squealed.
"I'm happy here. The spirits have been so kind. So very kind. It's
warm, Papa, soft and warm and filled with furry animals and little woollen things."

The Salisburys' eyes shone with tears. Moon stifled a yawn.

"Grandmama is with me," Innocenti went on. "Grandpapa,
too. Every day is Christmas and everything is wonderful. I am
floating, dear Papa, floating in amber and honey. I love you. I love
you. But I have to go now. Please. Please, join me soon."

The voice stopped. Innocenti slumped forwards and when she
spoke again it was in her Corcoran persona. "Forgive me," she
said briskly. "We lost contact. Who's next?"

Moon caught the Somnambulist's eye and they exchanged
sceptical smiles.

J'm almost certainly dead by now and your identity matters to
me not a whit. But whoever you are, I imagine you to be at best a
cynic, at worst a genuine, honest-to-goodness misanthrope. None
but the terminally cynical, after all, could have maintained your
interest in such a parade of thieves, crooks, fantasists and liars as
fill the pages of the present work. Consequently, I doubt anyone
with what I take to be your pessimistic view of life has a great deal
of time for the table-rapping, ectoplasmic nonsense of medium-
ship and seance. Am I correct? I thought as much.

*M*oon, of course, who had a strongly misanthropic streak
only occasionally tempered by acts of charity, would certainly
have agreed. Before Mr. Skimpole had destroyed his home
and livelihood, he had made his living by gulling people into

believing the impossible. Madame Innocenti, it appeared, did rather the same thing, only a good deal more lucratively and (if the albino's claims of the frequency of Directorate visits to Tooting were to be believed) with rather more influence.

If nothing else she was a first-rate performer. Her assumption of different voices—Corcoran the fusty Spaniard, the babyish tones of the infant Salisbury, her own beguiling appearance out of character—all were masterfully played and she possessed the ability (honed no doubt by years of end-of-the-pier mummery and mysticism) to tell her listeners precisely what they wanted to hear, to confirm in a few short lines of nebulous, comforting twaddle all they had ever dreamt and hoped was true.

After the Salisburys had spoken to their son, Corcoran presented Mrs. Erskine with the shade of her husband (lost at sea these past twenty years) and Miss Dolly Creed with the thin, pedantic voice of her late fiancé. Moon wondered what kind of man would consent to marriage with such a troglodyte and concluded that he must have arranged his own death purely in order to escape the altar. Trying enough, he thought, to be saddled with such a horse-faced creature in life—worse still to have one's carefree gambolling through the fields of Elysium interrupted by the same.

When Ellis Lister's turn came, however, he asked to speak not—as had all the others before him—to a dead relative, an old lover or a former pet, but to Corcoran himself.

"Mr. Lister?" Innocenti spoke in the Spaniard's dusty voice. "We have met before, I think."

"We have indeed, señor. I'm flattered you remember me."

"From the Service, yes?"

Lister smiled tightly. "Not something I like to advertise."

"Of course not. I myself dabbled in the intrigues of the secret world. I remember its etiquette too well."

Moon realised that he had started to forget Madame Innocenti's skill as a mimic and was beginning to accept her Corcoran voice as a separate and autonomous persona. He told himself in the sternest terms not to be so ridiculous.

"How may I be of assistance?"

"I need a name. We suspect a young man in our employ has been turned by foreign powers."

Madame Innocenti nodded sagely. "Okhrana?"

Lister was swift to shush her. "We are not alone."

"Indeed not."

"Can you tell me who it is?"

"Give me their names."

Obviously embarrassed, Lister gave the medium the Christian names of his five chief suspects.

Innocenti listened and fell silent. "Your man," she said at last, "is . . ." And with the slightly disdainful air of a local dignitary pulling the winning ticket from a tombola at the church fête, she repeated the third of the names. "He's been compromised for months."

"I'm in your debt, Señor Corcoran."

"Treat him mercifully. He is young and callow and not entirely to blame." She sighed. "I'm tired. But there is one here who has yet to speak. Mr. Moon? Is there somebody with whom you wish to converse? A loved one, perhaps? A parent or a sweetheart passed beyond the veil?"

The Somnambulist was visibly shocked when Moon answered: "Yes."

"The name?" Madame Innocenti asked.

"His real name is not known to me, but when he was alive he called himself the Human Fly."

A sharp pause, then: "There is one here who identifies himself as such. I must warn you, sir, that the Fly is not at peace. He is angry, an unquiet spirit."

"Nonetheless, I wish to speak with him."

A shadow passed across Innocenti's face. "As you wish." She squealed, her head jerked upwards and she squirmed in her chair as if in the grip of some invisible force. All at once her face crumpled and contorted itself as she transformed before their eyes into a slavering monster, the beast of Tooting Bec. To the shock of the assembled faithful, all traces of her former eloquence vanished and Madame Innocenti actually *growled*.

"Hello," said Moon with a nonchalance he did not entirely feel. "Remember me?"

"Moon," the medium muttered, her voice rattling and guttural. "Moon."

"How did you know my name?"

"Part of the pattern."

"Pattern? What pattern?"

"Did it easy. Enjoyed it. Like squashing a pea. A shove and a push and they tumbled into air. Easy. Easy."

Very little was capable of surprising Edward Moon, but Innocenti's performance seemed to stop him short. Slack-jawed and ashen-faced, he asked: "Who are you?"

"Prophet," Madame Innocenti gurgled. "Baptist. Lay straight the ways."

Moon recovered his composure. "Tell me more."

Innocenti grinned. In the semi-darkness it seemed as though her mouth was filled with far too many teeth. "Got a warning."

"A warning? For me?"

"Ten days till trap is sprung. Till London burns and city falls."

Moon leant forward. "Explain."

A long pause. Then: "Fuck." Madame Innocenti seemed to relish the word, swilling it around her mouth as though she were savouring the first sip of an unfeasibly expensive wine.

"I beg your pardon?"

"Fuck." Innocenti was being quite deliberate. "Fuck. Piss. Cunt." She spat out that last word with particular delight.

The Salisburys were appalled, Dolly Creed merely bemused, while Mr. Lister tried his best to suppress a nervous laugh.

"Mr. Moon!" It was Innocenti's husband. "This has gone too far."

"Shit," his wife said conversationally. "Cunty cunt cunt."

"Break the circle. Let go."

The party quickly disentangled hands and Madame Innocenti sat bolt upright, a fat gob of saliva dripping from her mouth unchecked. The Salisburys stumbled to their feet and Mrs. Erskine jabbed her forefinger angrily at Moon. "You're a liability," she said. "Someone ought to lock you up."

Innocenti opened her eyes and beamed. "I'm back," she said in her normal voice, wiping away the spittle which still hung in thick, ropy tendrils from her lips.

Everyone stared at her, astonished.

"I hope I didn't do anything to embarrass myself," she said mildly.

They had barely risen the following morning when the albino came to call.

"Anything?"

Moon glared. "I'm not your lackey."

"Just tell me what happened."

Slightly chastened, Moon gave his report as Skimpole drummed his slender fingers impatiently on the tabletop, evidently troubled by the news.

"Ten days," he said thoughtfully, once Moon had finished. "You think she's genuine?"

The conjuror spoke carefully. "If you'd asked me that yesterday afternoon, I would have said absolutely not. My instinct was that she was a charlatan like the rest of them."

"But now?"

The Somnambulist scribbled something down.

FLY

Skimpole was irritated by the interruption. "What does he mean?"

Moon confessed. "I asked to speak to the spirit of the Human Fly."

"And did you?"

Moon blanched. "Yes," he admitted. "I think perhaps I did."

Skimpole instructed them to return to Tooting Bec at their earliest opportunity, muttered a muted kind of thanks for their services to the Crown and shuffled to the door. Just as he was about to leave, he turned back. "By the way—there's a surprise for you in reception."

Moon and the Somnambulist walked to the ground floor where they found an old friend waiting. She squealed delightedly on their approach. "Mr. Moon!"

Even the conjuror allowed himself a small smile at seeing her again. "Hello, Mrs. Grossmith."

The Somnambulist, however, showed no restraint at all and he and the housekeeper fell immediately into a tight embrace.

"Skimpole found me," Grossmith explained, once they had disentangled themselves. "I'm to work for you here now."

"I see."

"Aren't you pleased?"

"I have much to concern me at present."

Someone coughed. A stranger stood half a dozen paces behind her, an untidy, gangling man some years her senior. Bulbous-nosed and endowed with disproportionately large ears, he had the appearance of an oversized toby jug. He shambled forward, tripped over one of his shoelaces and sprawled onto the floor. Picking himself up, he dusted himself down and asked, in a soft, nervous voice: "Well, Mrs. G. When are you going to introduce us?"

Mrs. Grossmith blushed. "Sorry," she said, uncharacteristically girlish. "This is Arthur Barge. My landlord. And now . . ."— a giggle escaped her and she spoke more shrilly than she had intended—"my special friend."

A long, awkward silence. Moon eyed the man with disdain and shook his hand half-heartedly.

Arthur Barge shuffled his feet, embarrassed. Mercifully, they were disturbed by the arrival of the hotel's concierge.

"Mr. Moon?" the man asked, discreet and subservient as ever. "You've another visitor. He's most insistent, I'm afraid."

"Who?"

Before he could reply, a curious figure strutted into the room. He began to speak almost at once, his words tripping over one another in their haste to be heard. "I hope I haven't called at a bad time. I'd hate to think I was interrupting a reunion. Still, considering what's happened, you're all looking very well." He stuck out his hand. "Edward. Good to see you again. Care for a stroll?"

It was Thomas Cribb.

11

*B*eneath the city, the old man dreams.

A phrase surfaces from the ether and forms itself in his mind.

"All poets go to hell."

A strange sentence but one he is certain he has heard somewhere before. Or read, perhaps. Even written it himself.

He dreams that he is back again in his bedroom at Highgate. Dr. Gillman is there, and someone else, a dwarfish figure who hangs back amongst the shadows that crouch malevolently at the edges of the room. Then the stranger steps into the light—the dark figure reveals itself—and the dreamer laughs with relief: it is a small boy not more than ten years old. He recognises him now. The child has a name and in the dream it swims determinedly towards him. Ned. But the boy's surname proves elusive and the dream shifts again.

He is on a beach, shoeless, wriggling his toes in the sand, feeling it rear up around his feet and work its way into the crevices of his skin. The wind catches playfully at him, flapping his coat like a cape, and almost succeeds in tipping the hat from his head. He watches an elderly woman stand at the edge of a wooden platform which has been wheeled out into the surf. She totters arthritically down to the shallows, squealing in matronly delight as the cold water touches her for the first time. The old man laughs and suddenly Ned is with him, his hot little hand clasped in his, and he laughs, too, though neither of them is quite sure why. Ned grips his hand tighter and they walk on.

The years roll back but the scene remains the same. The dreamer is on the beach again now no longer old. The boy has disappeared (doubtless yet to be born) and instead, another man is by his side, someone the dreamer feels certain is important, significant to many lives beyond his own. They are paddling together, breeches rolled up above their knees, shoes abandoned on the shore and guarded by an anxious entourage. The water laps hungrily at their calves and the dreamer grins at his companion. Suddenly the truth of it hits him. The Prime Minister. Could it be? Too fanciful, he decides, and shifts uncomfortably in his sleep. Could it be that he once paddled with the PM in the sea at Ramsgate?

Ramsgate? When did he remember that?

Probably not. Dreams lie.

The Highgate room again. Gillman and the boy. As usual the old man is talking, rambling incontinently on through another protracted anecdote. "All poets go to hell," he says, and the child listens intently, but Gillman seems bored—he's heard it all before, and more than once. Even in his own dreams the old man is aware of his reputation for garrulity.

Then he remembers. "All poets go to hell." Something said that to him once. Something less than human, not quite alive, its voice papery and insidious like wind through dry leaves.

And then he is young again, still a student, alone in his lodgings with this thing that has promised—for a price—to tell him certain secrets. "All poets go to hell," it says, its eyes like burning coals, and, maddeningly, the old man knows that this is all it will ever say, repeating ad nauseam and infinitum this same perplexing phrase.

Forty years later he tells the story and Gillman laughs as if it's just another yarn, another little story outrageously embroidered, but the boy, this strange, solemn, special little boy does not laugh and the old man thinks—the old man *knows*—that this, this is the one.

Above him, as he sleeps, the city roars turbulently on.

There was a faint scent about Mr. Cribb that Moon had never noticed before—not altogether unpleasant, not the smell of perspiration or the musky stink of an unwashed body but something altogether more unusual, comforting, redolent of age and must and damp. He smelt like leaves in October, Moon realised. Of Autumn.

They had walked some distance from the hotel before either of them noticed they were being followed.

"Friend of yours?" the ugly man asked, nodding discreetly towards a stolid, grey-suited gentleman skulking half a street behind them.

"My valet," Moon explained. "My keeper. Skimpole won't let me out without him."

Cribb waved with his left, four-fingered hand and, rather sheepishly, the man touched the brim of his bowler in reply.

"How are you finding Mr. Skimpole?"

Moon grimaced.

"I promise you. By the time all this is over, you'll have come to respect him."

Moon surprised himself by laughing. "I suppose you've seen it all before. In the future."

"Never forget," Cribb insisted, comically grave, "I know the plot."

The detective rolled his eyes.

"Of course, there are rules about this kind of thing, but I can tell you this: Skimpole does not die happy."

"Shame," said Moon, sounding anything but upset, at which Cribb unexpectedly roused himself to the albino's defence.

"He's not an evil man. He acts from what he believes to be honourable motives."

The corners of Moon's mouth turned themselves up into a sneer. "Monsters always do."

"He's not a monster."

Moon looked about him and saw that he was lost. The familiar streets had slipped away, the alien and unknown reared up in their place. "Where are we going?"

"Docklands," Cribb said, striding on. "Don't ask me why. I'll tell you when we get there."

"Is there a good reason why we can't hail a cab?"

"To understand the city you need to feel her soil beneath your feet, to breathe her air, to sample her infinite variety."

"You know you're a remarkably irritating man."

"It has been mentioned, yes."

They walked on, oddly content in one another's company, though dogged the whole time by Mr. Skimpole's familiar.

"What's your earliest memory?" Cribb asked at length.

Moon looked sharply at the loping, lopsided figure hunched beside him, this gawky Virgil to his reluctant Dante. "Why?"

"It may be important."

"My father," Moon said, "waking me in the night, shaking me awake to tell me my mother had gone."

Cribb all but rubbed his hands together in glee. "Wonderful!" he chuckled.

"And you?" asked Moon, faintly irritated by his companion's reaction. "Your earliest memory?"

Cribb frowned. "I sincerely doubt you'll believe me."

"Please."

"I remember the streets in flames. The city visited again by pestilence and fire. The great stone cracked. I am old and I am dying."

"You're *old*?"

"It's . . . complicated."

"I've just realised," Moon said with a start.

"Yes?"

"You really believe all this, don't you?"

Cribb would only smile in reply, and they walked on.

"I imagine you'll have met Madame Innocenti by now," he said a while later.

"Who told you that?"

Cribb brushed the question aside with a languorous wave. "I'm not in league with the Directorate if that's what you're thinking."

"It had crossed my mind."

"Well, banish it for ever. What did you make of her?"

Moon's throat felt itchy and dry and he swallowed, unwilling to reply.

"You spoke to the Fly, didn't you?"

"Truthfully? I'm not entirely sure who I spoke to. It was uncanny."

"You'll see her again," Cribb said firmly. "And next time you'll know the truth of it."

"How much further?" Moon glanced behind him. "I think our friend's getting tired."

"Almost there."

As they strolled on, the familiar turrets of Tower Bridge loomed into view and beyond them the wharves, warehouses and shipyards of the docklands. They seemed to Moon to resemble some industrial Baghdad, with its blackened spires, its grimy ziggurats and its smog-choked minarets. The Thames threaded her way amongst them, a discarded ribbon, dirty grey, strewn across the landscape.

"Walk closer."

Ignoring a legion of forbidding notices and signs and heaving themselves over innumerable gates and fences, they eventually clambered down beside the river. Moon wrinkled his nose at the omnipresent smell of decay, treading as carefully as he could along the bank as the filth and muck of the Thames oozed over his shoes.

"Mud," Cribb said, sounding just as he had on London Bridge, as though in the midst of delivering a sermon. "Glorious mud—"

"Have you got a light?" Moon asked, fumbling unsuccessfully in his pockets for a cigarette.

Cribb ignored him. "We've passed through the city's bowels. Now we walk the span of her intestine."

"Charming metaphor."

"A century from now all this will be torn down, this testament to industry, toil and sweat. In its place great temples are built, monuments to wealth and avarice and power."

Moon gazed in front of him, not really listening. A gull screamed overhead.

Cribb chattered on. "London is an inhibitor. You understand? She trammels and diminishes her inhabitants. The city is a trap."

"What's happening there?" Moon asked, pointing to what appeared to be a large marquee perched incongruously a few feet from the riverbank.

"Really, Edward. You can be infuriating at times. I'm trying to tell you something important."

Cribb tutted in irritation but Moon had already left him and he was forced to break into a run to catch up. He was amused to note Skimpole's man struggling along behind them, his shoes and trousers already sodden with the slimy jetsam of the river.

Moon reached the tent. Its canopy flapped noisily in the wind as though some great bird were trapped beneath the canvas, cyclopean wings beating frantically in an effort to escape. He peered inside and saw that the ground within had been thoroughly excavated, the soil potholed, cratered and covered with little marker flags, the earth itemised and ordered. What caught his attention, however, was a group of men—grubbily genteel, their clothes stained by silt and mud—gathered around a large spherical object placed on a table in the centre of the tent. Moon moved closer and it took a moment to acclimatise himself to the sheer peculiarity of the sight, to accept that what he was seeing was real.

He was looking at what appeared to be an enormous stone head, too large and unwieldy for one man to lift unaided, caked in dirt and river mud but otherwise intact. Giggling and chattering like schoolchildren abandoned by their teachers and left to run riot in the classroom, the men were all far too excited to take much notice of his intrusion.

"Who are you?" he asked.

"British Museum," one of them hissed. "You press?"

"Yes," Moon lied fluently, and the man nodded distractedly in greeting.

Cribb finally caught up, breathless, a flush of colour in his cheeks, its shade an exact match to his hair.

Moon ignored him and spoke to another of the men. "What is it?" he asked.

"It's quite remarkable," the man replied giddily. "It's got to be . . ." He turned to one of his colleagues bent over the head, which Moon now saw was made from some primitive sort of metal. "What do you think? Pre-Roman, at least."

"Has to be at this depth," his colleague replied.

"Look at the craftsmanship," the man breathed. "The sophistication."

"Who is it?" Moon asked as the man began to gently wipe the head clean of mud.

"Dangerous to theorise ahead of the facts but I might venture some supposition . . . a local leader, perhaps? Head of the tribe?"

"Seems too grand for that," said another, the most elderly of the group. "Too regal."

Then a young man spoke up. "A god, perhaps?" His voice was squeaky with nerves. "A king?"

"Wait," said another. "There's a name."

As the mud was wiped away from the bottom of the head, a three-letter word emerged.

The young man read it aloud. "Lud!" he cried. "The founder of London. King of the city."

"Impossible," said one.

"I can't believe it," said another.

"Lud?" Moon peered closer as the rest of the clay was brushed aside and he felt an acute, vertiginous sense that he had walked willingly into a trap. The head's features began to swim queasily into view—something disturbing and familiar brought inexorably into focus. The face revealed at last, several present gasped.

"Here," the old man said, belatedly suspicious. "Which newspaper did you say you were from?"

Moon ignored him. "It can't be," he murmured.

The bronze head was clean, history wiped away to reveal—calcified and perfectly preserved—an effigy of the first king of London. Lud unveiled.

And Edward Moon could only stare hopelessly down at it, biting hard on his lower lip in an effort to stop himself from crying out, as the unforgettably ugly features of Thomas Cribb gazed sightlessly back across the centuries.

He turned to confront his companion but, as though in some marvellous illusion, the ugly man had disappeared, vanished back towards the river, leaving nothing behind to prove that he had ever been there at all, nothing to say that he wasn't merely a figment of the city's imagination.

When Moon returned to his hotel, he found Mr. Speight waiting for him in the street outside. The tramp was dressed in his usual filthy suit and his face was covered with fresh sores, only partially hidden by his riotous, scratchy beard. A bottle of something yellow bulged from his jacket pocket and he had propped up before him his trademark placard:

SURELY I AM COMING SOON
REVELATION 22:20

"Afternoon," he said, ebullient but not yet quite drunk. The doorman gave him a dirty look and Speight nodded back. "This one's been trying to turf me out for hours."

"What are you doing here?" Moon was so bewildered that he felt half-convinced the man before him was a mirage.

"I've tracked you down," Speight said proudly.

Moon blinked, still not entirely certain that this exchange was really happening. "What can I do for you?"

"To be honest . . . money. Since the theatre . . . I've had nowhere to doss down. Things have got difficult. You were always so kind to me—"

Moon cut him off, reached into his pocket and passed the man a pound note. "Here. Spend it wisely."

"Actually," Speight admitted, "I'll only spend it on drink."

Moon pushed past him and clambered up the steps to his hotel. "Frankly, Mr. Speight, just at the moment, I'd happily join you."

"Something the matter?" Speight seemed genuinely concerned.

"Have you ever had everything you ever believed in ruined in a few hours?"

"Can't say I have, sir, no."

"Have you ever seen all logic and reason dissolve before your eyes?"

"Again, sir—I'd have to say no."

"Have you ever been thrust into the most acute existential crisis by the sheer impossibility of the truth?"

The beggar gave Moon an embarrassed look. "P'raps you'd better have a lie-down, sir. Thanks again for the cash."

With a heavy sigh, the conjuror stepped inside.

Six hours later, slumped at a table in the far corner of the hotel bar, a bleary-eyed Moon watched Arthur Barge shamble amiably past. The detective crooked his little finger and beckoned him across. "Mr. Barge?"

The human toby jug beamed. "Good evening to you." He walked across to Moon, tripping over a stray barstool as he did so.

"I've been meaning," Moon said with that ponderous solemnity unique to the seriously drunk, "to have a word with you."

"I suppose this is about me and Mrs. G. She's a wonderful woman, sir. A real lady. Frisky like, though, when she wants to be."

Moon steepled his fingers. "Mr. Barge. Mrs. Grossmith has given me years of faithful service. I am not entirely without feeling and I've no wish—to dabble for a moment in the vernacular— to see you break her heart."

Barge chuckled. "Are you asking me if my intentions are honourable?"

"Yes," Moon said, unsmiling. "How did you know?"

Barge blustered, "Rest assured. I'll do right by her."

Moon finished the last of his drink. "You'd better. If I find you've mistreated her in any way . . ." He paused, unable to think of a sufficiently menacing threat. "Believe me," he finished feebly, "I'll get you."

Barge looked back, astonished at this sudden burst of aggression so ineptly delivered. "Sorry if I've offended you. Really. I don't know what I've done, I'm sure."

Moon glared impatiently. "I'll be watching."

"I love her," Barge said meekly, then walked to the exit, narrowly avoiding spilling several patrons' drinks in the process. He struggled with the door, fruitlessly trying to tug it open when it would have submitted to the gentlest of pushes. Only the entrance of the Somnambulist afforded him an opportunity to escape. He stopped to whisper his thanks but the giant stomped grumpily past without acknowledging him.

When Moon saw his friend, he groaned and pushed aside a few of the legion of empty glasses lined up before him in a vain attempt to disguise the quantity of his drinking. The Somnambulist, however, was in no mood to be fooled. He pulled a stool up to the table, lowered his vast form upon it and wrote furiously on his blackboard, the ferocious tap of chalk on board sounding to Moon like the dull roar of distant cannon fire.

WARE WERE YOU

Moon squirmed. The Somnambulist gesticulated angrily at the message.

"Out," Moon said and stumbled to his feet. Faltering, he floundered and, his balance unsteady, fell heavily back onto the chair. The Somnambulist ignored these pratfalls.

CRIBB

"Yes," Moon admitted, a chink of emotion in his voice.

DONT TRUST

Moon looked up. "You recognise him, don't you?"

STAY AWAY

"I don't understand. Why won't you tell me what you know? Why won't *anyone* tell me what they know?"

TRUST ME

Moon sighed.

PLEESE

The Somnambulist frantically underlined the word.

Moon clutched his head. "Very well. If it makes you happy. I shan't see him again."

The Somnambulist nodded gravely.

"But you promise one day you'll tell me why?"

The giant shrugged.

"Fine," spat Moon. "If that's the best you can do." And he staggered up and lurched from the room.

Once he got to his suite, in a vain attempt to counteract the effects of the alcohol, he forced himself to consume three glasses of water before collapsing helplessly onto his bed. In the seconds before he passed out he watched, too weak to stir, as Skimpole's man peered into the room, realised his condition and pulled the door discreetly shut. His last thought was a drunken conviction that the strange events which had filled his life since Cyril Honeyman had fallen from the tower must have a pattern, that they shared some undiscovered connection, were bound together by an invisible plot. He could see only the tiniest part of its design—like looking at a single fila-ment of a spider's web through a microscope—but he felt cer-tain that all he needed was to step back, gain some perspective and watch as everything came into focus. He tried to keep hold of the idea but he was befuddled by drink and it leapt and wriggled away from him, struggling frantically like a mackerel

on a hook until, in the end, he gave in and the darkness came
to claim him.

Sleep did not come so easily in Newgate.

Barabbas stank and he knew it. Matters have come to a terrible
pass when the stench and toxicity of one's own perspiration are
enough to make one nauseous. Owsley had procured him many
favours, but it seemed that a decent bath was beyond even him.

Barabbas yawned, scratched at his shaggy beard and shuffled
his elephantine bulk across those few paces that measured the
floor of his cell. It was quiet now as the clock moved into the slow
hours of the night—the only time when the shrieks and lamentations of his fellow inmates died down. The next cell was currently
occupied by a member of a fundamentalist Methodist sect who
occupied his time in endless recitations of the Lord's Prayer, occasionally interspersed for variety's sake with a small selection of
the better known psalms. The man must have fallen asleep shortly
before midnight, exhausted and hoarse from his day's labours, as
Barabbas had heard nothing from him for almost an hour.

"Meyrick?" he hissed. "Are you there?"

Owsley's face appeared between the bars. "Always," he murmured, his tone that of a patient mother soothing a particularly
obstreperous child.

Barabbas sighed—a rattling, skeletal sound. "I'm bored. Do
you have any conception of what it's like for me in here? The miserable, numbing tedium of it all."

Owsley's voice was as obsequious as ever. "Yes, sir. I do sympathise."

"A man of my brilliance incarcerated in a space not fit for
beasts. A coruscating intellect penned in with criminals with
nothing to do but wait. It's one of the great tragedies of our age."

"Indeed, sir." Was there a hint of resignation in Owsley's

voice? A glimpse behind the disciple's mask, a momentary revelation of a man long-suffering, put upon, resentful? Perhaps.

"When will Edward come again?"

"I've no idea."

"When he comes, I'll—"

"Yes, sir? What will you do?" Just the faintest undertone of sarcasm, barely detectable.

"I'll tell him everything."

This had an unexpected effect on the listener. A thoughtful pause, then the carefully worded reply: "I should not advise such a course of action."

Barabbas spluttered, "I don't ask for advice. Yours is not to reason why."

Owsley, unruffled but insistent: "You would regret it."

"You are my creature. Never forget that."

But his disciple did not reply, and the prisoner heard only soft footfalls as Owsley padded away down the corridor in discreet abandonment of his post.

"Meyrick!" Barabbas shouted, but still the footsteps receded frustratingly into the distance. "Meyrick!" he screamed, desperate and confused at this sudden, inexplicable dereliction. "Come back!"

Too late. He heard the faint rattle of keys, then the uncaring clang of the iron door as Owsley left the innards of the gaol and headed back towards the outside world.

"Meyrick!" Barabbas rattled the bars of his cell in despair, then threw himself onto the stone floor, on the brink of tears. He heard a loud rustling from the next cell—a moan, stumbling footsteps, followed soon after by the first, familiar words of Psalm 130: "Out of the depths I cry to thee . . ."

At last Mrs. Puggsley's establishment was shutting up shop after twelve exhausting hours of business. Mina (always the darling of the salon) had been in great demand, and after dealing with her last john of the night she was grateful to walk downstairs to the reception room, hoping to sit with the other girls, gossip, chat and share a glass of wine or two. She was surprised, then, to find not a trace of them but only Mrs. Puggsley, who sat on her usual chair, her vast buttocks drooping gelatinously over the seat. A prim, precise, pale-skinned man stood over her.

Puggsley gave a weak smile. "Mina, my dear." She coughed, and as her enormous frame shuddered in sympathy, she wheezed like a worn-out steam train bound for the scrap heap. "I've sent the other girls away."

"Away?"

Mrs. Puggsley shuffled uncomfortably. "For their safety."

"Where?"

No reply. Mina transferred her attention to the pale man. "I've seen you before," she said boldly. "You're a friend of Mr. Gray's, aren't you?"

"Oh, we're old pals," he answered and smiled the way Brutus might have smiled the day he wielded the blade.

Mina began to fiddle absently with her beard, a nervous habit from childhood she had never quite managed to suppress. "What's going on?"

Mrs. Puggsley turned towards her. "Please," she said gently. "Go."

"Tell me what's happened," Mina protested, despising herself for the plaintive quality in her voice.

"I'm afraid it's bad news," the pale man said smoothly. "Your usefulness has come to an end."

Puggsley made a strange, uncharacteristic snuffling sound.

"I've decided to close you down. A terrible pity. But needs must . . ."

Mina looked at her employer, hoping for a denial, for some

shred of hope, but the woman was unable even to meet her gaze.

"You've been a great help. Mrs. Puggsley says you were quite his favourite. The details you supplied were invaluable." He paused to readjust the pince-nez that perched ridiculously on the tip of his nose. "It would be no exaggeration to say that there are those in the highest echelons of government who are grateful for your assistance." He gave an oleaginous smile. "Take heart. Even a wretch like you can serve King and country in your way."

"Get out," Puggsley said to Mina, hoarse now, almost whispering, not bothering to hide the desperation in her voice or stem the rising tide of hysteria.

"I suggest you take your mistress's advice. In a few minutes' time this place will be in flames. The Directorate has scheduled it for demolition."

Mrs. Puggsley did not move.

"My credentials as an arsonist are impeccable. You might say I've an eye for catastrophe." He smirked again but, still silent, Puggsley did not stir. Mina gazed at this tableau in horror.

"Do you know," the pale man said conversationally, "I fancy I can already smell the smoke."

Mina turned and ran, fleeing out into the street, bent almost double with sobbing, tears stinging her face and trickling down her beard.

She left Goodge Street and was some way towards Tottenham Court Road when she saw the smoke, stopped and thought of going back. Her loyalty was about to win out over her instinct for self-preservation when a gang of men rolled rowdily out of a nearby tavern and began to point at her and laugh. Her decision made for her, she did her best to ignore their derision and hurried onwards in the hope of finding some sanctuary in the city. As she walked she felt a cold, implacable certainty that, whilst the pale man was even now returning home, Mrs. Puggsley had never left her chair and sat there still, the flames licking about her feet, toying with her hungrily, her great fat frame shuddering and sweltering in anticipation of the inevitable roast.

$\mathcal{M}$oon woke three hours after he had lost consciousness, stumbled to his feet and vomited copiously in the basin. He washed the worst of it away and as the yellowed water spiralled down the plughole it seemed to mock him, chuckling quietly. He sank back onto his bed and surrendered himself to the pain, the interior of his skull assailed by battering rams, limbs rubbery like blancmange, mouth Sahara dry.

When he opened his eyes again, the physical pain had subsided but the tempest in his head was worse than ever. All at once the events of the past few months seemed to round upon him, jeering and ridiculing, crowding out his thoughts. He looked at the spotless, soulless luxury of his bedroom and under the influence of an ineluctable compulsion began—quite deliberately and with clinical precision—to smash it all up.

$\mathcal{M}$r. Skimpole arrived an hour later, perspiring, ill-tempered and smelling faintly of smoke. He was greeted at reception by the hotel's manager and by the man he had assigned to watch Moon. What they had to tell him did not raise his spirits.

He knocked at Moon's door but, predictably, got no reply. He tried again (still no answer), then gestured to his man to break it down. Ignoring the shrill protestations of the manager, the fellow did so in a single attempt.

"Mr. Moon?" Skimpole called out irritably. "Please come out. I'm not in an especially patient mood."

Moon emerged, not entirely without guilt, from the bathroom.

The suite was almost unrecognisable—glass strewn indiscriminately about the floor, lamps smashed, curtains gouged and torn, paintings brutalised and defaced, the carpet pulled from its fittings and thrown against the wall like a great wave lapping at the corners of the room.

Skimpole's tone was careful and even but masked a controlled fury. "What have you done?"

"You're holding me against my will."

Skimpole sighed. "We're on the same side. I acted as I did only because you left me with no other choice. Most of us would kill to live in this kind of luxury. You should see my house. This is a palace by comparison."

"It's a prison."

The albino looked exasperated. "I know you had a difficult time of it yesterday. Clearly you've had some sort of falling-out with your new friend. Mr. . . . . Cribb, is it?" Skimpole turned to his man to check the name. "Well, then. I'll have this room cleaned up and we'll no say no more about it. Surely you want to solve this case as much as any of us?"

"One condition: get rid of that ghoul." Moon pointed towards Skimpole's man. "I can't abide being followed everywhere. It's not even as though he's very good at it."

"Very well. But that's my only concession. You must stop acting like this, Edward. All I ask is for you to solve this one problem and then you can go back to your old life. If Madame Innocenti is correct we have just eight days left."

Moon collapsed onto the room's only surviving chair. "If she is correct," he muttered. "*If.*" He groaned. "In the past few days I've seen things I know shouldn't be true, things against the order of the world. Things that have no place in a rational universe."

"May I offer some advice?" Skimpole said gently. "You should do as I do whenever I'm confronted by the weird, by the uncanny, by the unexplained."

"What's that?"

"My job."

Skimpole turned to leave and, as he did so, the Somnambulist appeared behind him in the doorway. Seeing Moon and the carnage which surrounded him, the giant shook his head sadly, pushed past the albino and moved slowly away down the corridor. Moon did not even try to stop him.

When he finally emerged from his bedroom, the events of the past few hours were already receding happily into the past. His encounter with Cribb had the unconvincing quality of fiction about it, like something that had happened to someone else entirely. He washed, shaved, combed back his thinning hair and started gratefully for the Stacks.

The Archivist, at least, seemed pleased to see him. "Heard you'd been recruited," she said, once Moon had been ushered down into the basement by another nameless librarian. "Government work, is it? Mr. Skimpole's boys?"

Moon had learnt years before not to be surprised by the Archivist's apparent omniscience, but even he could not help but be startled by the coolly authoritative manner with which she delivered the specifics of his predicament.

"Yes, ma'am. Do you . . ." He hesitated.

"Yes?" The woman's sightless eyes seemed to swivel curiously in his direction.

"Do you know Mr. Skimpole, ma'am? Does he . . . come here?"

The Archivist turned away and began to search a shelf stacked high with mouldering copies of *Punch*, jaundiced WANTED posters and creaking, leather-bound encyclopaediae. "Now, now," she chided. "You know I have to be discreet."

"What you mean by that, I assume, is 'yes'?"

"I can't prevent you from drawing your own conclusions."

"No," Moon said pensively. "You can't."

"What are you looking for today?"

"Anything you have on a Madame Innocenti. Clairvoyant in Tooting Bec."

The Archivist said nothing, disappeared and returned shortly after with two slim volumes. "This is all I have. Seems she's fallen foul of the law once or twice before."

Moon thanked her and took them. "Archivist?"

"Yes?"

He paused uncertainly. "Have you ever heard of a man named Thomas Cribb?"

There was no reply. Moon had convinced himself that she had not heard him and was about to repeat his query when the Archivist spoke again, an unfamiliar, quavering tenor to her voice. "One moment. I may have something for you."

When she returned she was pushing a trolley piled high with records, reports, ledgers, dossiers and sheaves of what looked like nineteenth-century newsprint. She wheezed her way towards him, gripping his shoulder with surprising force to steady herself. Half a dozen pamphlets and a vast, dictionary-sized volume toppled from the trolley.

"What is this?"

"This?" The Archivist gasped for breath. "This is just the beginning. I've five times this amount waiting for you."

"Surely this can't *all* concern Mr. Cribb?"

"I'm afraid so."

Moon picked up some of the records and stifled a sneeze at the clouds of dust that mushroomed from the pile. "How far back do these go?"

The Archivist swallowed hard. "Over a century. Seems your friend has been with us longer than you thought."

The silence that followed, tense and oppressive, was broken only when Moon lit a cigarette, fumbling desperately in his pockets for box and lighter like a man deprived of tobacco for days. He told me later that it was the only time the Archivist had ever asked to join him, her aged, knotted hands shaking with quiet, unspoken desperation.

*W*hen Moon returned home the Somnambulist sat waiting for him. Rows of empty glasses stained with milky residue snaked their way along his table, the detritus of a long and lonely evening.

Even more than Moon, the giant had been damaged by the destruction of the theatre—the *ancien régime* had passed away, but under Skimpole's new republic Moon was at least given mysteries to unravel, missions to fulfil, the ongoing puzzle of the Honeyman business to divert him, whilst the Somnambulist had sunk into what might in any other man have seemed a profound melancholia. Communication between them had always been fragmentary at best, conducted via sign, gesture and the staccato correspondence of the chalkboard, but Moon had begun to suspect that the giant missed the performances—his nightly dose of spot-lit approbation—far more than he would ever admit.

He risked a pallid smile and the Somnambulist nodded sullenly back.

"I saw Speight yesterday. He seemed well. By which I mean, of course, not exactly *well*. But much as he always was."

The giant shrugged theatrically.

"I've spent the day in the Stacks. Uncovered a good deal on Madame Innocenti."

The giant shot him a reproachful look, sulky, like a child refusing to eat his greens. Moon pressed on regardless. "It would appear she's not been entirely truthful with us. Her real name is Ann Bagshaw. Before she became a prophet she used to be a seamstress—had a little shop by the Oval."

The Somnambulist scribbled something on his board and Moon, relieved at last to be getting some response, leant forward to read it:

SEE HER AGAIN

"Ah, yes. Well. Mr. Skimpole's arranged for us to attend another of her soirées tomorrow. Perhaps things will become clearer then."

The Somnambulist drained his final glass of milk, gathered chalk and blackboard to him and, with ponderous dignity, pulled himself to his feet.

"See you tomorrow?" Moon called out hopefully. "For the seance?"

The Somnambulist loped grumpily away, heading for his suite. They had not shared a room since the theatre blaze—a hotel as exclusive as this seemed to draw the line at bunk beds.

*I*n the morning, a gruff kind of rapprochement took place. The Somnambulist scrawled what might generously be construed as an apology, Moon plied him with further assurances and it was in the spirit of uneasy truce that they set off after lunch for Tooting Bec.

Madame Innocenti was waiting for them on the steps of her shabby home. "Gentlemen," she said, all smiles. "So pleased you've come back to us."

Moon bowed his head and said politely: "Mrs. Bagshaw."

The woman froze and Moon saw a look of fear pass across her face, but she recovered her composure almost immediately and walked into the house as though nothing had happened. As they moved down the corridor and towards the seance room, Innocenti's husband lurched from the shadows where he had obviously been eavesdropping, and shot them a look of pure animosity.

The seance took place exactly as before and Moon even recognised some of the same faces—Ellis Lister and the widow Erskine. With them were an elderly couple and a grim-faced, lugubrious man in mourning for his wife. In other words, the usual parade of misfits and delusionals desperate for their pain to be soothed away by the coos and sweet nothings of their hostess.

After half an hour or so of meaningless socialising, handshakes, introductions, tea and biscuits, the seance began in earnest, everything exactly the same as before—Madame Innocenti at the head of the table, the swift assumption of her Corcoran voice, those same nebulous, artfully worded missives from the spirit world. She turned first to Mrs. Erskine. "To whom do you wish to speak?" she asked, in the Spaniard's familiarly punctilious tones.

"My boy," Mrs. Erskine said, her voice weary and thin. "My little 'un. Billy. Sixteen when he died."

"Billy?" Corcoran whispered. "Billy? Is there a Billy Erskine amongst the spirits?"

Pause. Then, predictably: "Mother?" Innocenti managed a passable impression of a young man's voice, cracked and unsure of its register.

"Billy?" Mrs. Erskine asked, pain and hope intermingled in her voice. "Billy, is that you?"

"Mother! Why have you only come to me now? I've been here so long. I've been waiting."

Mrs. Erskine sobbed. "I'm sorry, Bill. Can you forgive me?"

"Will you join me soon? It's warm here and soft. You'll like it, Mother, I know you will." His voice had acquired a plaintive, wheedling tone. "But what's happened to you, Mother? You seem so old."

Erskine sobbed again and Madame Innocenti murmured: "Mother, I love you."

This exchange continued for what felt like hours and Moon felt himself on the verge of nodding off into a light doze when he heard the mention of his own name.

"Mr. Moon?" It was Innocenti in her Corcoran persona.

"Señor," Moon replied. "Such a pleasure to meet you again."

"I wish I could say the same. Seven days to go and you haven't done a damned thing."

"I've been busy."

"In little more than a week this city will be set ablaze and you've done nothing to stop it. The spirits are afraid, Mr. Moon. London is in great peril."

"So people keep telling me."

"Honeyman was a hook. You've taken the bait and you don't even realise it. You're being used."

"Go on."

"Underground." Corcoran's tone became more forceful. "Danger underground."

"Danger?"

Madame Innocenti arched her back. Moon and the Somnambulist felt her hands begin to tremble violently, as though galvanized by some invisible force. "The death of the city approaches," she chattered. "The poet dreams uneasy in his cot. The conspiracy moves against you. The sleeper wakes."

Despite his scepticism, Moon found himself enthralled. "What do you mean?"

"Skimpole is a pawn. You are their target. And it is you who are to blame."

*M*oon and I discussed Madame Innocenti's warnings at length. Of course, they sounded every bit as recondite and oracular as one might expect but they were also astonishingly accurate on a number of key points. Moon argued for a time—trying more to convince himself than me, I fancy—that she might have obtained the majority of the details from Skimpole, Lister or someone of that ilk, but in the end we were forced to accept that Madame Innocenti may well have been the real thing.

*I*nnocenti opened her eyes and what happened next took even Moon by surprise. Later, no one could be entirely certain what they had seen and witnesses disagreed on all but the most basic facts. Moon himself believed that Innocenti's eyes suddenly turned a profound shade of scarlet, others that they had become green or an iridescent yellow, and Mrs. Erskine insisted (though her testimony, as you will shortly discover, is not entirely to be trusted) that they turned a ghastly black. The colour itself, of course, is not important. What is significant is that something remarkable, something unquestionably preternatural, took place.

The medium screamed and fell to the ground where she lay in deathly silence. Some present even claimed to have seen tendrils of smoke emerge from her mouth and nostrils, as though some terrible engine were exhausting itself within her.

The spell was swiftly broken. Mrs. Erskine, a septuagenarian at the very least, leapt—genuinely *leapt*—to her feet and bounded around the table towards the psychic, whereupon she pulled the woman to her feet and slapped her hard in the face.

"Ann Bagshaw?" Erskine said, declaiming her words like a policeman collaring a suspect.

Madame Innocenti relaxed and her eyes returned to their everyday shade. "Not any more."

Mrs. Erskine turned to the other guests. "Ladies and gentlemen, forgive my intrusion. I represent the Vigilance Committee."

There were rumbles of disapproval from the faithful at this, but Mrs. Erskine went on, "This woman's name is not and never has been Madame Innocenti. Her name is Ann Bagshaw."

The woman's husband moved forward to protest but she waved him meekly away.

"Today I apparently spoke to my late son," Erskine said. "But I have no son, living or dead. If Mrs. Bagshaw is to be believed, I conversed this afternoon with a boy who never existed."

Innocenti recovered and seemed to direct herself not to her accuser but to Edward Moon. "What happened was real," she insisted. "The warnings were real."

There was such consternation and general bedlam at this that Moon had to shout to make himself heard. "Please. You've not been told the whole truth." A hush fell upon the room as everyone, psychic and punter alike, turned to listen. "Our hosts may not be exactly who they claim to be, but neither, I fancy, is Mrs. Erskine."

The old woman muttered something under her breath.

"Look at her hands, ladies and gentlemen. Too supple, too smooth and unlined. Too youthful, I fancy, to be real."

Erskine glared, pushed past Ann Bagshaw and dashed from the room at a speed quite impossible for a woman of her advanced years. They heard her clatter through the house and escape out into the street, like a rat making its obligatory exit from some leaky and waterlogged old hulk.

Moon turned to his friend. "Keep everyone here until I return. I've just realised who we're dealing with."

Outside it had begun to rain heavily and before Moon had run for more than a few yards he was sodden and drenched. Ahead he could see Mrs. Erskine dashing desperately through the rain, seeking sanctuary in the murky streets and mews of Tooting Bec.

The action of the chase took no more than five or six minutes but it seemed to both of them to last for hours. As the rain pelted down in unforgiving sheets, Moon could see no more than a few yards in front of him, but dashed on regardless, pushing past umbrellaed pedestrians, pursuing Erskine by sheer instinct, a tracker dog after a scent.

He finally cornered her in an alley. Like weary boxers after the final bell, they stood panting and embarrassed at this anticlimactic finish to their flight. Mrs. Erskine's make-up had been all but obliterated by the rain—dye, powder and greasepaint streaked down her face, its thick lines of colour lending her the appearance of a clown caught in a thunderstorm. From behind the remnants of Mrs. Erskine a much younger woman peered out—in her early thirties, not quite pretty (she had too large a nose for that), but the hint of a pulchritudinous figure was apparent in the sopping, clinging silhouette of the old lady's clothes.

Moon stared, his suspicions confirmed, and caught somewhere between shock and elation, he felt violently sick. "It *is* you!" he cried. "Oh my dear. You've come back to me." He sank to his knees. "Oh my darling. Oh my angel."

She looked down, her eyes cold and devoid of pity. "You're embarrassing yourself," she said. "Get up, Edward."

12

*M*r. Skimpole had spent much of his life trying to be good. Naturally he'd had his lapses and temptations, as a younger man in particular, but nowadays he strove for a pure and virtuous existence, a life of temperance, decency and moderation, free from sybaritism and excess. But he allowed himself a single luxury— once a day, every day, he smoked a cigar. Of course, there was nothing ordinary about his vice; these cigars belonged to an exclusive brand beloved of the connoisseur, imported at great expense from an obscure region of Turkey and sold only to a select few customers through a deliriously overpriced shop in the centre of the city.

Skimpole took out his cigar of the day and rubbed it beneath his nose, making a great show of smelling it. He had never entirely understood the necessity of this olfactory ritual but he always did it anyway, going through the motions for the benefit of any cigar experts who might coincidentally be watching. He pushed the thick brown tube gently into his mouth, felt it slide smoothly between his teeth and let out a small sigh of pleasure.

Moon and the Somnambulist sat opposite him at the edge of the bar observing his performance, their expressions pitched somewhere between amusement and distaste.

"Forgive me," the albino murmured. "A small failing." He savoured the sensation of the smoke as it coiled its way down his throat, the rich, dry scent of it sinking deeper into his body, and he shuddered a little with joy. The cigar was half-done before he turned to the matter in hand. "The Innocenti problem. My sources suggest that she and her husband left the country two days ago, just after you caused that fracas in her parlour. We think they were bound for New York but I'm rather afraid we've lost them."

"It was not my doing," Moon said tightly. "She was exposed before I could act."

Skimpole dabbed self-consciously at the corners of his eyes. "I gather there was some involvement from the Vigilance Committee."

"Correct."

"What's your opinion? Do you think her warnings were real?"

"I ought not to. I should be able to dismiss her as a charlatan and a fraud. But there are questions. The things I saw . . . The Fly . . ."

"I consider myself a man open to the improbable," Skimpole went on. "I don't see how friend Bagshaw could have obtained the information she did without some kind of—how shall we say?—some supernatural advantage. Some etheric help."

"I agree."

Skimpole snorted. "I should say that the Vigilance Committee have a reputation. I've heard it suggested that if they can't uncover their evidence by conventional means, they're more than happy to fabricate it. Just last year they planted sheets of muslin on a psychic we believe was capable of producing genuine ectoplasm."

"The veracity of the woman's exposure is not in question," said Moon. "But her warnings . . . *bother* me."

Skimpole shifted uncomfortably in his chair and sucked on what was left of his cigar, teasing out those final precious few drags.

"She told me I was being used," Moon continued. "Said something about a sleeper. Danger underground. In point of fact, Mr. Skimpole, she told me that you were just a pawn."

The albino finished the last of his cigar and left the butt to smoulder on the ashtray before him. "I know my place."

"Something worries me."

"Madame Innocenti?"

"There's a connection we're missing."

"What do you intend to do? You should know that whatever you decide, you have the Directorate's full support." He smirked. "We're not an agency entirely devoid of influence."

"I need to see Barabbas again. He knows something, I'm sure of it."

"That can be arranged." Skimpole rose. "But move fast. We're running out of time. If Madame Innocenti was right, we've only four days before whatever it is happens. Incidentally, you may like to know I've authorised the first payment to your account." At this, he mentioned a remarkably generous sum—even today, all but the most highly rewarded of public servants would not baulk at so substantial a fee. "Naturally, your stay here and all related expenses are being paid for by my department. You may divide the money with your associate as you see fit."

"Money?" Moon said contemptuously. "You think I'm doing this for money?"

Skimpole stared blankly at him, faintly offended. "No need to be uncivilised about it. If you must, think of the money as a bonus. A gift from a grateful government."

Moon did not reply.

"Work fast. And keep me informed. I'm watching." Skimpole gave a formal bow and left the room. The Somnambulist pulled a childish face behind his back.

Moon walked across the room to where a young woman sat alone, a glass of red wine half-drunk before her. The Somnambulist watched, unable to hide his surprise as his friend paused before the lady in question, exchanged some polite words with her, smiled, motioned her to her feet and brought her back across the room. When the stranger drew closer, he realised that he recognised her as Mrs. Erskine, agent of the Vigilance Committee—but made young, stripped of her disguise and dressed in clothes suited to a lady of elegance and youth.

"This is my friend, the Somnambulist," Moon said, and his pretty companion curtseyed in greeting. Moon grinned. "I don't believe," he said, his hand reaching for the lady's, "that you've met my sister."

Skimpole left the hotel at a brisk, pedantic trot. Already late for an important meeting, he chose not to hail a cab but hurried through the city's streets, half-running along her crowded walkways and thoroughfares, darting in and out of shoals of pedestrians, pushing his way amongst swarms of indigenous urbanites. One might most naturally expect a government employee to head towards Whitehall or Westminster, but Skimpole turned towards the East End, careful at all times to ensure he was not followed, and headed instead for Limehouse and the Directorate.

SISTER

the Somnambulist scrawled hastily on the blackboard, then rubbed out the word and wrote again, in even larger, bolder letters:

SISTER

Moon explained. "This is Charlotte."

Miss Moon smiled as winningly as she was able. "I'm delighted to meet you."

The Somnambulist frowned. He felt strangely as though he were in the midst of some elaborate practical joke and began to hope that his friend and the stranger would burst out laughing, slap him on the back and thank him for playing along. He sat patiently and waited for the punch line.

"Is he really a mute?" Charlotte asked, rather rudely.

"He's never spoken to me. Nonetheless, it's one of my fondest hopes that one day he shall. And I've little doubt that when he does he will astonish us all."

She gave the Somnambulist a cursory glance and seemed unimpressed. "Not as handsome as his predecessor."

"Believe me," said Moon, sounding pained, "if you saw him now you would no longer call him that."

"I suppose not."

"The Somnambulist is a brilliant illusionist," said Moon, doing his best not to sound patronising. "Did you ever see the show?"

"Three times," Charlotte said lightly. "Once as an old woman, once as a drunken Pole and once as a dwarf. That last was rather a challenge, I admit. It's no joke taking three feet off your height for hours at a time." She paused and chewed her lower lip awkwardly. "I'm sorry about what happened to the theatre."

"Skimpole," Moon said, as if that explained it all.

"He really doesn't like you, does he?"

Moon looked away. "You never told me you were affiliated with the Committee."

"You never told me what happened in Clapham. I had to read about it in the papers."

"Must have slipped my mind."

The silence was broken by the familiar tap of chalk on board. The Somnambulist had begun to feel left out.

DRINK

"Capital suggestion," Moon exclaimed, in an abrupt and unexpected burst of jollity. "Charlotte?"

"Just a small one," she said doubtfully. "Nothing too strong."

But Moon was already out of earshot and racing hungrily over to the bar. As he gave his extensive, expensive order, he offered the bartender his sharkiest smile. "Make sure," he grinned, "that you bill all this to Mr. Skimpole."

Limehouse, unique amongst the districts of the city, does not belong to England. The curious smells which fill its streets are resolutely foreign in nature, its placards, signs and boardings are thick with hieroglyphics baffling to the uninitiated, and its people, whilst welcoming and well-mannered enough, are nonetheless alien and sallow-skinned to a man. If you've ever walked along its frantic, lurid streets, you will doubtless think of the place much as I do—as a piece of some exotic metropolis sliced from the Far East and set down wholesale amongst the boroughs of London, a vision of an impossible England where the Empire has fallen and the Orient is king.

Strange, then, to see Mr. Skimpole walk with such confidence and ease through those selfsame streets—his appearance quite as outré as ever, pince-nez perched upon his nose, his hair and skin bleached graveyard white. One might reasonably assume that he could not be more out of place amongst those multitudinous yellow faces, but they seemed happy to accept him as one of their own and he attracted no open curiosity, no inquisitive stares, no muffled laughter.

Less than half an hour after leaving the hotel, the albino reached his destination, coming to a halt outside a dilapidated butcher's shop. It was the kind of place which looked as though it had existed for years without customers, its windows cobwebbed and soot-streaked from neglect, filthy with the greasy rime of oil and what appeared to be dried blood. A bird was roasting on a spit in the window, its featherless cadaver turning slowly in the light, browning and crisping for passers-by to gawp at. Skimpole could not be entirely certain what species of fowl it had been in life—a duck, perhaps, or a chicken, or some other, nameless bird unique to the peoples of the East—but as he watched the thing revolve plumply behind the glass he thought unwillingly of Mrs. Puggsley and felt a momentary flicker of guilt. Struggling with his conscience, kicking against the tug of the past, he thrust the image from his mind and stepped inside. As he pushed open the door a bell rang and a young Chinaman materialised, greeting him with a bow and the words "A pleasure to see you again, sir."

"Good day," Skimpole said imperiously. He had never bothered to learn the name of his host or that of the young man's father, who had owned and run this place before him. The albino saw no reason to defy tradition at this late stage. Sins of the father and all that.

He strode through the shop. Slabs of meat, salted and of indeterminate origin, hung on hooks behind the counter; something old and sour bubbled and broiled in a pot and the smell of blood was all-pervasive. Skimpole ignored it, too familiar with the place to allow himself to be unsettled by its magic-lantern menace, its storybook smoke and mirrors. "Is he here?" he asked.

"He's waiting," the Chinaman said, unfailingly placid and respectful.

Skimpole noticed a fluffy down on the man's upper lip. "Trying a moustache?" he asked sarcastically.

The Chinaman blushed.

"Good luck." Skimpole smirked. "Incidentally, is that a chicken in the window?"

The proprietor looked confused.

"Chicken," Skimpole repeated, becoming irritated at the man's apparent lack of comprehension. "Chick-en." Still entertaining the long-standing misapprehension that his host had only the most tenuous grasp of English, the albino did his best to mime the actions of a chicken, flapping his arms like a bird and squawking.

The man did not seem to react, so Skimpole took his leave of him and walked through a door at the back of the shop. Incongruously, there was an elevator behind it. A Chinaman squeezed into a tight red uniform stood inside. He hauled back the metal grille when he saw Skimpole approach. "Morning, sah."

"Good morning."

"Noughth Level?"

"Thank you, yes."

The man operated the controls and, with a nauseating heave, the lift lurched downwards, eventually reaching its destination with a creak and a shudder.

"Noughth Level," the man said in a toneless, mechanical voice.

"Thank you," Skimpole snapped. "I can see that." He stepped out into a well-furnished room, smart, modern, dominated by a vast and ostentatious circular table. This, then, was the Directorate.

A bulky, broad-shouldered man strode forward to meet him, four or five Orientals standing deferentially behind him.

"Skimpole!" There was a warmth to his voice which suggested he was pleased to see him, but the albino knew it to be feigned for courtesy's sake—suspected also that it masked a lifetime of disdain, even loathing.

Without thinking, he deployed a sleek, professional smile. "Dedlock."

They shook hands. Skimpole's palm was damp and sticky from his exertions and Dedlock was far from successful in masking his discomfort.

"Forgive me," Skimpole said, taking off his coat and passing it without a glance to a hovering lackey. "I had business at the hotel."

"Ah." Dedlock's eyes glittered with undisguised inquisitiveness. "Mr. Moon?"

"That's right," Skimpole replied stiffly.

"Sit down, old man, and tell me all about it." His curiosity had dissipated and Dedlock sounded bluff and jolly again, like a retired colonel proposing nothing more vexatious than a postprandial round of gin rummy.

They sat opposite one another at the round table, Dedlock busying himself rustling a sheaf of official-looking papers, Skimpole reaching for cigar and lighter only to return them reluctantly to his pocket when he remembered that he had already enjoyed his little piece of luxury for the day.

Dedlock had the meaty look of an ageing rugby player about him, the kind of man (and the albino knew this for a fact) who had excelled at games at school—one of those heroes of the playing field who possessed in spades that peculiarly English composite of brutishness and impeccable manners. An unsightly scar intersected the space between his nose and left ear, a relic from some long-ago conflict. It was so vividly coloured and Dedlock took such perverse pleasure in displaying it that Skimpole had long suspected him of exaggerating its ferocity with greasepaint and makeup—a touch of vanity far from uncharacteristic of the man.

"Drink?" the scarred man asked.

Skimpole hauled out his pocket watch. "It's a little early," he said, in a voice which clearly indicated his willingness to be persuaded.

"This may take some time. Why not indulge yourself for once?"

The albino acquiesced. "Very well."

Dedlock snapped his fingers and one of the Chinamen stepped forward. Dressed as a butcher, his face was a strikingly lurid shade of yellow, his hair styled into glossy black pigtails and he had tied about his waist a filthy apron spattered with gristle and blood. The man bent close to Dedlock and whispered obsequiously: "Yes, sah? How may I help?" Unlike the proprietor, he had a strong, all but unintelligible accent, speaking his halting, uncertain English as though he were saying each word for the first time.

"A whisky for me," Dedlock said. "You know the way I like it."

"Whis-kee?" the Chinaman repeated doubtfully.

Dedlock leant across the table towards Skimpole. "You?"

Thinking it unwise to commit himself to any more complicated order, the albino asked for the same.

The Oriental screwed up his face perplexedly. "Same?"

"That's right."

"Velly good, sah." The Chinaman scurried away, but Dedlock stopped him before he reached the door. "Now, now, what do we ask?" he chided, as though he were addressing a small child still being trained in the niceties of the adult world.

The man looked horribly confused before understanding flooded across his face. He giggled. "Yes, yes. Mistah Simpole want ice? Ice?"

The albino was transparently amused. "No ice, thank you."

"Incidentally," Dedlock said, before the man could disappear, "I think we can dispense with the accent, don't you? Mr. Skimpole's not likely to be impressed."

Embarrassed, the Chinaman stood up straight, cleared his throat and spoke at once in an English accent so plummy and rich that it could only have emerged from one of our most prestigious public schools. "Terribly sorry, sir," he said briskly. "Had no idea. Thought I was doing rather well, as it happens."

Skimpole sniffed disparagingly. "I'm sure you could afford to be a little less theatrical, Mr. . . . ?"

"Benjamin Mackenzie-Cooper, sir."

"Well, then, Mackenzie-Cooper, at present, your delivery's pure music hall. It's corn, frankly, and silly with it. And your make-up . . . florid and overstated." The man looked disappointed and Skimpole softened. "Still. It's a promising start."

Mackenzie-Cooper thanked him and left the room.

"New man?" Skimpole asked.

Dedlock nodded. "Eton and Oxford. Just come down from Oriel. Promising, don't you think?"

"Oh, I think so," Skimpole said (though of course he didn't).

Dedlock adopted a curt, businesslike tone. "What news of Moon?"

"He's proving a little recalcitrant. You know he and I have . . . history?"

"You have history with us all."

Skimpole bristled.

"I gather the Bagshaw woman's left the country. Dear, dear, poor Lister will be disappointed."

"She knew something," Skimpole protested. "One of our best leads and we've lost her."

"Another mess, then?" Dedlock tutted. "I've warned you before about your obsession with Moon."

"Edward Moon was not the man who exposed her. We believe it was a member of the Vigilance Committee. You know yourself they've shown no compunction about framing psychics in the past."

"This Committee member—do we have a name?"

"As I understand it, the woman was in disguise. I've no direct evidence but I believe her to be an associate of Moon's—possibly more."

"A friend?"

"Perhaps."

Mackenzie-Cooper returned with their drinks, set them discreetly down upon the table and vanished. Skimpole took a demure sip of his whisky; Dedlock swallowed half of his in the first gulp. It was the albino who spoke first.

"Moon seems to have struck up a friendship with a man called Thomas Cribb."

"Can't place him. Is he affiliated?"

"He appears to be an independent. I suspect their association's rather set the cat amongst the pigeons with the Somnambulist."

Dedlock grinned. "Oh yes? Has he spoken yet?"

The albino shook his head and Dedlock brayed a laugh—a callous sound, devoid of any genuine mirth.

"And you?" Skimpole broached the subject carefully. "Any movement?"

"The Okhrana have been busy," Dedlock said flatly, as though he were describing nothing more thrilling than team tactics to his favourite centre forward. "They've been getting reckless of late. Something's got their agents excited. We suspect they've got wind of the conspiracy. Perhaps they have access to an Innocenti of their own."

Skimpole drummed his fingers thoughtfully on the table. "Agents?" he said. "By which I take you to mean *anarchists*?"

"Oh, I do hope not. I've had enough of men making a nuisance of themselves up on the Embankment to last me a lifetime. I had to scrape the last one off the pavement myself. Little bits of him got stuck between the cobbles. Besides, it isn't who they send we need to worry about."

"No?"

"We know who they are. We can track their movements as soon as they enter the city. Our biggest problems are the sleepers."

"Sleepers?"

"The Russians have seeded agents in this country, dormant for years. I do wish you'd read the files."

Skimpole ignored the rebuke. "Do the Okhrana know of our involvement?"

Dedlock looked away. "It seems likely."

"How did that happen?"

Dedlock muttered something about a mistake.

"Then we may be in trouble."

"I know," he replied, and there was a moment's bleak silence. A heartbeat later, Dedlock continued cheerfully, as though nothing had been said at all, "Incidentally, the Bagshaw woman—did Moon get anything out of her before the end?"

"Just a few words, though I'm quite sure he doesn't understand their worth. She talked about the plot, told Moon he was being used—as if he didn't know that already."

Dedlock began to clear away his papers. "Anything more?"

Skimpole took another sip of his whisky, a larger one this time, and felt a giddy, honeyed surge of pleasure at the taste of it. "She said we have ten days. We have four of them left."

Dedlock grimaced.

"Something else . . ."

"What?"

"Danger," he said. "Danger underground."

Trying his best to ignore the frenzied recitation echoing down the corridor, Meyrick Owsley tapped on the door of a killer's cell, as politely and discreetly as a delivery boy calling at some fine country house, bearing a telegram, perhaps, a wedding gift or an expensive bouquet. Barabbas's voice drifted from inside, ravaged and diseased, riddled with immorality. "Meyrick?"

Owsley's face was blank and expressionless, a tragedian's mask. "I'm here, sir."

"Am I forgiven?"

"Quite forgiven, sir."

A pause, a snuffling noise, then: "Thank Christ." Owsley heard what might have been a sob. "It was just a spat, wasn't it? Just a nonsense?"

"That's right, sir. A spat, sir. It meant nothing."

A grateful sigh. "Good."

"Sir?"

No reply (although his neighbour had begun again his favourite psalm).

"You have visitors."

A sudden stirring, a pacing, shuffling sound, then Barabbas appeared at the tiny aperture of the cell, his bloated, toad-like face segmented by its bars. "Edward?" His breath was fetid and rank.

"He's here with me," Owsley said calmly. "He wants to speak to you. Stand back, sir. I'm letting him through."

On hearing the iron rattle of keys, the mocking creak of the door, Barabbas fell to the floor and cowered in a corner of his tiny world. Somebody stepped inside, the door clanged shut and when the prisoner looked up he saw that not one but two figures stood before him in the gloom.

"Edward?" he murmured again.

"I'm here." The voice was strong, compassionate, but with a hint of unworthy pleasure at seeing him reduced to such a condition.

"Edward? Who is this?"

Moon stepped forward. "You remember my sister?"

"Charlotte?" he breathed. "My, but you've changed. When we last met you were still a girl. Barely out of school. But you're a woman now."

Charlotte stared at him, fascinated, repulsed.

"Please forgive the mess," the prisoner said, slouching back against the wall. "Try to ignore the smell. I had no idea you were coming."

"What have you done to yourself?" Charlotte asked, curiosity winning out over disgust.

"You've grown, haven't you?" said Barabbas, ignoring the question. "Swollen in all the right places. Ripened and budded." His tongue darted lasciviously in and out of his mouth and he winked. "You feel safe with me, don't you?"

With admirable self-restraint, Charlotte replied, "I feel sorry for you."

"Barabbas," Moon began, then stopped himself, exasperated. "Do I have to call you that? Charlotte—she . . . We knew you by another name."

"Like poor Edgar's, my name is lost."

Moon sighed, reached into his pocket and pulled out a small padded box. "I brought you something."

"A bribe," Barabbas muttered sulkily.

"A gift," Moon said firmly. "Here." He held out the box. "Take it."

The killer shuffled his behemoth frame across the floor, grabbed at the box and tore it open. "A tiepin?" he said once he'd examined its contents. "For me?"

"It was very dear. Gold-plated. Thought you'd like it."

"You were right." Barabbas stared avariciously at the thing. "Oh yes, you were quite right. You'll have to excuse me whilst I put it with my collection." He slithered back across the room and added the gift to his stash of precious things. "Thank you," he said, then added: "I shall wear it the day I die."

"They may not let you. They have strict rules here about that sort of thing."

"I'm sure Meyrick can make the necessary arrangements. He's awfully good at organising these things."

"I've been meaning to ask—how did you and Owsley meet?"

"He came to me, sought me out, to offer his services—said he'd been transformed by what I'd done. He's—dare I say it?—an admirer of mine." Barabbas glanced suspiciously at his guests. "Surely you're not jealous?"

"I wouldn't trust a man like that."

"You trusted me," Barabbas snapped. "Now what do you want?"

"We need to talk."

A sneer stretched itself across his suety face. "I knew you'd come back."

"You spoke of a plot against the city, of a guiding hand behind the murders. You knew about the fire at the theatre."

"You want to ask me how I came to know such things?"

"If it's no trouble," Moon said lightly.

"Magic," Barabbas replied, and laughed.

Moon tried not to rise to the bait. "When was the last time you saw the albino?"

Loathing clouded the prisoner's face. "Not for an age. You still blame him?"

"I blame him for your corruption, yes."

Barabbas sounded thoughtful, like a dictionary editor searching for the perfect, the Platonic, definition of a word. "I don't think 'corruption' is right. He bored me by the end. But I had been introduced to a new world—one above morality, where all experience and sensation were mine for the taking. I drank deep, explored the outer reaches of transgression. The only truly sinful act left to me was murder. What I did in that room in Cleveland Street, Edward, it was the high-water mark of my existence—nothing before or since has measured up. It was the death of my old self, the birth of Barabbas."

"That's history," Moon insisted. "I came to talk about the future."

"You may have a future. I do not. Nonetheless I have some small compensation."

"What?"

Barabbas whispered: "In the end I was glad it was you who caught me."

Moon sighed. "You were a worthy opponent. The last worthy opponent. Ever since, I've been beset by minnows. Unpersuasive confidence men, murderers who can't shoot straight, would-be bank robbers who burrow into sewers."

Barabbas grinned. "I heard about him."

"I wish I could remember his name," Moon said, allowing himself to become distracted. "I don't suppose you . . . ?"

Barabbas gave a desultory inclination of his head. "You saw Mrs. Bagshaw?"

"You knew?"

"Of course."

"She's a fraud," Charlotte said sternly.

"Ah, but then you would say that, as a loyal devotee of the Vigilance Committee. I'd expect nothing less. I must say, Edward, that you ignore the Madame's warnings at your peril."

"What aren't you telling me?"

"It's close now," the killer said quietly. "Four days. The disappearances start soon."

"You know, don't you?" Moon sounded as though he hadn't quite believed it before. "You really know what's going on?"

Barabbas laughed. "Lean closer," he said, and Moon scrambled across to where he lay. The fat man spoke quickly. "Naturally, I was approached. They needed someone like me. P'raps I should be flattered. They've great plans for us all, Edward. They're engineers. They want to change the world."

He was interrupted by the ostentatious rattle of a key in the lock. The door swung open and Owsley appeared at the mouth of the cell. "Time's up. Visiting hours are over."

"Visiting hours?" Barabbas protested.

Owsley ignored his master and favoured Moon with a glacial stare. "You have to go."

"I'm not finished."

"Leave at once or I shall alert the prison authorities."

Quickly, Barabbas rummaged around in his stash of beauty for a few moments and pulled out a slim book. "You brought me a present," he said, at which Owsley shot Moon a look of barely controlled fury. "I'd like you to take this in return."

Moon was surprised. "What is it?"

"The *Lyrical Ballads* by Samuel Taylor Coleridge and William Wordsworth." He sounded like a provincial schoolmaster introducing the poetry of the last century to a class wary and suspicious of verse. "It's been my most constant companion here. A beacon in this abyss. It opened my eyes, Edward. As I hope it will open yours."

"Thank you."

"Edward?" Barabbas tapped the book's cover. "Ask him. Ask the poet."

"Poet?" Moon snapped. "What poet?"

Barabbas giggled, then pointed towards one of the names on the front of his book, chuckling to himself as if this were the punch line to a joke of which only he knew the beginning.

"Coleridge?" Moon snapped. "Why should I be interested in Coleridge? The man's been dead for sixty years."

This time Barabbas's smile was positively demonic. "Oh, Edward," he cooed. "You have so much to look forward to."

With that, he lurched towards Charlotte and planted a slobbering kiss on her cheek. She writhed away in disgust and the prisoner transferred his attentions to the conjuror, who did not pull away but allowed the captive to kiss him on that secret, intimate space behind the ear just between flesh and hair. The killer whispered something, and for a moment both men seemed unutterably distraught, their sorrow lacerating, acute, grief beyond words. Charlotte even found herself wondering whether they might not be about to fall into one another's arms.

It was Owsley, of course, who broke the spell. "You have to go," he insisted. Later, Edward was to remark that the man had sounded almost scared.

Barabbas wailed in anguish at their departure but the Moons filed out in sober silence.

Once the door was safely locked behind them and the monster returned to the blackness of his cell, Owsley, sounding smug and not a little officious, said: "Thank you for your cooperation. I trust you shan't be troubling us again."

Edward Moon began to complain but Owsley strode away, the plait of hair dangling limply at the rear of his egg-bald scalp flapping absurdly as he walked.

Charlotte and her brother were relieved to leave Newgate behind them and start back towards the hotel. They walked for some time before either of them spoke.

"He wasn't how you expected?" the brother asked.

"I knew he'd changed. I know what he did. I thought I'd see something evil. But I felt sorry for him. And you? Have you forgiven him?"

"There's nothing to forgive," Moon replied tonelessly.

"You were friends."

"It's not him I blame."

"He has to bear some responsibility."

No reply.

"I'm sorry," Charlotte said. "Crass of me."

Still nothing.

"Have you . . . have you tried appealing to his better nature? Called him by his old name?"

"You heard what he said."

"Seems Skimpole's washed his hands of him."

"Of course. He can't be seen to be responsible for aberrations like that."

"Do you think he knows something?"

"I'm sure of it."

"What was the significance of the book? Seemed a pretty rum sort of gift."

"I think he's given us a clue. Where it will lead, I'm not sure."

"May I see?"

Moon passed her the book and Charlotte flicked it open. "There's an inscription," she said. "'*To my dear Gillman, with profound gratitude and love.*' It's signed '*STC.*'"

"Good grief," murmured Moon. "Must be his own copy. Worth a small fortune."

"What does that mean? Why's he given it to you?"

"If only Owsley hadn't interrupted. I'm sure he was about to tell us something significant. He said he was approached. Mentioned disappearances. 'Ask the poet,' he said . . . Why doesn't any of this make sense?"

"Edward," Charlotte said ruefully, "if *you* can't make sense of it, I'm not sure anyone can."

"I'm glad you've come back," Moon said, then added tentatively: "Will you stay?"

"You know I can't."

Before he could reply they reached the hotel where an old friend stood waiting.

"Mr. Moon!"

The conjuror managed a polite smile. He gestured towards the uninvited guest. "Charlotte. This is Speight. A friend from the theatre. A former tenant, you might say."

"Pleased to meet you."

The tramp blinked and tried a bleary bow. "Pleasure's all

mine." He took Charlotte's hand, kissed it, and the lady, unlike in her encounter with the Fiend of Newgate, had the good grace not to flinch.

She noticed a heavy wooden placard propped up raggedly beside him.

SURELY I AM COMING SOON
REVELATION 22:20

"What brings you here?" Moon asked, as politely as he was able, discreetly reaching for his wallet.

"I came to thank you," Speight interrupted. "There's not many men as would have tolerated me the way you did."

Moon looked surprised. "It was my pleasure."

"I'm going away now."

"I don't understand."

"I'm needed. The suits have come for me."

"You mean you've found a home? Someone who'll take care of you?"

Speight thought for a moment. "Yes," he said, sounding surprised at his own answer. "S'pose I have."

"Well, it's been good seeing you again . . ." Moon began and made for the entrance to the hotel.

"I've come to give you this." Speight reached for the board and thrust it towards him. "Here. It's yours."

"What?" Moon asked, but it was too late. Speight had pushed the placard into his hands and walked away.

"Thank you," he shouted again. "Thank you!"

Moon shook his head in bemusement. "What the devil will I do with this?"

"I like your friends," Charlotte said playfully as they walked inside. "They're . . . unusual."

They went directly to Moon's suite where Mrs. Grossmith was waiting for them, her gangly beau by her side.

"There's a visitor here to see you," she said. "He's been waiting for almost an hour."

"I've just seen him," Moon said briskly. "Mr. Speight, yes?"

Mrs. Grossmith sniffed. "I wouldn't let that one in if he tried. No, this is quite another class of gentleman. The inspector."

Moon turned to his sister. "What were you saying about my friends?" he asked, and, as if on cue, Merryweather barrelled into the room, accompanied by peals of laughter, the kind one usually hears only upon feeding pennies into seaside mannequins. The Somnambulist strolled beside him; both men had half-empty glasses of milk in their hands.

"Well, well," the inspector said, once the handshakes and introductions were over, "this is an improvement on your old lodgings and no mistake."

"I loathe it," Moon said evenly.

"What's that sign you're carrying? Looks familiar."

"I doubt it's important." Moon propped the placard up beside the door. "So, is this purely a social call?"

"No such luck," the inspector said ruefully. "You remember the Honeyman case?"

"Of course."

"Seems I owe you an apology. You were right, Mr. Moon, and I was wrong. It's not quite as finished as I'd thought."

Moon was suddenly alert. "What's happened?"

"The boy's mother . . ."

"Tell me."

Merryweather cleared his throat. "It's Mrs. Honeyman," he said. "She's disappeared."

13

Mrs. Grossmith bent over the kitchen sink and busied herself with the final dishes of the day, brown soapsuds swilling greasily about her wrists. With uncharacteristic stealth, Arthur Barge crept in behind her and nestled himself snugly against her amply proportioned frame. Silently he stroked her sagging cheeks, smoothed away a stray strand of iron-grey hair and entwined his wrinkled hands with hers. She said nothing but he could feel her beneath him, trembling and pulsating with secret pleasure. Awkward, graceless, out of practice from years of bachelorhood, he tried to manoeuvre his mouth around to meet hers. Grossmith made a perfunctory effort to shoo him away, muttering something about the washing-up, but soon allowed herself to be silenced by his ardour, his lips, his plunging, delving tongue.

Hesitant at first, wary, but growing in confidence and vigour, they came blissfully together. Locked in an embrace, they kissed long and hard, resembling two antediluvian lizards mating for the final time on the blasted plains of primeval Africa.

This at least was the colourful image which sprang unbidden to the mind of Charlotte Moon as she stood and watched them from the doorway. She cleared her throat as noisily as she could and, like characters in a farce, the couple sprang apart. Bashful and flustered, Mrs. Grossmith's cheeks flamed a hectic shade of red, but Barge just stood there dumbly, a smirk flickering across his face, like a schoolboy whose embarrassment is mostly feigned, a child perversely proud to be discovered in the midst of impropriety.

"Mrs. Grossmith," Charlotte said icily. "So sorry to interrupt."

"Forgive me, miss." The housekeeper smoothed down her skirt and fumbled an awkward curtsey. "I thought you'd gone out, with your brother and the policeman."

Charlotte ignored the question. "Why are you washing dishes? Surely that's up to the hotel staff?"

"Mr. Moon is my responsibility. I like to look after him the best I can."

Charlotte passed her a folded slip of paper. "Will you make sure my brother gets this?"

"You're leaving us?" The housekeeper didn't sound especially disappointed at the prospect. "Can't you stay an hour or so? Mr. Moon will be back soon and I'm sure he'd like to say goodbye himself."

"It's best I go now."

"If you're sure."

"Quite."

"Can I ask you something?" Mrs. Grossmith paused uncertainly. "In all the years I have been in his employ, he has never once mentioned you. I don't mean to pry but—"

"You want to know why?"

"Suppose I do."

"My brother and I have an unusual relationship. If we spend too long together, *things* have a habit of happening around us. The kind of things one would prefer not to happen, if you understand me."

"No, dear. Frankly, I don't."

"Believe me, it's for the best we stay apart." Charlotte turned towards the door. "Goodbye, Mrs. Grossmith. Mr. Barge."

Arthur gave a gawky wave of farewell and Charlotte stalked from the room.

"Strange little girl, isn't she?"

"Can't say as I noticed," Barge said. "I was looking at the other lady in the room. The one that has my heart." He reached out to touch her but Grossmith brushed him firmly aside.

"Later," she said, stowing Charlotte's message discreetly in the sleeve of her pinafore. "There's plenty more pots need scrubbing before bedtime."

*M*r. Honeyman was almost exactly as Moon remembered him—a stubborn, grey-skinned man, permanently harassed. He seemed rather bolder on this occasion, due perhaps to the absence of the gorgon who passed as his wife.

Moon and Merryweather had barely been ushered in before the man started to complain: "I believe I insisted on seeing an official investigator," he barked, glaring at Moon.

Merryweather did his best to placate him. "I can vouch for his trustworthiness, sir. He's helped me out on more occasions than I care to remember and I don't mind admitting there's a goodly number of villains behind bars today who'd still be out and fancy free if it weren't for his assistance."

"Is that so?" Honeyman snapped sarcastically. "I haven't allowed you into my home, Inspector, so you can stand here and eulogise this amateur. Besides, my understanding is that since that deplorable incident in Clapham, Mr. Moon is no longer considered quite as infallible as he once was."

"My apologies," the inspector said gently and changed the subject. "I've no wish to hurry you, sir, but could you tell us a little more about the circumstances of your wife's disappearance? Try to remember as much as you can. Anything might prove important. What may seem an insignificant detail to you, sir, could be a vital clue to the trained eye of a policeman."

"I woke early in the morning," the man said stiffly, "at around six, as is my habit. Often walk the grounds, you understand. Admire my fish. And she'd gone. It was as simple as that. Taken a suitcase with her and just upped stumps. None of the servants saw her go."

"You think she chose to leave?"

"I've no idea."

"The suitcase would seem to rule out abduction. Don't you think so, Mr. Moon?"

The conjuror yawned, bored by the predictable plod of police procedure.

"Mr. Honeyman," Merryweather persisted, "do you have any idea where your wife might have gone?"

"None. Her whole life was here. I'm worried she might have done something . . . unnecessary."

"You'll forgive me," Moon said acerbically, "but when I last met your wife she hardly struck me as the kind of woman predisposed to self-harm. Neither did she appear noticeably bereaved. She behaved more as if she was profoundly relieved at being rid of some irritating encumbrance."

Honeyman turned to the inspector. "This is intolerable. Am I expected to stand in my own home and allow myself to be insulted by this rank amateur?"

"Believe me," Moon pressed on, "your wife was not in mourning."

"Can you tell us, sir," Merryweather said, his voice almost comical in its excessive deference, "had your wife been behaving strangely at all before she vanished? Had she done anything unusual or out of character?"

"She'd been particularly involved in her church work of late. She's a great philanthropist, you see. Most devout."

"Church?" Merryweather said. "Can you tell us the name of that church, sir?"

"More of a charity, I think, properly speaking. Somewhere in the city. Of course, I'm perfectly happy with our little parish church but then she was always far more serious about all that than me. She was quite besotted with this new lot. Lord knows why."

"The name of the church, sir?"

Honeyman harrumphed. "I'm afraid I couldn't tell you without looking it up."

Merryweather favoured the man with his best professional smile. "We're happy to wait, sir."

Muttering under his breath, Honeyman trudged from the room.

"Inspector?" Moon said suspiciously. "Do you know something I don't?"

Merryweather was unable to hide his excitement. "It's a rare day I'm ahead of you, Mr. Moon, but I fancy this time I might just have managed it."

"Tell me," Moon said sharply. "Now."

"Patience."

Before Moon could frame a sardonic reply, Honeyman returned, brandishing a sheaf of papers. "Just as I said. They're a philanthropic organisation. Missionaries, I think. Something of that sort."

"Their name?" Merryweather asked again as he reached for his notebook.

"I have it here." Honeyman flicked vaguely through his papers until he came across the information. "The Church of the Summer Kingdom." He wrinkled his nose. "Ridiculous name. You think it could be significant?"

Merryweather scribbled furiously. "Yes, sir. I think it just might be."

They left with a promise to keep him fully informed of their investigation and strolled outside to the grounds where the Somnambulist was loitering about by the fish pond, listening to a groundsman chatter incontinently on about tree surgery. He gave them a quizzical look.

"The inspector's keeping something from me," Moon explained sulkily.

"Wait till we're in the coach. Then I'll tell you everything."

They were halfway back into the city before he finally told them the truth. "You remember Dunbar?" he began as the coach lurched with fearless rapidity in and out of the jostling ranks of traffic. "The Fly's other victim?"

"Of course."

"Seems his mother disappeared around about the same time as Mrs. Honeyman."

Moon sounded almost disappointed. "I see."

"Wait for it, Mr. Moon. Wait for it. This is the really interesting part."

"Let me guess," the detective interrupted swiftly. "She was also a member of this gang of philanthropists—the Church of the Summer Kingdom?"

Merryweather clapped his hands together in delight. "Precisely so."

"Well, then. It seems at long last that we have a new lead in the murder of Cyril Honeyman."

*T*he Directorate.

Skimpole had never liked the name. He thought it was ostentatious, pompous and unnecessarily melodramatic. It originated from the founding of the agency in more theatrical times, days of blood and thunder. Since the death of the Queen, Skimpole had harboured hopes that the excesses of the past would not continue into the new century. He felt that a secret organisation (if it were to have a name at all) ought to take pains to make itself sound as commonplace and as unworthy of notice as possible—certainly not revel in a title like "the Directorate," which sounded as though it had been torn from the pages of popular fiction and seemed to him to reek of showmanship and cheap sensation. Dedlock, however, had always heartily approved of the name and, as it happened, considered himself a man who positively thrived upon showmanship and cheap sensation.

It was late in the working day and they sat in their usual places at the round table, Dedlock doggedly working his way through a bottle of wine, Skimpole struggling with a set of dense and tiresomely exhaustive surveillance reports.

"This is quite like old times," Dedlock said, all of a sudden gregarious.

"How so?"

"You hard at your studies, me bunking off for a drink."

"I don't want to talk about it."

"Like being back at school, isn't it?"

"I said I don't want to talk about it."

"Sorry I spoke."

The albino went back to his work, only to be interrupted again.

"Don't sulk, Skimpole, for God's sake. You never talk about

the old days." After the consumption of the best part of three-quarters of a bottle, he seemed in a ruminative mood.

Skimpole slapped down his reports on the table. "What news of Madame Innocenti?" he asked, pointedly ignoring Dedlock's overtures of nostalgia.

"She was last seen in New York. After that—poof!—disappeared."

"Damn."

"You're convinced she was the real thing?"

"It doesn't matter what I think. But if there's the slightest chance she was genuine—and frankly, I can't believe that all the information she gave us was entirely a string of lucky guesses—then the very last place we want her is New York. Power like that in the hands of the Americans is unthinkable."

Mackenzie-Cooper emerged from the shadows, dressed in his usual unconvincing guise of a Chinese butcher. "Drink, sah?" he asked, speaking in that risible accent. Irritated, the albino waved him away.

"You should join me," Dedlock said. "It's surprisingly good."

"Far too early for me." Skimpole turned to Mackenzie-Cooper. "I'll have a cup of tea."

The man bowed and disappeared to the back of the room. Although neither of his superiors noticed it at the time, he seemed oddly nervous. Dedlock was later to claim that he saw the man's hands tremble and shake as though palsied, but this particular detail was one he was only able to recall a number of months after the incident and—suspiciously—during a dinner party at that.

"What's Mr. Moon up to?" Dedlock asked.

"Following a lead on the Honeyman case. He's still convinced it's connected."

"Do you agree?"

"I've learnt by now to trust his instincts."

Dedlock scratched idly at his scar. "He's your agent," he said.

"I shan't try to interfere. But if Madame Innocenti was correct, then we've only got four days left."

"I hardly need to be reminded."

"I'm thinking of moving my family out of the city. You know, before it happens. Have you made any arrangements?"

Before he could reply, Mackenzie-Cooper returned with a large pot of tea. He poured Skimpole a cup and, offering the same to Dedlock, stressed in rather more forceful tones than really behoves an underling the efficacy of the drink in combatting insobriety. Dedlock grudgingly accepted and a cup of the rehabilitative brew was set beside his wine.

As Mackenzie-Cooper was pouring, Skimpole swigged from his own cup and frowned. Far too much sugar. Still, he drank again, a bigger sip this time, taking a guilty pleasure in the saccharine rush.

Dedlock leant across to the phoney Chinaman. "You all right, old boy? You don't seem quite yourself."

Startled, Mackenzie-Cooper snatched the pot away, clumsily spilling a good deal of its contents in the process.

"Velly sorry, sah," he muttered, frantically searching his pockets for something to mop up the mess. "Velly sorry."

"No need to get yourself het up about it. It was an accident."

At last Mackenzie-Cooper produced a dishcloth, but as he reached across to clean up the tea, he succeeded in toppling his superior's wineglass. Dedlock cursed as rivulets of tea and wine ran across the table and Niagaraed onto the floor.

"Sorry, sah. Sorry, sah." Beneath his greasepaint and disguise, Mackenzie-Cooper had begun to sweat.

Dedlock started to clear away the spillage, but barely had he begun before he observed a most curious effect. As the wine and tea combined and intermingled on the table before him, the liquids seemed first to bubble, then to steam and stew in some unnatural reaction.

Mackenzie-Cooper saw it, too. For an instant, they stared open-mouthed at each other, the one astonished that he had been found out by so petty an accident, the other trying desperately to understand the precise nature of what had occurred.

With a Greek-wedding clatter, Mackenzie-Cooper threw the teapot to the floor, its china splintering expensively, and ran at full pelt for the exit. Dedlock bounded to his feet (with surprising athleticism for a man of his age) and raced after him, an unexpected blur of motion. Mackenzie-Cooper yelped in fear. Just before he reached the door, the older man rugby-tackled him, hurling his quarry to the ground, pinning the interloper to the floor.

"Why?" he snarled. Mackenzie-Cooper said nothing, his eyes darting about him in fear. Dedlock slapped his face hard. "Why?" he asked again, and the man looked as though he might be about to cry. Another slap. "Why?"

At this, Mackenzie-Cooper began to contort his face, gurgling, dribbling like a teething infant. Dedlock looked on. "What now?"

By the time he realised what was happening it was too late. Mackenzie-Cooper screwed up his face again, swallowed something, then shuddered and convulsed, his face turning a mottled purple, white foam bubbling at his mouth. Seconds later, his body seemed to crumple in upon itself and he spasmed a few times before falling still. Dedlock screamed his frustration. Flinging the corpse aside, he staggered to his feet.

"Cyanide capsule," he explained (superfluously, in Skimpole's opinion). He reached across to the spilt tea, dabbed a finger in the pool and smelt it carefully. "There was enough poison in that pot to kill us both. How much did you drink?"

Skimpole lied. "Nothing."

"Are you sure?"

"Of course," the albino said, too quickly. "I drank nothing."

Dedlock nodded vaguely.

Skimpole gazed down at the twisted body on the floor. "Thought you told me he went to Oxford."

Dedlock bent over the body and tugged away the man's disguise to reveal not the callow Oriel alumnus they had expected, but a bald, middle-aged stranger, lugubrious-looking, ill and wasted. "Somehow I doubt he's an Eton man," he said.

You may be interested to learn that the real Mackenzie-Cooper—a genuine, amiable old Etonian with far too trusting a nature ever to have enjoyed much success as an agent of the Directorate—was found three days later locked in a bathroom in one of the most squalid of the city's lodging houses, half his head caved in and a look of abject terror on his face. No happy ending, then, for him.

Who is this?"

"You don't recognise him?" Skimpole asked, surprised.

"Enlighten me."

"Declan Slattery. Formerly a Fenian agent till he went independent a few years back. Bit of a legend in the field. Past his best now, of course. Gone to seed. This must be the first time anyone's hired him in ages."

"But who?" Dedlock asked. "Who would want us dead?"

Skimpole shrugged. "Could be a long list."

The Church of the Summer Kingdom was run out of a small third-floor office in Covent Garden which smelt strongly of dust and halitosis. On their arrival, Merryweather, Moon and the Somnambulist were met by a man whose bluff, ruddy-faced looks seemed to owe more to the taproom than the pulpit.

"Donald McDonald," he said, sticking out a meaty paw and adding with a twinkle: "Me mother had a sense of humour."

Moon shot him a disdainful look and he withdrew his hand unshaken.

"What's this about, gentlemen?"

"We'd like to talk to you about one of your flock," Merryweather said. "A Mrs. Honeyman."

"I'm so glad someone's finally doing something. We're awfully worried here. I've been absolutely frantic."

The inspector took a notepad from his pocket. "How often did you see her?"

"She was one of our most devout members. One of the cornerstones, you might say, a bedrock of our little church."

"Forgive me for asking"—Merryweather scribbled frantically—"but what is the exact nature of your association with the church?"

"Oh, I'm nothing special," McDonald said, his modesty unconvincing. "I do a little lay preaching . . . help out where I can . . . assist our pastor in his good works."

"And who is he?"

"It's him you should be talking to by rights. Our leader, sir. Our shepherd. The Reverend Doctor Tan."

Merryweather dutifully wrote down the name. "May we speak to this Tan?"

"He's out of the city at present. I'm a poor substitute, I know, but you'll have to make do. Incidentally, I must apologise for the condition of our office. Normally we're so much tidier than this."

Merryweather saw the thick layer of dust blanketing the place and tactfully decided not to comment. "Where is your church, sir? Surely you can't take services here."

"Oh." McDonald sounded vaguely irritated by the question. "We worship . . . nearby."

Growing tired of the seesaw of their conversation, Moon had

begun to examine the room for himself, nosing about the cupboards, shelves and bookcases, openly curious, brazen in his rummagings. A crucifix hung above the door; below it was a discreet plaque depicting a black, five-petalled flower. Printed beside it were the words "If a man could walk through Paradise in a dream, and have a flower presented to him as a pledge that his soul had really been there, and found that flower in his hand when he awoke—what then?"

Donald McDonald wandered across. "I see you've found our motto."

"Motto? I'm afraid I don't see the relevance."

"Paradise, Mr. Moon. Elysium. The condition to which we all aspire."

"This isn't scripture."

"S. T. Coleridge. The Reverend Doctor's a great admirer. Our church reveres him and his work."

"Coleridge?" Moon was incredulous. "Might I ask what kind of church venerates a secular poet?"

McDonald simpered. "No doubt you find that strange. Many do. Though I can assure you that anyone who spends time amongst us soon comes to appreciate our point of view."

"The flower beneath the crucifix," Merryweather asked, trying to wriggle back into the conversation. "What does that represent?"

"A motif we've appropriated from Greek mythology." Donald McDonald summoned up a faraway look. "The immortal flower which blooms in Paradise for poets—*amaranth*."

"What's the point of this?" Moon spat. "What is it you people do?"

"We're missionaries."

"Missionaries? In Covent Garden?"

"The Reverend Doctor sees no reason to travel out of England when there is so much spiritual poverty, so much pain and deprivation, on our doorstep. London is in greater need of the cleansing light of revelation even than the darkest recesses of the Congo. Our work is done here amongst the forgotten people, those abandoned by the city, left to rot in the slums and in the hopeless places."

"We've heard enough." Moon turned smartly on his heel and headed for the door. "Come along, Inspector."

"You will let us know if there are any developments?" McDonald asked, his voice dripping spurious concern, ersatz sympathy. "Mrs. Honeyman is in my prayers."

The inspector followed Moon from the room. "Didn't believe a word of it," he said once they had emerged onto the street. "Man knows more than he's telling. You?"

"I'm not sure," Moon admitted. "This latest development is—I confess—unexpected."

"What was all that business about the plaque?"

"Coleridge," Moon said mysteriously.

"Is there some significance?"

"Are you a poetry-lover, Inspector?"

"Not seen a word of the stuff since school."

"Then at least you've learnt one valuable lesson today."

"What's that?"

"Read more."

Later that evening, lulled by the rhythmic snoring of his wife, just as he was about to go to sleep, Inspector Merryweather would think of rather an amusing retort to this. But he would know that the moment had passed, and would roll over instead and hope for pleasant dreams.

Moon seemed excited. "Did you recognise the flower beneath the crucifix?"

"Seemed pretty unremarkable to me."

"We found the same sigil daubed outside the Human Fly's caravan."

Merryweather shrugged. "Coincidence?" He looked about him. "Besides, aren't you forgetting somebody?"

"Who?"

He grinned. "The Somnambulist."

*R*egretfully, Mr. Skimpole put aside his fourth cup of tea since he had left the Directorate for the day, reflecting as he did so that the sound of a teacup clinking into its predestined place on a saucer was one of life's small but perfect pleasures. There was something indefinably comforting about it, something soothing and warm and British. "Are you sure you don't know when he'll be back?"

On hearing the question, Mrs. Grossmith felt a deeply uncharacteristic urge to unleash a scream of rage and frustration—in part at the albino's bloody-minded persistence but also at a bottled-up lifetime of tireless obedience to the whims of infuriating men. She restrained herself. "No," she said, trying not to let her irritation show. "I've no idea where he is or when he'll be home. Mr. Moon's quite capable of disappearing without warning for days or weeks at a time. Once, when he was investigating that Crookback business, he was gone for the best part of a year."

After the unpleasantness of the morning, Skimpole had wanted to speak to Moon, only to find him vanished. It was at times like this that he regretted honouring his promise to retire the conjuror's shadow.

"More tea?" Mrs. Grossmith asked, secretly willing the man to refuse.

Skimpole waved the offer away and relief showed immediately in Grossmith's face.

"I've outstayed my welcome, haven't I?"

"Not at all." The housekeeper's smile was strained but still in place. Strange to think that there was a time when she had found this man a figure of menace.

The albino heaved a maddening sigh and sank further back in his chair. "Changed my mind," he said. "On second thoughts I'd love another cup. Is there any chance . . . ?"

"Of course," Mrs. Grossmith said wearily.

As the housekeeper ministered to the teapot, Skimpole murmured: "I almost died today."

"Sorry?" she asked, palpably uninterested. "What was that?"

Before he could reply, Arthur Barge strolled into the room. "Still here?"

"Evidently."

"It's just that I was planning to take Mrs. G up to town. Give her a little treat. I reckon she deserves it. We're both men of the world, Mr. Skimpole. I'm sure you understand my meaning."

"Not entirely, no."

"Lord knows if Moon will be back tonight. If I were you, I'd go home."

Grudgingly, Skimpole got to his feet. "Then I'll go."

"I'll be sure to tell him you were here, sir," said Mrs. Grossmith.

"I'll be back first thing tomorrow. It's imperative I speak with him."

Barge ushered their guest to the door. "We'll see you then, sir. I'll look forward to it."

The albino had barely stepped from the room and the door closed behind him before the air was filled with squeals of delight, shrieks and wails of lascivious pleasure—the earthy sounds, strangely troubling to Skimpole's ears, of senescent romance. He rolled his eyes and headed home.

Home, as it happened, was Wimbledon—an hour distant and a world away from the silver-plated comfort of Moon's hotel.

Unlike Mr. Dedlock, Skimpole had never fancied himself a glamorous or powerful man. Dedlock liked to put on airs, to dress up his job as something exotic and exciting, but Skimpole was happy, proud even, to be seen for what he was—a Civil Servant, and a damn good one. His colleague swaggered through the world as though he was the most important thing in it, but Skimpole had always remained content with his life of quiet duty and routine. That this duty and routine often involved arson, blackmail, espionage and state-sponsored murder seemed not to occur to him.

The Service offered a respectable if hardly generous salary and Skimpole had been able to afford a modest terraced house situated a street or so from the Common. An hour after leaving Mrs. Grossmith in the saggy arms of her suitor, Skimpole let himself into his home and winced at the sounds of revelry emanating from next door. The walls were thin and Skimpole's neighbours fonder than he of raucous company and popular music.

Above that noise, there came other, more welcome sounds: a persistent tap-tap, a metallic jingle and with it a series of fitful stammers, gasps and wheezes. Skimpole hung up his hat, and for the first time that day, he actually smiled. Limping towards him was a sandy-haired boy, eight or nine years old, sickly and pallid, his progress severely impeded both by the metal callipers which encircled and armoured his legs like a homemade exoskeleton and by the two heavy wooden crutches on which he leant for support.

"Dada!" he called plaintively, his voice shivery and hoarse from his exertions. He stopped short, gave a pitifully feeble cough and, caught off balance for a moment, tottered uncertainly on his feet. The albino bent down to steady the child and kissed him tenderly on the forehead.

"Hello," he said gently. "Sorry I'm late." He removed his pince-nez from the tip of his nose and filed them away in his jacket pocket.

"Missed you," the boy murmured.

"I'm home now," his father said and rose cheerfully to his feet. "Hungry?"

The boy laughed. "Yes! Yes! Yes!"

Skimpole ruffled his hair affectionately and was about to head for the kitchen when, without warning, he was struck by a terrible wrench of pain in his innards, a blistering burst of agony flaring deep in his guts as the poison began to stir. He bit down hard on his tongue to stop himself from screaming, lost for a second in the most acute agony he had ever known. Mercifully, the sensation disappeared as quickly as it had arrived.

He was in no doubt, of course, as to what it signified.

Poleaxed by grief and fear, Mr. Skimpole surprised himself by weeping. Racked by noisy sobs, he stood in the hallway of his second-rate home, hot, shameful tears running down his face whilst his son gazed up at him in quiet bemusement all the while.

Meyrick Owsley was pleased with himself. He had waited a long time for this, counting down the days and hours, hoping and praying that the moment would come. For months he had waited, and now, at last, the Fiend was condemned. Tonight was the last time he would ever see Barabbas alive.

"Sir?"

The killer slumped in the corner of his cell, elephantine, all but naked, luxuriating in his wickedness and sin. He had prised his stash of beauty from its hiding place in the wall and had spread before him a dozen or so of his favourite items—rings, coins and Moon's tiepin amongst them. "Come in, won't you?" he said, barely bothering to look up. "I was just admiring my collection. Flashes, little fragments of beauty in a world of misery and care."

Owsley looked disdainfully at the meagre pile. "I'll make sure they're distributed to charity after your death."

"My death. Is it come already?"

Owsley grinned. He seemed hungry suddenly, cruel, his mask of servility wrenched aside. "In a manner of speaking."

I fear I may not have been entirely honest about Mr. Owsley.

*B*arabbas seemed not to notice the change in his disciple. "When?" he breathed.

Owsley licked his lips. "Now."

The prisoner made no attempt to move away, but rather slouched further onto the floor. He scrabbled in front of him to gather his collection and clutched it to his heaving, blubbery chest. "It's you, then?" he asked, although he already knew the answer.

"Me," Owsley snapped back. "It's always been me." He bent over the convict, malevolence boiling off him in ugly black waves. "You should have accepted our offer. You could have had Elysium. Instead you chose this."

"I know my level," Barabbas murmured. He added, almost conversationally: "Can I ask you something?"

"I suppose."

"Why now? I had hoped to see how everything turns out."

"You ought never to have given him that book."

"Edward will work it out. His faculties are almost the equal of my own."

Owsley laughed. From his pocket he drew out a long, slender surgical knife, coolly vicious, precision-tooled for death. "Your punishment has been decided," he snarled, relishing the drama of the moment. "And the sentence is death."

Barabbas yawned, waved a pudgy hand languidly. "Then get on with—" he began, but before he could finish, Owsley, his face convulsing with pleasure, plunged the knife deep into him.

Barabbas gave a wet gasp. Owsley twisted the blade, pulled it loose, then thrust it in again. The fat man moaned and a trickle of blood emerged from his mouth like lava, staining his lips and teeth a murky scarlet, spattering messily down his chin.

Still alive, he whispered something to his disciple that even Owsley, in all the innumerable times he had rehearsed and played this scene out in his head, had not foreseen.

"Kiss me."

Owsley had never killed a man before. He felt overwhelmed by the power of it, caught up in the giddy thrill of his transformation, possessed by the sublime transgression of the deed. No doubt it was this which made him think he would be safe and assured him of his invulnerability as he leant forward to kiss Barabbas full on the lips. Triumphant, drunk on his murder, he was about to pull away when he felt the dying man stir. With one vast hand, Barabbas held firm his erstwhile servant's head; with the other he reached for his stash of beautiful things and pulled free Moon's tiepin, sharpened and honed in anticipation of this inevitable moment. Owsley thrashed and flailed as, with his final flicker of strength, Barabbas brought the pin up to Owsley's throat and dragged it pitilessly across, feeling the arteries snap with a series of satisfying pops. He closed his eyes as a torrent of blood gushed stickily onto his face. Meyrick Owsley tried to scream in rage, agonising pain and frustration, but could succeed only in gurgling. Helpless, he fell onto his former master and they lay there awhile in a macabre embrace— mutilated, ragged things, bound together for the underworld.

Just before he died, Barabbas tried to whisper the name of the man he loved, an act which had always seemed to him to be appropriate before the end. Whenever he had imagined his death, he had always envisaged an attendant degree of pathos, for it to play out as the sort of strange and tragic scene which might inspire some artist to daub a study in scarlet or a poet to pen a mournful stanza or two. Much to his disappointment, as he lay choking on his own blood, his life dripping away from him with terrible speed, he found himself too weakened even to speak.

Consequently, the Fiend died silent.

*M*erryweather and Moon found the Somnambulist in the first place they looked—the taproom of the Strangled Boy. The pub had withstood the worst of the fire, but across the street the theatre remained a blackened, burned-out husk, bleak testament to Moon's failure.

The conjuror bought his friend a pint of milk and asked, as politely as he could, why he had disappeared. The Somnambulist took out his chalkboard.

SAW SPEIGHT

"Speight?" Merryweather peered nosily over Moon's shoulder. "The tramp?"

The giant nodded.

"How was he?" asked Moon, slightly bemused.

SUIT

"He was wearing a suit?" Moon asked carefully.

SMART

"Are you sure?"

The Somnambulist nodded, evidently frustrated.

BANK

"He was outside a bank?" the inspector offered.

The Somnambulist shook his head vigorously.

"He works in a bank?" Moon asked, incredulous.

The Somnambulist nodded gratefully.

Merryweather snorted. "Preposterous."

CAMOUFLAGE

"Camouflage?" Moon was about to ask the meaning of this when the faint cry of a paper boy floated in from outside.

When he heard the headline, Moon dashed out of the pub and into the street.

"Horrible Murder in Newgate!" the boy shouted again. "The Fiend Is Dead!"

Moon seized a paper and riffled furiously through it. When his friends ran out to join him, they found him staring dully down at the newsprint, tears edging the corners of his eyes. Discreetly, they kept their distance. Moon let the paper fall from his hands and drop onto the street, where it was trampled underfoot, sodden, torn and kicked away, another piece of city flotsam. Suddenly, acutely aware that the forces of coincidence were marshalling themselves against him, Moon stood alone and silent. Then he surprised himself by laughing. There was no humour in the sound, no genuine mirth, but in the face of all that had happened it seemed to him by far the most logical reaction. To the impartial observer, of course, it may have appeared more like the act of a man whose sanity, like desert earth baked dry, has begun at long last to splinter and to crack.

Through it all, the old man sleeps beneath the city.

Some conscious part of him may be aware that things are changing in the streets above, that events are progressing towards their inevitable crisis. Perhaps he knows that he will soon have to stir from his slumber and face the waking world. But for now he remains mired in dreams.

First, he is a young man again, in the company of friends,

before any of them had been touched by life's realities. Southey is with him—brave, dear Southey—at a time before his betrayal and their feuds. Their talk is earnest, too solemn, perhaps, but typical of the way they were.

The old man sighs and stirs uncomfortably in his sleep, remembering happier times.

The young men talk of their hopes and ambitions, of the great experiment. Southey speaks loftily of a brotherhood, of their plans to escape and perfect themselves.

The dreamer sees himself talking fervently, fire blazing in his eyes, of poetry and metaphysics and the need for a better world.

Susquehanna. The word surfaces without warning. It means nothing to him but he enjoys the sound of it, its pleasing rhythm. He repeats it to himself. *Susquehanna.*

Then Edith emerges beside Southey, interrupting them with cake and wine, and the old man sees that the chasm between them is already widening. Sara brushes up against him and he is distracted. The dream shifts again.

He is old now, his friendships withered like fruit on a rotten vine, the clear vision of his youth fogged and obscured by the compromises of age. He is a different man, gripped in the coils of penury and afflicted by an evil longing. Naked to the waist, his breeches pulled down below his knees, he sits straining over a privy, clenched and groaning, sick in the knowledge that he has afflicted this poisoning, this acrimony of the bowels, upon himself, that he is to blame for his condition. "My body is deranged," he writes—his madness the product of a fondness for medicine, a folly, a treacherous lover in whose thrall he has been too long held tight. He mutters to himself as, humiliated, he sits and heaves and pushes.

At last, he returns to the garret room in Highgate, to Gillman and the boy. Ned is there, not so young now. He holds out his hand. Feverish and dying, the old man takes it. He tells Gillman to leave them, and the doctor, respectful of his patient's whims, obeys.

Ned seems fearless of him now that death stares back through the old man's eyes. He wants to tell the boy what he means to him, how the boy has brought him to life again and rekindled his dreams. Surprisingly, for one so voluble in life, he cannot find the words. He stutters awhile, then contents himself with clutching the proffered hand, but he is sure nonetheless that the boy—this special, chosen boy—*knows*. He has bequeathed him a legacy. Ned is to be his successor, his champion. He squeezes his hand, blinks back a few final tears.

Gasping in his sleep, shuffling uncomfortably on his iron cot, the dreamer knows the end is near.

Perhaps, if he were aware of the passing of time, the exact chronology of his incarceration, he might care to know precisely how long he has left before he wakes.

But I have faith in you. You'll have worked it out by now, I'm sure.

Four days. Four days before the dream ends, the old man wakes and the city falls.

14

*P*rofessional pavement artists are a modern phenomenon. In London, they sprang into being only as the guardians of the city's streets and thoroughfares began to favour the economy of tarmacadam over the quaint impracticality of cobblestones. By the time of Moon's last case, the pitted, pot-holed character of the old city had given way to the flawless asphalt of the new century. Accordingly, the city had seen an unwelcome increase in vagrants and down-at-heel needies plying their trade as roadside artists. One especially pernicious breed had acquired the name *screever*, a title given to those alms-seekers little better than beggars, the type that had they not possessed the barest modicum of artistic ability would doubtless have been selling matches or accosting passers-by with an outstretched cap and a forlorn look.

The day after Barabbas died, Mr. Dedlock was thrusting his way through the crowds which, quite without reason, had chosen this morning in particular to pack the streets of Limehouse and block his path, all of them pushing and shoving and struggling like a Far Eastern football team jostling for drinks at the after-match bar. This must be a religious festival, he thought, some heathen public holiday or other which has resulted in this thoughtless and distracting inconvenience. By the time he reached the familiar shop front, he had to pause, sweaty and wheezing, to catch his breath. His triumphs on the rugby pitch were years behind him; that world belonged now to fitter, leaner, younger men.

A screever sat a few paces from the butcher's door. Unkempt to an almost grotesque degree, his artwork was chalked half-heartedly on the pavement before him. Dedlock strode past, determined not to give the man the merest flicker of acknowledgement, but as he glanced down at the screever's handiwork, something stared back—a word which made him stop short in shock.

Dedlock

Wrinkling his nose at the smell, the gentleman in question stared down at the screever. "Do I know you?"

"Danger," the beggar hissed. "Danger."

"Danger? What danger?"

"Danger."

Dedlock gave him a haughty stare. "You're drunk."

"Don't you know me, sir?"

Dedlock snorted dismissively and was about to walk away when something about the creature drew his eye, something uncomfortably familiar. He peered closer. "Grischenko? Is that you?"

The screever nodded, a little sheepishly.

"What the devil are you doing here?"

"Danger," he repeated solemnly. "Danger."

"So you said."

"Danger."

Dedlock rolled his eyes. "Wipe that muck off your face and come with me. Whatever it is, you might as well tell me inside."

The tramp stumbled to his feet and followed Dedlock as he swaggered into the building. Inside, Mr. Skimpole was already seated and waiting at the round table, fretful and restive. Given the albino's permanently pasty complexion it was difficult to tell, but Dedlock thought he looked especially sickly today.

At the entrance of his colleague, Skimpole waved away a group of Civil Servants dressed as Chinamen who had been clustering round him, anxiously proffering reports to be read, letters to be signed, schemes and plots to be initialled. "Who's this?" he asked, looking suspiciously towards the screever, his voice filled with the vexed tenor of a man whose pet dog has just dragged a small woodland creature into the drawing room, dead but still bleeding.

"This is Mr. Grischenko," Dedlock said, and the man nodded distractedly in greeting. He seemed jittery and furtive and kept looking about him as though terrified of some unseen menace lurking just beyond the borders of his vision.

"One of yours?" Skimpole asked witheringly.

The scarred man was unapologetic. "One of mine."

"Who?"

Dedlock lowered his voice to an absurd stage whisper: "He's our 'in' with the Russians. A double."

"What in God's name is he doing here? After the Slattery fiasco I'd have hoped you might be more wary about this kind of thing."

"I think he has information for us." Dedlock pointed to a chair and barked: "Sit down." Grischenko, still whimpering, his vagabond disguise only partially removed, did as he was told.

"Why are you here?" Dedlock snapped. "Why that ludicrous disguise?"

Grischenko spoke carefully. His English was slow and thickly accented, his vocabulary antiquated and fussy. "I have to warn you," he began. "I come here in this most brilliant disguise because the men who track me, they are dangerous. Most probably they watch us even now. I could not allow myself to be seen as Grischenko. You understand?"

Dedlock crossed his arms. "You're quite safe here, I assure you. And I suspect that Mr. Skimpole and myself are more than a match for anything your people might care to throw at us."

"No, no." Grischenko suddenly seemed animated. "Of course, I understand that my fellow countrymen would not alarm men so courageous as yourselves. But I am not followed by my own people. Not Russian. No, sir, these men you do not know, though I think you are aware of their activities. They are powerful, sirs. Very powerful. They have long been plotting against the city. You know to whom I refer now, I fancy?"

"Perhaps," Skimpole said evenly.

"We've heard rumours," Dedlock admitted, blunter than his partner. "We'd be grateful for any information you might be able to offer. The Directorate is a powerful ally. We can guarantee your safety. Who are these people? What do they call themselves?"

"They have no name, sir, but I believe that they are quite without scruple. They hired the Irish Slattery to stop you. He failed, I know, but they will not hesitate to try again. They will not stop until the Directorate is defeated and dead."

"How do you know this?"

"Mr. Dedlock," the Russian hissed, "I know because they have tried to turn me."

"You?"

"Me," Grischenko repeated, a hint of pride in his voice. "I resisted, of course. I threw their filthy offer back in their faces. I am a man of principle."

"But of course."

"There is more."

Dedlock gestured for him to continue.

"They failed with me but they have succeeded with another. An old associate of mine."

"What do you mean?"

"They have a sleeper."

"A sleeper?"

"Our deadliest. And now this man, this killer, a man we ourselves planted in this country many years ago, now he is recruited to their cause."

"Who?" Dedlock snapped. "Give me a name."

"He has many aliases," the Russian said doubtfully. "His real name has disappeared."

Dedlock frowned.

Grischenko brightened. "But he has code name."

"Tell us."

Grischenko muttered something which sounded like "The Mongoose."

"The Mongoose?" Skimpole repeated incredulously.

Dedlock swallowed a laugh. "The Mongoose?"

The Russian shrugged. "We were running out of names."

"Means nothing to me." Dedlock sniffed.

"He has killed many dozens and he has yet to fail. He is the worst of men, Mr. Dedlock. Please, gentlemen, on this matter you must be absolutely certain: he is coming for you."

"Coming for us?" Skimpole echoed.

Grischenko nodded vigorously. "Like a pale rider," he murmured. "Upon a pale horse."

Skimpole shivered. Grischenko scrambled to his feet. "I must go," he said and scuttled to the door, readjusting his disguise as he went.

"Wait," the albino protested, but Grischenko ignored him.

He paused. "Be watchful. Promise me, sirs. Be watchful." With this final, gnomic advice, he disappeared through the door and into the street.

"We should have him stopped," Skimpole said. "Bring him in. Interrogate him properly."

"Let him go. He's told us everything he knows."

"You believe him?"

"It would seem he risked his life to warn us. To be frank, I think we should expect the worst."

"Who are these people?" Skimpole asked angrily. "What do they want? Good God, if only we hadn't lost Bagshaw."

"You don't look well. Go home. I'll keep you fully informed of developments."

"I'd rather stay."

"Go," Dedlock insisted, not unkindly. "But be careful. We should both be on our guard. From now on, it seems, the Directorate is under siege."

The Strangled Boy opened early for business. Even arriving shortly after ten, Edward and Charlotte Moon were far from being the first customers of the day—that dubious honour had already been claimed by those patrons who were even now on their second or third glass of the morning. Charlotte was discomfited by the beery, musky, masculine smell of the place but Moon appeared not to notice. Waving his sister towards a rickety barstool, he ordered drinks.

"You see they're rebuilding the old place?" he asked as he sat down beside her.

Charlotte peered from the window across the square to the

burned-out hulk of the theatre where squads of workmen swarmed about its scaffolding like carrion flies on a corpse.

"This isn't especially convenient, Edward. I thought we'd agreed not to see one another for a while."

"It's an emergency."

"I'm busy."

"With what? More 'debunking'?"

"There's a psychic in Bermondsey who reckons she can move household objects by the power of thought and bring back the dead in her front room."

"You think she's a fake?"

"The objects are raised up on strings, the dead people are her accomplices in white sheets and cheesecloth."

"Charlotte, if I've learnt anything from my recent experiences it's that it is as dangerous to believe in nothing as it is to believe everything."

"Stop pontificating and tell me why I'm here."

Moon reached into his briefcase and pulled out a folder swollen fat with paper. He swallowed, ill at ease. "I have a favour to ask of you," he said, extricating a sheaf of documents and placing them carefully upon the table. "The Somnambulist and I have not been idle. Whilst you've been off running table-rappers to ground, we've been pursuing an old obsession of mine."

"Honeyman?"

"You know about his mother? Also that of Philip Dunbar— the Fly's other victim? Both of them gone. Vanished into the city without trace."

"People go missing all the time."

"I've since discovered that both women were prominent fig-ures in a small but extremely affluent religious group called the Church of the Summer Kingdom."

"I've heard of them."

Moon seemed surprised. "You have?"

"Silly name, of course, but harmless from what I can gather."
She paused. "Presumably, you disagree."

"I suspect they're not as benevolent as they appear."

"What makes you say that?"

"Too many coincidences. Too many connections. They're
linked to the Fly, I'm sure of it. Their sigil—a black, five-petalled
flower—was daubed on his caravan. From what I can make out,
it's practically the symbol of the church. Coleridge, too."

"Coleridge?"

"Barabbas gave me a copy of the *Lyrical Ballads*. The church—
if that's really what it is—seems centred on his ideology."

Charlotte sighed. "Edward," she began, speaking much as one
might to a beloved elderly relative, formerly alert and intelligent,
but now sunk into befuddled senility, "you can't believe a word
that man told you. Not for nothing did the popular press call him
'the Fiend.' "

Moon, turned ashen, did not reply and Charlotte was glad of
the distraction when a serving girl brought across their drinks,
slammed down the glasses and shuffled truculently away.

"You mentioned needing a favour," she said, once Moon had
taken a fortifying sip.

"I spent the night in the Stacks."

"You spend half your life there."

"The Church of the Summer Kingdom is one of the richest
organisations in London."

Charlotte pursed her lips. "Are you sure?"

"No question. They've hidden it well. I had to wade through
oceans of paperwork. But they've left a trail. It only needed someone with enough persistence to follow it to its source."

"And what did you find?"

"That the church is funded almost entirely by a single body. A
corporation which calls itself . . . 'Love.' "

"Love?"

"Bankers and brokers. Moneymen of some kind. Massively wealthy and a major player in the city. Their full name—believe it or not—is Love, Love, Love and Love."

"Sounds like a joke."

Moon did not smile. "The Somnambulist and I went to their offices. He recognised the building. Said he'd seen Speight of all people walk inside, dressed in a suit and behaving as if he owned the place."

Charlotte laughed. "He must have been confused. Or drunk. He strikes me as the kind of man who might be."

"The Somnambulist is far and away the most sensible person I know. Besides, I've only ever seen him drink milk."

"The mystery thickens. You must be delighted."

"Don't you see that something's happening here?"

Charlotte drained her cup and spoke again, calm and in control. "I agree it's suspicious. How can I help?"

"I've arranged a job for you at Love."

"Presumptuous of you."

"Forgive me. Time is short."

"How did you manage it?"

"Skimpole. The Directorate has its uses."

Charlotte sighed. "What do you want me to do?"

"Infiltrate Love. Discover their connection to the church. Find out what they're planning."

"Nothing *too* demanding."

"Report everything back to me, no matter how extraneous or irrelevant it may seem. Please, be scrupulous. I'm relying on you."

"And what will you be up to whilst I'm doing all this?"

"The Somnambulist and I have to pursue another lead but—rest assured—I will be watching." Moon fished a business card from his pocket. "Here's the address. Be careful. I hope to God I'm not putting you in danger."

"Danger? What are you expecting?"

"If Madame Innocenti was right we only have three days left."

"You believe her?"

"I hope I'm wrong. But I think the pattern is beginning to make itself clear."

Irritation rose in Charlotte's voice. "You're being mysterious again."

"I know." He shrugged. "I can't help it."

Dedlock took a cab to the centre of the city and alighted amidst the bustle of Piccadilly Circus, that Mecca for the sybarite, the pleasure-seeker, the good-time girl. He did not stop to sample the delights of the place but headed instead towards the genteel calm of St. James's Park, at the borders of which was situated his club, a well-heeled oasis scant seconds from the populous commotion of the city.

There had been an atmosphere of disquiet in the Directorate for days, a tangible sense of menace in the air. The Slattery incident had unsettled them all, the business with Grischenko even more so. Dedlock had sent the "Chinamen" away (vetted more carefully since the Mackenzie-Cooper debacle) and Skimpole had slouched off home for the day, gloomier and more grisly-looking than ever. Clearly something was up with the man, but in all the years they had known one another Dedlock had always found it difficult to sympathise with him, had never had much stomach for the spindly palpitations of his permanently sickly colleague.

He walked down a narrow avenue just off Pall Mall, stopping outside a house halfway along the street. A bronze plaque had been placed by the doorbell and read, in neat, black, unassuming letters:

THE SURVIVORS' CLUB
STRICTLY MEMBERS ONLY

Dedlock rang the bell and an elderly man hobbled to the door.

Shrivelled, hunched and wizened, he had huge eyebrows—vast white things like spiky tadpoles mutated to a dozen times their normal size—which hung precariously beneath his brow and cast strange shadows across his face. He recognised Dedlock at once. "Pleasure to see you again, sir. Do come in."

Inside, Dedlock was immediately assailed by the familiar scents of the place, its indefinably comforting cocktail of whisky, port, stale tobacco smoke, musty carpets and the aroma of manly perspiration.

"It's rather quiet today, sir," the man with the eyebrows apologised as he took Dedlock's coat. "You're just a little early."

"That's fine. I'll go straight through."

"Very good, sir."

Dedlock sauntered down a long corridor and into the last of four open rooms. "Afternoon," he said, by way of a general greeting. A chorus of grunts and murmurs ensued, emanating from the half-dozen gentlemen sitting inside, all of whom clasped cigarettes, cigars or pipes.

Dedlock took his usual armchair by the door. Opposite him, engrossed in the *Gazette*, was a tall, rangy man, besuited and wholly unremarkable—but for the fact that most of both his legs were missing, the lower part of his body reduced to a flabby stump hanging impotently over the front of his chair.

To his right sat a man so grotesquely disfigured that most of us would probably have screamed or swooned at the sight of him. Dedlock, however, only nodded with the same nonchalant courtesy he might have afforded any other, more recognisably human acquaintance—a friend passed in the street, perhaps, or a workmate encountered at the bar. Evidently the victim of a terrible fire, half the man's features had been ravaged and deformed, his hair entirely scorched away, his skin dyed a livid shade of purple. Doubtless, Dedlock thought, this fellow was an object of pity in the world at large, doubtless he was jeered at by children as he went about his daily business, pointed out and stared at and made an object of ridicule. Fishwives (it would not surprise him to learn) cast aspersions on his sexual capabilities whenever he so much as raised his hat in greeting. But here in this most exclusive of the city's clubs, here the man could relax without shame and hold his head up high amongst his peers. Today, in fact, he seemed positively cheerful, puffing enthusiastically away on an ancient briarwood pipe. Dedlock waved and the man smiled lop-sidedly back.

A few yards away sat a chap with an eyepatch and a ragged red hole where his nose ought to have been; his neighbour was a man with half an arm who seemed subject to repeated bouts of violent shakes and shudders. Close by sat a scrawny fellow whose face resembled that of a dog or badger in the aftermath of an especially bloody fight.

Dedlock wriggled in his chair, feeling suddenly uncomfortable and out of place. Giving in gratefully to temptation, he took off his tie, unbuttoned his shirt and stripped naked to the waist to reveal a body criss-crossed by a pair of gargantuan milk-white scars. He passed his fingers over their deep indentations, caressed their worn, familiar lines. The man with the pipe looked over and nodded approvingly. Dedlock reached for his cigarettes and set-tled back into his chair, a rare smile of contentment on his face, home at last.

*W*hen he awoke, the room had grown silent, dark and empty. Dedlock's first thought as he stretched himself into a vague ap-proximation of consciousness was a question: why had the man with the eyebrows not woken him? He felt stiff and uncomfort-able and his joints ached from sitting too long in the chair. He rubbed his eyes and was giving serious thought to clambering to his feet when he became uncomfortably aware that he was being watched.

"Who's there?" he asked, his fingers fumbling for the revolver he kept concealed in his waistcoat, only to remember, too late, that he had stripped half-naked in a show of solidarity with his fellow Survivors.

"You're awake," said a voice.

"Who is it?" he asked again.

A figure moved towards him and Dedlock thought he could make out two others flanking the first.

"Do you know who we are?" said a second voice.

"Can you guess?" said a third. Each of the three men spoke with a different, distinctive accent. Together, they were instantly recognisable.

"I know who you are," Dedlock said, pins and needles pirouetting up and down his spine.

"Bet you didn't think we were real," said the first man.

"I knew."

One of them laughed and the others joined in.

"Mr. Dedlock?"

The scarred man swallowed hard, determined not to show his fear. "Yes?"

"We've been hearing stories. Something about a conspiracy, a plot against the city."

Dedlock cleared his throat and tried to force himself to speak as levelly and calmly as if he were delivering a report to one of the innumerable boards and committees to which he was accountable. "The Directorate knows of a threat to London. We have our man investigating—Edward Moon. Perhaps you've heard of him."

In the blackness, three men shook their heads as one.

"Dedlock? We need you to be certain. Has this anything to do with the Secret? Is the Secret out?"

A cold trail of sweat snailed its way down his back. "The Secret is safe."

"You realise what would happen if it were to get loose?"

Another voice. "This affair would seem a storm in a teacup in comparison."

Dedlock could no longer tell which of the men was speaking. "I promise you, the Secret is safe. Even Mr. Skimpole doesn't know."

"It's imperative it stays that way."

"You have my word."

Even though it was pitch black, Dedlock felt certain that all three of the men were smiling and that the smiles they wore were not benign ones. "Then we must place our faith in that."

Then with a rustling, clicking sound, the three were gone. Curiously, Dedlock found that he no longer had any desire to lever himself out of his chair, but fell asleep again almost immediately, the encounter already fading into dream.

When he woke again, the birds were singing.

*P*ity Mr. Skimpole.

An odd request, I know, given his previous showing as a blackguard. But it would take a heart of stone not to feel sorry for him as he trudged forlornly home to Wimbledon, his breathing ragged and irregular, unsteady on his feet, weaving as he walked like a drunkard trying to persuade himself he's sober. There was something terribly beleaguered about him, something Sisyphean and doomed.

He let himself into his little house and almost called out his son's name, only stopping when he realised that today was a school day, that he was at his lessons and—if the tales the boy had told him were true—was even now the subject of whispered jibes and catcalls. The albino sympathised. His own school days were a blur of sneers and note-passing, name-calling and impromptu playground beatings, all the petty humiliations and habitual cruelty of childhood.

As if in reaction to this unsought nostalgia, Skimpole felt another rending deep in his stomach, another surge of agonising pain. He staggered to a chair, sucking in wheezy lungfuls of air, struggling to stay calm and trying not to think about the implications of his distress. But he knew all too well the meaning of the slimy tugging in his guts, had realised its significance from the moment Slattery had expired upon the floor of the Directorate. Time was getting away from him—a few days were all that were left to him now—and he was determined to make the best of that time, to leave a legacy of which he might be proud.

I will be remembered, he decided, as he sat, grim-faced, too weak to move, as the blood thundered through his head and the pain welled up again. *I will be remembered.*

These were his final thoughts before he drifted into an uncomfortable sleep, a merciful release from pain. He woke to find his son standing before him.

"Dada? What's the matter?"

With an enormous effort of will, the albino pulled himself upright in his chair. "Nothing. Nothing's the matter. Just napping, that's all. How was school?"

The boy looked awkwardly away.

"Come here." Skimpole patted his knee. His son limped across the room and clambered awkwardly onto his lap. The child had almost become too large for such treatment, but this was an old, much-loved ritual they were loath to surrender lightly. Skimpole pulled him closer and, trying not to betray the merest flicker of his own discomfort, began to sing—crooning a familiar lullaby, a favourite since infancy. The boy laughed and smiled. In the soft cadences of his father's voice all the horrid travails of school were forgotten, and for a few sweet, fleeting moments, Mr. Skimpole smiled, too.

*Y*ou will recall that, at the beginning of this narrative, I promised there would be several points in the story at which I would tell you a direct lie. I'll be honest and confess that this is one such juncture. Everything you have just read concerning Mr. Skimpole and his crooked child is a fiction.

Gruesome old sentimentalist, aren't I?

*B*ack to the truth.

More often than not, the Somnambulist did not appear to require food at all; the pleasures of the dinner table were a foreign country to him and he would go for days or weeks without so much as a morsel passing his lips. But on those irregular occasions when he appeared to require sustenance, he invariably ate in style.

Late in the morning after Barabbas's death he sat in the hotel dining room enjoying a leisurely breakfast, ladling pink strips of bacon into his mouth, shovelling in egg, tomato, bangers and fried bread and washing it all down with glass after glass of milk. Moon had yet to put in an appearance and the Somnambulist had been more than happy to scoff his meal for him in his absence. A number of other guests, put off by the giant's noisy mastication, had given him their own plates, still brimming with the greasy bulk of a Full English, with the result that by the time he was finished the Somnambulist had polished off the best part of five or six separate courses. Wondering what was for lunch, he gestured to a nearby waiter. The man walked reluctantly across, disdain etched upon his face.

MORE MILK

With that combination of resentment and superciliousness unique to British serving staff, the man bowed his head and vanished, though he accomplished even that only grudgingly. The last of the other guests left soon after, dropping a final few rashers onto the Somnambulist's plate as they went. Finally, Moon arrived, tiresomely excited—so much so that, to the giant's relief, he seemed not to notice that all his breakfast had been eaten.

"Come along," he said, not even bothering to sit down. "We have an appointment."

The Somnambulist gazed regretfully at the food still lingering on his plate. He was able to summon up little excitement for this mysterious appointment and had, in fact, been toying with the idea of hibernating for a week or two.

Moon persisted. "We're expected in Highgate."

The Somnambulist shrugged.

"It's important. I think we're close."

The giant pushed aside his plate and got to his feet.

"Good man."

The waiter came back into the room bearing a large jug. "Your milk, sir."

The Somnambulist looked longingly at it but Moon stood firm.

The giant pulled a face.

Moon relented. "Bring it with you," he said. "You can drink it on the way."

*T*hey arrived in Highgate just over an hour later. Their destination was a nondescript little cottage set back from the road, halfway up a hill so steep it was practically vertical and mere paces from the spot where Whittington was said to have turned back and returned to the city, powerless against the pull of its gravity.

WHY?

the Somnambulist asked, trying his best to wipe away the flaky dark milk stains which had accumulated on his shirt like the first spatters of rain on a dry pavement.

"Coleridge lived here."

The Somnambulist's expression made his feelings on the relevance of this remark quite clear. He gesticulated again at the chalkboard.

WHY?

"Remember the book Barabbas gave me? There was a name in the dedication. Someone called Gillman. I've done a little reading. I think he may have been trying to direct us here."

The giant scrubbed out his message and hurriedly wrote:

MR. COLERIDGE—HE DEAD

"I shan't take issue with your grammar," Moon scolded.

The Somnambulist looked as if he were about to punch him.

Swiftly, Moon tried to explain. "I think that in some manner, Coleridge may be at the heart of this." He was about to say more when the door swung open and a grey-haired woman peered out.

"Mr. Moon?"

"Miss Gillman? A pleasure. This is my associate, the Somnambulist."

The giant proffered an awkward wave and the woman nodded back. "Come inside. I've tea and biscuits waiting."

"Marvellous. The Somnambulist is absolutely famished."

But the giant did not reply. Distracted for a brief moment from the prospect of food, he felt a strange, inexplicable certainty that it was here—in this unremarkable little cottage smelling faintly of lavender and soap—here that the end would finally begin.

My dear Edward,

I hope this letter finds its way safely into your hands. As a result of those circumstances I am shortly to relate, I have found myself unable to deliver it in person and have been forced to entrust these words to a "go-between," a young woman whose acquaintance I have made here. A tentative friend, let us say, and perhaps an ally—though unfortunately I cannot tell you her name. That, too, I will explain in time.

These, then, are my first impressions of Love, Love, Love and Love (known henceforth, for brevity's sake, simply as Love). The past few hours have convinced me that this is, by some considerable distance, quite the most eccentric organisation in England. I am certain now that your instincts are correct—something seems very wrong here, but so far, whatever the truth of it, I have been shown only a tiny portion of a much greater picture.

I think you mentioned that you have seen the building yourself—a great black citadel just off Eastcheap, beneath the shadow of the Monument. Close by is the church of Saint-Dunstan-in-the-East—a minor Wren but one which still has about it his characteristic beauty and brilliance. On the next occasion you and Mr. Cribb are enjoying yourselves on one of your historical walks, you really ought to stroll by and see it for yourself. Did the giant ever reveal the reason for his animosity towards the ugly man? In my opinion, all most suspicious.

I have joined the firm in the capacity of a clerk with a

number of minor secretarial duties. I must say that this company is astonishingly egalitarian in its choice of employees—there are three other ladies on my floor alone. The work is tedious but easy, the nine-to-five routine a far cry from the giddy derring-do of my assignments for the Vigilance Committee.

Edward, I think I could easily suffocate here, that it wouldn't take long, weighed down by documentation and paperwork, correspondence, ink and dust.

Superficially Love operates much like any other large city firm—old-fashioned, moribund and staid. However, there are two remarkable facts which render the organisation unique.

Firstly, accommodation is provided for its entire staff on site—by which I mean that we actually reside in the building itself, deep in the basement levels. This is not a generosity one may choose to decline: it is compulsory for all members of staff, and, more than that, even leaving the building at any time and for any reason is frowned upon. We are all of us expected to remain here and are fully provided for within these walls. I had no choice but to accept such terms and I write this in the tiny room I share with another girl. This is the first time I have ever spent the night in a bunk bed, though doubtless you would find it a home from home. I trust that whatever mysterious "lead" you and your giant friend are pursuing from the comfort of your singularly well-appointed hotel room is important enough to warrant forcing your only sister to endure these primitive conditions.

Strange though these arrangements may be, there is a sense of community here. That we all eat, sleep and work together seems to engender an atmosphere of fraternity not unlike being back at my old college, or how I imagine it must be for mariners at sea. More troubling is the mood of anticipation which hangs in the air. I am convinced that these people are waiting for something. They resemble a rugby team before the first match of the season or an army awaiting the order to advance.

Needless to say, it is not simply the idiosyncrasies of its domestic arrangements which mark this firm out as unique. Odder by far is the enforced practice of replacing one's real name with a number. Lunatic though I know it must sound, every single person in this building shares the same name: Love.

To aid identification we are all assigned a number. Consequently, Charlotte Moon is no more and in her place sits Love 999. My tentative friend is Love 893. You see now why I was unable to give you her name.

All this strikes me as awfully strange and not a little sinister. It need hardly be remarked upon that I shall be greatly interested to hear your opinion of the matter.

Another puzzle: the Somnambulist was right.

I met Mr. Speight today, tidied up, clean-shaven and smartly dressed in an alarmingly expensive suit. "Love 903," as he styles himself, failed to recognise me and gave me not a second glance when we passed in the corridor. He seems important, a bigwig, and works on one of the higher floors, his days of placard-carrying long behind him.

I am not sure why but we were asked today to burn a good deal of paperwork. I stole a look at it before it was consigned to the flames and the material was all very recent, relating, I think, to some kind of consolidation of the firm's considerable assets. I have not the slightest idea why Love should be destroying documentation nor why it is marshalling its funds. Perhaps I will simply have to ask, although I have done my best, according to your instructions, to appear as inconspicuous as possible. I do not wish to seem curious and therefore provoke suspicion.

That is all I can tell you for the present. I shall write again as soon as I am able.

Your affectionate sister,
Charlotte

15

I have long believed the city, the country, indeed the world at large to be run by precisely the wrong kind of people. From the government to the great financial institutions, the peerage to the police force, our lives are controlled without exception by the stupid and greedy, the venal, the rapacious and the undeservedly rich. How much more comfortable would it be if the rulers of the world were not the cognoscenti of the bank balance, the ballot box, the offshore account, but were drawn instead from the ranks of the everyday—honest, kind, stout-hearted, commonplace folk.

In the course of this narrative we have encountered few such paragons. Mrs. Grossmith, perhaps. The Somnambulist. Mina the bearded lady. To that list we may now add one other: Miss Gillman, the mild-mannered sage of Highgate.

When Moon and the Somnambulist arrived on her doorstep, she and the giant took to one another immediately, sensing perhaps that they were kindred spirits of a sort, that they shared the same benign outlook on the world at large.

But the Somnambulist was confused. He had to struggle hard to resist the urge to scratch his head—in part from genuine befuddlement, in part because his wig itched abominably. He was a little comforted, however, to note that Miss Gillman seemed every bit as bewildered as he. And as was so often the case, the only person who understood what was going on was Edward Moon.

"Miss Gillman," he asked, as their hostess sipped her tea, "do you recognise this?" He pushed into her hands the slim black book Barabbas had given him in Newgate, his copy of the *Lyrical Ballads*.

The old lady flipped back the cover and read the dedication within. "It's mine." She sounded surprised. "Do you know, I'd thought it lost for ever."

"The dedication . . . It's for your father?"

"How did you come by this?"

"It was a legacy," Moon lied fluently and without compunction. "I believe its last owner acquired it at auction."

"Really? I must confess I never knew you were such a lover of poetry. Your reputation precedes you, of course, but this . . . this is most unexpected."

"It's a new interest of mine. Recommended to me by an old friend."

"I'm afraid I'm rather at a loss as to how I can help. It's a great pity my father is no longer with us. He would have been of so much more use to you than me."

"Tell us what you can. Tell us about Coleridge."

"It was so long ago," she said doubtfully.

"Of all those who had the honour of knowing the poet personally," Moon said, slapping the Somnambulist's hand as the giant reached out for his ninth digestive of the day, "I understand you're one of the last still with us."

Miss Gillman gave a watery smile. "I suppose that's a distinction of sorts. Of course, I was still a girl when he died. Did you know he's buried close by in our little churchyard? He was a kind man despite it all."

"I understand he stayed with you here?"

"Oh, he lived upstairs for years. I'd be happy to show you his room. My father cared for him there until his death, paid, I believe, by some sort of stipend, though I think he did it mostly out of love. Mr. Coleridge was one of the family. A second grandfather, if you like. He had stopped writing by then, almost entirely. His best work was long behind him. And as you know, he had become a slave to that disgusting opiate. It was a great source of pain to us all."

"Go on."

Miss Gillman spoke for the best part of an hour, happy to relive her memories of the remarkable man with whom she had shared her childhood. She told them how, abandoned by his wife and child, fugitive from an unhappy love affair and disowned by his friends and admirers, the poet had come to Highgate to live as a lodger-cum-patient in the Gillman household, where it was hoped he might heal himself and extinguish his addiction. He stayed, as it turned out, for the rest of his life.

Moon listened politely, the Somnambulist made short work of the remaining biscuits and time flowed by in a stream of anecdotes and reminiscences. They were in a bubble there, the giant thought, far removed from the world outside, and on hearing Gillman speak, he felt as though someone else's story, some other narrative, were impinging itself, suddenly and without warning, upon their own.

"There was the boy, of course," the old woman said. "At the end."

Moon looked up. "Tell me about him."

"He was an apprentice, still a child, not more than nine or ten. He used to bring the old man his prescription up to the house. *Prescription*—that was the word he used. We never liked to actually name the thing out loud."

Moon urged her to continue, peculiarly convinced of the importance of her story.

"He was a delivery boy. That was how he first came to us. But Coleridge became fond of the lad. Took him on walks, read him poetry. My family used to own a house in Ramsgate where we'd spend our holidays and I remember he even visited us there once. They played together on the beach. Relations with his own son had always been strained, so Ned became a kind of surrogate for him. 'Ned's my heir,' he used to say. 'My successor.'"

"Ned?"

"That was his name."

"And his surname?"

Miss Gillman finished her tea. "Love," she said. "Ned Love."

Moon and the Somnambulist stared back in slack-jawed astonishment.

"Oh," she said. "Does that mean something to you?"

*P*olitely refusing further rounds of tea, biscuits and nostalgia, they took their leave of Miss Gillman soon after. Before they went Moon gave her back the book.

"I think this belongs to you."

"Are you sure? It must be valuable."

"I've no need of it now. Please. Take it."

Gillman looked doubtful.

"I'll be offended if you don't."

She took it, of course, and sent them on their way with her blessing.

Despite his myriad faults, Moon was occasionally capable of feats of good nature, which peered out from beneath his carapace of misanthropy like a splinter of sun glimpsed through clouds.

They departed Miss Gillman's cottage and walked the half-mile or so to Highgate Cemetery. The Somnambulist—still yawning, replete from his multiple breakfasts—repeatedly asked the purpose of their journey, but Moon would give nothing away, marching ahead at a punitive pace, a marathon runner nearing the end of the race and hungry for the finish.

They arrived at the church and waded through the tall, unshorn grass of the graveyard, amongst crooked ranks of crucifixes, stones and slabs, many of them askew and at oblique angles, as though they had been displaced by some crazy ruction of the earth. There was no sense of peace there, of gentle rest well earned; rather there was a neglected, minatory air. They paused before a nondescript grave. The inscription read:

HERE LIES

SAMUEL TAYLOR COLERIDGE

1772–1834

Out of the depths I cry to thee

The Somnambulist bowed his head, oddly reverential, as though by having heard so much of the man who lay in the ground beneath them he felt an inkling of grief for his passing.

Moon showed no such sentiment. "See here," he murmured as he squatted beside the tombstone. Gently he tugged away at the grass which lay on top. The turf came up easily in his hands, unfurling in precise, regular strips, the soil beneath it freshly turned over.

The Somnambulist felt confused for the third or fourth time in as many hours.

VANDALS

he suggested hopefully.

"Too clinical. Too clever."

As the giant stared down at the ground, certain terrible possibilities began to suggest themselves.

Moon scrambled up. "It's worse than I thought. We should hurry. I have the distinct impression that time is running out."

They strode away from the churchyard, leaving the dead behind and returning, for now, to the world of the living.

Edward,

Another dispatch from the lion's den.

My second day at Love, Love, Love and Love has proved almost exactly like my first. Eight hours of clerical drudgery, a meagre half-hour for lunch and the evening spent underground in this ghastly communal recreation room, praying, listening to the poetry recitals of my colleagues and reluctantly making up a hand of whist. In order to write these words I have had to slip away to my shared bedroom. My friend——Love 893——has agreed (if asked) to make up some story about my being ill. There is only a finite amount of these people's piety I can stand.

I am astonished that Mr. Skimpole was able to secure employment for me here at all. Everyone else has been working at Love for months, many for years. As the newest recruit, I can sense a certain coolness directed towards me. Clearly there is a great deal I have yet to discover and none of them seem at all keen to tell me. Even 893, when I question her on Love's financial intricacies, becomes taciturn and close-lipped. Not, I should add, that I have shown much overt curiosity so far. As promised, I have done my utmost to appear as inconspicuous as possible and I doubt I am thought of as anything more than an unremarkable clerical assistant. Perhaps I have been less inquisitive than I ought. Perhaps my apparent lack of curiosity is in itself suspicious. Maybe I should pry a little more.

I saw Speight again today, striding along the corridor, coattails flapping self-importantly, a cloud of lackeys in his wake. The transformation is so remarkable that I fancy you would barely recognise him now—he seems half-naked without his placard. I wonder how it was that these people brought about so complete a metamorphosis. More to the point, I wonder *why*.

Even he is not the most bizarre of Love's employees. I saw the most extraordinary thing this morning: a bearded woman busying herself with books and ledgers, a freak attracting no stares of curiosity or muffled guffaws. Her natural milieu is surely the circus tent, but here she is accepted as one of us. For all its eccentricity, Love is a broad church. Although a relatively recent recruit (Love 986, I believe) she seems to be held in high regard, as a rising star, someone of whom great things are expected.

Now for my news. Towards the end of my shift I was approached by my immediate superior, a plump, hairless man named Love 487. After some small talk about how well I was settling in, he told me that I have been selected to meet, in person, the Chairman of the Board. Apparently this is considered a great honour and I was the subject of many an envious stare at dinner tonight.

It seems that the Chairman (or Love 1 as he is known to my superiors) is something of a recluse. Few of my colleagues have ever met the man (it *is* a man, of course— even Love are not quite that forward-thinking). This momentous meeting is set for the day after tomorrow. As soon as I return I shall tell you all.

Once again, I am sending this letter with 893. She has been nothing but kind and generous to me, though I cannot help but wonder how deeply mired in it all she is. Edward, I think she may have known the unfortunate Mr. Honeyman. Last night, in her sleep, I heard her murmur some lines of Shakespeare. Paris—from *Romeo and Juliet*—the fat actor's final role. "Immoderately she weeps for Tybalt's death / And therefore have I little talked of love . . ."

I have been promised that I shall be able to leave the building at the end of the week, so perhaps I will post my next message to you then.

The atmosphere seems more intense than ever. These people are waiting for something, and whatever it is, I am starting to suspect that only Love themselves will welcome its arrival.

I will write again as soon as I am able. My cordial regards to the Somnambulist.

Charlotte

Mr. Skimpole limped forlornly into the offices of the Directorate, already in a filthy temper thanks to the elevator's stubborn refusal to work and the subsequent necessity of taking the stairs. Despite his best efforts to disguise them, his symptoms were acute, inexorable, irreversible. Husky, permanently short of breath and unsteady on his feet, he was forced, like some old lush, to apply all his powers of concentration just in order to walk in a straight line. Some might find it ironic that a man whose life had been dedicated to temperance and moderation should end it so closely resembling a chronic drinker. Needless to say, I'd stop well short of making so crass and callous an observation.

Whilst dressing that morning, Skimpole had discovered the presence of five or six fresh and angry red lesions which had scattered themselves about the lower half of his body, speckling his genitals with an itchy, flaking rash. Worse still, the attacks had become more frequent and he often found himself having to leave the room whenever he felt their onset, before their pincers of pain began to rummage mercilessly about in his guts.

But he did not walk into the Directorate alone that morning. His son was with him, the boy's crutches click-clacking like ancient joints as he hobbled down the stairs and across the room to the round table. Together they cut a pitiful pair, refugees from a home for cripples, rejects from some unusually cruel workhouse.

Dedlock was already there, waiting in his usual place, but sitting beside him was a stranger—a tall, smartly dressed, smooth-featured man, emanating discretion and good taste. Set against these, Skimpole felt more spindly and puny than ever. He took a handkerchief from his pocket, wiped his forehead dry and breathed in deeply, determined not to appear weak. In the event, he just about managed a "good morning" before he lapsed into helpless spluttering.

Dedlock was staring in disbelief at the boy. "Who is this?"

Skimpole attempted a smile, only for it to fade half-formed from his lips when he saw the granite expressions of the others. "Have you met my son?" he asked as lightly as he could. The Skimpole boy tried to say something in greeting but could only produce a wretched, wheezing cough.

"Your son?" the stranger asked, sounding as though this were the first time he had ever heard the word. "Your *son*?" he repeated (probably just to check he hadn't misheard the first time). "Are you seriously telling us you've brought a child here? Fewer than three dozen men even know of the existence of this place and you bring your son? Grief, man, what do you think you're playing at?"

"I'm sorry," Skimpole stuttered. "I just wanted to be with him."

"I'm afraid you'll have to send him home," Dedlock said, his tone gentler and less aggressive than the stranger's.

Skimpole fought back tears. "I can't. I need him with me. He mustn't go home alone. I'm sure we were followed on our way here. Oh, we shook them off, but this isn't the first time. Not by a long shot." Frantic, he turned to Dedlock. "Don't you agree? Whoever they are, they've set the dogs on us."

"Send the child home. Or I'll have him removed." The smooth-featured man clicked his fingers and four fake Chinamen materialised obediently at the back of the room.

Dedlock tried to defuse the tension. He gestured towards the stranger. "This is Mr. Trotman."

"I'm from the Ministry," the man said darkly, as though that explained it all.

Skimpole seemed uncharacteristically cowed. "I see. How can we help?"

"The Directorate has recently come under my purview . . ." He tailed off delicately. "There will be changes."

"Changes?"

"Remove the boy," Trotman demanded. "Then we can talk."

Skimpole bent down and whispered in his son's ear: "Go upstairs. Wait for me there."

The lad nodded and lurched uncertainly away, manfully tackling the mountainous staircase alone and unaided. Throughout his son's short life, Skimpole had never ceased to marvel at his courage.

"Take a seat," Trotman said once the child had left. "This won't take long."

Meekly, Skimpole did as he was told.

"I shan't be coy," Trotman said. "I'm a plain man." (Judging from the expensive cut of his clothes and general air of affluence, this was transparently untrue.) "I expect frankness from my subordinates and I intend to grant you that same courtesy."

Dedlock and Skimpole nodded, mock-appreciative.

"The Directorate has become a liability. Your methods are

unorthodox, your agents unaccountable, your security laughably easy to penetrate. Slattery should never have got within spitting distance of this room."

Dedlock began to protest but Trotman motioned for him to be silent. "Let me finish. You'll have your say in due course." He cleared his throat before continuing. "I query the necessity for all this cloak-and-dagger behaviour. Hiding beneath a butcher's shop in Limehouse. All these agents of yours running around in fancy dress." He tutted, appalled at the flamboyance, the show-manship of the place. "I'm sure if that particular foible of yours had never become policy, Slattery would never have got so far as he did. I have to be honest, gentlemen—the perception amongst my colleagues is that the Directorate is run by men who delight in wasting time, money and resources and who take altogether too much pleasure in dressing up."

"Can I say—" Dedlock began.

"You may not," Trotman countered briskly. "You know the correct procedure for registering your views and I think it's time you used it. You've operated above the law for too long. I understand my predecessor had some sentimental attachment to you. Rest assured, I do not share that weakness."

"What will you do?" Skimpole asked quietly.

"The Directorate is to be dissolved, effective immediately. If it ever becomes necessary to reactivate it, I can assure you it will be under different management." Trotman softened. "Gentlemen, you needn't worry. Your pensions have been arranged. You'll both be provided for. And if I might be entirely honest, Mr. Skim-pole, you really don't look well. A man in your condition ought never to have been allowed so much responsibility. I suspect re-tirement will suit you."

"Haven't you read our reports?" Skimpole protested. "We've got two days until the city comes under attack."

Trotman favoured the albino with a withering look. "I think

this crisis of yours has been vastly overstated. I've seen no hard evidence of a conspiracy. I've had absolutely no intelligence of any substance from you whatsoever. I find your reports to be recklessly alarmist and I seriously question your methods of information-gathering. I'm appalled that any government department should rely upon the word of a fortune-teller. We owe the Vigilance Committee a debt of gratitude in that affair, I think."

"It will happen," Skimpole insisted. "Innocenti was right."

Trotman smirked. "I doubt we need concern ourselves with a nebulous threat conjured up by a table-rapper, do you? In my opinion, this Mrs. Bagshaw is far better off in America. They're a credulous people on that side of the Atlantic. No doubt she'll make a killing." Trotman got to his feet. "Pleasant though it is chatting with you, gentlemen, I have to go. I've three other meetings this morning."

Dedlock stumbled up. "Please—"

Trotman waved him away. "If you wish to register a complaint you may speak to my secretary. Thank you for your attention. My department will be in touch shortly. Good day to you."

Trotman sauntered from the room, whistling softly to himself (he was the kind of man who whistled a lot), apparently oblivious to the devastation he had left in his wake. Uniquely, Dedlock was lost for words.

"It's outrageous," he said at last. "They can't do this."

Skimpole didn't seem to hear. "Stupid," he murmured. "He's left the city open to attack."

"We'll appeal. Speak to his superiors. Go to the top."

Skimpole's voice sounded distant and muffled. "Won't do any good. He needs to be dealt with immediately. I know of only one body with such power. Highly unofficial . . . and not without an element of risk."

"Who?" Dedlock asked eagerly.

"You know their names. I shall not speak them here."

Dedlock sank slowly back onto his chair, suddenly ashen, the ruddy health draining from his face. "You're not serious?"

"Afraid so."

"You've no idea what they can do."

Skimpole leant forward. "I can't allow all this to be torn down. It's the only thing left to prove I ever lived."

"Bit morbid of you, old man."

The albino staggered up. "I must go. My son is waiting. Leave this to me."

Dedlock let him go, not trying to stop him despite his suspicions about what he was planning. He snapped his fingers and one of the ersatz Chinamen appeared at his side. "You heard everything?"

The man bowed. "Yes, sah."

"Well, then. Bring me a bottle of brandy." He grinned. "Two glasses."

Skimpole had barely got clear of the room before the attack hit. He grabbed at the stair rails and jackknifed in agony, clutching his stomach impotently and biting hard on his tongue to stop himself from crying out. He hoped desperately that Dedlock wouldn't leave the room and find him like this. As soon as he was able, once the worst of the pain had passed, he began the ascent to the shop above. He arrived to find his son chatting amicably to the proprietor, mercifully innocent of all that had transpired below.

"Thank you," he said, wheezing his way across to the boy. "Thank you for looking after my son."

"My pleasure."

Skimpole began to shepherd his charge to the door when he stopped and turned back. "Do you know," he said, "I've never asked your name?"

The Chinaman grinned. "No, sir." So he told him his name, something monosyllabic that began with a *W*. The albino forgot it, of course, almost immediately, but at least, just once, he had asked.

Out on the street, the two of them hailed a cab. Several passed by empty, refusing to accept so grotesque-looking a cargo, and it was some time before one finally stopped.

"Where are we going?" asked the boy as they clambered aboard.

"A special place, underground."

"What's it called?"

"I'd be breaking the rules if I told you."

"Oh." The child looked disappointed, but even at his young age he had begun to appreciate the necessity for discretion.

Skimpole ruffled the boy's hair affectionately and decided to relent. No time for secrets any more. "The Stacks," he whispered. "They're called the Stacks."

*M*r. Cribb peered across the café table at Edward Moon.

"It's good to see you," he said. "Last time we met you weren't quite this friendly."

"We have to be quick. The Somnambulist doesn't know I'm here."

"Would he mind?"

"He has this . . . It sounds ridiculous . . . This *bête noire* about you."

"Really? Do you have any idea why?"

"None whatsoever."

"Ah, well."

"Listen, you tug me along through London, you tease me with clues and intimations. You seem to delight in cropping up in my life unannounced and tantalising me with slivers of the truth.

Why, sir? To what purpose? That business by the docklands—
you led me to Lud on purpose, I'm sure of it."

"I did?" Cribb looked genuinely bemused. He scratched at his
left hand, which, Moon noticed, was bandaged up as though he
had been recently injured. "Rather, you mean I will. You seem to
forget that your past is my future." He smirked. "And vice
versa."

"What was it? A prank? Are you laughing at me?"

He tutted. "I've no idea. You ought to have asked me at the
time."

"I feel as though I am travelling into the dark and that it is you
who has led me there."

"Come, come. There's no need for all that."

Moon snorted and, at long last, Cribb did his best to explain.

"Perhaps you're right. Maybe I do owe you an explanation."
He sighed. "I've seen the future, Edward. Not by travelling but
by living. Forgive me, I'm not sure how to phrase these con-
cepts in a way that will make sense to you . . . Look at it like
this. Yours is a single chronology, rosy and predictable. Tuesday follows Monday, Wednesday follows Tuesday. Not for me.
I walk backwards through my life. I wake on a Wednesday
morning and the day before was Thursday. My life is a constant
slipping away, a losing touch. From your perspective we will
meet twice more. The next time I shall not be myself, the time
after that I'll barely recognise you. I'll say goodbye the day we
met."

"Ridiculous."

"You know it's true."

"Then you know what happens to us? To the Somnambulist
and me, to the city?"

"Know but can't tell."

"Why?"

"There are rules I cannot break. My position is a privileged one, and though I have the utmost respect for you and your methods, I will not jeopardise it."

"Do you ever speak plainly?"

"Believe it or not, I am never deliberately oblique. I have always done my best for you."

"Was Innocenti right? If she was, we've only two days left."

"Well, then. Perhaps we should save the recriminations for another time. Why am I here?"

"I need your help."

"I'd assumed as much."

"There is a man I have to locate, the final link in the chain I have forged."

"His name?" Cribb asked, sounding as though he already knew the answer.

"Love." Moon watched his companion intently for any sign of recognition. "Ned Love."

"Ah." Cribb sounded pleased.

"Ah?" Moon repeated, infuriated. "What do you mean by 'ah'? Do you know him?"

"I can tell you only that you're close. Very close. No more than that."

"But can you find him? He'd be an old man by now."

"If he's somewhere in the city, then yes, you may rely upon me. As soon as I have him I'll send word."

"Excellent."

"Well, then." The ugly man got to his feet.

"Thomas?"

He turned back.

"Please. Tell me how it ends."

"Sorry." Cribb smiled. "You've no idea how complicated it is being me." He touched the brim of his hat and walked from the café.

Moon settled the bill and wandered home, troubled in his mind and anxious for a resolution. This case, singular though it had been, had hung over him for far too long. High time to bring an end to it.

E,

I apologise if this letter is to be shorter than the rest. Love 893 has been removed from my room and a new woman put here in her place. Older by far, a long-term employee, Love 101 is a hatchet-faced crone who has assumed an immediate dislike of me and seems determined to act more as my gaoler than my roommate. Why 893 was summarily evicted I am not entirely certain, though naturally I have my suspicions.

I am watched all the time and I am no longer permitted to absent myself from the evening prayer meetings. It seems more and more as though I am a prisoner here, one neither liked nor respected by my fellow inmates. Needless to say, I do not sleep well—my nights are fitful, my dreams troubled.

Tomorrow I am summoned into the presence of the Chairman of the Board. His name is spoken amongst the faithful in the most absurdly hushed and reverential tones—he is as royalty to these people, small god of their little realm.

He is Love 1, the alpha company man, Ur-Love. It seems as though a thousand is some predetermined limit for the company, a quota to be met. That number is almost attained, and as soon as a Love 1000 is found it seems certain that whatever it is these people have been planning will come to fruition.

I cannot for the life of me make out how much in earnest these people are. At times I am convinced that, with their poetry and prayers, they are harmless zealots who delight in schemes and plots which can have no reality beyond their own fevered minds. But more and more I feel as though I am in danger here, that my colleagues are working towards some terrible and devastating end, some outrage to be perpetrated upon the city. Whatever evidence led you to place me here (and I refuse to acknowledge any part the charlatan Bagshaw may have played in the matter) you did well to heed it. Whatever they are planning, they mean for it to happen soon.

My work was as uninteresting today as ever but I did happen to stumble upon one small item of note. Whilst working through an especially tedious ledger, I came upon a record of the company's transactions. Until recently Love, Love, Love and Love were buying up a great deal of property underground. Disused pieces of the sewer system mostly and some stretches of tunnels abandoned by the railway. I have no doubt that you will find this suggestive, though its precise significance eludes me at present.

I shall endeavour to find out more when I am able, but for now I must tread carefully. I am under close observation and I should not like to guarantee my own safety in the event of their discovering my true purpose here. When may I leave? I feel like the dim heroine of some shilling shocker walking blithely into peril.

But I must go. My time alone has ended. I hear my warder approaching.

C.

16

$\mathcal{N}$o man alive knew the city better than Thomas Cribb. Like an old and faithful lover, he knew her every curve and crevice, her every aperture and inlet, all the intimate places of her body. He was custodian of her secret and hidden terrain. In a few hours he was able to find any individual in London from the lowliest street-sweeper to a peer of the realm, regardless of how well they believed themselves to be hidden. He boasted that on numerous occasions he had assisted the police in precisely this manner, bringing to justice dozens of wanted criminals who, in their vanity, had believed themselves disappeared for good.

But Ned Love was a different matter. It was almost as though the city were hiding him. No one had ever proved as elusive—not even in the far-flung future when (Cribb assured me) the metropolis would be still more densely populated than it is today.

Consequently, it was late in the afternoon on the following day when Moon and the Somnambulist received word from the ugly man, and by the time they found themselves standing on the threshold of their quarry's singular residence, light was already fading.

Ned Love lived in a low, mean district of the city. His house, with its boarded-up windows, its doors heavily bolted and barred, had the appearance of being utterly abandoned, so much so that the Somnambulist angrily scribbled that Cribb might have sold them a pup and led them on a fruitless expedition for some mischievous purpose of his own. Ignoring the suggestion, Moon knocked as loudly as he was able. "Mr. Love!"

The giant looked carefully about, checking to make sure they were unobserved. In such an area as this, surely it did not pay to draw attention to themselves.

Moon was about to shout again when the letter box creaked open. Suspicious eyes peered out. "Go away," a voice croaked.

"Mr. Love?"

"Who wants to know?"

"My name is Edward Moon. This is my associate, the Somnambulist."

"Don't like visitors. Got no time for guests."

Moon looked at the house, derelict and shuttered-up as if awaiting demolition. It astonished even him (no stranger to unconventional accommodation) that anyone could seriously conceive of living there.

"It's vital that we speak to you," Moon said urgently. "Many lives could be at stake."

"Go away. You can't get in. Shan't let you."

"I have . . . questions. Concerning the poet."

"Poet? Don't know any poets."

"You knew him when you were a boy," Moon snapped, his patience already wearing thin. "I've no time for games. If my sources are correct, we've little more than twenty-four hours before the city is attacked."

"Is it come, then, at last?" He muttered something, too quiet for anyone else to hear, then: "I feared it must be close."

Moon bent down to address the letter box. "Mr. Love. This is not the most comfortable position in which to conduct this conversation. Please let us in. We need your help."

"Wait." The face vanished, the letter box snapped shut and groans and clankings ensued as an improbable number of locks and bolts were undone. All this took far longer than it ought—Barabbas himself had not been so secure within Newgate's walls as was Ned Love at home. In the event of a fire he would assuredly perish before he could open his own front door. Moon made a mental note not to inform Mr. Skimpole of the fact—given the man's predilection for arson, it might put some nasty ideas in his head.

At last the door swung open and a very old man ventured out to greet them. His face was lined and weathered like a piece of fruit left in the sun too long; he was dressed in an ancient brown suit which showed unmistakable signs of having been habitually slept in, and clutched in his left hand a half-finished bottle of noxiously cheap whisky. "I am Love," he said grandly. "But you may call me Ned."

They followed him inside and he led them down a corridor which smelt of mildew and animal hair, into what must once have been a sizeable morning room. If gas had ever been laid on, it had long since been disconnected and the place was lit by a dozen or so candles, flickering half-heartedly against the gloom, their wax puddling onto the floor. A mass of blankets had been pushed up against the wall, a small stove sat in the centre of the room and the remnants of several rough meals lay scattered about on the ground. *Surely a magnet to vermin*, thought the Somnambulist (his instinct for cleanliness and hygiene cultivated over the years by the meticulous house-sense of Mrs. Grossmith).

"Take a seat, gentlemen, please." Love scuttled about them, stepping nimbly over the debris with a dexterity that belied his advanced years. "Might I offer you a drink?"

"I'll have whatever you're drinking."

Love produced a grubby glass and poured the conjuror a tot of whisky. "And for your friend?"

MILK

"Milk?" He looked astonished. "My, what a curious request. Well, never let it be said that Ned Love doesn't do his best for his visitors. Invited or otherwise." After hunting around under blankets and pillows, sending up great clouds of dust and feathers in the process, Love emerged with a filthy milk bottle, a quarter full of a grey-green liquid. He passed it to the Somnambulist. "You're welcome to this," he said doubtfully. "Though I can't vouch for its quality."

The giant took the bottle, sniffed it with barely concealed disdain, then placed it discreetly to one side.

"Well, then," Love began once they were all seated. "What can I do for you? I ought not to have admitted you but you did seem so very keen. Should I be flattered? The fact you've found me at all, you know, speaks volumes for your tenacity."

"Why do you live like this?"

"I know it must strike you as strange. I often think so myself when I am awakened in the morning, usually by some small creature or other nibbling at my toes for its breakfast, roving about my cuticles for its eggs and b. Ned, I say, Ned, old man, why do you live like this? Good God, I think. This isn't worthy of you. You'd planned so much more than this."

Moon arched an eyebrow. "Quite."

"It was always my intention, you see, after I was removed, that I should shut myself away from the world entirely. I had a fancy to become a hermit, here in the midst of the city. An anchorite in the old tradition. I decided to abjure the material world in favour of a meditative life. I had discovered the eternal truth that one cannot serve God and Mammon both. I'd hoped never to see or speak to a human soul again. Though perhaps I didn't think the matter through all that thoroughly. I have to make frequent excursions outside. For provisions, you understand. Oh, only for the most absolute essentials. I'm not the kind of hermit who goes dashing out every time he fancies a loaf. Absolutely not. No, no, I'm terribly strict with myself. Try to limit my forays to once a week or so. Still, that *does* mean I'm not quite the ideal anchorite. Not that that's my only sin. I get visitors, too. Men like yourselves. By rights, I oughtn't to speak at all. I've started to wonder recently whether I'm really cut out to be a recluse. But despite it all I continue to aspire. Saint Simeon, you know, spent thirty-seven years up a pillar. Best years of his life, he said. Remarkable, don't you think? Absolutely remarkable."

"Mr. Love," Moon said gently, "I need to ask you some specific questions. You mentioned that you were 'removed.' May we assume that this was from the corporation Love, Love, Love and Love?"

The man paused to take a noisy swig from his liquor bottle. "So you know about the firm? My, you have been diligent. What else do you know? Or should I say . . ."—he wiped his mouth with a grubby sleeve of his jacket—"what do you *think* you know?"

"I know that the city is in imminent danger from a plot masterminded by Love in collusion with a religious group known as the Church of the Summer Kingdom. I know that this same firm is responsible for the deaths of Cyril Honeyman and Philip Dunbar, for the disappearances of those men's mothers, for the execution of Barabbas and for the assassination attempt upon the heads of the Directorate. I know that they are utterly without scruple and that they will stop at nothing to achieve their ends. The only thing I do not know is the nature of their plan."

"Or why," Love breathed softly. "You don't know that."

"You don't deny it, then?"

"Deny what?"

"That the firm which bears your name is behind the blood-shed."

"I'd hoped and prayed they wouldn't stoop to this. You must believe me when I say that the company in its present form represents the most monstrous perversion of its original conception." He paused for breath. "You've guessed no doubt that I am the founder of Love, Love, Love and Love."

"We had assumed as much."

"You will know, too, then, that the firm was established according to the stipulations of a will made by Samuel Coleridge. To enable you to understand his motives in making such a curious request, I shall have to explain it from the beginning."

"Pray be as precise as you can."

The old man took another long swig of whisky. "You were quite correct, of course, when you said that I knew the poet when I was a child. In the last years of his life he dwelt in Highgate with a kindly medical man—one Dr. Gillman. In fact, the doctor's young daughter lives there still. Bit of a looker. She might be able to furnish you with more facts about the old days. My memory has grown a little hazy."

"It was she who told us of you."

Love seemed not to have heard. "I was a lad of eight or nine when I met him, from a humble family, a harum-scarum youth, no great shakes at my studies and always with an eye on making money. The Gillmans took me on from time to time as an errand boy—odd jobs, little chores and suchlike." Another swig of whisky. "I'd worked there for a month before I met the poet. He lived upstairs in the garret room and more often than not he kept to his bed. You have to appreciate that by this time he was almost completely addicted to opium. Gillman had done everything in his power to curb the craving, but so far as I could see it never came to anything. The old man was completely in thrall to the stuff, and it was his need for the poison which first drew me to him. I'd been carrying out some minor task or other for the doctor's wife when Coleridge called me upstairs. He had an errand for me, he said, and would pay handsomely for it. He ordered me to hurry down to the shop and buy what he referred to as his 'prescription.' He'd never call it by its real name, you understand. He was almost superstitious about that. Anyway, I did as I was asked. Gillman turned a blind eye, the old man got what he wanted and we all of us were happy. It became a regular arrangement, and over time the poet and I grew friendly, became pals. He loved to talk, you see—he was a great man for a chat—and I was his favourite audience." Love sighed. "The things he told me. When I knew him he was close to death, but still he enraptured. How he must have been at the height of his powers I cannot imagine." Another retreat to the whisky bottle.

"He spoke of the adventures of his youth, of his disastrous spell in the army, of his time at university where he conjured up the ghost of Thomas Gray. Oh, he could spin a yarn. Of course, I knew they were exaggerated like as not, embroidered for effect, but still I lapped them up. What boy wouldn't? He even took me on holiday. We walked together on the beach at Ramsgate. But what he spoke of most of all was an old dream, something he had imagined as a young man with his best and closest friends. *Pantisocracy*. That was what they called it. No doubt you've heard the name?"

Moon inclined his head to suggest that he had not.

"It was a scheme of enormous audacity, an experiment, he said, in human perfectibility. There were twelve of them, fresh from the university. They planned to create the perfect society, to

quit England and live in America on the banks of the Susquehanna in absolute self-sufficiency. It was to be a utopia based
equally upon agriculture and poetry. They thought they'd discuss metaphysics as they chopped wood, criticise verse as they
hunted buffalo, write sonnets whilst they followed the plough."
Love laughed, all but clapping his hands in glee. "Wonderful!
Quite, quite perfect."

"It sounds admirable," Moon said briskly. "If a little idealis-
tic."

"Ah well, there you have it. That's the rub. It could never have
worked. They fell out over money, weren't able to raise enough
capital to make the trip. The whole project was abandoned."

"I'm afraid I've yet to see a connection with the firm."

"The abject failure of Pantisocracy had become the old man's
greatest regret, and towards the end it came to dominate his
thoughts above all other things. He felt he had squandered his
only opportunity to change the world for the better. And as we
grew closer, the old man somehow got hold of the notion that I
was his successor, that I'd be the one to succeed where he had
failed—that I would revive Pantisocracy. I knew he was dying,
of course, so I did the decent thing and told him what he wanted
to hear—that I would do everything I could to carry out the
plan, that I'd move to America and live out his fantasy. All bun-
kum as far as I was concerned but if it made a dying man happy
I reckoned it could do no harm. What I didn't realise was this:
Coleridge was not a rich man, but most of what he possessed
was placed in my care for me to do with as I would when I eventually came of age. It's only due to the old man's generosity that
I was able to go to one of the universities. The remainder, he
said, should go to the formation of a company dedicated to the
resurrection of his Pantisocratic dream. In his will he insisted
that I name it after myself. I can see you wondering, Mr. Moon.
There are four Loves in the title. Time was, I had sons of my

own." At this mention of his family, he reached again for the bottle.

"I graduated with a good degree and found, much to my astonishment, that I had a way with figures. I did as I'd been told and established the company according to Mr. Coleridge's instructions. But I could muster little interest in Pantisocracy, and whilst the firm ostensibly remained loyal to his intentions, I was able to make a good deal of money over the years by investing in property and playing the markets. At the peak of our success, I employed nearly a hundred staff and enjoyed considerable profits."

"You betrayed the ideals of your benefactor for the sake of money."

Love seemed upset. "Harsh words, Mr. Moon. Very harsh. You have to understand that the old man was very ill when he died. Some might say not quite in his right mind. I did what I was able with my inheritance and doubled it—doubled it dozens of times over. I'm not a selfish or an avaricious man. I was generous with our earnings. There was a time when I was one of the most prominent philanthropists in London. I did feel guilty. But a few thousand a year will help a man forget his duty."

"So what happened?"

"Five years ago, the golden times had passed. I'd got too old to run the company and, like me, it had grown somewhat decrepit. None of my boys showed any real interest in succeeding me, and I was at my wits' end as to what to do when I was approached by a consortium. They were men of God, they said, representatives of an organisation called the Church of the Summer Kingdom. I see you recognise the name. So did I, as it happens, since I had donated money to their cause on more than one occasion. Their names were most improbable—Donald McDonald and the Reverend Doctor Tan. They said they were devotees of Mr. Coleridge, said they venerated the man and were almost embarrassing in their effusive deference to me—one of the last men alive, they said, who had actually known the poet personally. They knew all about the will, about the old man's plans for the company, and they made me an offer. They promised to keep the firm operating exactly as it was, to retain all my staff and instate me as Chairman Emeritus on the one condition that we return to Coleridge's original intentions. They actually planned in the fullness of time to live as Pantisocrats. It was an old man's weakness and no doubt you'll think me foolish, but I took them at their word. I see now that they were silver-tongued rogues, but I had wearied of the place and I felt guilty, so I allowed them some measure of power. It seemed the right thing to do."

"Let me guess," Moon said. "The church took absolute control of the company and ousted you."

"They threw me out onto the street. I thought the only path left to me was one of meditation and repentance. And so you find me like this, an unsuccessful anchorite."

"Could you not appeal? Surely the company still belonged to you?"

"They had clever lawyers. In my stupidity I had signed documents which gave them complete control. I admit it—I was thoroughly gulled. Cuckoos, Mr. Moon. Cuckoos in the nest. And my boys were under their spell. I was told they took part in my downfall, though I can't bring myself to believe it. Can you blame me for hiding myself here?" He reached again for the whisky bottle and drained it dry.

"Courage, Mr. Love. What changes did they make in the firm? This McDonald, this Reverend Tan?"

"Those are not their real names, are they?" Love asked, rather sadly.

"Aliases, I'm sure of it. But tell me—what happened to Love, Love, Love and Love?"

"From the start, they went against their word. They fired most of my staff and brought in their own men—and women, if

you can credit it. Oh, they were a queer lot and no mistake. Peculiar creatures, all of them. Some looked like they'd been
plucked straight from the gutter. Knowing Tan, I wouldn't even
put that past him. Then they started building. Underground.
Lodgings, they said, for the staff. By the time I left, most of
them were living there. Names, too. They began to frown on
names, of all things, started insisting everyone take a number.
Sinister. Sinister and most unchristian. I only wish I might have
stopped it."

"I have an associate on the inside at the firm and it would seem
that since your departure matters have got very much worse."

"Worse?"

"The place sounds more like a commune than a business.
They've all been numbered. Branded like cattle. They seem to be
waiting for something. Like an army before a battle, so I hear.
Tell me, Mr. Love—what are they planning?"

Love seemed exhausted by the effort of talking for so long and
the drink had finally begun to work upon him. He slumped back,
confused. "I'm not entirely certain. Once, in his cups, Tan made
insinuations about his real plans. The old man would not have approved. You can take my word on that. I may not have done as he
wished but I would never go so far as the church. Something terrible is afoot. But tell me, who is this ally of yours inside the
firm?"

"My sister."

"Your sister?" Appalled, Love struggled to his feet only to lose
his balance and collapse onto the ground. "You don't know what
you've done."

"Explain."

Love shook his head. "How could you send your own sister in
there? You'll have to get her out immediately. She's in terrible
danger."

"Danger?"

"They have a way of . . . turning you. They're extremely persuasive. She's not safe. You must fetch her at once."

"Are you sure?"

"Go now, gentlemen. I shall wait for you here."

Moon stood up and gestured for the Somnambulist to join him. "We'll come back."

"Please go. I couldn't bear it if something awful happened." Love's speech had become slurred and when he'd finished speaking he rolled slowly onto his back, like a turtle, close to passing out.

Moon and the Somnambulist left him there, and at something approaching a run they headed back towards the old city and the black gates of Love.

The Archivist was filing a series of reports on the notorious Finchley Cannibal of 1864 and thinking about retiring early for the night when she was disturbed by a sudden sound: the telltale clump and clatter of visitors feeling their way into the gloom of the Stacks.

"Archivist?" The voice was familiar.

"Mr. Skimpole? Is that you?"

More graceless sound and fury. Strange. This one was usually so quiet, practically feline in his stealth. "It's me."

"You have someone with you?"

"My son," the voice admitted.

The Archivist was annoyed. "You know the rules. Visitors not admitted under any circumstances. I might also add that it's very late and that you haven't made an appointment."

"I need your help."

Something was different about his voice. There was a hoarse quality to it, a strained sound and a huskiness which had never been there before.

"My apologies. I may have put your life in danger even coming here."

"You're not making sense, Mr. Skimpole."

"The Directorate is in danger. Dedlock and I . . . We're targets. Someone's put a killer on our trail. An assassin they call the Mongoose."

The old woman tried not to smile.

"Worst of all. I'm . . . I'm not feeling my best. I should have seen you yesterday. But I was so very tired."

"How can I help?" the Archivist asked finally, sensing the true seriousness of the situation.

"Desperate measures, I fear. I need to contact them."

"Who?"

"I shan't speak their names here, but you know who I mean."

"I suppose I do."

"I need the Directory."

"Things are really that bad?"

"Worse."

The Archivist tried to warn him. "You're not the first to have made this mistake, Mr. Skimpole. Those creatures . . . They say they are for hire. Offer their services as mercenaries or killers or solvers of problems. But you won't be able to control them. And you'll never be able to afford their fee."

"I've heard they carry out certain worthy tasks for free."

"Oh, Skimpole. Nothing is for free. And the cost of hiring them is always far too great."

"I'm begging you."

"They're impossibly dangerous, Mr. Skimpole. They're agents of chaos and destruction. No man has ever employed them and escaped unscathed."

Someone coughed. The child.

"Please," Skimpole pleaded. "My son is not well."

The old woman sighed. "Come with me." She moved away

into the permanent dusk of the Stacks. "I keep it locked up. It's on the Home Office's forbidden list, you know. A black book. In my opinion, even here it's dangerous." She reached a glass-fronted cabinet, unlocked it with the key she kept hung about her neck and took out a slim, leather-bound book. "I had hoped never to touch this again."

Skimpole grabbed it from her eagerly. "I'm grateful."

"All you need is there. But be careful. They will lie and do their best to trick you. Whatever you wish to ask of them, they will twist it to their own advantage."

But her warning fell on deaf ears. The albino and his son hurried away, stumbled noisily up the steps and out of the Stacks. As the Archivist locked the cabinet she felt an icy pang of certainty that she had just spoken to Mr. Skimpole for the last time.

*V*ast, grand and marble-floored, the foyer of Love, Love, Love and Love was approximately the size and shape of a ballroom, filled with echoes and empty space. An elaborate design was set into the centre of the floor—Moon and the Somnambulist lacked the perspective to appreciate it, but had they viewed it from a better vantage point, from that ubiquitous, hypothetical bird's eye, they would have recognised the pattern immediately: styled in marble and stone, a black five-petalled flower. On the far side of the room, otherwise deserted and devoid of the whirling masses for which it had surely been intended, a small, dark pinprick of a man sat upright behind his desk.

The receptionist looked up as they walked in and gave them only the briefest of glances before dismissing them with that uninterested sneer which typifies his breed. Moon and the Somnambulist walked towards him, the tap-tap of their shoes ringing out accusingly like gunfire. The receptionist tutted audibly.

"My name is Edward Moon."

"Really?" the man asked, polite—scrupulously so—but somehow managing to convey an utter contempt for anyone who had ever stood on the wrong side of his desk.

"I wish to see a member of your staff."

"Oh?" The incredulity of the man's tone suggested that Moon had asked for an audience at the Vatican. "Does sir have an appointment?"

"I do not."

"Then I'm afraid I am quite unable to help you."

"It's my sister—"

"Here at Love, sir, one needs an appointment even to visit one's sister." All this delivered in the same infuriatingly cool, automaton tone—impossibly bland but with just the barest hint of amusement.

Moon persisted. "Can I make an appointment?"

"Of course, sir." With a crisp flourish, the man produced a sheet of foolscap. "If sir would just be so kind as to complete this form . . . I should add that no one will be available to see you until next Wednesday at the earliest." He leant forwards as if about to confide some great secret. "This is our busiest time of year."

Moon was beginning to sound agitated. "I need to see her today. Her name is Charlotte Moon."

"I'm terribly sorry, sir. We've no one here of that name."

"I know she works here, man. Don't be obstructive."

"I assure you, sir, I have never heard the name before in my life and I am intimately acquainted with all nine hundred and ninety-eight of my colleagues. Besides, as you may be aware, here at Love, Love, Love and Love we have dispensed with the cumbersome necessity of surnames. Here we all share the same glorious appellation. I myself am Love two hundred and forty-five. Though I permit my closest intimates to call me 245."

"My sister is Love nine hundred and ninety-nine."

The receptionist smiled. "Sir must be mistaken. Love nine hundred and ninety-nine is a writer of sentimental dramas for the stage, formerly known as 'Squib' Wilson."

"Were you born this aggravating or did you learn it here?"

"I like to think a little of both."

"Where's my sister? I'm quite prepared to beat it out of you."

Love 245 looked pained. "There's no need for sir to lower himself to threats. I have only to call for attention and a dozen of my colleagues will leap to my aid. You'll be charged and prosecuted for trespass and threatening an employee. Consequently, we'll be quite within our legal rights to take punitive action. The last man who asked the wrong questions at my desk spent nine months in a mental hospital. Even now he's convinced that his mother's Labrador plots to kill him."

"I wish to see my sister."

"Sir must be mistaken. Sir's sister is not here."

"Is she downstairs, is that it? In those catacombs you've got down there?"

The receptionist looked at the Somnambulist. "Is your friend quite well?"

The giant glared back.

"One hesitates to suggest such a thing, of course, but one has to ask—has sir been drinking?"

With an enormous effort of will, Moon swallowed his rage and turned back towards the door. "I shall return," he called out as he walked away. "I swear I'll uncover what's going on here."

"Goodbye, sir. So sorry I wasn't able to be more helpful."

As Moon and the Somnambulist reached the exit, a man walked in from the street, shoving past them in his haste to reach reception. Shiny and smart, a briefcase clutched in one hand, he resembled a black beetle forced upright and dressed by Savile Row. Every inch the Love employee—but not, as it happened, a stranger.

Moon shouted his name. "Speight!"

The man turned back to reveal a face no longer unkempt but

clean-shaven, even handsome, the grime of the doorstep wiped away. He stared at the conjuror and the giant as though they were a couple of acquaintances he hadn't seen for years, their faces faintly familiar but their names impossible to recall. "Can I help you?"

"I shouldn't trouble yourself, sir," murmured the receptionist.

"No trouble."

"Speight!" Moon cried again. "It *is* you."

The man walked back towards them. "Mr. Moon, isn't it? And the Somnambulist."

"Surely you remember us."

"I'd rather you call me nine hundred and three," Speight said flatly.

"I prefer Speight."

"Then we have an impasse."

The Somnambulist scribbled on his board.

WHY YOU HERE

"I'm working," the man said tersely. "This is a busy time for the corporation."

"So I'm told. But what I don't understand is why."

"Good day, gentlemen. Pleasant though it is to stand here and chatter, I'm afraid I am required elsewhere."

"Tell me what you're planning."

"Be careful," he hissed, his blank façade momentarily replaced by something approximating the Speight of old. "A great tide is about to break upon the city. Stand aside, sir. Or be drowned." And with this, the ex-tramp strode away, vanishing into the depths of the building.

Moon walked out into the street, utterly bemused by what had just taken place.

WHAT NOW

"Back to Ned. There are questions I need answered. After that . . . You've no objections to breaking the law, I take it?"

The Somnambulist shook his head.

"Well, then. Tonight we break into Love."

Something had changed when they arrived back at Ned Love's hermitage. Everything seemed the same—the windows were still boarded up, the place tightly sealed, locked and barred—but with one notable exception: the front door gaped wide open.

"I suppose he might have gone out," Moon said doubtfully.

The Somnambulist shot him a cynical look and pushed past into the house. If there was to be danger, the giant always insisted on being the first to face it.

The place seemed undisturbed at first, but as they moved back along the corridor, Moon felt a growing conviction that something was not as it ought to be.

Consequently, neither man was surprised when they found the body.

Poor Ned Love, an empty whisky bottle in his hand, lay slumped against the wall, crooked, ugly and unnatural in death. Moon thought he heard movement when he entered the room. It was only later he realised that this almost certainly denoted the scurrying departure of those rats and other vermin which had come already to nibble on the corpse.

"Mr. Love?" Moon crouched down beside the body. "Ned?" For tradition's sake he checked the body's pulse.

DEAD

"Afraid so."

FROTTLED

Moon tried hard not to sound impressed. "How can you tell?"

The Somnambulist gestured towards the pinkish marks at the man's throat, fading but still visible.

"Wouldn't have been difficult given the amount he'd drunk. Evidently he said too much."

LOVE

"I'd put money on it."

Leaving poor Ned where he lay, they strode back out into the open air. "This is it," said Moon once they were outside, perversely sounding almost cheerful. "Time for the end-game."

$\mathcal{B}$eneath the city, the old man dreams, turning uncomfortably on his steel cot, drifting out of sleep and into a strange half-wakefulness, an unhappy hallucinatory consciousness. Faintly, he becomes aware of movement around him, of faces glimpsed through the murk of sleep, lips forming his name, eyes watching. Often he feels that he is being scrutinised and observed and that the manner of those who watch him is weirdly reverential— pilgrims at the foot of his bed come like the Magi to pay homage and to worship.

As before, his dreams are filled with the boy Ned, with glimpses from his past, but now they seem to darken, showing him old mistakes come back to him in evil new shapes. Old hopes, too, the paradise of Pantisocracy turned sulphurous and rank. He sees a feverish mob of Pantisocrats careering through the streets, eager for blood, slaughtering all who stand in their path. And others with them, strange, incongruous figures, mon-sters in the skin of schoolboys who turn upon the dreamers and rip them to shreds. A world he barely recognises congealing into bloodshed.

Pity the dreamer! If only he had known what was unravelling above him. If only he had known what Mr. Skimpole was about to set into motion, of the serpent who had entwined himself around poor Grossmith, of the dark path down which Moon and the Somnambulist were travelling. Had he but known the scope of what awaited him, I have little doubt but that he would have remained safely underground, away from the corruption of the surface. He would have stayed asleep. He would have stayed, blissfully, in Love.

17

A little over an hour after the death of Ned Love, two advertisements appeared in the personal columns of the *Echo*, the *Gazette*, the *Times* and the *London Chronicle* (evening editions only).

The first read:

INFORMATION WANTED

Anyone who works or has worked

in the Underground tunnels

in the areas of

Eastcheap and the Monument.

SUBSTANTIAL REWARD

Apply in person to Mr. M.

There then followed the address of a celebrated city hotel which, for obvious reasons, I have elected to censor.

The second, far shorter and more enigmatic entry read simply:

LUD

Come at once. Much at stake.

E.

Regrettably, the man for whom this last, cryptic message was intended never had an opportunity to read it. At the time of its publication he was being detained against his will in a manner he had entirely failed to predict.

Cribb had been walking alone, his head full of a jumble of ill-considered thoughts and half-digested philosophies, when he was surprised to see a carriage pull up beside him and its driver beckon him across. Cribb played his part, walked over to the vehicle and listened as its occupant asked him for directions to the Tottenham Court Road. Needless to say, Cribb was quite unable to resist such an invitation, or the temptation to add a number of interesting historical titbits. He was still speaking, and in the midst of a droll anecdote about the mediaeval witch of Kentish Town, when the stranger invited him into the carriage, the better (he said) to consult a map in his possession. Cribb did as he was asked, but given his talent for prognostication ought perhaps to have recognised the insignia stencilled discreetly on the carriage door—a black five-petalled flower.

Two men sat inside—thuggish, burly types, the kind who break people's arms for a living, professional maimers. As Cribb entered the carriage, one of them plumped a fist meaningfully into his outstretched palm and smiled greedily.

"I was expecting you, of course," the ugly man noted. "I've seen the future, you see. I know the plot."

At this, one of the men shoved him against the back of his

seat and began what many of us have long harboured aspirations of doing. He pummelled Cribb repeatedly in the head until at long last (and still stammering something about time flowing in a different direction for him) the ugly man fell unconscious.

Mrs. Grossmith, meanwhile, felt happy. Wonderfully, improbably, deliriously happy.

She all but skipped into her employer's bedroom, not even bothering to knock before she entered.

"Mr. Moon!" she trilled in a girlish falsetto. "Mr. Moon!"

But as she came into the room she felt chastened and ashamed, like a wedding guest who gatecrashes a funeral by mistake. Transparently irritated by the interruption, three men glared back at her—Mr. Moon, the Somnambulist and a loutish-looking stranger.

"What do you want?"

In the decade or more that she had spent in his employ, Mrs. Grossmith had become accustomed to Moon's testiness and abrasive manner, and she took this latest snappish remark, delivered like a prosecuting counsel hurling questions at a defence witness, as she had all the many other slights and dismissals over the years—by pretending not to notice, by giving him her biggest smile and carrying on regardless.

"Sorry to disturb you. I wonder if I might have a word?"

"Not a good time."

Mrs. Grossmith persisted. "I've news. It can't wait."

"Mister?" the stranger interrupted. He nodded towards Grossmith. "'Scuse me, but this is important."

He was a grimy, lean, leathery man, engaged in unfolding a series of maps on the table in the centre of the room. The Somnambulist, apparently fascinated by all this cartographic paraphernalia, peered, enthralled, over his shoulder.

Moon waved vaguely towards him. "This is Mr. Clemence. He answered my advertisement."

"Call me Roger," the stranger said and offered Grossmith a lascivious wink.

"Mr. Clemence," Moon said, "what was it you were about to tell me?"

Clemence gesticulated at one of the maps. "See here. Here's where it happened."

Mrs. Grossmith began to protest but the conjuror cut her short. "Please. This is of the utmost importance." As he strode across to examine the map, Mrs. Grossmith could only sniffle forlornly, her earlier ebullience quite gone.

Moon relented slightly. "This gentleman was formerly employed by the city railway. Love have their headquarters underground. We're trying to find a way down."

The housekeeper sighed. "Very interesting, I'm sure."

Clemence pointed to a section of the map. "See there. Under the Monument. All that's abandoned track. They'd planned an extension to King William Street Station. It would have been directly beneath Love's offices. Never happened, of course."

The Somnambulist, eager to be a part of the conversation, nodded in sober agreement.

Clemence leant across the table, rustling the maps. "If you're serious about going down there, you've a right to know the truth."

Mrs. Grossmith cleared her throat. "I really need to tell you something."

"Not now," Moon growled. "Wait."

Clemence lowered his voice to a conspiratorial whisper. "I knew some of the men who worked on the King William Street extension. All trustworthy, believe me. Oh, one or two of them might have liked a drink from time to time, but they can't all have been wrong. They saw something down there. No question."

"Tell me. Tell me what they saw."

"Tunnels—tunnels that weren't never on any plans, tunnels that ain't been built for no railway. Great, fantastic warrens of them, like giant rat holes leading into the dark. Some sort of jade door, set into the ground itself. And something lived down there—that's what they said. Two of the men went missing—just vanished, never seen again, like. After that, the rest of them got nervous, superstitious, started saying they didn't want to work there no more."

"What happened?"

"The work got abandoned in the main. A few of 'em wanted to stay on, of course. The brave ones, or the stupid. Still, maybe not so stupid. Most of 'em are rich now—far richer than any railway-man has any right to be. Those that didn't end up in the nuthouse, that is."

"Nuthouse?"

"Something happened. One of the men had to be committed. Poor beggar started seeing things and babbling like an idiot. Course it might just have been that place. Down there, under-ground, in the dank and the dark . . . Your mind plays tricks on you."

"Some vanished, some became rich. And some went mad." Moon sounded as though he was thinking aloud. "Thank you, Mr. Clemence. This has been invaluable."

"Pleasure."

The conjuror proffered a handful of coins, but as Clemence reached forward to grab them, Moon closed tight his fist. "Can you take me there?"

The railwayman looked uncertain. Moon glanced meaning-fully down at his clenched hand.

"I'll take you to the entrance of the tunnel," the man said doubtfully. "No further. What I've heard . . . I wouldn't go down there for anything."

"You won't have to. The Somnambulist will be with me. Can we do it tonight?"

Clemence thought for a moment. "Shall we say midnight, at the Monument?"

"Excellent," said Moon, shepherding him to the door. "I'll see you then."

Clemence nodded politely again, then sloped away, incongruous against the spotless beige of the hotel corridors. On his way, he passed a beaming Arthur Barge, bustling towards Moon's rooms.

Barge knocked politely, sauntered in and made a beeline for Mrs. G., immediately clasping her hand in his, as unselfconscious as lovers half their age meeting after a long separation. In fact, they had seen each other at supper barely an hour earlier.

"Have you told him?"

Mrs. Grossmith sighed. "I haven't had a chance."

"Told me what?" Moon asked testily.

"I've been trying to say ever since I got here, sir. You wouldn't listen."

Moon softened. "Then tell me now. You have my full attention."

"It's good news."

"Delighted to hear it."

When she spoke, Mrs. Grossmith gripped Arthur's hand all the tighter and the words tumbled out overeagerly, scrambling over one another in their haste to be heard. "Earlier this evening, Arthur did me the honour of asking me to marry him . . . And I've accepted, Mr. Moon, I've accepted. I'm going to be his wife!"

There was a moment's silence. The detective managed a thin-lipped smile. "Well done," he said eventually, speaking as one might to an old dog who has finally mastered a new trick.

The Somnambulist tried his best to write CONGRATULATIONS

but misjudged the length of the word and got in a terrible muddle with his spelling, with the result that it actually read:

CONNGRATT

followed by an indecipherable scrawl.

Mrs. Grossmith understood enough, however, to appreciate the sentiment. "Thank you."

Barge disentangled himself from his fiancée and stepped up to Moon. "It must seem awful sudden to you," he began. "We've only known one another for a month or so, but something just seemed *right* between us from the first. We understood each other. And at our time in life you can't afford to wait, if you catch me meaning. We all deserve some happiness. And I think we're going to be happy, Emmy and me."

It was obviously a well-prepared speech. Moon listened as graciously as he was able and, when it was over, added rather pompously: "You have my blessing."

"Well, thank you, sir," said Barge. "That means a lot to me. Truly it does."

Moon turned to his housekeeper. "But am I to understand, whilst these glad tidings mean that Mr. Barge is to gain a wife, that I am to lose a housekeeper?"

Grossmith looked embarrassed. "I don't . . . That is, we haven't decided."

"I've enough to keep us both," Barge said proudly. "Her skivvying days are over."

"Well, then. I wish you joy." Moon turned away and busied himself with clearing up the maps and plans of underground London. "Eggs and bacon if you please, Mrs. Grossmith. We've a long night ahead of us. And I sincerely hope that at the end of it we'll finally have some answers."

✿

Emmy," he murmured once the couple had left, no doubt to canoodle in the kitchen over a frying pan. "Short, one presumes, for Emmeline . . . I must confess that, until today, I never even knew that was her name."

There is something both melancholy and oppressive about a schoolyard at night. Melancholy because one sees only silence and empty space where, according to the natural order of things, there ought to be laughter and movement and learning; oppressive because despite its desolation there is a strong and persistent sense of *other people*, of strangers present but unseen. Stand alone in a deserted playground at midnight, long after its daytime inhabitants have been tucked up in bed, and it is easy to imagine oneself surrounded by a thousand ghostly schoolboys— easy, too, to glimpse the whirl and bustle of their play, hear the shouts of their games, the thud of ball on bat, the groans of disappointment as the bell calls them back to study. Mr. Skimpole had never been an especially imaginative man—had prided himself, in fact, on his regimented common sense and rigorously practical mind—but even he could feel something of this eerie sensation as he waited alone in the playground of Gammage's School for Boys.

He had never liked schools, of course, whether fully occupied or not. Evil memories crouched behind the blackboard; they strutted along the cricket pitch and strolled with deceptive nonchalance across the yard, where the spectral outline of a long-abandoned game of hopscotch could still be dimly traced.

He shivered and checked his watch again. They ought to be here by now.

A sudden gust of wind, a cloud edged across the moon and all at once the shadows crowded eagerly about him. Skimpole felt a surge of dizziness and took deep, gulping breaths, but still he felt queasy and uncomfortable. He had no desire to check but he was certain that some of his sores were bleeding. The stains, he reflected, would be impossible to get out.

Over the course of the day, the lesions had grown infinitely worse. He had changed after dinner and found them—flaky, livid, puckering red—covering most of his belly and moving inexorably up his chest, towards his neck. One had already appeared on his face, high on his left temple, though Skimpole was relatively confident that he had managed to disguise it by the artful positioning of a stray strand of hair. He hoped that his son hadn't noticed.

Where were they? They must come soon or he feared they would arrive only to find him sprawled unconscious (or worse) upon the asphalt.

"Hello?" the albino called out to the darkness. He coughed. A small amount of phlegm came up, but the vulgarity of spitting in public having been instilled in him as an infant, he forced himself, with some discomfort, to swallow.

"Hello?" he said again, more gingerly this time. "I'm here. I'm waiting."

Still nothing. He pulled his coat tighter about him, did his best to remain calm and, not for the first time that day, wondered whether he was truly doing the right thing.

At last he was disturbed by the sound of an unfamiliar voice calling his name. Two strangers stood before him, and he realised with some astonishment that they must have crept up without him hearing, a feat he had long believed impossible.

"Well, chop off my legs and call me Shorty," said one, peering curiously at Skimpole. "What a deuced queer-looking johnny. I was expecting someone taller. Bit less pale, ruddier of cheek. Weren't you?"

"Abso-bally-lutely, old chum," said the other. "He's a rum 'un and no mistake."

In all his extensive experience of the weird and grotesque, these two men were by far the most singular individuals Skimpole had ever encountered. The first was big and brawny, the other small and neat, and they spoke in cheerfully upper-crust, well-bred accents, their voices thick with money and casual privilege. But what was most striking about them was the fact that whilst they were evidently well into middle age, both were absurdly dressed in matching school uniforms. They wore identical bright-blue blazers, school ties and grey flannel shorts cut off just above their gnarled and hairy knees. The smaller man wore a little stripy cap.

Skimpole stuttered in disbelief. "Are you really them?" he managed at last.

The big one grinned. "I'm Hawker, sir. He's Boon. You can call us the Prefects."

His companion frowned. "Hang it all. That's my speech you've just pilfered. I always say that. It's practically a tradition."

"Don't I know it," Hawker protested. "About time I had a crack."

"But we always agreed *I'd* say it. You're a wretched sneak to go back on your word. If old Skimpy weren't here I'd give you a sound hoofing."

"I'd like to see that, you silly young josser. Little Poggie Thorn and 'Baby' Wentworth from the lower fifth could trounce you in a scrap *and* you jolly well know it."

"You can be the most priceless idiot sometimes, Hawker."

"Rather that than a born sniveller, Boon."

"Pipsqueak."

"Beast."

"Hog."

Skimpole could only stand and blink in bemusement at this remarkable exchange. Briefly, he toyed with the idea that these apparitions might be some by-product of his illness, phantasms conjured by his febrile mind as his body sped towards total shutdown.

Boon broke away from his argument and turned back to the albino. "Awfully sorry, sir," he said. "You must think us the most fearful asses to stand here joshing like third-formers."

"Jolly decent of you to call," Hawker said, their spat seemingly forgotten as quickly as it had flared up. "Boon and me had been bored to tears on our hols and we'd been simply dying to bunk off for a bit of fun."

"Why here?" Skimpole asked.

"We thought it apposite, sir," Boon replied.

"*Apposite*," Hawker mused. "Good word. Might write that down. Boon's a veritable thesaurus, Mr. S., once he's in the mood. Oh yes, he knows how many beans make five. Though I've never been so hot at study myself. Between the two of us, I'm rather a prize dunce. Boon here rags me raw about it."

Skimpole tried to steer the most bizarre conversation of his life back towards some semblance of normality. "I meant to ask about the book—" he began.

"Confused you, did it, sir?"

"Bamboozled, were we? All of a fluster?"

Skimpole struggled to understand. "It's blank, apart from the page which had this address on it."

"Devilish tricky thing, that book," Hawker said, with faux gravitas.

Boon agreed. "Can't let it out of your sight, sir. Heaven knows what mischief it gets up to when we're not around."

"I don't understand," Skimpole said weakly.

"All you needed was an address," Boon said. "We got your telegram and hey presto, here we are. In this day and age there's no need for anything more complicated."

Hawker brought out a bright-green apple, rubbed it against the lapel of his blazer and took a big, crunchy bite. "Course, in other times and places it might have looked different. Might have been stuffed with funny symbols and sigils and squiggles and suchlike."

"Or rows and rows of numbers," Boon added helpfully.

"Do you always . . ." Skimpole whispered. "Do you always look like this?"

"I've always looked like this, haven't I, Boon?"

"More's the pity. You're the ugliest man in the first fifteen."

"Bosh, tiffle and pish." Hawker punched Boon playfully on his shoulder and the little man reciprocated in kind.

"Please," Skimpole said, "we haven't much time." He coughed again.

"Nasty cough you've got there, sir."

"Hacking, sir. Positively grisly, if I might say so."

"You ought to get that looked at, sir. Go along to Matron and let her take a gander. Might get a chit for games."

"Please," Skimpole muttered.

"Quite right, sir," Boon said.

"Awfully sorry. Just horsing around," Hawker added.

"We might seem like a couple of young scamps to you," Boon insisted, "but believe me, ask us to run an errand and we'll do it better than any other boy in school. They didn't make us Prefects for nothing. Spill the beans, Mr. Skimpole. We're dying to know—what is it we can do for you?"

Before Skimpole replied there was a pause in which he considered for the very last time the possibility of taking another path, making a different choice, a quieter, more mellow death. But he ignored the screaming of his conscience and pressed on. "There are men I want . . . removed," he said. "I need you to murder them for me."

*T*homas Cribb opened his eyes.

By virtue of his curious existence, memory must have worked rather differently for him than it does for the rest of us. Presumably he was able to remember what was about to happen to him rather than what had already taken place. Assuming, of course, that you believe him.

Whatever the truth, when he opened his eyes and saw where he was, he had no idea how he had got there. "There," as it happened, was completely unfamiliar to him. A gloomy room, dank and airless, its walls peeling, sweaty and blistered.

"Hello?" he said, not really expecting an answer. "Anyone there?"

Nothing happened. Feeling foolish, he fell silent.

Numbed by pain, cold and the journey, only now did it come to his attention that he was sitting upright, somehow stuck to a chair. Experimentally, he tried to move a leg.

No good, of course—he was bound tight. His hands, too, were trussed to the chair's arms, rope cutting hard into his wrists, sensation fading from his extremities. Evidently he was being held captive and, strangely, he wasn't altogether surprised by the fact—in the course of his long, long existence he had made innumerable enemies. He had a sensation of weightlessness, a woozy, floating feeling as though he had been removed from his life and was staring down at it from some great distance.

He heard a thundering rumble, painfully loud and coming from somewhere nearby. A train? He couldn't be sure.

Suddenly he was aware of another presence. A match flared before him in the gloom, a lamp was lit and he saw exposed at last the grim dimensions of his cell. He wasn't altogether certain he didn't prefer it in the dark.

A woman's face, familiar but maddeningly nameless, swam in front of him. "Mr. Cribb," it said. "Welcome to the Summer Kingdom."

He managed a defiant kind of mumble. "What do you want?"

"We want to help you," she said in a singsong voice. "We want to show you Love."

Cribb remembered. "You're Charlotte Moon."

The face gave a sweet, seraphic smile. "You must be mistaken," she said, still in that same hypnotic tone. "My name is Love."

It was then that Cribb heard himself scream. During that impossibly long night it was to be the first of many.

*H*awker and Boon—known collectively as the Prefects—had long been objects of terror in the city: implacable, remorseless purveyors of death and destruction to anyone foolish or unwary enough to cross their path. Nobody had ever suffered their ire and survived. Even criminals—the worst, most brutal and perverted recidivists the city had to offer—all were scared to death of those two men. The smallest rumour of a sighting set the underworld quivering as one.

I should add that their notoriety was far from being restricted to London. Baba Abu, the infamous Bombay assassin of the last century, was said on one occasion to have vomited copiously at his dinner table at the mere mention of their names.

It was two living legends, then, with whom Mr. Skimpole found himself confronted in the playground of Gammage's School for Boys. By rights, their appearance ought to have been comical—the albino should have had great difficulty keeping a straight face—and yet the emotion evoked upon encountering these curious men-children was not laughter but its polar opposite. There was something horribly, indescribably *wrong* about the pair of them. They seemed to exist a little outside reality, hovering an inch or two above the real world.

Boon smiled at Skimpole the way a poultry farmer smiles at a turkey the week before Christmas. "Murder, sir? I say. What larks."

Hawker chortled in agreement. "Topping."

During their long and highly successful career, the Prefects had encountered men and women who had seen fit to laugh at their speech patterns, to mock the unmistakable patois of the playground, their trademark idiolect. Needless to say, few of these would-be satirists were ever able to laugh again. Dribble, yes. A thin moan, perhaps. Blink their eyes once for yes and twice for no, without a doubt. But laugh? Never.

Mr. Skimpole did not feel like cracking so much as a smile. His clothes were soaked with sweat, and those parts of his body which were covered in lesions wept and itched abominably. "Please," he said. "I'm in deadly earnest. I need you to kill two men."

"Wrong 'uns, are they, sir?"

"Ne'er-do-wells?"

"Bounders?"

"Rotters?"

"Cads?"

"Give us their names, sir. Do."

"You understand that I do this not out of revenge," Skimpole said carefully, "but only to protect my work."

"Absolutely, sir."

"Say no more."

"Well, then." Skimpole coughed painfully, at which Hawker and Boon tutted in noisy sympathy. "The Directorate is under attack. A man has been set on our trail. Ex-Okhrana. The best assassin they ever had. And the only real intelligence we have on him is his code name."

"Tell us, then, sir."

"Let the cat out of the bag."

"Spill the beans."

Skimpole swallowed hard. "The Mongoose."

Hawker let out a low whistle. "Coo!"

"You'd like us to deal with him, would you, sir?" Boon asked.

"Give him a dashed good slippering?"

Skimpole nodded weakly.

"You ought to be at home, sir."

"Tucked up in bed with a hot-water bottle and a steaming rum toddy."

"Wait," Skimpole said. "There is someone else."

"My my. You *are* in a bloodthirsty temper."

"The Directorate has an enemy in Whitehall."

"Shifty lot, those politicians."

"Nasty glints in their eyes."

"Never trust them, sir. Never."

"His name is Maurice Trotman. A man from the Ministry. He wants . . ." Skimpole sniffled. "He wants to close us down."

"Gosh." Hawker sounded sympathetic. "Are you frightfully raw at the chap?"

"Had words, did you, sir?" Boon asked.

"Fisticuffs, were there?"

"Can you do it?" Skimpole gasped. "Can you kill them?"

"Deuced if I can't see why not," said Boon. "How about you, Hawker?"

"Absolutely, old fruit. Point of fact, I'm looking forward to it."

"You've asked the right chaps, sir, coming to us. There's none better in the sixth form."

"Boon's an absolute brick in a scrap. Take it from me—he's a real game cock when his dander's up."

"What do I owe you?" Skimpole asked.

"Owe us?" Hawker affected incomprehension. "Owe us? Whatever do you mean by that, sir?"

"We'll let you know our fee, sir, soon as the job's done," Boon said.

"You ought to get back home now, sir. Check on that young lad of yours. You'll catch your death if you stand out here much longer."

"Can't you give me any idea?" Skimpole pleaded. "Of the cost?"

Boon beamed. "Oh, I think you'll find our price quite within your means, sir. Quite within your means."

"We'll be in touch."

"Goodbye, then," Skimpole managed.

Boon touched the brim of his cap. "Tinkety-tonk."

With this last perplexing valediction, the two anachronisms turned and vanished into the dark. Shaking with a mixture of pain, confusion and the cold, and trying not to think about the nature of what he had set in motion, Skimpole pulled his jacket tight about him and started for home.

No doubt Mr. Clemence did not intend to appear as suspicious as he did whilst he waited beneath the shadow of the Monument. But as he paced shiftily up and down, two dimmed lanterns by his feet, checking his pocket watch far more often than was necessary, he could scarcely have drawn more attention to himself had he worn a placard around his neck proclaiming his imminent intention to break the law.

Without warning, the shadows disgorged Edward Moon and the Somnambulist.

"My apologies if we've kept you waiting," the conjuror said.

"Not to worry. Though if we could hurry, gentlemen, I'd be grateful. The sooner we get out of here, the better, if it's all the same to you."

"We're ready."

Clemence led them away from the Monument and towards the darkened flight of steps which led to King William Street Underground Station. A metal grille, padlocked shut, was pulled across the entrance. Clemence produced a key from his pocket, snapped open the lock, pulled back the grille. It groaned and complained in response and they all stood still and silent, waiting to see if the noise had attracted any attention. Nothing.

This was the financial district of the city, invariably deserted at night as the bankers, brokers and moneymen scurried home to their supper and an evening by the fireside. Besides, all this took place on a Sunday, when even the most fiscally devoted stayed in with their wives and children or (in at least two dozen cases of which I am personally aware) with their mistresses and lovers.

The last time Moon was there he had been walking with Cribb, as the ugly man kept up a steady stream of fantastical chatter, speculating wildly about London's history, anecdotalising about the great Stone and propounding the most curious notions concerning the relative heights of the Monument and Nelson's Column. But now, at midnight, the place was a ghost town, barely recognisable but for the great needle of the Monument keeping its silent vigil like some landlocked Pharos.

Clemence passed one of the lamps to the Somnambulist. "Follow me."

Looking around for a final time to check they were still unobserved, the three men stepped through the gateway and into the gloom, down the staircase, past the ticket office and onto the deserted platform. For an instant the Somnambulist fancied that he could hear the familiar clank, whistle and chug of a locomotive, but when he listened again the sound had vanished.

Clemence beckoned for them to follow. "It's not far." He clambered down off the platform and onto the tracks.

"You're quite sure they don't run trains down here?"

"At this time of night?"

Moon sighed. "We're in your hands, Mr. Clemence."

The railwayman strode away and they followed, leaving the relative safety of the platform behind as they headed into the tunnels, those mysterious warrens beneath the city, glimpsed by her inhabitants only as a monochrome whirl passed during the course of a journey back to the light.

Moon felt a sudden need to fill the silence. "Mr. Clemence? Are you a superstitious man?"

"Can't say as I am. I'm a practical sort. Level-headed."

"Then you don't believe in fortune-tellers? Clairvoyants?"

"Not given it much thought. Why do you ask?"

"I knew one."

"That so?"

"And if she was correct, then today is the day that the city shall fall."

"Ah, she were probably just making it up. Most of her sort are jokers, I shouldn't wonder."

"Perhaps."

They walked along the track for what Moon estimated must have been about half a mile, brushing past the grime and dirt encrusted onto the walls like plaque on rotting teeth. The Somnambulist felt a strong sensation that they were being watched: he could hear the skittering and scratching of the little creatures whose home this was.

Clemence stopped short as the track split into two. "We're about halfway between stations. Here's where the men were working when the trouble started." He pointed ahead. "That track leads on to the next station. But this"—he gestured towards the track which curved off to the left into a narrow tunnel—"this was abandoned." He walked on, the lamplight straining against the darkness which down here seemed thicker and more complete than ever.

The track petered out a few minutes' walk from the main tunnel. Clemence apologised. "They stopped in a hurry," he said, moving past the remnants of the track and into the dirt and shale. "Here's why."

Set into the ground was a wooden trapdoor, painted a faded green. If one were to have chanced upon it above-ground, one would most naturally assume it to be the entrance to a cellar or a basement, containing nothing more sinister than firewood, or coal, or a collection of half-forgotten old junk. But here at the end of a tunnel far beneath the surface, it was distressingly peculiar, filled with incongruous menace.

Clemence seemed unaccountably pleased with himself. "This is it."

Moon said nothing. Struggling for a moment, he eventually succeeded in pulling up the trapdoor. Darkness yawned beneath them, a deep vertical tunnel with a flicker of light gleaming distantly at the end of it. The Somnambulist moved his lantern closer, revealing a metal ladder clinging to the inner edge of the hideous drop.

Clemence gave a nervous cough. "Here's where I leave you."

"Thank you." Moon passed the man his handful of coins. "You've been a great help."

"Pleasure." Clemence began to move away, transparently eager to depart. "Mr. Moon?"

"Hmm?"

"Be careful."

He vanished back into the outer tunnel. Moon watched him go. "We climb towards the light," he said and swung himself into the tunnel, grasping the ladder firmly, and began to move slowly downwards. He called up to his friend. "Coming?"

Frantically the Somnambulist tried to remind Moon of his fear of heights, but his efforts were rendered invisible by the gloom.

"Don't worry," Moon said lightly. "It's too dark to see how high we are." He clambered further down and the giant followed suit. Had he been able to mutter resentfully under his breath, no doubt he would have done so.

*R*oger Clemence emerged back onto the station platform to find a well-fed, ruddy-faced man waiting for him, clutching what looked like a half-eaten pasty.

"Evening, Mr. Clemence."

"Mr. McDonald."

The fat man took a meaty bite, chewing noisily like a dog truffling through a bowl of leftovers. "It's done, then?"

"Signed, sealed, delivered."

"At last. We were starting to wonder if he'd get there at all."

"He's not what he was, you know. He's past his best. Worn out. Used up. Shop-soiled."

"I know." Donald McDonald smiled. "That's precisely why we want him."

❀

After an age of climbing, Edward Moon and the Somnambulist emerged into the light. Shaking a little from his ordeal, the giant stepped with obvious relief from the final rung of the ladder back onto solid earth. They looked around them, drinking in the sounds, sights and smells of Love.

At last, Moon broke the silence. "I have to admit, I'm a little disappointed."

The Somnambulist just looked glum. They were in some kind of storeroom, surrounded by empty boxes, old bottles and rotting sacks. There was an unpleasant odour, too, as though meat had been allowed to spoil. Moon walked towards the door. "Let's hope things prove more interesting out there."

They found themselves in a big round room, currently deserted but evidently used as a dining hall or refectory of some kind. Chairs and trestle tables were set out before them in regimented rows, and at the far end of the room, beneath a balcony arranged for public address, a gigantic banner hung upon the wall. It depicted a symbol they had seen many times before: a black, five-petalled flower.

Moon could not resist an exclamation of delight. "At last."

The Somnambulist looked less overjoyed—already suspecting, perhaps, the true nature of what they had stumbled into.

"Edward!" The voice reverberated across the room.

Moon turned round. A gloriously familiar figure stood before them.

"I'm so glad you made it."

Moon laughed with a mixture of gratitude and relief. There may even have been tears nudging the corners of eyes. "Charlotte! Thank God. Are you all right?"

Miss Moon gave a beatific smile. "I'm fine. In fact, I've never been better. Though I'll thank you not to call me by my old name."

The Somnambulist shot Moon a concerned look.

"Old name?" Moon said carefully, as though by slowing this conversation down he might somehow delay his fast-approaching realisation of the truth.

"That woman is dead," his sister said cheerfully. "I've been reborn in her place. From now on you must call me Love."

Moon was appalled. "Charlotte."

"There's someone I'd like you to meet."

Moon edged gingerly away, as if backing off from some savage animal for whom sudden movement would be an incitement to kill. "Oh yes? Who's that?"

"He's a very, very dear friend. A great leader. A hero. And my inspiration."

At last Moon began to understand what was happening. "Then he's the man behind it all," he said, suddenly furious. "The prime mover in the murders of Cyril Honeyman and Philip Dunbar. The mastermind behind the attacks on the Directorate and the plot against the city."

"You'll like him," Charlotte said sweetly. "I'm sure you'll get on famously."

"What have they done to you?"

She looked up. "He's here now, Edward. He'll explain everything."

A stranger glided onto the balcony. He had been waiting outside, biding his time in order to make the most dramatic entrance possible. Slight and narrow-featured, he was an unassuming little man, his skin pockmarked, lined and swollen. But despite these shortcomings he was not without a certain nobility, an innate dignity. When he spoke his voice was soft and low and seemed to pulse with a hypnotic power. It was the voice of someone accustomed to being obeyed without question, whose every utterance was treated with reverence and awe.

"My name," he said, "is the Reverend Doctor Tan."

*B*ut you will know me better, dear reader, as your narrator.

18

I fear I may not have been entirely honest with you.

Of course you'll say I ought to have been truthful from the start, that I should have owned up on page one, come clean from the outset. But stay your verdict a while longer; don't judge me for withholding a few minor details, a name or two, for fudging some of the minutiae.

I never revealed my true identity to you because I didn't want you to think *The Somnambulist* is in any way a biased account. The great majority of what you have read is the absolute, unalloyed truth. Where I have embroidered or embellished, I have admitted it; where I have indulged in fabrication, I have immediately confessed.

However, you may be able to detect a slight unevenness in my portrayal of one particular character. I have done my utmost to write as impartially as I am able but—sweet Christ—how I hated that man by the end.

Nonetheless, when the two of us met again in the great hall beneath Love, Love, Love and Love, I tried my best to be civil, though it was with no small difficulty that I resisted the temptation to gloat.

"Mr. Moon. Delighted you could make it."

"Have we met?"

"Edward," I chided. "How can you have forgotten?"

"Reverend Doctor Tan," he replied (in what I felt to be an unnecessarily sarcastic tone). "Can we assume that's not your real name?"

"My title is an honorary one," I admitted, "but I must say I'm hurt you don't remember me."

Moon spoke to his sister. "Who is this man?"

I cannot claim the honour of having known her well, but during the course of our all-too-brief acquaintanceship, Miss Moon always struck me as a thoroughly decent sort. Intelligent as well as pretty and (after a few days' gentle persuasion) no mean convert to our cause.

"He's a hero," she said again. "A leader and a great friend."

I blushed at this undeserved praise. "You really don't remember me?"

Moon shook his head. "Never seen you before in my life." He turned to the Somnambulist: "He ring any bells with you?"

Infuriatingly, the giant merely shrugged.

I felt cheated. For years, I had looked forward to our meeting, anticipating it with all the sick excitement of a child on Christmas Eve. On so many occasions I had mapped out the ideal version of this conversation—I would be magnanimous in victory, witty, wise and inspirational. I planned to dazzle.

But then I had expected Moon to recognise me at once, for the

Somnambulist to shrink back in horror, for both of them to treat me with just a little bit of respect, as a formidable rival, an adversary to be feared. Instead they just gazed blankly at me as they might at some rank stranger accosting them for money on the street.

So I told them my real name.

I shan't repeat it here. It's a prosaic, everyday thing which does no justice to a man of my talent and ambition. You may continue to think of me (if you care to think of me at all) as the Reverend Doctor Tan.

The Somnambulist grinned in recognition, but still Moon looked none the wiser. The giant scribbled something down, and at long last the light of understanding flickered into Edward's eyes.

SEWERS

Moon laughed—the despicable little man actually *laughed* at me. "Of course," he said and proceeded to relate a highly exaggerated account of how (as a much younger man) I had attempted to rob the Bank of England but had burrowed mistakenly instead into the London sewer system.

"I've been trying to remember your name for months." He chortled. "Even Mrs. Grossmith wasn't able to recall it and she's always had an excellent memory for nonentities."

I think I said something then about the wisdom of Moon taking quite so antagonistic a tone with me when he was trapped in my underground lair, unarmed and entirely at my mercy.

He demanded an explanation, and as soon as I had recovered my composure, I did my best to answer. I told him that there is a hierarchy even amongst criminals, and that following the regrettable incident outlined above, I had become something of a standing joke amongst my peers. Artfully avoiding self-pity, pitching my tone perfectly between pathos and determination, I told them this: "I wearied of being the pettiest of petty crooks. I saw I had to improve myself. You might say I found religion." I chuckled at this, thinking it an amusingly ironical quip. Charlotte smiled (dear girl) but the other two stood resolutely stony-faced.

"We've put our society out of joint, Mr. Moon. Here at Love we have a solution."

"Tell us, then." He yawned. "But don't let's take too long about it, there's a good chap." He spoke to me as one might to a child, and though I bristled at his manner I chose for the time being to let his impertinence slide.

"You're a part of it," I said carefully. "I summoned you here for a reason."

"I came here of my own volition. You had nothing to do with it."

I confess I was unable to restrain a squeal of delight at his ignorance (though I think I was able to disguise the sound as a light cough). "No, no," I corrected him softly. "*I* have brought you here."

Three people were waiting by the balcony door for their cue. I beckoned them in.

Mr. Clemence. Mrs. Honeyman. Thomas Cribb.

"I laid down the clues, Edward, and you followed them just as I knew you would."

Something like fear flickered across his face as the final pieces of the puzzle were pressed into place. I cannot be certain whether it was at this moment that Moon realised the sheer scale of the trap into which he had been expertly led. Certainly he seemed deliciously broken, and as I watched him come to grips with the parameters of his failure I found it almost impossible not to laugh.

Despite what you might think, I am not entirely devoid of compassion. Moon had experienced a considerable shock, and even the Somnambulist—he of the granite face, the Easter Island visage—now wore a look of stunned surprise at my casual revelations.

Dismissing Cribb, Charlotte and the rest, I led my guests to my modest private rooms where I offered them food and drink and promised that when they were ready I would explain it all. The Somnambulist was manifestly grateful for the food, but Moon, rather churlishly, declined. He pushed aside his plate and announced, petulantly: "I have questions."

"What we're building here," I said, "is the future. A new community inspired by the dream of Pantisocracy."

"Why does this dream necessitate murder?"

"My conscience is quite clear. What I do, I do for the poor and the abandoned in this great city of ours, for the indigent who exist at the very precipice of society, forced there by circumstances not of their own making. The 'edge-people,' if you like, life's marginalia, footnotes in flesh and blood. The meek, Mr. Moon—the meek who will inherit the earth."

"Men like Speight."

"Precisely so."

He sounded angry. "The Speight I saw last week was not the man I knew."

I tried to make him understand. "He's changed. He's found a better way to live."

"Whatever you did to him, you've done to my sister."

"She came to us willingly. When she realised that she had spent her life in darkness, Love led her into the light. All we desire is to live our lives according to Pantisocratic principles. And we're very close to achieving our dream. How many men in history have been able to say as much? We're going to build Paradise on Earth, Mr. Moon. Why do you persist in opposing us?"

"Because you have murdered and cheated and corrupted. Because you are a twisted failure deluded into thinking you can recreate the world in your own image."

I smarted a little at these harsh words and Moon pressed home his momentary advantage. "You had Barabbas killed."

"We asked him to join us."

"Join you? What place does a killer have in Paradise?"

"You never believed him to be irredeemable. Neither did we."

"But he refused?"

"It seems he was happy to die in the dark."

"And Meyrick Owsley?"

"Meyrick was placed there to watch over him. Barabbas knew a great deal about our operation."

"Is that why you had him killed?"

"It wasn't that he was telling you the truth. It was the speed at which he was doing it. I must admit to being surprised," I said, "that you haven't asked me about Cyril Honeyman. It was his death, after all, which first set you on this path."

Moon glared resentfully at me.

"No theories?" I asked lightly. "No elegant suppositions? No brilliant deductions pulled out of the hat at the last moment?"

He all but shouted, "Tell me!"

"It was a hook, Edward. A wicked, grotesque crime which was bound to attract your attention. A piece of theatre we knew you couldn't resist. As a means of drawing you to us it could scarcely fail."

"Are you saying all this was for me? A set-up?"

"Essentially, yes, that's true."

"Men have died," Moon spat, "so that we can have this idle conversation?"

"There's no need to be quite so self-centred. Mrs. Honeyman and Mrs. Dunbar had little love for their feckless sons. They wanted those blights on their lives removed, lopped off as harmlessly as one might an unsightly mole. I think they rather enjoyed the experience."

"Mrs. Honeyman. Mrs. Dunbar. Hardly edge-people, are they?"

"I confess there have been times when Love has not been entirely solvent. We needed money. They were useful assets."

"Were?"

"They're not fit to enter Paradise," I admitted quietly.

"And the Fly? Why him?"

"The kind of deliriously improbable touch I thought might appeal to you. How were we to know you'd kill him?"

"So you have me here at last. What do you want? Has this just been about my humiliation?"

"Oh, I shan't say I haven't enjoyed it. But this is about more than revenge."

"What do you want?"

"Why, Edward." I smiled. "I want you to join us."

*M*rs. Grossmith (soon to be Mrs. Barge) woke suddenly just before dawn with no immediate idea of why she had done so. The room was silent, though she could hear the birds in the garden trilling their perennial songs, their avian arias, their feathered canticles and hymns. For much of her life, Grossmith had wondered precisely what it was they had to be so cheerful about first thing in the morning. Since meeting Arthur she finally knew. A small sigh of pleasure escaped her at the thought of him, something between a conscious snore and a moan of satisfaction. She reached out her hand to touch him but found only empty bed-sheets, still warm but distressingly devoid of fiancé. "Arthur?"

Now, if you've any Victorian qualms about a loving couple sharing a bed out of wedlock then I trust you'll keep them to yourself. I've no truck with such antiquated prudery and I can assure you that in the new state of Pantisocracy there'll be no place for your morality. The repressive codes of our parents and grandparents will be swept away to be replaced with something far more organic, more beautiful and true. Liberated from the cages society has constructed for itself with such self-defeating ingenuity, human nature will flourish and prosper. In the new age, we shall all be as Emmeline Grossmith and Arthur Barge.

The housekeeper felt uneasy at her lover's absence. She sensed the first faint intimation that the day ahead was about to go horribly wrong, and all at once the merry chirping at the birdbath ceased to seem quite so inspirational. She sat up in bed, pushed the pillows behind her and brushed from her eyes that hard, flaky substance which accumulates during sleep. Unable to resist, she deposited a crumb of the stuff in her mouth and chewed thoughtfully, although, unusually, this ritual failed to improve her mood. She called again. "Arthur?"

The door to the bedroom opened and her fiancé appeared, scrubbed, clean-shaven and fully dressed. "Yes, my dove, my angel?"

"It's early. What are you doing?"

"Did I wake you?"

"Arthur, I'm worried."

"No need, my dear. I'm just going out for an hour or so. There's a little matter requiring my attention. A chore I've been putting off. Nothing for you to concern yourself over."

The cool, deliberate manner with which he said it, the studied nonchalance of his tone, immediately convinced her that the reverse was true—that whatever the love of her life was getting up so early for was something she should worry over and, more than that, that it was worth getting frightened about.

Barge wandered over to the bed, sat down beside her and stroked her cheek. "Go back to sleep. I shan't be long. And I'll have a surprise for you when I come back."

"A surprise?"

He put a finger to his lips. "Wait and see."

Mrs. Grossmith allowed herself to be soothed and reassured, and for a time she was even able to ignore that persistent sense of imminent catastrophe. Arthur left to carry out his mysterious errand and she retreated back under the bedclothes to let sleep wash over her. As she dozed, she dreamt, and her dreams were restless and black.

Bad enough that dear lady should suffer such nightmares at all—worse still that their vague, amorphous horror should be eclipsed upon her waking by the terrors of the real world.

❧

*A*rthur Barge hailed a cab and instructed the driver to take him to Piccadilly Circus. His errand had been long delayed—a reprehensible lapse in a man who had always prided himself on his professionalism and timekeeping.

Once in Piccadilly, Barge stopped the cab and stepped out onto the street. The object of his errand did not lie there, of course, but he had no wish to give the driver an exact address. He passed his fare up to the cabbie and, as he did so, turned his face away. It wouldn't do for the man to be able to identify him later.

He stepped away from the cab, waited until it had driven out of sight, then set off towards St. James's Park. It was early morning, just light, and the streets were largely empty, save for those unfortunates who spend their evenings crumpled in the doorways and gutters of our metropolis. Barge strode past them all without a second glance—understandable enough, given the ubiquity of such sights, but it's worth noting, perhaps, that these things would never occur in a Pantisocratic state.

Barge reached the borders of St. James's Park, headed down a narrow avenue just off Pall Mall and paused before a modest house situated halfway along the street. The plaque hanging by the doorbell read:

THE SURVIVORS' CLUB
STRICTLY MEMBERS ONLY

Needless to say, Barge was not a member.

He pulled a spindly metal tool from his jacket pocket, a thin, delicate thing bristling with sharp, serrated edges. With the stealthy ease of a man who has performed the action many times before, he inserted the instrument into the keyhole, turning it first one way and then the other until the lock sprang open with a solid clunk. As quietly as he could, he pulled the door open and crept inside.

He edged his way down the corridor. Ahead of him lay the Smoking Room, out of which emanated a stream of ear-shattering snores and wheezes. Barge peered inside to see an old man asleep in one of the armchairs, yesterday's *Times* open in his lap, a half-empty decanter of brandy by his feet.

Barge turned away and moved towards the end of the corridor where he knew Mr. Dedlock's quarters to be situated. He had been observing the club for weeks, eventually coming to the conclusion that membership must be restricted to the very oddest men in London. Everyone he had seen entering or leaving the premises looked like an escaped detail from a painting by Hogarth, barely three-dimensional, so grotesque they were scarcely believable. Once he had glimpsed Dedlock himself, strutting naked around the Smoking Room. That he appeared to be the most normal person present spoke volumes for his fellow members.

Barge tried the handle to Dedlock's room—stupidly left unlocked, it opened easily. The joint chief of the Directorate lay prone on his bed, sweating, turning, mumbling in his sleep. The bed stood close to a large bay window, its curtains billowing suggestively in the early-morning breeze. Bed-sheets were strewn over his naked form and his thick white chest-scars were visible even in the gloom.

As Barge walked over to the bed, he reached into his pocket

and pulled out what looked like a surgeon's knife. Nonchalant as a dentist about to commence his dozenth examination of the day, he leant over the victim.

In the course of his career, Arthur Barge had killed thirty-four men, thirteen women and two children (twins). During this time he had cultivated certain habits and superstitious rituals, chief amongst which was the fact that he always liked to look into the eyes of his victims before he slit their life away. It made it more real, somehow, gave it a certain tangy flavour.

With his free hand, he shook Dedlock awake. The man's eyes flickered open. Bleary and befuddled, he started to struggle up only to be pushed easily back down again. Thrashing about frantically, he tried to call out, but the jug-eared man brought up his knife. Then, like a cow docile before its slaughterer, prescient of the inevitability of the blade, Dedlock fell still. Barge pushed the knife up against his target's throat and was looking forward to increasing his tally—wondering how many more there would be before he finally retired—when, amid an apocalyptic smashing of glass, something burst through the window.

Or rather two things.

Once they had disentangled themselves from the curtain, idly brushing shards of glass from their clothes, two deeply improbable figures stepped into the room.

"Hullo, sir."

"What ho, Arthur!"

Barge dropped his knife in shock. Dedlock struggled upright in bed, gasping for breath, suddenly hopeful that he might yet live.

Barge stared at the two intruders, too stupefied at first to speak. "Who are you?" he managed at last.

"I'm Hawker, sir. He's Boon."

The Prefects grinned as one.

"Evening, Mr. Dedlock. Beastly sorry to drop in on you like this."

Dedlock hugged a stray pillow for comfort. "Did . . . did the albino send you?"

"Certainly did, sir. Pal of yours, is he?"

"He's an absolute brick, old Skimpers."

"Tip-top."

It was around this time that some understanding of what was taking place finally dawned on Arthur Barge. He was about to make a run for it when the larger of the two men gripped him by the shoulders and steered him firmly across the room. Barge tried to fight back, only for the stranger—quite casually—to break his right arm. As Barge screamed in agony, Hawker began to whistle.

"Thank you," Dedlock said weakly, his words barely audible over the sound of his assailant's torment.

Boon touched the brim of his cap. "Pleasure, sir." He and Hawker bundled Barge swiftly out of the window, then disappeared the same way themselves.

A moment's silence, then Dedlock swung himself out of bed and peered through the shattered remains of his bedroom window. The old man with the eyebrows doddered into the room, his hair dishevelled and askew. "What happened here? Are you all right?"

Dedlock barely spared him a glance.

"There's the most ghastly mess," the old man moaned.

"I was almost murdered in my bed."

"Sorry to hear that."

Dedlock snapped, "Fetch the brandy. I've an awful feeling today's about to get worse."

A deferential twitch of the eyebrows. "Very good, sir."

When Arthur Barge came to, Hawker and Boon were leering over him like a couple of prep-school gargoyles. He was lashed to a chair with twine which cut into his wrists and ankles, drawing blood. Aside from the bright light shining in his face, all was darkness.

"Good to have you back, sir. Marvellous to see him, isn't it, Hawker?"

"Marvellous, Boon."

"Who are you?" Barge mewled. "What do you want?"

"He's not heard of us, Boon."

"Not heard of us? I'm disappointed. Thought we were living legends."

"Silly old josser."

"How much have you been paid?" Barge asked desperately. "Whatever it is, I'll double it."

"Don't bandy words with us, sir."

"What do you want?"

"I'm afraid we've been told to give you a bit of a wigging."

"A . . . *wigging*?"

"A damn good slippering, that's what he means."

"A sound hoofing."

Barge began to cry. "Please—"

"What's your name, sir?"

"My name?"

"That's right, sir."

"Arthur Barge. My name is Arthur Barge."

Boon looked disappointed. He nodded towards his companion, at which Hawker rooted around in his blazer pocket and retrieved an immensely large knife, two or three times the size of the one with which Barge had intended to murder Dedlock and far, far too large for the size of the Prefect's pocket.

Barge boggled at it in fear, a sticky yellow warmth coursing unchecked down his left leg.

"Cor! Hawker's got a wizard new penknife."

"It's a smashing knife, sir. Look—it's got a bottle-opener and a corkscrew and all sorts."

Barge wept.

"Tell us your name, sir."

"I told you. I'm Arthur Barge."

Boon raised his voice just ever so slightly. "Don't be an ass, sir."

"Please. Please, I—"

"Name, please, sir. Your real name."

Barge could see no alternative but to tell the truth and submit to the uncertain mercy of these creatures. Strangely, after all these years, it actually felt good to admit it out loud, to own up at last. He groaned: "I'm the Mongoose."

Boon beamed. "Thank you, sir. You understand, of course, that we had to make sure." They laughed. Hawker leant over Mr. Barge and, with enormous gusto, began to saw away at his neck.

I should put up my hand here and confess that I was, at least in part, responsible for all the above unpleasantness. I needed to stop the Directorate becoming too interested in our activities, and following the failure of that old soak Slattery, I set this killer on their trail, a former Okhrana sleeper agent living in deep cover as Arthur Barge. I allowed Donald to take care of the specifics and I fear he may have been a little overzealous in his duties. Certainly, I never intended matters to go so far or for poor Mrs. Grossmith to suffer as she did. But how was I to know? I'm an important fellow, and delegation is a necessary evil of my job.

*M*uch as I had enjoyed explaining to Moon the ease with which I had manipulated him, I had begun to weary of exposition.

Moon spluttered, "You want me to join you?" His face had turned an interesting shade of mauve, puce with righteous indignation.

"When you see what I have to show you, I think you'll understand."

I sauntered from the room, certain that Moon and his companion would follow—led on now not by fear or even simple curiosity but by the most basic and primal desire of all: the need to know how everything will end.

I have long had a fascination with underground London, her secret subterranea, for the dark places of the earth. Since wresting control of Love, Love, Love and Love from its odious President, Donald McDonald and I had constructed an entire world beneath our headquarters. We had sculpted great vaults and chambers to be a hiding place and refuge from the tumult of the world above.

I led Moon and the Somnambulist back to the balcony above the great hall. The place had filled up with my people, men and women packed shoulder to shoulder, crammed against the walls. It seethed with life, it brimmed with Love. Standing before us were London's edge-people, the poor, the ugly and the deformed, the indigent, the dispossessed, the ragged and the hopeless, all the marginalia of the city. At my appearance a mighty roar went up, which I acknowledged as best I could with a modest bow and a diffident wave.

Moon stared down at the multitude, trying no doubt to spy his sister amongst them, or Thomas Cribb, or Mr. Speight.

"So many," he murmured. "I had no idea there'd be so many."

"Love assembled," I said, unable (I admit it) to entirely hide my pride. "The foot soldiers of Pantisocracy."

"Soldiers?" Moon was being contrary again. "Why would Paradise need soldiers? Why the violence? Why the death? Why not simply take your followers and go? Build your Eden by the banks of the Susquehanna and leave the rest of us be."

I marvelled at the man's obtuseness. Despite all I had told him, still he hadn't realised the truth of it. "The Susquehanna?" I tried to keep the contempt from my voice. "You really believe we're going to America?"

"That was Coleridge's plan, was it not?"

"America is unsuitable. Corrupt."

"Where, then?"

"Here, Edward. Here, in the city."

"I thought you hated London."

"No city is irredeemable. We shall rebuild. Start again. A new city where we will live as true Pantisocrats. I'm giving London a second chance."

"What happens to anyone who doesn't qualify for your utopia?"

I had to be honest. "They shall be put to the sword."

Moon said something predictable about my mental state. I told him he was being short-sighted and patiently explained that we could wipe the city clean, begin again.

"What would your precious Coleridge make of this? I doubt he would ever have condoned such bloodshed."

I felt an attack of hysterical laughter surge up inside me and it was only with a Herculean exercise of will that I was able to re-strain myself. Calmly, I told Moon that I wanted to introduce him to my superior—to the Chairman of the Board.

"I had assumed you were the Chairman," he snapped.

I did not reply, but instead left the balcony, led them away from the hall and deeper into the underground tunnel system, down to the lowest levels, to a large locked room located in the most inac-cessible part of Love, our holy of holies. The door was fastened with padlocks and chains, and a small sign was all that proclaimed this to be the province of the

CHAIRMAN OF THE BOARD

I unlocked the door and ushered my guests over the threshold. Evidently, they had not expected anything so grand as what lay beyond. Even I, who ought to have been inured to the sight, never failed to be awed and humbled by it.

An enormous metal sphere filled the room, a great iron egg panelled intermittently with glass portholes against which a greasy yellow liquid lapped hungrily. Attached to one side was a small steam engine, its working parts skeletally exposed, its tubes and metal lines snaking umbilically between the two machines. All the awesome modern technology of electricity and steam was at the service of the sphere, all its valves and slides, its crank-pins and pistons, its pumps and its flywheels, its cylinders and packing rings and pillow blocks.

But it was not the object itself which aroused such wonder but rather what lay inside—its most singular occupant.

An old man floated in the sphere, dressed in clothes not fashionable for almost a century, his wispy white hair yellowed from nicotine and decay, his skin mottled, torn in places and showing signs of minor putrefaction. He was immediately recognisable nonetheless as the foremost poet of his age.

Moon realised at once, I think. The Somnambulist took a little longer. A line of poetry sprang unbidden to my mind: "*Could I revive within me that symphony and song . . .*"

Moon gasped, and it was with a small spurt of pleasure that I saw he had finally comprehended the full magnitude of my achievement. "How is this possible?"

"Galvanism," I said triumphantly. "The wonders of electricity and steam."

The Somnambulist scribbled furiously on his slate.

GRAVEROBBER

I shrugged, beyond such petty morality. "I liberated him. No doubt he'll thank me for it."

"He seems . . . damaged," Moon said uncertainly.

The Somnambulist peered through the glass at the old man's hands.

STITCHES

"When I found him," I explained, "parts of his body had badly deteriorated. They had to be replaced . . . Of course, we used his friends where we could. His left hand belonged to Robert Southey. Several toes were donated by Charles Lamb. Other organs, best left unspecified, originate from the late Mr. Wordsworth."

MONSTER

"A thing of shreds and patches, perhaps," I said. "But no, not a monster. A saviour. The lord of Pantisocracy."

Moon seemed transfixed. "What is that liquid?"

"Amniotic fluid. Or at least my best approximation of it. *'For he on honey-dew hath fed, /And drunk the milk of Paradise.'"*

"He's alive?"

"Dreaming. Recovering his strength. Often I've asked myself what he sees in his dreams. What wonders he must witness in his sleep." I pointed towards an ostentatiously large red lever at the side of the sphere. "I have the means to awaken him."

The three of us looked through the glass at the face of that re-markable individual, that titan of poetry and philosophical thought—the last man, it was said, to have read *everything*. He floated serenely in the golden liquid, magisterial despite the im-perfections wrought by his sojourn in the grave.

Moon gazed on, tears forming at the corners of his eyes. "I understand," he breathed. "Forgive me. You were right."

You'll think the less of me for this, I know, but I admit it with-out shame—when I heard him speak those words, I clapped and I jumped up and down, I cheered and I squealed with childish joy.

*M*rs. Grossmith woke again at breakfast time, some hours after her fiancé had departed the house. Groggy, she rubbed her eyes, scratched herself vigorously all over and was about to clamber out of bed to make the first cup of tea of the day when she heard a curious sound emanating from the kitchen: children's laughter and, mingled with it, male voices, gruff and unfamiliar. She armed herself with the nearest heavy implement (seeing no pokers or vases to hand she was forced to make do with her chamber pot) and tiptoed through into the next room.

Two extraordinary figures slouched before the stove—grown men dressed as schoolboys. They were playing with a soft, round object, kicking it between them as though it were a football. It made a squelching sound as they did so.

The burlier of the two men grinned when he saw her. "What ho, Mrs. G."

"Hullo, miss," said the other, rather more politely.

"Hope we didn't wake you. We were just having a kick-around."

"Playing keepy-uppy."

It was then that Grossmith saw the true nature of the "football." Strange, she thought distantly, as though she were somehow divorced from the horror of the thing, how a human head could look so much smaller when removed from its body than it did when securely in place on top of a good pair of shoulders. She tried to scream but no sound would come.

"Bad news, I'm afraid, miss," Boon said courteously. "Your fiancé was a professional assassin known to his masters as the Mongoose. 'Fraid Hawker and I had to give him a bit of a wigging."

"Sawed his head orf." Hawker sniggered. "We fairly howled with laughter."

"Still." Boon brightened. "I wouldn't worry. Sometimes life's just like that."

𝒥t was around this time that I made my first mistake.

A change had come over Moon. The cynic in him had vanished before my eyes; the logician, the proselytiser for ratiocination and reason, all that had made him what he was, evaporated as I looked on. In his place stood a convert to our cause, a new Saint Paul, with Cannon Street as his Damascus.

Such a reaction on encountering the Chairman was far from unique. Speight, Cribb and Moon's own sister had all seen the light only when setting eyes upon the dreamer.

"I see it," Moon said softly. "I see it."

Feeling much as Jesus must have felt once Thomas had finished rummaging about in His ghostly wounds, I tried hard not to seem smug. "So you understand now?"

Moon seemed oddly deferential towards me, all trace of his earlier disrespect gone. Perhaps I should have realised then that all was not as it appeared to be, but at the time it just seemed so right.

Astonished at his friend's volte-face, the Somnambulist seemed about to write something down, some objection, some weasel words of doubt, but, wisely, he stood back and kept his own counsel.

"I'm flattered," said Moon, then more forcefully, as though I might doubt his sincerity, "Really. I'm flattered. Everything you've done for me . . . To bring me face-to-face with this. All this trouble just to show me the truth. I'm in your debt."

I licked my lips. "I have a mission for you."

He grinned. "Thought you might."

Quivering with excitement, I explained what I wanted him to do. I intended the conjuror to be the voice of Pantisocracy in the outside world, chief propagandist for the new order, spokesman for the Summer Kingdom. Like all the great leaders of men, I knew my limits. Who would listen to me: failed thief, former gaolbird, serial incompetent? I know first-hand the cruelty of popular opinion, its perverse, bovine insistence not on listening to the message but on ridiculing the messenger.

Moon was different. They would listen to him, a celebrated detective, star of the Theatre of Marvels, once a fixture of society.

It's that "once" of course which was important. I hoped he retained enough influence to be heard, but it was the marginalization of the man which intrigued me. He was turning into an edge-person. Whether he knew it or not, Edward Moon was becoming one of us.

"Let me go," he said. "Please. Let me spread the word. The people must be prepared. The city must be made ready for Pantisocracy."

It was a convincing performance and I've no doubt it came easily to him. Probably you think I was a fool to be taken in at all, but since I was overwhelmed by righteousness at the time, you'll have to forgive me.

So I let him go.

I gave him fourteen days to spread the word, a fortnight in which to prime the city. But even in my sublime state of belief I was not entirely without guile—doubts lingered at the corners of my mind. "You'll go alone," I said, and as Moon started to protest, I cut him off with a gesture. "The Somnambulist has yet to be converted. He'll stay with us here until he sees the truth of things."

Moon argued some more but eventually he gave in and agreed to abandon his friend below-ground. Perhaps the two of them exchanged a secret message, a code or gesture, something to allay the giant's fears and assure him that Moon was faking. If there was such an incident, it was one I failed to detect.

I like to think that a small portion of him really did believe, that despite his cynical play-acting, some fragment of decency recognised the truth. Naive, I know. Naive and too trusting. But that's the kind of chap I am. The cynical perfidy of a man like Moon could never come easily to me.

I left the Chairman still sleeping and ordered the detective to be escorted to the surface (Donald McDonald and Elsie Bayliss, a one-armed former charlady, did the honours). We shook hands warmly before we parted.

"Fourteen days?" he asked, apparently still effusive, super-charged with belief.

"Two weeks. You have my word."

He thanked me and strode away. The Somnambulist watched him go, his silent eyes betraying the barest scintilla of fear. "Don't worry," I said, touching him lightly on his shoulder. "You'll see the truth before long."

We walked back to the Chairman of the Board. Despite his sleeping state I hoped that he was aware of my presence, that he understood who I was and thanked me for it. Sometimes I even dared to hope he loved me. I spoke softly into the glass. "Fourteen days. Then you shall walk through the Summer Kingdom."

A brisk tap on the door. "Reverend Doctor."

I turned to face a vision in chiffon and lace. "Charlotte."

She managed a thin smile. "Call me Love."

"Of course," I said, slightly embarrassed.

"I'm concerned." She spoke in that enchanting singsong voice of hers—the kind of voice, I mused, which might in earlier times have led mariners to their deaths, lured generations of sailors onto the rocks. "My brother. Have you let him go?"

"He's one of us now. Love one thousand has returned to the surface to spread the good news."

Charlotte seemed impatient. "He was feigning. He's lied to you."

"What?"

"I know my brother. He hasn't gone back to spread the word. He'll have the police down here, the army. They'll wipe us out. You've humiliated him and he'll want revenge."

"I'm sure he's genuine," I insisted, though I could feel the fault lines already widening in my belief. "He was changed."

"Nonsense," Charlotte said briskly. "He'll betray you. You've not sent out a Baptist but a new Judas." It was an interesting side effect, I noticed, that those faithful who had encountered the

Chairman seemed in the wake of the experience to become far wordier and more verbose.

"You're sure?"

"Indubitably."

For a moment I was lost. "What do we do?"

"Bring the plan forward. Forget the fourteen days. Do it now."

"We're not ready."

"You've been planning this for years. Of course we're ready. In fact, I have already dispatched a crew to stop the trains."

"Without my permission?"

"Forgive me. I thought it best. Time is short. The Underground trains shan't trouble us today." She glanced at my companion. "There's something else. The Somnambulist. My brother will come back for him. He may prove useful as . . . leverage."

*I*t took twenty men to restrain the Somnambulist once he realised what we were planning, but eventually we succeeded in herding the giant into the main hall, forcing him onto the ground and staking him down. He was practically invulnerable, of course, and we knew that ropes and chains alone would not bind him. In the end it was Mr. Speight who came up with the solution.

We skewered the Somnambulist twenty-four times over; passed two dozen swords through his body, pressing them deep into the floor below. Stoically, without making a sound, he withstood these multiple lacerations and I wondered again precisely what he was, what nature of being could withstand such torture without shedding the merest drop of blood. As I watched, I found myself reminded of Gulliver staked out on the beach by the Lilliputians, of Galileo's portrait of man, perverted, pinioned, reduced to the status of a lepidopterist's specimen.

Love gathered about the giant, curious and not a little afraid.

I called them to order—all nine hundred and ninety-nine of them, the infantry of the Summer Kingdom, my troops of Pantisocracy. I knew these might be the most important words I would ever speak, the culmination of a decade's dreaming.

I began by apologising. "I confess," I cried, "that I have been misled—betrayed by a man I thought had become one of us. And because of my short-sightedness he has gone to warn our enemies. Thank the Chairman, then, for Love nine hundred and ninety-nine, who opened my eyes before it was too late." A gratifying cheer at this.

"But something wonderful has come even out of treachery. Our plans have changed. Pantisocracy begins today. The Summer Kingdom is upon us sooner than we dared to hope." More whoops and cheers. "Go forth," I said, my voice rising to a crescendo. "Reclaim the city, eradicate the symbols of impurity and evil. Wreak havoc—but a pure and holy havoc. Use the sword—but sparingly, not as a weapon but as a surgeon's tool to remove sickness and disease, for we walk amidst a new Eden. I have faith in you." I looked down at almost a thousand lonely faces, the detritus, the dispossessed of our society, and I felt a great surge of power and affection.

"I love you all," I said, before adding mischievously: "God be with you."

And with a great roar they ran from the hall, through the tunnels and out onto the streets, antibodies ready to do battle with the city's cancer.

❋

Alone, I walked back to the Chairman of the Board and observed him silently through the glass of his womb until the excitement became too much to bear.

Then I finally did it. I pulled the red lever.

A shower of sparks flew from the machinery, firecracking

across the room. The sphere filled with bubbles and a terrible light shone out from its innards, so piercingly bright that not mere stars but whole galaxies seemed to dance before my eyes.

The old man's head jerked upwards, his body shuddered and flailed and his hands reached out to claw at the inner surface of the sphere. I could hardly credit it that I should be there to see such a sight, akin to witnessing the first birth, Eve's bewildered heaving and writhing as Cain crawled forth from her womb.

The old man's face was mere inches from my own when his eyes flicked open, and it seemed that when he saw me, he smiled.

The dreamer had awoken.

Overwhelmed with joy, I unscrewed the portholes of the sphere. Waves of fluid crashed about me and I screamed in triumph as the old man lurched forward. I caught him before he fell and he leant against me, struggling for breath. I clapped him hard on the back, he coughed, then breathed in great lungfuls of air. He said nothing but only gurgled and hissed like a leaky pair of bellows, spumes of liquid dribbling from his mouth as I held him in a tight embrace.

Moon would not defeat me. I had transformed failure into triumph. The dreamer had awoken, the Chairman walked amongst us and Love was loose at last upon the streets of London.

19

*M*aurice Trotman was eating breakfast when destiny came knocking at his door. Mr. Trotman, you will recall, was the man from the Ministry, the Civil Servant who had succeeded, where so many others before him had failed, in closing down the Directorate. He was a precise, punctilious man, typical of his breed—those passionless, blank-faced automata who tirelessly maintain the grim machinery of state. His ambitions were limited, his vistas modest and he saw life prosaically, as a ladder, a career, a comfortingly regular sequence of promotions and preferments.

He was midway through a poached egg when he heard a determined rap at his front door. Still a bachelor, despite his half-hearted wooing of a colleague's daughter, he had no servants and lived and ate alone. Consequently, still clad in his fawn-coloured dressing-gown, it was Maurice himself who opened the door onto death.

"What do you want?" he asked sharply. Like any proper gentleman, he was rarely at his best before eight o'clock.

His visitors made an outré pair. Grown men, one burly, the other slight, both clad in flannel shorts, their legs knobbly and ridiculous.

"Morning," said Boon.

"What ho," said Hawker.

"Awfully sorry to bother you so early."

"Couldn't be helped."

"I'm afraid we're something of a deus ex machina."

"Don't chatter on in Latin, old man. You know it's all Greek to me."

Boon chortled dutifully. "Hawker's got a wizard new penknife. Corkscrews and bottle-openers and a how-do-ye-do to get stones out of horses' hooves. Would you like to see it?"

In the course of their unfeasibly long and bloodstained career, the Prefects had rarely been surprised by much. Strange, then, that they should have been so easily outwitted by a glorified clerk.

Maurice Trotman had not clambered so far up the Service ladder without learning a good deal of guile along the way. He had recognised the Prefects from the first, and as they stood there trolling through their usual blather, their carefully scripted crosstalk and banter, he was formulating a plan of escape. No good fleeing back into the house, of course. There they'd have him cornered, track him down and finish him off in moments. But out in the open he might still have a chance.

While Hawker and Boon talked on (something about conkers), Trotman carefully snaked his left arm around the door and towards the umbrella stand where he skilfully extricated a family heirloom—a slender black umbrella three generations old, passed down from father to son through sixty proud years of Civil Service.

He looked back at the Prefects. Hawker had drawn his knife and was advancing noiselessly upon him when, with surprising dexterity, Trotman produced the umbrella from behind his back and struck the knife from the creature's hand. Taking advantage of their momentary surprise, he thrust past the Prefects and out into the street where, barely believing his luck, he ran frantically into the centre of the city, towards what he mistakenly believed to be safety.

Whilst Hawker howled in surprise and frustration, Boon merely simmered with rage.

"By the living jingo!" Hawker cried. "He's done a bunk. Rotter's gone and scarpered. What'll we do now?"

Boon set his face in an expression of grim determination. "We follow. And when we catch him, we clobber the brute to death with that blasted umbrella."

The Prefects turned in pursuit and loped silently after their prey, determined as bloodhounds on a scent, implacable as fate.

I suppose I had better tell you what happened to Moon. For all I know you've ignored my warnings and gone and got attached to the man, so it's just possible you might care.

No doubt he was feeling mightily pleased with himself as he left the headquarters of Love and sauntered back to the surface by way of King William Street Station. Oh, he must have thought he had me fooled with that play-acting of his, that fraudulent Damascene conversion. But as we have already seen, he had not counted upon the perspicacity of his sister.

Above-ground again, he hailed the first cab he saw and instructed the driver to deliver him directly to the Yard, promising a sovereign if the fellow could get him there in a quarter of an hour. In the event it took almost double that time, the detective drumming his fingers impatiently all the while. Once he arrived he dashed straight to the office of an old friend, flung open the door without knocking and cried: "Merryweather!"

The inspector looked up from his desk, surprised. "Edward. What is it?"

Desperate to get out his story but uncertain where to begin, Moon sounded like a human telegram, his message fragmented and nonsensical: "Conspiracy . . . underground . . . Love assembled . . . the dreamer . . . Somnambulist . . ."

"Calm down. Tell me slowly what happened."

Moon took a deep breath. "Underground, a man calling himself the Reverend Doctor Tan has assembled an army. He has some crackpot scheme to destroy the city, to reduce it to ashes and begin again."

I suppose I should feel some slight at the "crackpot" description. But I'm a bigger man than that. Prophets, after all, are never recognised in their own country.

As Moon finished speaking, a bulky shadow stepped from the corner of the room. "So it's begun," he stated flatly.

Merryweather rose to his feet. Moon was later to say that this was one of the very few occasions that he had spent any length of time with the inspector when he had not seen him laugh or smile or crack some faintly inappropriate joke. In the face of brutal crimes and fearful murders, assassinations, bloody riots and deliriously horrible killing sprees, Detective Inspector Merryweather had never once lost his sense of humour. That today he was unable to manage even the ghost of a smile was perhaps some measure of the situation's gravity.

He introduced the stranger. "This is Mr. Dedlock."

The scarred man made a nominal inclination of his head. "I work with Skimpole."

Moon stared and seemed to sniff the air, like a fox sensing the approach of the hunt. "You're Directorate," he spat. "What are you doing here?"

"*Ex*-Directorate," Merryweather murmured.

"The agency has been closed down," Dedlock admitted. "This morning an attempt was made upon my life. Skimpole's gone missing. I've had to come to the police for assistance." He wrinkled his nose in distaste.

"Love has outwitted you," Moon said (and I confess to feeling some pride at the casual certainty with which he made the claim). "They're ready to make their move. Two weeks from now they'll burst from underground to destroy everything in their path. The city's in terrible danger."

"Sounds incredible," Merryweather said. He was interrupted by a brisk tap at the door. A police constable, flushed and out of breath, peered nervously into the room. "Sorry to bother you, sir."

"What is it?"

"We've had reports of a . . . disturbance in the financial district. Fighting on the streets. Fires and rioting. It sounds like—" The boy swallowed hard. "It sounds like an invasion."

Rather unfairly, Dedlock rounded on Moon. "You've been tricked. Two weeks! You bloody fool. It starts today."

Merryweather shouted orders. "Get every man we have down there at once. *Everyone*."

Moon was appalled. "You don't understand the scale of it. These people are armed to the teeth. You're sending truncheons and whistles against an army."

The inspector swore. "We should have been prepared." He turned to Dedlock. "How many men can you raise?"

"Twenty. Thirty, maybe, who might still be loyal."

"Twenty or thirty!" Moon exclaimed. "My God, they'll be slaughtered."

Dedlock looked afraid. "I'm sorry . . ." he whispered. "I've no power any more."

The detective turned towards the door. "Do what you can. I'm going back."

Merryweather stepped in his way. "Edward, you can't stop this on your own."

"The Somnambulist is with them. My sister, too. I owe it to them both to try." He clasped the inspector's hand, then pushed past him. "Good luck."

He left the Yard at a run, heading back towards the heart of the city.

No cab would take him anywhere near the scene. He was forced to hire the temporary use of a hansom and drive there himself, careering lunatically through the streets, little caring what damage he caused as he drove. As he drew closer, his path became blocked by fleeing and panicked crowds and he could go no further. Abandoning the cab he ran on, racing ever closer to disaster.

When I emerged from King William Street Station, the Chairman by my side, I saw a sight very few of us are ever privileged enough to witness—my dearest dreams given form, my hopes made real before me.

Fires had been lit and the sky was illuminated by bursts of scarlet, iridescent even against the watery light of the morning, an anarchist's Guy Fawkes display. The foot soldiers of Love, the faithful of the Church of the Summer Kingdom, poured through the streets, dispensing justice wherever they could, revelling in their freedom, in the epochal change they were to induce upon the city.

The morning was frosty, our breath fogged up the air like smoke, and to my astonishment I saw that my companion's exhalations appeared to be tinted a vivid green—a phenomenon I unwisely dismissed at the time as a trick of the light or mild hallucination, brought on by excitement and overwork. The old man looked blearily about him, bewildered by all the sound and fury. "Ned?" he asked hopefully.

"Yes," I lied. "I'm here."

"What's happening?"

"Come with me. We need a better view."

I took him by the hand and led him to the Monument, up its corkscrew staircase to the top. Lithe and gazelle-like, I scampered up the stairs, but I was often forced to a halt in order to let the old man recover himself. I all but carried him the final leg of the journey. Eventually we emerged into the open air, to witness a Monday morning unlike any other, unique amongst all the centuries of the city's long life.

"Behold," I cried (surely you can forgive me some grandiloquence under the circumstances), "the dawn of the Summer Kingdom."

And from our eyrie, our Wren's nest, we saw it all. Smoke rose up in mighty plumes. The sounds of war clashed about us and the air was filled with the screams of the dying. Dying? I'm afraid so. When opposing ideologies meet upon the battlefield some bloodshed is inevitable. No doubt you think such a view harsh but there are people devoid of any potential for redemption. If the city were to be reclaimed I had no choice but to put them to the sword.

The working day had barely begun before it was abruptly and bloodily curtailed. The bankers, the brokers and the clerks, the businessmen, the dealers, the accountants and the moneylenders—all were dragged screaming from their rooms and offices. A few were spared, most were executed. I would like to assure you that their deaths were swift and painless, that they were treated with some measure of dignity at the end, but in truth I doubt that this was so. An orgy of cruelty unfolded below us, a frenzy of murder and bloody reprisal for generations of injustice as the destitute shareholders in Love, my cockney bacchants, reclaimed the streets at last.

As for the bankers and their kind—some of these unfortunates were beaten to death, some cut down by axes, picks and scythes. Others were thrown into the river to drown, and I saw at least one choke to death as members of my flock stuffed his mouth with bag after swollen bag of silver coins.

Of course, I anticipate your objections. But why should these men have been granted mercy when they showed none to their innumerable victims? They had abused the city for far too long. Their time was past, a new age was upon us, and around them London's topography seemed to reconstitute itself in sympathy.

The great temples to avarice and greed were set alight. The banks were torched to the ground, the too-expensive restaurants and wine bars, the gentlemen's barbershops and outfitters—all were impregnated with cleansing flame. The gold reserves in the Bank of England were looted and my people hurled their contents carelessly into the blackness of the Thames or threw them deep into the dank recesses of the sewers. One prominent city man was thrashed to death with a shiny ingot of the stuff. The air was thick with the stench of burning currency.

The old man's voice was hoarse and weak; he gurgled as though he were speaking underwater, but still he managed to murmur a few lines of verse—not his own, alas, but words not entirely without relevance. "The king was in his counting-house, counting out his money. The queen was in the parlour, eating bread and honey."

I squeezed his hand, he squeezed mine ("Ned," he murmured), and below us the terror raged on.

*M*oon struggled through the crowd, fending off attacks from the faithful, stepping where he had to over the bloodied corpses of the fallen. He never once stopped to help but strode onward, searching for a single person amid the mêlée. "Charlotte!" he shouted. "Charlotte!"

He found her eventually, standing demurely by as the chief executive of a large firm of stockbrokers had his arms torn from their sockets. Moon left the man to his fate and grabbed at his sister. "Charlotte. What are you doing?"

She gave him another of her wonderful smiles. "Hello, Edward." She paused. "You ought not to have lied to us, you know."

"What's happened to you?"

"You don't understand."

"You're right, I don't."

Behind them the broker gave a final, feeble moan before he expired in a spreading pool of crimson. Charlotte seemed enthused by the sight. "This is the start of something wonderful. A new age. A second chance."

Moon pointed to the dead man. "There'll be no second chance for him."

"But there will for you," Charlotte insisted. "You can still be saved."

Moon pushed her aside in disgust. "Where's the Somnambulist?"

"Underground. We bound him."

Moon was defiant. "You know I'll rescue him."

She shrugged. "You're welcome to try. It scarcely matters now."

"Where's Tan?"

Charlotte pointed upwards to the Monument, at the pinnacle of which the Chairman and I stood silhouetted against the skyline, emperors of Pantisocracy. Moon left his sister and ran towards us, intent, it seemed, upon a further confrontation.

*H*e emerged minutes later, wheezing, hissing, gasping for breath. He glared at me, fury blazing in his eyes.

"Edward!" I waved. "You're just in time." The Chairman and I peered over the parapet. "It seems the cavalry has arrived."

Below us, help had come to the moneymen's aid. Several dozen policemen led by the redoubtable Detective Inspector Merryweather and accompanied by a handful of the Directorate's false Chinamen poured into the financial district.

Now, I say "poured," though the description is not entirely an apt one. My men—the troops of Love, Love, Love and Love—now *they* "poured" onto the streets. They were a great tide breaking at long last upon the city, a dam bursting, spilling open after years of miserable and unnatural confinement. But the police force, the men from the Directorate, they didn't really "pour" so much as seep and trickle into the fray, dripping over the cobblestones like water from a leaky tap.

But then Moon was complaining again, self-righteous all of a sudden. "Those men don't stand a chance."

"By my estimation they are outnumbered approximately ten to one," I said mildly. "You're right. They'll be slaughtered."

Below us a blue-coated policeman was dragged under a seething tide of Love. His screams carried up to us, 202 feet above ground. Moon was of course tiresomely sentential about the incident. "This blood is on your hands."

"On the contrary. It was you who betrayed me."

"I can't stand by and allow you to inflict this atrocity upon the city."

"This is a natural process," I chided. "Is it not written that the sheep are to be separated from the goats? The meek, the weak, the despised and the forgotten—we've been suppressed too long. This is our revenge."

"Why does it have to be like this?"

Behind us, the old man murmured, *"About, about. In reel and rout the death-fires danced at night. The water, like a witch's oils, burnt green and blue and white."*

"Do you recognise it?" I asked, something of the proud father in my manner. "It's his own work."

Moon turned on me. "Do you think he approves? Do you think he's flattered by what you've done?"

"Ask him," I said simply.

Moon tugged the Chairman away from the parapet, pulled him roughly across to me and pushed his face into mine. I recoiled from the old man's rank, electric halitosis.

"This *thing* is not alive," said Moon. "It's a corpse, barely animated by your perverted science."

"He's still just a child at present. He's confused."

Moon forced the old man to look down at the carnage and sneered: "Tell me, sir. Do you approve? Is this a fitting tribute?"

The dreamer gazed glassily, perplexedly at the street. *"The many men, so beautiful. And they all dead did lie. And a thousand thousand slimy things lived on, and so did I."*

"All this," Moon persisted, "is being done for you."

For the first time the old man seemed to notice us, to show some real awareness of his surroundings. It was as though he had finally woken up. "For me?" he murmured. "Me?"

Teary-eyed, I flung myself at his feet. "Yes!" I sobbed. "All this for you. For Pantisocracy."

"Consider well," Moon said. "Everything that is unfolding beneath us, all this suffering and agony, is being done in your name."

The Chairman shook his head. "No, no," he muttered. "No, no, no. Not like this."

"Please, sir. You have the power. Stop this."

The old man seemed to grow in stature before us, becoming taller and broader as though at the mercy of some invisible rack.

"Chairman!" I cried.

He looked at me as if I were a stranger. "I am not your Chairman." Enraged by Moon's words, his anger seemed to revitalize him. "No," he shouted (really shouted, too, not the senile mutterings he had managed till then). "This is not my fault."

"But it is," Moon whispered, like Claudius pouring poison into the ear of a better man. "This will be blamed on you."

And it was then that something extraordinary happened. Given that the day hadn't been exactly routine so far, you'll understand that I do not use the word lightly.

The Chairman roared with fury, and as his anger grew, a change began to manifest itself in his body, a fresh transfiguration. Gangrenous streaks of green appeared on his face and hands as though all of his veins were suddenly visible to us, pulsing not with the healthy ruby of life but with something hideous, diseased and dying, his face lit up with phosphorescence.

Edward Moon looked at me in horror. "What have you done?"

I admit that I was surprised by this development. The amniotic fluid which had revivified the old man must have had some special properties I had not foreseen. Nowadays, I find myself unable to recall its precise constituents. Perhaps it is for the best—I would not wish for anyone else to repeat those vile experiments.

When I had dug the old man from the ground, his left hand had been severely damaged and I felt I had no choice but to amputate, attaching in its place a hand which had once belonged to one of his closest friends and colleagues, Robert Southey.

But now I noticed that my stitching was coming undone and that the hand had begun to dangle like a child's mitten from the stump of the old man's wrist. One by one the stitches popped out and I saw oozing slime where blood and cartilage should have been.

It was around this time that I first began to worry that things were no longer going according to plan.

Since the old man's rage seemed fuelled as much by pain as anger, I became concerned that other stitching may have undone itself on the old man's person. Sick of the sight of the fighting below, he left the parapet and windmilled his way towards Moon.

Unwisely, the conjuror attempted to block his path, the gesture as fruitless as trying to halt a speeding locomotive by standing in its way.

"Wait," he said. "Please."

With a single swipe of his good right hand, the Chairman batted Moon aside, displaying far more strength than ought to have been possible. Like a boxer woozy from the fight but determined to beat the bell, Moon stumbled to his feet only for the old man to hit him again, a flicker of green playing across his hand as he did so. This time Moon crumpled to the ground and lay still.

Clearly the amniotic fluid had given the old man far more than mere life, and I considered myself fortunate that it was a comparatively mild-mannered poet whom I had succeeded in resurrecting. Even now I shudder to think of the consequences had I gifted such weird power upon, say, Lord Byron or mad Blake or that oikish fraud Chatterton.

Moon was down, unconscious or worse, and the old man marched away, disappearing back into the Monument, heading towards the streets, imbued with awesome power and purpose. Leaving Moon for dead, I saw no choice but to follow, my dreams in tatters around me.

I moved down through the spiral heart of the building, eldritch light emanating from the Chairman as he descended below me, casting strange green shadows on the walls.

At least, I *think* that is what I saw. I fear I may not have been in my perfect mind.

What happened next was a series of horrible coincidences.

You needn't worry yourself about Moon (as if you care). He was merely unconscious. Having betrayed me once that day, then goaded the Chairman into madness, a knock on the head was the very least he deserved. Personally, I should like to have seen him eviscerated.

We'll leave him lying there for the time being, lost to the world. He's done enough for now.

❧

At around the time that the Chairman had begun to display the earliest signs of his disintegration, Mr. Maurice Trotman re-enters our story. He had run through the streets for more than an hour, his umbrella clutched fearfully in one hand, his heart clenching and unclenching itself frantically inside him. His supply of courage had been used up, had leaked from him during his long flight like air from a punctured tyre.

It was his bad luck that when he made his escape from the Prefects he ran towards the centre of the city, into what he hoped might be the sanctuary of the business district. It was his bad luck that the day he chose to make such a flight was also the day that we at Love finally showed our hand. But it was all of our bad luck that he brought the Prefects with him.

Trotman finally came to a halt halfway down Cannon Street. As he struggled through crowds of flustered clerks and maddened bankers he wondered whether he might not inadvertently have stumbled into a nightmare. People were fighting around him, brawling and scrapping and—good God—was that a body in the street? Like Cyril Honeyman before the end, he toyed with the idea that the events of the morning might have been nothing more than an unusually vivid dream. He wondered, too, if the hysterical warnings of the Directorate could have had some truth in them after all and, for the first time in a life otherwise unimpeded by any colour or interest, even considered the possibility that he might be going mad.

Whimpering, his dressing-gown gaping open, he hunkered

down onto the pavement, curling up into a foetal ball. He hoped that if he crouched there long enough he might be ignored and neglected by the mob. No such luck, of course.

Somebody tapped him on his shoulder. Refusing to turn around, hoping to deny the inevitable, he squeezed shut his eyes and hugged himself tighter.

"Come on, sir. Play up, play up and play the game."

Trotman opened his eyes. Hawker and Boon loomed before him, evincing not the slightest sign of fatigue from the long pursuit.

"What ho, Maurice," said Boon.

"Thanks for the run, old thing. Rather exhilarating."

Boon snatched the umbrella and Maurice Trotman sobbed.

"Oh, be a man," chided the smaller of the killers. "Face up to it like one of the chaps." With this, he held the umbrella high above his head—a commuter's sword of Damocles.

"Why?" asked the Civil Servant feebly. "Just tell me that."

"We're doing it for a favour."

"Old chum of ours."

"Real brick."

"P'raps you know him."

"Funny little chap."

"All white and queer-looking."

"Skimpole?" Trotman managed as, moments before his extinction, understanding flooded too late into his brain.

"Quite right," said Hawker.

Had he lived longer, Trotman might have protested at the injustice of it all, at the unfairness of being hunted down and murdered for nothing more than doing his job. As it happened, he had no time left to think. Boon brought the umbrella down hard upon his chest and its spike entered his body, neatly perforating his heart with a crisp snap. It was, at least, over quickly.

Cackling with delight, Boon pushed the umbrella fully through the body of his victim and forced the thing open. Trotman cut a strange, undignified sight, all but naked, an unfurled umbrella sprouting from his chest like a fancy cocktail stick skewering an olive. The Prefects stood back and admired their handiwork.

Hawker clapped politely. "Bravo."

Boon rummaged around in the pockets of his blazer and drew forth a couple of lollipops. He passed one to his friend and they stood sucking contemplatively for a time, gazing at the carnage unfolding around them with the mild anticipation of men waiting for a late bus.

Hawker pulled the lolly from his mouth, making a slurping noise as he did so. "Looks like a proper scrap."

Boon crunched and swallowed. "Fancy causing a ruckus? Bit of mischief?"

A fat man came wheezing past them, an axe clutched in one hand, the arterial spray of two dozen prominent bankers congealing on his suit. You may remember him as Donald McDonald, my oldest and most faithful lieutenant.

"I say. 'Scuse me, sir."

McDonald careered to a stop.

"Could you tell us what the deuce is going on?"

"We're taking back the city," my friend gasped. "Reclaiming it from the moneymen. The age of Pantisocracy is here."

Boon yawned. "Politics."

"Pantisocracy?" Hawker asked, only mildly interested. "What's that, then?"

"Freedom, food and poetry for all," McDonald replied. "The death of commerce. A new Eden at the heart of the city."

Hawker smirked. "It'll never work."

McDonald began to frame some objection but it was too late. He had already bored them.

"Your turn," Boon said. The big man turned to McDonald, grabbed him roughly by the throat and with a desultory twitch of his hand—exerting no more force than you or I might employ to open an especially recalcitrant bottle top—snapped the unfortunate fellow's neck.

"Another?" Hawker asked.

"Why not? Might kill an hour or two."

They set off into the heart of the fighting, towards the Monument, killing indiscriminately as they went—police, bankers, Love, Directorate men—wild cards gleefully disrupting the game, spreading fear and disaster wherever they trod.

Like I said: a series of horrible coincidences.

*P*lease don't think I've forgotten about the Somnambulist. We left him underground, you'll remember, deep in the vaults of Love and pinioned to the floor by twenty-four swords. You'll have realised, of course, that something like this was never going to stop him for long. By the time the Chairman had left me, the giant had already freed himself from half a dozen of the things, tugging them out of himself one by one, like a porcupine pulling out its own quills. He worked steadily, certain that the city was in danger, knowing it was his duty to protect it.

I, meanwhile, was following the Chairman. Puffed-up, bloated and enraged, the old man was wading through the battle, knocking combatants aside regardless of their allegiance. He proved easy to follow, since he left in his wake a trail of body parts (fingers, an ear, lumps of flesh and skin) as well as a lurid green track, like a giant upright snail.

Those members of Love who encountered him were appalled by the sight of a roaring monster in place of their leader and inspiration, and as his rampage continued I could sense, palpable as smoke, the spread of dissent amongst my followers, the crumbling of their collective faith.

It now became my priority to return him to his tank in the underworld, where I harboured hopes that he might yet be saved, revivified, restored. The day may not have gone as I had planned but there was still hope for the future. And so I followed, hoping to shepherd him back underground.

"Sir," I cried. "Sir, it's Ned here."

He stopped what he was doing and let out a gargantuan groan. "Ned?"

"That's right."

"Is that you?"

"Come with me, sir. I can take you somewhere safe."

To my great relief, he decided to do as he was told.

*M*oon regained consciousness some ten minutes after we had departed. Doing his best to ignore the pain, he left the Monument and ran as hurriedly as he was able back onto the street.

The fighting had thinned out—the moneymen were either dead or had escaped into another part of the city—and the battle had become a two-way affair, the forces of Love, the police and the Directorate joined against the Prefects.

Hawker and Boon had burst onto the scene, a hurricane of penknives and inky fingers, dead arms and Chinese burns. They had already butchered several hundred men, felling them like skittles. As it gradually dawned upon the assembled troops that the Prefects meant to destroy whatever was closest to them without discrimination, several strange alliances were joined. Mr. Speight, for example, was seen to fight side by side with an ersatz Chinaman. Dedlock took up arms with Mina, the bearded whore.

Detective Inspector Merryweather had withdrawn from the fray and was trying to marshal his men into a concerted attack when he saw Moon appear at the foot of the Monument. "Edward!" he shouted above the din and chaos. "Over here!"

Moon ran across to join him. "What's happening?" he gasped. "What are those things?"

"No one seems sure. I've heard . . . rumours."

A voice called out: "*I* know."

They turned to see a squat, wizened figure walking towards them. His flesh was tugged tight about his face, his eyes hollows of pain, his skin covered with a multitude of fierce sores and lesions. Mr. Skimpole was very close to death, his life seeping almost visibly away. "They're the Prefects," he rasped. "And they're my fault." Without acknowledging either man further, the albino stumbled on towards the centre of the mêlée, for the eye of the storm, for Hawker and for Boon.

"Where's my sister?" Moon snapped. "Where's the Somnambulist?"

"She's in the thick of it," Merryweather said bemusedly. "But I've not seen the giant. Shouldn't worry, though. Practically indestructible, isn't he?"

"Have you seen the Chairman?"

"Who?"

"Never mind." Moon set off towards the fighting, following the green trail of the poet.

I was only a few minutes ahead of him at the time, trying to manhandle the old man back underground. It was tough and unforgiving work as parts kept dropping from his body without warning. We reached the mouth of King William Street Station and I led him inside, down past the ticket booths, along the platform, onto the track and towards the headquarters of Love. I tried not to think about how badly things had gone wrong, how my schemes and dreams had been undone, but simply did my best to concentrate on saving the Chairman, on preserving the cornerstone of my vision. I didn't know it at the time, but as I grappled with the old man, the Somnambulist, with a look of intense concentration on his face, was pulling the final swords from his body, almost free at last.

Like most schoolboys, the Prefects were easily bored. Half an hour was all it took to rout the combined forces of the Directorate, the Metropolitan Police Force and Love, Love, Love and Love. The streets around them were upholstered with corpses; the gutters ran red with the blood of the fallen. Hawker and Boon were in the midst of removing a man's eye with the horseshoe attachment on their penknife when they caught sight of Mr. Skimpole tottering uncertainly towards them.

"Skimpers!" shouted Boon. "What the devil are you doing here? Hawker, look. It's Mr. S."

Stepping over a dozen or so dead bodies with fastidious care, the albino finally reached their side. "What have you done?" he hissed.

"Pretty much what you asked, haven't we, Boon?"

The other man nodded in fervent agreement. "The Mongoose is down, Maurice Trotman's snuffed it and we've tidied this lot up as a bonus. Practically done your job for you, I'd say."

"Please go," Skimpole gasped. "You've done enough."

"Well, I like that."

"Dashed ungrateful's what I call it."

"What . . ." Skimpole stopped, his face screwed up in pain, until he managed at last a feeble: "What do I owe you?"

"Owe us, sir? Jolly decent of you to ask about payment at a time like this."

"You don't owe us a bean, sir."

"Not any more."

"What?" Skimpole wheezed.

"Point of fact, we've taken what you owe already."

"Shouldn't worry, sir. It's quite within your means."

"Rather a bargain, I'd have said."

Boon ruffled his hair affectionately. "I'd get home, though, sir, if I was you. He doesn't look at all well, does he, Hawker?"

"Positively peaky."

"If you're going to die, sir, I'd do it at home, Keeling over round here's just going to look like you're following the crowd. No, no, place to do it's back in Wimbledon. Mortality's unusual there. Out of the ordinary. People might take a spot of notice."

A voice floated across to them. "Stop!"

Amused, the Prefects craned their heads to look. "Oh, I say, who's that?"

"Isn't he the fat johnny from the club?"

"Could be."

Dedlock stepped forward, a revolver clasped tightly in his hand. "Let him go."

"You don't understand," the albino murmured.

Hawker moved towards Dedlock.

"Don't move. I know what you are."

Boon grinned. "I doubt that."

"It's all right," Skimpole muttered. "They're working for me."

"For you?"

Stifling a yawn, Hawker sauntered across to the scarred man and knocked the gun from his hand. "Name's Hawker. Don't think we've been properly introduced." And he gripped the older man's hand in a parody of a handshake.

At once, Dedlock felt a terrific burning sensation which began at his fingertips and rushed over his entire body, a broiling, intense, pulsating heat. He fainted almost immediately.

Hawker shrugged and let him fall to the ground. "Just a little gift," he explained. "No extra charge."

"What's happened to that funny green fellow?" asked Boon.

"Did a bunk down the Tube, I think," Hawker replied.

"Shall we have a look-see?"

"Why not?"

"I'm too tired to walk."

"Agreed."

They turned back to Skimpole.

"Ta-ta, then, sir."

"Tinkety-tonk."

The Prefects linked hands, looking for an instant oddly innocent, like real children. Boon crumpled his brow, apparently deep in concentration.

I expect by now that your disbelief is not so much suspended as dangling from the highest plateau of credulity. Even so, I regret that this next incident requires a further extension of that capacity.

*T*he two men seemed to shimmer slightly, flickering like a reflection in rippling water. This effect lasted for no longer than a few seconds before they disappeared. Oh yes, disappeared. I can't put it any more plainly than that. One moment they were there, the next they had been erased from existence. The sole sign that they had ever stood in that spot, their only residue, was a pungent smell of fireworks and the lingering aftertaste of sherbet dip.

They left maybe three dozen people alive. The living were outnumbered by the dead.

*T*his, then, was the final horrible coincidence of the day, as all the strands knitted together to ensure the total failure of my plans. It is as well that I am a good and patient man and not prone to bitterness—somebody with a greater propensity towards self-pity than I might justifiably consider themselves a second Job.

I hurried the Chairman along the tunnel, back towards the sphere. He was degenerating fast, half his face gone, his body oozing and excreting spurts of that terrible green liquid. I tried to keep clear of the stuff but inevitably a little of it reached my skin, fizzing and sizzling like acid. Where it touched me, my body smelt like burning sausages.

We reached Love at last and I tried to get the old man inside. Behind us, I could hear someone running in our direction. Then a faint cry: "Tan!" It was Moon, of course, looking for revenge or some such. I bundled the Chairman through the green door and into the main hall.

What happened then was confused and difficult to follow. Even today I have great difficulty arranging events in their correct order.

The Chairman recognised the great hall as soon as he saw it, and I must say that his reaction was not one of grateful homecoming. Presumably he associated it with his long incarceration, with the tank and the amniotic fluid. In consequence, he became suddenly frantic to leave and return to the surface.

He roared something which I imagine was intended to be "No," but, so thoroughly had his innards been eaten away by that viscous green slime which still oozed from his every pore, the words that emerged from his ravaged throat sounded more like animal roars than human speech.

Heroically, I tried to reason with him. "Mr. Chairman, please. I can repair you. Believe me, it's for the best."

"Sur-face," he growled, more coherent now. "SURFACE."

"Stay. I beg of you."

He seemed to calm down a little at this and I stepped closer, hoping to lead him by the hand and return him to the tank. Very probably, it was the worst move I could have made. With one swipe of what was left of his right hand (technically now more of a stump) he hit me hard across the face and sent me sprawling to the ground. I still carry the legacy of that blow today—a purple mark on my left cheek, around the size and shape of an apple, often mistaken for a birthmark.

I lay there, unable and unwilling to move, as the Chairman, dripping with poisonous green fluid, turned back towards the door and the outside world. How much indiscriminate havoc would he wreak before he was stopped? Given that his slightest touch was potentially lethal, I fancied the cost would be high indeed.

What I hadn't bargained on, however, was another man, just as deadly as he.

Later, I reasoned that I must have reached the main hall just as the Somnambulist had removed the final sword from his belly. As I was thrown to the floor, he stood up, dusted himself down and looked over towards us.

The Chairman gaped at the Somnambulist. He pointed and screamed something which sounded at the time like *"My God,"* though it has since been put to me that it was something else entirely.

Spewing green acid, the Chairman staggered forwards and flung himself at the giant. The Somnambulist, weakened by his ordeal, was taken aback at first, but soon fought back, and furiously.

There was a crash and a stumble behind me. Edward Moon appeared by my side, intending no doubt to challenge me to a duel or bring me to justice. Mercifully, we were both distracted by a far more terrible sight.

Surprisingly, the green fluid seemed to affect the Somnambulist just as badly as it had me, and his face contorted in pain. Moon and I could do nothing but watch. It was like seeing two lions fight for dominance of the pack—no, more than that, grander—like two ancient reptiles, megalosaurs clashing on some primeval killing ground, twin gods, colossi grappling for the fate of worlds.

Another sight distracted us even from this awful vision, at first nothing more than a wispiness, then a faint disturbance in the air, then a swirling, shimmering rush of colour. A foot or so from where the conjuror and I stood transfixed, the Prefects flickered into existence. In their hands they carried four absurd sticks of dynamite—the kind you see in newspaper cartoons, great red sticks of the stuff, their enormous fuses spitting sparks.

Oh, you'll say that they couldn't possibly work. Explosives don't actually look like *that*, those are just comical representations intended for the amusement of children.

Of course you're entitled to your opinion, but I was there and I can assure you of their efficacy. Hawker or Boon (one of them—I get confused) flung the dynamite into the centre of the great hall.

Leaving the red sticks spitting on the floor, the Prefects fled from the hall, peals of cackling laughter in their wake.

Moon stumbled forward, hoping, I imagine, to help his friend, but it was already too late. The first piece of dynamite exploded in the far corner of the room, bringing half the roof down with an ear-splitting roar. I could hear the whole of the building's structure creak and groan in protest and begin to fall in upon itself. Thick clouds of dust all but obscured our vision, but from what I was able to make out the giant and the dreamer ignored it all and fought on.

I have no shame in admitting that I picked myself up and ran, back through the tunnels and out onto the street. I have many faults, but at least I know when to cut my losses.

The last thing I saw as I glanced back was the Chairman and the Somnambulist—monsters locked in conflict, an emerald miasma hanging about them, whilst Moon, not knowing what to do, gazed helplessly on.

He ran away in the end, just like me, though he stayed, I believe, to see the second explosion. He was later to claim that, before the great hall fell utterly in upon itself, the Chairman's acid had begun to eat its way through the rock itself and that the adversaries had begun to sink into the earth, swallowed up as if by quicksand. He called out for the Somnambulist but the giant fought wordlessly on, and Moon had no choice but to flee. I

wonder sometimes what he might have shouted before everything fell down, what final words he might have had, and I wonder, too, if the Somnambulist called back, if—at long last—he
spoke.

All I know is that Moon escaped just before the last explosion.
Behind him he saw the headquarters of Love, all that I had worked
for, buried for ever by rubble. I was glad not to be there to see that.

$\mathcal{F}$or the second time that day I emerged panting back onto the
street. The fighting was over; police, medics and other professional busybodies were arguing over what to do with all the mess
and corpses. Even the press had started to sniff about.

On seeing all this commotion, I felt a sudden surge of hope. I
thought I might still escape and slip away in the midst of the confusion. No such luck. I felt a revolver pressed hard against the
back of my head.

"The Somnambulist is dead."

"Edward?" I asked feebly.

He spun me round, placed the gun at my forehead. "The Somnambulist is dead," he repeated in a flat, toneless voice.

I wondered how I could possibly apologise without sounding
insincere. "Sorry," I said eventually, and shrugged. "Thought he
was indestructible."

$\mathcal{I}$ doubt you'd have done any better under the circumstances.

$\mathcal{M}$oon pushed the gun harder against my head and seemed on
the cusp of pulling the trigger when he was interrupted by a familiar voice.

"You must be Edward Moon."

"What do you want?" Moon hissed.

"My name is Thomas Cribb." I realised that the ugly man was standing behind me, facing the detective. "I would offer to shake hands but I can see you're a little tied up."

"What?"

"You're about to make a considerable mistake."

"I thought you'd joined Love."

"Me? Well, I suppose I may do. But that will happen tomorrow."

"Give me one good reason why I shouldn't shoot him."

"Only this." Cribb smiled. "You don't. I've seen the future and the Reverend Doctor here is languishing in a prison cell."

Out of the corner of my eye I could see the approach of several policemen and the inspector. They hung back, waiting to see how the situation would play itself out. I suppose I've no right to be angry but I rather think it was their duty to save me, not stand by and watch my murder.

"Does he die?" Moon asked, sounding—I have to say—unnecessarily bloodthirsty. "Is he executed?"

Cribb pulled a face. "They won't hang him."

"No justice, then?"

"I can promise you this: He gets punishment enough. He suffers. Please. Put down the gun."

For a moment, Moon looked as though he still might go through with it.

"Please," the ugly man said again. Moon seemed to relent and started to return the gun to his pocket. But at the last second he brought the gun back up towards my face.

"No!" shouted Cribb.

Moon, distracted by the sound, pulled the trigger too soon. The bullet went wild, missed me (though I fancy I felt it brush my cheek) and hit the ugly man instead. The damage can't have been all that serious but he fell to the ground nonetheless, whimpering like a soccer player hoping for sympathy, clutching at his left hand and muttering to himself.

The police finally appeared (not before time) and I was wrenched roughly to my feet. Handcuffs were slapped on me with little or no consideration as to how they might chafe. I was led away and Moon said nothing.

As I walked, however, I heard him call out to someone. Cribb? Perhaps, but I have always felt a strange certainty that he was addressing someone else entirely. "The Somnambulist is dead," he cried, then more quietly: "The Somnambulist is dead."

20

It happens every morning underground. Chances are you've noticed it yourself.

In the rush hour, as all those beleaguered commuters fight their way off the trains at Monument Station, pinstriped and bowler-hatted to a man, ready to submit themselves to the merciless grind of another day's work, they bear witness to an extraordinary phenomenon.

Shit. The choking stench of it becomes on some mornings almost overpowering. I am reliably informed that there is many a nose wrinkled in distaste, many a copy of the *Times* folded into an impromptu fan, many a handkerchief pressed discreetly against the face. But so used are these passengers to the city's creaking, dilapidated railways that they make no comment at this indignity but, teeth clenched and pride swallowed, travel stoically onwards. I've no idea why such an effect should occur, though I imagine it has at least something to do with the tunnels' unfortunate proximity to the sewer system.

I think this is significant. It seems to me that London reveals something of its real self at such moments, shows the skull beneath its skin, its true cloacal nature. It is meant as a warning, I think, and as a rebuke.

How different things might have been had we succeeded! Poppies and daisies would grow now where the banks and counting-houses stand. London in its corrupt state would have passed away and in its place the state of Pantisocracy would flourish and bloom. A dream, you say? A childish fantasy? Perhaps.

Two and a half hours after Hawker's searing handshake had rendered him unconscious, Mr. Dedlock opened his eyes and hoisted himself groggily to his feet. Happily, he had awoken from his stupor without any obvious ill effects, save for a faint, throbbing ache in his head, no worse than he had endured on countless occasions after a night's overindulgence.

Around him, the fires had been extinguished, the dead were being cleared away and the walking wounded bandaged up—everything polished and cleaned and made tidy. Within a day the battlefield would be restored to its usual condition and the citizens would try to pretend that nothing had really happened there at all. It was as though after Hastings the survivors had simply swept up the debris, stowed away the casualties and hoped everything would be back to normal again tomorrow. Such small-minded behaviour—London had come within a hair's-breadth of being saved, and her people had responded like children afraid of the dark, by squeezing shut their eyes and begging it to go away.

The Church of the Summer Kingdom had offered them salvation but they were content to live on just as they always had, in iniquity, in ignorance and sin.

Not, of course, that Dedlock thought about any of this when he looked approvingly around him. No, he was merely relieved that the incident was over and that he had survived unscathed. Just a little self-consciously, he cleared his throat, walked across to the nearest group of policemen and began barking orders.

But Dedlock had changed. It wasn't until hours later, when he was back home and undressing for bed, that he happened to glance into a mirror and see for the first time exactly what the Prefects had done to him, the subtlety of their promised gift.

The scars on his torso had gone and with them the marks upon his face—those milk-white indentations which had once so strikingly crisscrossed his body—all had been wiped away, erased as easily as the Somnambulist might remove chalk marks from his slate. Dedlock looked down at his chest, unlined and newly smooth, and was disgusted by what he saw, now so commonplace, so unbearably everyday and unremarkable.

Suddenly short of breath, he shrugged off the last of his clothes, slumped down upon his bed and did something he'd not done for almost twenty years.

In the morning, when he called at the Survivors' Club to tender his resignation, his eyes were still puffy and red from weeping.

The Prefects knew exactly what they were doing. But compared to the albino, Dedlock got off lightly.

I'm not sure how much I can bring myself to tell you about what happened to Mr. Skimpole. Where should I begin? At which point in that protracted and humiliating death? The long and agonising journey back to Wimbledon? The moment when he was ejected from his hansom cab after spewing a glutinous red substance over the seats? When he looked down at the mess and wondered, almost idly, whether some of that putrescent slime might not be the last remnants of his stomach lining?

No. I'll spare you that—we'll begin, I think, as the man arrived back at his house, wrestled with key and lock for the final time, the roar of pain in his head blocking out even the sounds of his neighbours' revelry. To steady himself, he leant against the front door for a moment, then half-walked, half-stumbled inside, rasping out his son's name.

Of course, there was no reply and Skimpole tottered further inside, determined to be with his only child as death collected her due. Reeking of vomit and bleeding from at least a dozen separate places, he stumbled into the kitchen, wailing for his son.

It was then that he saw him. Or rather what was left of him.

Even I (scarcely a squeamish man) can hardly bear to describe the thing. No doubt you have a good idea yourself—you will have guessed by now the nature of the Prefects' "fee."

The Skimpole boy lay supine on the floor, pale and clammy, a pitiable look of terror on his face. His skin and clothes were spattered with crimson and every bone in his body was broken. He had been expertly battered to death with his own two crutches.

Numbly, Skimpole wondered if they had taken turns.

Too weak to scream out his rage and grief, too tired to cry, the albino fell to his knees and collapsed upon his son's ruined form. With his last remaining strength, he clasped the corpse's hand (still wet with blood), squeezed it tight and waited patiently for the end.

❧

As for the murderers themselves—no policeman will ever track them down nor any court try them for their innumerable crimes.

After they disappeared, a half-hearted manhunt was arranged but nothing came of it and the matter was swiftly dropped. To be frank, I doubt anyone *wanted* to find them.

To the best of my knowledge, the Prefects have appeared twice more since then, though I've no doubt that they figure in many other stories as yet unknown to me—lurking at the corners of other narratives, some very old, some still to be told, some more strange perhaps even than this.

Twelve years ago, witnesses of an atrocity carried out under the auspices of the new Russian government claimed to have seen two men bizarrely dressed as English schoolboys take a leading role in the massacre. No one believed them, naturally, but those of us who were there beneath the Monument that day recognised at once the handiwork of Masters Hawker and Boon.

They have surfaced again more recently—some appalling bloodbath in New Zealand. I saw a newspaper story about the incident, illustrated by a blurred photograph taken at the aftermath of the scene. Most likely it was my imagination but I could have sworn that Hawker stood at the periphery of the frame. He was fuzzy and indistinct but it seemed to me as though he was grinning delightedly at his handiwork, at the destruction unravelling about him. Sadly, I am unable to verify this, as the paper was taken away from me before an hour had passed. They seem oddly strict here about reading matter.

It should go without saying that, despite all the years that had passed since the Battle of King William Street Station, the Hawker in the photograph looked not a day older. It was as though he had been frozen in time, unaging, like a fly trapped in amber.

Should you ever have the profound misfortune to encounter these creatures, I need hardly caution you to run (not walk) away from them, to block your ears so as not to hear their lies, to flee in giddy desperation for your life.

*N*ot for me the picturesque death of Mr. Skimpole. I have been subjected to a far longer and, in a sense, more gruesome execution. There was talk at one time of my being hanged for treason (I believe Detective Inspector Merryweather was especially vociferous on the subject) but I was able to outwit my captors without a great deal of effort. After some faintly degrading play-acting on my part, they put me here, in a sanctuary where the supposed mental condition of its inhabitants places me beyond the reach of the state's bloodier excesses.

Time is notoriously difficult to judge in a place like this, the passing of night and day almost impossible to mark save by the irregular rationing of food and drink. When I first arrived, they locked me up on my own for . . . how long? Days? Weeks? Even now I can't be entirely certain.

It's testament to my tremendous resilience that I was able to endure such solitary incarceration without my mind cracking under the strain. As it was, I emerged from my confinement all the stronger, if, admittedly, rather lonely. I am a sociable creature and I found that I had missed the warmth of companionship and camaraderie, the sound of voices other than my own. Consequently, I was permitted—under strict conditions—to receive guests.

I confess I was surprised that he came to see me at all.

*Th*omas Cribb," he said and reached his left hand (unbandaged, five-fingered) across the table. One of the guards, his beefy arms folded, observed us truculently from the other side of the room.

"We've met before," I said.

Something like a smile flickered across his face. "So I gather."

I had never previously enjoyed an opportunity to study the man at close quarters, and I cannot stress enough quite how remarkably striking was his ugliness, how compellingly repulsive.

"What do you want?" I asked.

"I want to make you a promise."

I noticed that he had brought a newspaper with him and I caught a glimpse of its headline—a report, it seemed, of recent events beneath the Monument. I saw my own name and below it an insulting likeness of my face.

Cribb leant forward across the desk towards me. At the gesture, the guard unfolded his arms and reached instinctively for the truncheon which hung from the belt about his waist. The ugly man fixed me with his most piercing gaze.

"I do not care to see my city threatened," Cribb said.

"*Your* city?"

"I promise to do everything in my power to stop you. I'll help this . . ." He glanced down at the paper as if to check some minor detail: "This Edward Moon. I'll teach him how to thwart you."

I yawned. "Sorry. Don't follow."

"I'll guide him. Use him to ensure you don't succeed."

I grinned at the guard. "Maybe he ought to be in here with us," I quipped, and gratifyingly, the man smirked in response.

I've built up a good rapport with my gaolers. I think they've taken to me and I suspect that many of them (though it would be more than their jobs are worth to admit it) know that I really shouldn't be in here at all.

My visitor rose to his feet. "By the way," he said, "history will not remember you."

I chose not to reply to this last, childish barb and Thomas Cribb walked silently away.

Perhaps, in retrospect, I should have said more, kept him talking, found out more about his claims. As it was, I never saw him again.

Frankly, I don't consider it a great loss. There was always something so bloody smug about the man.

A week passed before I received my second visitor (I say a week; of course, it might just as easily have been a fortnight or a month). You'll think it strange, and at the time it certainly surprised me, but even after everything he'd done, some part of me was actually pleased to see him.

"Edward," I said, and smiled.

For a man who had suffered so much, he looked well. A little older, perhaps, greyer, with some of the swagger gone out of him, and some of his vanity, his preening self-confidence, satisfyingly punctured. All in all, I thought it an improvement.

We sat in silence for a while.

"Why have you come?" I said at last.

"I need to ask you something."

"Anything," I said, perhaps a trifle overeager.

"I need to know why."

To my—and I suspect to *our*—surprise, his visits became a regular fixture.

I like to think we both gained a good deal from the encounters. I tried my utmost to give him an insight into what I had intended to achieve (though, needless to say, I was never actually able to convert him) and he brought me news from the outside world, about what had happened after I was led away in chains. Between us we were able to stitch together a complete overview of events, a comprehensive narrative of all that had transpired in the months leading up to the Battle of King William Street Station.

The body of the Somnambulist has yet to be found. In a conviction born of grief, Edward has come to believe that the giant still lives, that he sleeps somewhere beneath the surface, waiting, Arthur-like, for the city's hour of need. It might be of some interest to you that when I last saw him, Moon had begun to hold some eccentric notions as to his friend's identity. He showed me a postcard which depicted the two giant stone statues that guard the Guildhall—Gog and Magog, as Cribb correctly identified them—and swore that he recognised something of the Somnambulist in their features. Personally, I could never see the resemblance.

Publicly, Moon announced him dead. There was even a funeral, though it was sparsely attended and I was not invited. The inspector was there, along with Charlotte, Mrs. Grossmith, a few well-wishers and general idlers. They used an empty coffin (constructed to unusually large specifications as though the giant really did lie in state within) and buried it, ironically, in Highgate Cemetery, scant feet from where another, more celebrated plot lies similarly uninhabited.

But Moon also brought me happier news. The Church of the Summer Kingdom lives on; the light of Pantisocracy has yet to be extinguished. Some time ago, a small group of the faithful—six men, six women—travelled across the Atlantic with the intention of founding a community upon the banks of the Susquehanna just as the old man planned. They have my blessing and my prayers—or would do had they asked for them. You may have seen in the popular press that these pilgrims have disowned me and my methods—understandable, of course, under the circumstances, but I'd be lying if I said that such disloyalty didn't sting.

Edward does not share my sentiments. He thinks the venture a fool's errand which can only end in disaster. And he has good personal reason to disapprove—it was his own sister, you see, my dear Charlotte, once Love 999, who orchestrated the whole thing.

Edward always believed that his sister's conversion to my cause was only temporary, an aberration brought about by the unusually persuasive recruitment techniques of Love, Love, Love and Love. As it turned out, the transformation is permanent and irreversible. She remains my truest convert. Curious, is it not, how it is often the worst sceptics and bitterest cynics who become the most zealous of us all.

But Edward has further reason to be distressed at his sister's defection. She has taken poor Grossmith with her. Deprived of a husband and confronted with evidence of his duplicity in the most upsetting manner, the housekeeper decided to throw in her lot with the new Pantisocrats. I wonder what use she can be to them, since she is well past child-bearing age and unlikely to be much good as either a poet or a farmer. Perhaps she can organise the cooking or busy herself with some light cleaning.

It is a source of concern to me that I have not heard any news of the Pantisocrats since their departure. I have scoured the papers to no avail, begged the guards and the doctors for any whisper they may have heard in the outside world, but it seems that they have disappeared. Pity. I should like to have known how it all turned out.

The last time I saw Edward Moon he had said goodbye to them all that very morning, come hotfoot from waving them off at the docks. I asked if Charlotte had mentioned me and he assured me that she had not. Something in his manner, however, coupled with the suspicious speed of his reply, convinced me that he was lying. He would admit only that there had been further tears and recriminations at their parting. It was, as I understand it, a final goodbye.

Moon told me that he intended to travel. A certain respect had grown up between us in the months of our conversations and we were able to bid one another a civil farewell and shake hands almost amicably. I told him that I intended to write a full account of all that had happened, to which he replied that I should do precisely as I pleased.

The last I heard, he had gone to Africa, wherein he travelled widely, eventually forming something of a bond with a particular tribe of its indigenous people. For all I know, he lives there still. I am reminded of some lines by the poet:

And ne'er was heard of more: but 'tis supposed,
He lived and died among the savage men.

I have a deal more time on my hands. My hosts have continued to be accommodating and I am allowed light and space in which to write, as well as a limited number of foolscap sheets and a single pencil. No pen, unfortunately—I have often requested an inkwell and nib, but there is some petty rule here about spiked implements and sharp points. They do not discourage my work, though at the end of each day everything is taken from me for safekeeping. I feel sure that my skill has grown with the tale's telling and I am concerned that the opening sections must seem amateurish and crude in comparison with later chapters. I have repeatedly asked if I might not be allowed the complete manuscript, if only for an hour or two, so that I might make some revisions and clarifications from which the work can only benefit. To date, they have denied my every request.

No doubt you can tell from the clinical manner in which I have related this narrative that I am not a man inclined to excesses of the imagination.

However, I have been much troubled of late by a recurring dream.

It is not as other dreams—no fragmentary jumble of dredged-

up memories and half-forgotten faces, no meaningless kaleidoscope of impossible juxtapositions and incongruities. Nor does
its detail fade and vanish in the morning but lingers in my mind
long after I have woken, acquiring such permanence and solidity
that I wonder if what I have seen is not somehow more than the
fantasies of sleep but a piece of reality. The truth.

Every time it is the same. It begins deep in a forest, all light
beneath the canopy of trees tinted a dusky green, strange birds
screeching overhead, creatures chittering unseen in the under-
growth. I see twelve people—six men, six women—trekking
through the woods, often having to hack and battle their way
through the foliage but, rather wonderfully, always endeavouring
to walk forward in pairs, in crocodile formation, like schoolchildren on a day trip to the zoo. Some of them I recognise—Mr.
Speight, Mrs. Grossmith, Mina the bearded whore. Dear Charlotte is with them, too, radiant even as she battles, perspiring,
with tree-roots and recalcitrant branches, her natural beauty
complemented and enhanced by that of her surroundings.

At the head of the party is a man I do not recognise at first.
Completely bald, his pate gleams with sweat as he leads the others
through the trees. Baffled, I watch his progress for a while until at
last it comes to me. Even though I have had this dream dozens of
times before, on every fresh occasion I am astonished by the realisation. It is the Somnambulist, stripped at last of his sideboards
and wig, of the props and make-believe of his life with Moon,
come at last into the cleansing light of revelation. His skin is un-
tanned and, as ever, he says nothing.

At length, the party emerges at the edge of the forest on a small
promontory some feet from the ground. They look down and see
below them the great expanse of the Susquehanna, its thick blue
ribbon coiling through the landscape, framed on either side by
lush, glorious swathes of perfect green, unpeopled, fertile, poised
for Pantisocracy.

The Somnambulist gazes upon this sliver of Eden and smiles. Then he opens his mouth and—to my everlasting surprise and joy—he speaks. His voice sounds nothing like what I had expected.

"Well, then," he says. "Where do we start?"

Enjoyed *The Somnambulist?*

Turn the page for more

A deeper look into Edward Moon's world,
including an interview with the detective himself and
an essay from the author on the history behind one of
the main themes of the novel.

A Short History of Pantisocracy
(and Other Possibilities)

*T*he dream of Pantisocracy was always bound to be a mayfly thing. Cooked up by two young Englishmen – the twenty-one-year-old Samuel Taylor Coleridge and the future poet laureate Robert Southey, then still only nineteen – in the summer of 1794, the idea was born, flowered briefly and hopelessly before withering away, within months, into disappointment, frustration and bungled compromise. The plan was naïve, ambitious and flawed from the start, but, more than that, its originators were fundamentally ill-suited to collaboration. Whereas Southey had drive and self-discipline in abundance, coupled with an ineradicable core of common sense, Coleridge was always a dreamer and a fantasist, a weaver of illusions and visions and peculiar jokes, the man of whom E. M. Forster once wrote, "if life is a lesson, he never learnt it."

The year had not begun well for Coleridge. A bibulous drinker, heavy user of opium and recklessly promiscuous lover, he had fled his Cambridge college just before Christmas under thunder-clouds of debt, having contrived to find himself in arrears to everyone from his violin teacher to his wine merchant. Desperate to

pay off his clamouring crowd of creditors, he took the extreme
step of enlisting in the army, signing up, with a typical flourish,
under the deliberately ridiculous nom de plume "Silas Tomkyn
Comberbache."

A lanky, maladroit scholar, prone to an indolence which was
punctuated only occasionally by bouts of frenetic activity,
Coleridge made an exceptionally poor soldier – tumbling from
his horse, failing to keep his kit in acceptable condition, suffering
from saddlesores and boils and generally proving, on an almost
daily basis, to be singularly ill-suited to military life. He was res-
cued by his brothers after four disastrous months, and the Regi-
mental Muster Roll records his departure on 10 April 1794 with a
kind of grimly humorous relief. "Discharged: S. T. Comberbache," it reads and then, by way of explanation, "Insane."

The poet was returned to Cambridge the next day, insisting that
he had sworn off all madcap schemes, daft plots and catastrophi-
cally ill-advised adventures for good. Two months later, on 17
June, Coleridge made the acquaintance of Robert Southey, and
shortly afterwards, their plans for Pantisocracy were under way.

The new friends shared a horror at the savage inequalities of society ("I am sick of this world and discontented with everyone in
it," Southey had complained the previous year. "I look round the
world and everywhere find the same mournful spectacle. . . . The
strong tyrannize over the weak. . . . The same depravity pervades
the whole creation."), and they resolved to find a way to escape the
institutionalised corruption of English life. Coleridge would later
call it an "experiment of human perfectibility" – the establishment
of an egalitarian society to be located (after a brief flirtation with
Kentucky) by the banks of the Susquehanna River in the state of
Pennsylvania. Ever the showboating polymath, Coleridge coined
the word "Pantisocracy" from the Greek roots *pant-isocratia*, meaning "the government of all," and as his enthusiasm grew ("Pantisocracy!" he exclaimed in a note to Southey. "O I shall have such a

scheme of it! My head, my heart are all alive."), the details of the adventure swelled in complexity and ambition.

They proposed to lead a party of twelve married couples to America (both were bachelors at the time, so it would be a pleasant necessity for them to find wives before they left), where they would live as a single family with all their property and goods held in common. Their days would be split between physical and intellectual labours, each of them working two to three hours on the land before retiring indoors to write, debate and educate their children. Poetry and philosophy would inform everything they did. "When Coleridge and I are sawing down a tree," Southey wrote, "we shall discuss metaphysics; criticize poetry while hunting a buffalo, and write sonnets whilst following the plough" — and it was to be an altogether better kind of life, even for animals, whose cruel bondage Coleridge had not overlooked. In October he wrote a poem in honour of a donkey, in which he pledged to rescue that "innocent foal" and "take thee with me in the dell / Of high-soul'd Pantisocracy to dwell."

Incredibly, there appeared to be no shortage of volunteers who were willing to join the band of what were becoming known as "Pantisocrats." Southey was especially keen on recruiting his pretty young neighbour Edith Fricker, and when Coleridge visited him in Bristol in August, he was eager to introduce his friend to Edith's sister Sara, a tempestuous brunette who, it was suggested, might make an ideal Pantisocratic wife. The attraction between the couple was genuine, at least at first, and over the course of that summer certain promises were made, certain pledges exchanged, which both parties hoped would shortly be redeemed by the verdant banks of the Susquehanna.

On hearing of it all, Coleridge's long-suffering brothers found their patience stretched to the snapping point and wrote to their wayward sibling to tell him precisely what they thought. Their disapproval meant little to Coleridge — he was, after all, well used to it – but by this time he and Southey had taken up residence in a house in Bristol and the first cracks were already beginning to show in the edifice of Pantisocracy.

To begin with, they fell out over the nature of the tasks that the women would perform, Southey assuming that they would be happy to do the lion's share of the domestic chores whilst Coleridge was adamant that they should do only light and minimal tasks. "Let the husbands do all the rest," he wrote, "and what will that all be? Washing with a machine and cleaning the house. One hour's addition to our daily labour – and Pantisocracy in its most perfect sense is practicable." They argued over servants: Coleridge had always planned that Pantisocracy should be entirely classless, but Southey announced his intention to bring with them a number of workmen whose status would be subtly inferior to that of the Pantisocrats themselves. "Let them dine with us and be treated with as much equality as they would wish," he wrote, "but perform that part of the labour for which their education has fitted them." Coleridge replied, disgusted, "to be employed in the toil of the field while we are pursuing philosophical studies – can earldoms or emperorships boast so huge an inequality?"

It soon became apparent that the magnesium flare of their friendship had burnt itself out, and after a year of being close to inseparable, the two men began to drift apart. Southey, frantically trying to prove himself in the face of parental opposition to his marriage to Edith Fricker, announced that he would return to the Pantisocratic dream "in about fourteen years." Soon afterwards, amidst bitter recriminations from Coleridge (who characterised his friend as "low, dirty, gutter-grubbing") and following some short-lived, half-hearted talk of a commune in Wales, the idyll of Pantisocracy was laid aside forever, though its shadow was to stretch across the rest of Coleridge's life.

So paradise was cancelled, but the promises Coleridge had made to Sara Fricker in that heady summer still stood. In the end, it was more out of a sense of gentlemanly duty than from any tender feelings that he married Sara on 4 October 1795. Their union cannot be called a happy one, and the damage that it was to do to their lives and to those of their children can perhaps be counted as Pantisocracy's most enduring fruit.

Something about this story, and the strange, doomed folly of its players, has gripped and fascinated me from the moment that I heard about it – first, when it was mentioned by an inspirational teacher during a classroom discussion of "The Rime of the Ancient Mariner" and then again, years later, when I encountered a complete version of these events in Richard Holmes's superb biography of Coleridge. I even had an idea once of writing a novel on its theme, a fantasia on the old poet and Pantisocracy, although the book that you hold in your hands is manifestly not that story.

The springboard for my original idea was the following question: What if the Pantisocrats had made it to America after all? The novel would have begun with the sea voyage and their arrival in Pennsylvania before going on to chart the establishment of their colony. In a series of leisurely, understated chapters, I would have chronicled the successes and disasters of Pantisocracy: the trials that faced Samuel and Sara, Robert and Edith and the rest; the difficulties they encountered in farming land and keeping livestock; their quarrels and their fallings-out; their love affairs, fistfights and curdled friendships. In the end, I doubted (and still doubt) that I would have had the maturity or skill to coax so domestic a scenario into life upon the page, and the novel that I eventually wrote was, as you have discovered, quite different in subject and tone.

Yet for all that *The Somnambulist* turned out to be a giddy love letter to stories and genres that I've always loved (*Frankenstein*, Sherlock Holmes, *The Picture of Dorian Gray*, *Bleak House*,

Doctor Who and the London histories of Peter Ackroyd, to name just a few), traces of that seedling idea survive. It is there in the story of poor Ned Love, in the swirling memories of the old man who sleeps beneath the city and, most of all, it is there, quite palpably, in the very last page, as the giant leads his ragged gang of outcasts down to the banks of the Susquehanna.

Some readers have asked how literally this final scene should be taken. Can it be explained away as a delusion in the head of the narrator (already addled, of course, undoubtedly paranoid and hardly to be trusted)? Or should it be read as something more than that — as a vision or a prophecy? The only answer I give is that the scene represents a possibility, a ghost of something which might have been or which is yet to come — like my half-abandoned story, perhaps, or the mad, joyous, wonderful dream of Pantisocracy itself.

I met Edward Moon only once.

We had certain common acquaintances at the Metropolitan
Police Force, gentlemen whose trust and company I had taken
pains to cultivate and who, from time to time, had found themselves, grudgingly and with reluctance, turning to Mr Moon for
advice. It was through these mutual allies that I was able to com-
municate my request for an interview.

I think the notion touched his vanity. Certainly, he was a man
who relished any opportunity to speak at length upon his favourite
subject: the life and works of Edward Moon. This would have been
towards the end of 1898, around the time that his reputation had
begun to fade and his name, already mired in scandal and disgrace,
was already on its way to becoming a byword for a certain kind of
dishonourable failure. Not that Moon's behaviour revealed any obvious cognisance of these facts. His manner was loftily assured
throughout our meeting and he propounded his opinions with a
confidence that some might call arrogance, apparently wholly

unaware of the degradations which were being heaped upon his character in every drawing room in London, happily oblivious to the plummeting nature of his fortunes.

At that time, he still lived in a set of specially constructed rooms beneath his theatre. It was there, in the so-called "Theatre of Marvels," that, every night except Sunday, he performed his act – a curious hybrid of conjuring, illusion and grandstanding displays of deductive reasoning. I was met at the door by a small, grey-haired woman with an air of weary servitude who appeared to be my subject's housekeeper and who gave her name, with a sigh, as Grossmith. She led me through a warren of interconnecting rooms to a cramped and darkened library in which every conceivable inch of space had been filled up by books. Here, Mr Moon sat waiting – tall, a little stooped, his dark hair just beginning to grey – with his associate sitting beside him, a freakishly large man of indeterminate age upon whose lap lay a miniature blackboard and a tiny stub of chalk. You will have guessed this personage's name by now, I fancy. The Somnambulist.

I began by asking Mr Moon about his conjuring act. He was polite enough in his replies but did not trouble to disguise his boredom. He did, however, pay tribute to the indispensability of his assistant with what sounded to me to be unfeigned emotion and at this apparently unexpected compliment the giant grinned lopsidedly in pleasure.

I asked Moon about some of his most celebrated successes – the Limmeridge Park Murders; the killing spree of the Warminster curates named Weddlebeach, Fickling and LeStrang and the extraordinary sequence of events of the late 1880s that the popular press of the day had called "the Miracle of Mile End." He answered my questions at length and with almost clinical precision, although I noted that he was not above positioning himself as the story's hero in every instance despite the considerable evidence that has since amassed to the contrary. It was only when I asked about "the

Fiend," the demented murderer for whose capture and subsequent incarceration he was undoubtedly responsible, that the mood darkened and my host became evasive and suspicious. The Somnambulist looked down at me and shook his head in silent rebuke.

I made a note to myself at the time to investigate exactly why my mention of this notorious killer had met with so strange a reaction, though when I subsequently attempted to do so my efforts were forcibly rebuffed at the highest levels. I chose to let the mystery lie. If my career has taught me anything it is that there are times when it does nobody much good to know the truth.

The mood had soured irrevocably and Moon seemed tired of my interrogation, sullenly batting away my enquiry about the debacle in Clapham and indicating, rather brusquely, that he and his companion would shortly have to retire in order to prepare for that evening's performance. He said that I might be allowed one final question.

I thought for a moment. "Do you think that you will ever solve a crime again?" I asked. "Do you still have it in you?"

The Somnambulist winced and, as his friend began to answer, I saw him write something on his chalkboard, seemingly scarcely aware that he was doing so.

When he spoke, Moon had never sounded more serious. "I know I do," he said. "I feel certain that there is still one last, great case. Somewhere in this city is a mystery worthy of my talents – a puzzle more devilish, more labyrinthine than any I have solved before. Somewhere up there –" he gestured vaguely above him, "is the case which will test me to the breaking point." He gave a complicated smile. "Perhaps even beyond."

We said our goodbyes after that and I took my leave of the Theatre of Marvels. Just before I left, I leant surreptitiously over to see what the Somnambulist had scrawled upon his chalkboard.

It was just one word:

PRIDE

I have thought of our meeting many times in the past few years, especially since the exact nature of the events that eventually overtook Mr Moon have come to light and we have learnt at last precisely what that last great case of his was to cost him. He should have stayed in his theatre, I think. He ought never to have gone looking for mystery and danger, especially not in this new century where the rules have proved so very different from anything to which he was accustomed.

Most of all, I wonder about the Somnambulist. I wonder exactly how much he knew, about what compelled him to write "Pride" upon his blackboard that afternoon, about all the secrets that he must have kept. Only now do I realise that I was talking to the wrong man. It was the Somnambulist, I think, of whom I should have asked my questions all along.

And don't miss . . .

THE DOMINO MEN

by Jonathan Barnes

Coming February 2009 from

WILLIAM MORROW
An Imprint of HarperCollins*Publishers*

I'm horribly aware, as I sit at the desk in this room that you've lent me, that time is now very short for me indeed. Outside, the light of day is fading fast; in here, the ticking of the clock sounds close to deafening.

I've come to terms with the fact that I won't have time to write everything that I'd hoped – my definitive history of the war, from its origins in the dreams of the nineteenth century to the grisly skirmishes of my granddad's day to the recent, catastrophic battle in which you and I played modest parts. No, I simply have to hope that there'll be time enough for me to set down my own story, or at least as much of it as I can remember before the thing which sleeps inside me wakes, stirs, flexes its muscles and, with a lazy flick of its gargantuan tail, gives me no alternative but to forget.

I know where I have to start. Of course, I wasn't present in person – wasn't even born then – but I'm sure that it was there, for all intents and purposes, that it began. I can picture it so clearly, as though these events are calling to me across the years, pleading with me to set them down on paper.

It's probably no coincidence that I've been thinking a lot lately about the old flat, the place in Tooting Bec where I lived with Abbey in happier times and which, in a strange sort of way (although I didn't realise it back then), was always at the heart of the business. Our house was built at some point late in the 1860s. I had other things on my mind whilst I lived there and I never looked into its history, but Abbey did once, in an offhand, mildly curious sort of way, spurred on, I think, by some TV show or other. Her findings were faintly disquieting although she never discovered what I now know about the place. But then, how could she? The Directorate kept those records locked up safe and everyone who was present or who knew anything about them is long dead.

It happened late one night towards the end of April 6th, 1967. Years before the house was divided into flats and a decade or so before I came into the world, a long, dark sedan motored to a stop outside the flat in Tooting Bec. Although spring should have been in full bloom, it had felt more like winter for almost a week and everyone had started wearing thick coats, hats and scarves again, shouldering their way to the backs of their wardrobes to tug out winter outfits that they'd hoped not to see again until October.

It had been raining for hours and the streets, lit up by the unforgiving yellow of the lamps, seemed to shine and dully glisten as though they'd been smeared with some grease or unguent. No-one was abroad and the only sounds were the distant wail of a baby and the plaintive whinnies of urban foxes, padding through the darkened city, foraging for anything that might prove edible amongst the junk and wreckage so carelessly abandoned by humanity.

The car door opened and a tall man unfolded himself from the driver's seat – middle-aged, sharply, almost dandyishly dressed in a dark blue, single-breasted suit and still handsome, albeit with a cruelly vulpine quality to his features. With him was a woman, about the same age, but already moving like someone much older, a brittle spinster decades before her time. Both wore expressions of stoic professionalism mingled (and I suppose we must consider this to be to their credit) with a kind of distasteful disbelief at the unconscionable demands of their jobs.

They had a passenger with them, lolling in the back seat, apparently drunk almost to the point of insensibility. It was a woman, very young and even then, after all that had been done to her, still extremely beautiful. Most of her hair had been shaved away, although a few scattered, tufty islets remained. Her scalp was marked out with scorings, scars and half-healed incisions, and she seemed only dimly aware of what was happening to her, clinging to the man in the same way in which a child clutches at her father's hand on the way to her first day at school. He pulled her out onto the street and helped her stagger towards the front door of the house, letting her slump and flop against him, an arrangement which lent him the appearance of a shop boy grappling (not a little salaciously) with a storefront dummy.

When they got to the door, the older woman reached into her handbag, first for a key and then for a pair of torches. Once the door was open and the torches were switched on, the man steered the girl over the threshold, whispering declarations of love into her ear, honeyed fictions designed for the sole purpose of keeping her moving, saccharine lies told only to propel her onwards. Inside, the house was stripped and empty. The man dragged the girl down the corridor towards the dining room, the bobbing light of his torch picking out their way. His companion, after surveying the street with baleful eyes, busied herself in locking and bolting the door and ensuring, with the painstaking paranoia of the career professional, that the place was completely free of all listening devices, surveillance equipment and sundry bugs.

In the dining room there was an old white wooden chair, a few unlit candles and a brand new television set. The floorboards were bare and seemed to have been daubed with strange signs and symbols in what I can only hope and pray was red paint. There was a strange quality of power in the room, a sense of energy crackling in the air, its presence understood in the same distant way in which one might sense the throb of an engine or the humming whine of a generator.

The man helped the girl into the chair. She was moaning a little now, grizzling like a baby in the grip of a bad dream. He patted her head before producing a length of rope and binding her to the chair, winding it so tightly around her wrists and ankles that he drew blood. At this, she started to whimper and complain, but the man cooed softly, stroked her lips and ran his fingers along the bridge of her nose in the kind of intimately soothing gesture which only a lover could perform, until she fell silent once again.

They had a moment alone together then. He could have begged for her forgiveness, he could have wept tears of shame and regret, he could, at the very least, have said something to try to make amends. But he didn't. She stared up at him with dull accusation in her eyes, and he found himself unable to return her gaze. Head bowed, he walked to the other side of the room and began, with sacerdotal reverence and intensity, to light the candles. A few minutes later, the woman came into the room, closed the door behind her and suggested, with only the barest tremble in her voice, that they begin.

What they did next sickens me to think of, no matter how many times I've been vociferously assured of its necessity.

The handsome man stood over the chair and, reaching down to a leather pouch that he kept out of sight and strapped to his flank, produced a knife. Its blade gleamed in the candlelight.

There may have been a ritual of some kind. Who can say? I never understood the specifics. But I feel certain that the older woman would have said a few words, that, in that clear, precise schoolmarm's voice of hers, would have issued an invitation into the dark.

Once she had finished speaking, the man moved closer to the girl and, in a few swift motions, lifted the knife into the air and brought it slicing down. Just before the blade bit into her flesh, he told her the same thing that, four decades later, he would say to me.

"Trust the Process," he said.

Then again, as though repeating a lie somehow makes it true: "Trust the Process."

I don't want to imagine what came next, but I find it almost impossible not to – the cutting of her wrists, the animal screams of pain, the awful, unstaunchable flow of blood.

Once the bleeding stopped, once the poor girl ought, according to any biological law, to have slid gratefully into death or unconsciousness, she sat up quite straight in her seat with a sticky, fleshy popping sound, like the noise one hears on pulling the heads off shrimp.

Whatever it was that stared out at them then from behind that girl's eyes, it wasn't remotely human. When it spoke, it was no longer in the voice of the girl at all. It would have been impatient, I think, a little peevish and annoyed, as it asked why it had been called to this place before it was time, before the city was ripe.

Then – the springing of the trap. Realising too late what had happened, the thing that wore the girl's skin screeched in rage and fury. It hissed and thrashed and struggled in her chair as, quite impossibly, the cuts on her wrists began to knit themselves together, the skin miraculously reconstituting itself over the slaughterhouse confusion of flesh and blood until, at last, it came to understand the parameters of its entrapment.

The man and the woman watched until the creature in the chair fell silent and the change began. Unable to bear witness to the alterations wrought upon the body, they left the girl where she sat and retired to the nearest public house, where, on taxpayers' money, they proceeded to fortify themselves with a generous martini apiece.

*F*orty years later, I moved into that same building. I ate my meals, read the newspaper, kicked off my shoes, leant back on the sofa and watched TV in the room where they cut the wrists of that poor girl. All the time I was oblivious of what had happened there, foolishly (and, as it turned out, tragically) ignorant of the circle of history which was almost complete.

But I'm getting ahead of myself. Until very recently, I knew none of this, and for a long time, I believed that the story of the Domino Men started last year, in slightly more prosaic circumstances, when everything in my life still seemed broadly normal. I thought that it began with my granddad and with what happened to him in *The Queen's Head*.

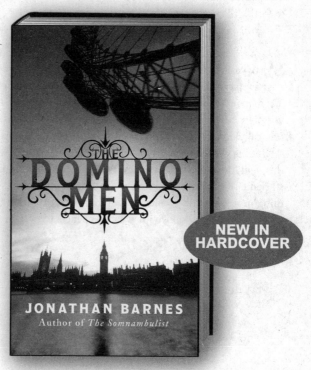